"From the very first page, *A Moonbow Night* charmed me into its story, a story as earthy, rugged, and beguiling as the early American terrain upon which it has been laid. The book offers everything this reader wants: fidelity to history with rich, sensory details of time and place; names we've known fleetingly from the annals of the past who quicken on the page; fictional friends for whose happiness and romantic redemption we yearn. Tempe is a Kentucky heroine worth our time and heart's investment—a waif on the outside, steel on the inside, kind in every situation. In Sion we find a hero worthy of the title, willing to grapple with his past to own his present and claim his lady. The plot is complex, tense, and layered and resolves in a most satisfying conclusion. This remarkable, elegantly written novel pulses with life and is a must-read for all who love historical romance."

—**Sandra Byrd**, author of *A Lady in Disguise*

"*A Moonbow Night* captures the wilds of a young and unyielding American frontier with breathtaking action and Laura Frantz's signature mastery in storytelling. The effortless merging of narrative with intelligent dialogue allows the spot-on historical research to shine. Sion's understated valor is in perfect step with Tempe's independence, making them a pairing that will keep readers turning pages and rooting for them to the end. This is an exquisite novel of love and loss, and a sweet reminder that even in an untamed world, the gentle grace of God heals all wounds."

—**Kristy Cambron**, author of *The Illusionist's Apprentice* and the Hidden Masterpiece series

"As timeless as it is historical, *A Moonbow Night* is the shining embodiment of everything Laura Frantz does best, from her trademark attention to detail to the unfolding of rich and textured love in a setting no less complex. To read this novel is to take a journey along with the characters, inhabiting the story with all five senses. Truly, a book to savor and revisit."

—**Jocelyn Green**, award-winning author of *The Mark of the King*

"Laura Frantz is a master at transporting readers back in time! From the first page to the last I was swept away to the frontier and captivated by its beauty, danger, and romance. Tempe's bravery and tender heart make her an admirable heroine, and Sion's strength and determination make him her perfect match. *A Moonbow Night* is an all-around delightful read for lovers of historical romance."

—**Carrie Turansky**, award-winning author of *A Refuge at Highland Hall* and *Shine Like the Dawn*

Books by Laura Frantz

The Frontiersman's Daughter
Courting Morrow Little
The Colonel's Lady
The Mistress of Tall Acre

THE BALLANTYNE LEGACY

Love's Reckoning
Love's Awakening
Love's Fortune

A Moonbow Night

LAURA FRANTZ

Revell

a division of Baker Publishing Group
Grand Rapids, Michigan

Published by Revell
a division of Baker Publishing Group
P.O. Box 6287, Grand Rapids, MI 49516-6287
www.revellbooks.com

Printed in the United States of America

Library of Congress Cataloging-in-Publication Data
Names: Frantz, Laura, author.
Title: A moonbow night / Laura Frantz.
Description: Grand Rapids, MI : Revell, [2017]
Identifiers: LCCN 2016031262 | ISBN 9780800728571 (cloth) | ISBN 9780800726621
    (pbk.)
Subjects: | GSAFD: Love stories. | Christian fiction.
Classification: LCC PS3606.R4226 M66 2017 | DDC 813/.6—dc23
LC record available at https://lccn.loc.gov/2016031262

Most Scripture used in this book, whether quoted or paraphrased by the characters, is taken from the King James Version of the Bible.

Scripture quotations marked ESV are from The Holy Bible, English Standard Version® (ESV®), copyright © 2001 by Crossway, a publishing ministry of Good News Publishers. Used by permission. All rights reserved. ESV Text Edition: 2011

Scripture quotations marked NASB are from the New American Standard Bible®, copyright © 1960, 1962, 1963, 1968, 1971, 1972, 1973, 1975, 1977, 1995 by The Lockman Foundation. Used by permission. (www.Lockman.org)

Published in association with Books & Such Literary Agency, 52 Mission Circle, Suite 122, PMB 170, Santa Rosa, CA 94509-7953.

In memory of my hero,
Daniel Boone.
From one true Kentuckian
to another.

I remember the devotion of your youth,
your love as a bride,
how you followed me in the wilderness,
in a land not sown.

1

Come to a turabel mountain that tried us almost to death to git over it.

> —William Calk, His Jurnal
> March ye 25th 1775 Satterday

April 1777

What cannot be cured must be endured.

There was no cure for the whirling April snow, the cold seeping through thin, trail-worn moccasins from the frozen forest floor. No cure for the tender back of his favorite mare now courting a saddle sore or the dog fight that had just occurred over the paltry remains of a winter-starved deer. No cure for the beef-and-biscuit Englishman at the rear of their small party whose every labored breath was an epithet.

Sion Morgan's own breathing, honed on numerous forays, was heavy. But he reckoned it was more the beauty that stole both his wind and speech. Underfoot was a tangle of cress and purslane and clover. On every side redbud and dogwood were blossoming, breaking through the avalanche of greens with blazing bursts of purple and cream.

Ahead was the saddle of the Gap, the gateway to Kentucke, a whirl of windy white. They'd come three hundred miles since Fort Henry. Only one hundred more to go. The crude maps Sion had pored over, crafted by Walker and Boone and the few men who'd gone before, blurred in his weary brain. A few details lured him.

A sandy cave . . . a seasonal waterfall . . . a staggering vista. All to be had but a few rods more.

"Morgan! Will you drive us like livestock?" Cornelius Lyon paused to spit out another curse, this one the most colorful by far. "By all that is holy, this mountain's the devil's own stairway and naught else!"

Setting his jaw, Sion pressed ahead, shrugging aside his aggravation. He couldn't fault Cornelius's logic. The climb *was* brutal, each step so steep, so treacherous, one dared not look down or pause or speak.

But Cornelius wasn't done with his bellowing. "Why such haste? Surely the savages wouldn't be out on such a day!"

The clipped, bitter words bore a challenge. Heat rising, his gait unbroken, Sion shifted his rifle to his other hand and squinted as a stinging wind slapped his face. He was glad six packhorses, two chain carriers, and a marker separated them, lest he give vent to his temper and send Cornelius Lyon over the cliff.

The uncharitable thought had barely cleared his head when a commotion arose from behind, sudden enough to chill the blood. He'd seen Indian sign farther back but had said nothing, the snow obliterating the Warrior's Path. Now he swung round to see a packhorse lose his footing and tumble from the trace. Down, down, down the big bay went, skinning hide and hair in a vicious descent against jagged rock. Its anguished whinny set the dogs to howling, a mournful chorus that carried on the wind.

For a few dizzying moments Sion felt woozy. Seeing the animal's deathly struggle, he shouldered his flintlock and sighted, firing down past rock and brush to where the horse lay bleeding and broken. When the animal stilled, he gritted his teeth against the jarring impact as he leapt from the trace onto a slick ledge of limestone below, gun held high in his right hand, all in an ungraceful attempt to rescue the provisions the bay had been carrying.

Reaching bottom, he looked up to find eight wide eyes on him—all but Nate Stoner, who kept his back to the chasm, his rifle trained on the hills above in case of ambush.

Fingers cold and cramped, Sion set his rifle aside, took out his hunting knife, and sliced free the precious stores of gunpowder and bullet lead. Once they were secured to his back, he began the slow uphill climb. Twice he nearly tumbled backwards, his footing unsure, gaze clouded with snow. By the time he reached the top and his chain carriers rushed to lighten his load, he was bruised and bloody-knuckled, the earth driven deep beneath his fingernails, the mournful weight of a lost packhorse pressing down with a vengeance.

A warm, wet nuzzle to his hand brought comfort. Smokey, his collie, leaned into him before bounding ahead with a sharp yip to spur him on. The trace couldn't climb much higher. The tree line was thinning, the snow miraculously slowing. His muddy moccasins sank into sand, a strange sensation after so much rock. Overhead was a cavern.

Sand Gap.

The tumult of falling water met his ears, the mist of the

falls like ice. He looked back to make sure all was in order. All was, yet he was unable to shake that shadowed feeling. Truly, who would be out on such a forbidding day? Other than a bunch of witless surveyors bent on Indian territory?

Facing forward again, Smokey beside him, Sion crossed the cavern, eyes west, the cave's dimness offset by a startling burst of light. Years earlier he'd heard of this place. But Boone and Walker hadn't done it justice. Their tales of its grandeur seemed tattered and lackluster.

Sion stood in the Gap, wordless, barely aware of his surveying crew fanned out around him. The wind had ceased its bitter sighing. Before them was pewter sky. A bluish haze of mountains and then . . . endless, untrammeled, unredeemed wilderness.

Sion hated that Cornelius broke the spell. "Here we shall rest, surely."

"Here, aye," Sion answered. "For a quarter of an hour or so."

Shooting him a black look, Cornelius retreated into the cavern with his manservant, Lucian, and the two chain carriers.

Nate stood shoulder to shoulder with Sion, gaze unbroken. "I misdoubted I'd live to see such a wilderness. But I'm glad I did." He drew in a ragged breath. "'O Lord, how manifold are Thy works! In wisdom hast Thou made them all; the earth is full of Thy riches.'"

The Scripture chafed, intruding on Sion's appreciation. Tearing his attention from the view, he began to reload his rifle, distracting himself with powder and shot.

"This here Gap's the best—and the worst of it, I reckon," Nate mused, still agape.

"You reckon wrong." Sion poured powder down the barrel

and rapped it with his hand to set the charge. "There are three choke points on Boone's Trace. The Narrows are next—and a spring-soaked river to ford farther down."

"Don't sound so gleeful." The gleam in Nate's eyes eclipsed his worry. "I know you'd like to get shed of us and go your own way, just like you been doin' thirty years or better."

Sion grinned and drove the ball home. "The way I figure it, I'm saddled with the lot of you till the surveying's done."

Nate scratched his silvery chin. "You see any sign back there at the spring?"

With a nod, Sion closed the gun's frizzen. "Shawnee. Six or so. Mayhap a couple of Wyandot thrown in."

Nate's shoulders convulsed in a shiver. "Outnumbered, then."

Meeting the older man's gaze, Sion decided against confessing his certainty they were still being watched, even as their frosted breath plumed between them. "We'll make a cold camp. Stand watch through the night. Indians don't usually care for a wintry fight."

"Well, they do like horses. And we got some fine ones left." Nate darted a wary eye at the woods. "I'll be glad to get to Boone's and Harrod's forts."

"A hundred miles more." Again Sion looked square at Nate, unwilling to withhold a last way out. "It's not too late to turn back."

"And leave you without a marker?"

Committed, then. Despite Nate's Scripture spouting and hymn singing, the graying borderman was the only member of the surveying party Sion was sure of. Still, he felt an odd twinge. An old man should be at home, surrounded by life's last comforts. But Nate Stoner had little to return to in Virginia. He was a widower of ten years, and his only daughter had died in childbirth, leaving him without family. Sion was the closest thing to kin Nate had.

"No need to worry about my old hide. I'll keep. 'And even to your old age I am He; and even to hoar hairs I will carry you.'" Nate gave Sion a reassuring grin. "It ain't me I'm fretted about but you. We'd best head down and make camp."

Sion admired the camp, the way it nestled against a rocky ridge near a spring just below Sand Gap off the Warrior's Path. He could hear the hobbled horses foraging, free of their loads, somewhat protected from the northwest wind by a stand of pine. The snow had left off, leaving a miserable cold, everything muddy and damp. Sion craved the smell of wood smoke and browning meat. A fire to warm his backside. A dry bed.

But comfort might bring calamity.

As it was, their party sat hunched in saddle blankets, rifles near at hand, and partook of parched corn and jerked meat, warming themselves with a dram or two in battered tin cups and aiming for camaraderie at least.

Once again Sion was struck by their mismatched party. An old man. A dandy and his servant. Two gangly-legged boys. As many dogs as horses. He was most gladdened by the dogs. Mostly foxhounds and curs, they were ever alert to danger. Smokey rarely left his side, nose in the air, tetchy to a fault.

Weather permitting, they'd soon be running the line below the Gap, chaining through dense forest, using the levels on the steepest inclines, always recording measurements and computations in tattered field books.

But for now the talk shied away from the work ahead.

Leave it to Cornelius to turn fanciful, the lot of them hanging on his every word like coons after pawpaws. The dark soon masked their rapt expressions if not Cornelius's crisp British tones.

"A gentleman by the name of Johnathon Swift, some fifteen years past, is reported to have had a secret silver mine within these very mountains." Cornelius was gesturing now, adding to the drama. "A revered Shawnee chief led some white traders near the mine only to become ill and refuse to go farther, saying the Great Spirit was displeased."

Spencer Rankin's eyes went wide. "Why would the Great Spirit get riled up?"

"Why, indeed," Cornelius replied coolly. "Because of their greed, boy. Even the Indians' god abhors selfishness. Silver."

"We ain't any better than them nosy traders, the way I figure." Spencer elbowed Hascal Mullins, whose hand rested uneasily on his gun. "We're chain carriers and axemen for you surveyors, all of us paid in land. I reckon the Great Spirit ain't too happy about that neither."

Cornelius cleared his throat. "Be that as it may, our mission is more benevolent. We're marking land for soldiers and settlers. Not merely ourselves."

"Is it true what they say about the Indians? That they call surveyors *land stealers*?"

Cornelius reached into his waistcoat and withdrew a pocket compass, holding it aloft. "*This* is what they're referring to, yes. The savages have no concept of ownership, I'm afraid. Kentucke is their hunting ground and has ever been. We're trespassing, in their eyes. Uninvited guests."

"Seems not even the king can keep us out with his proclamations," Hascal said. "We be comin' over the mountains, like it or not."

"Daniel Boone—a God-fearing woodsman of solid Quaker stock—has come before us," Cornelius replied. "Others will follow. I see no stopping the land-hungry masses."

All quieted. They were shadows now, swallowed up by pitch darkness. A lone wolf howled and Sion tensed. But the sound rang true, like a woman's cry, the last haunting note an eerie echo. He eased, assured no human throat could make that noise. Still, someone was out there, waiting. Watching. He sensed it sure as his blood ran red.

Nate shifted. "Whereabouts exactly is this here silver mine?"

"Somewhere between Piney Mountain and the Big Sandy River," Cornelius answered.

"Swift's journal states that the richest ore is to be found in latitude 37 degrees minus 56 minutes north." Sion studied the sky, intent on the North Star. "By astronomical observations and calculations, the vein is just a little west of the longitude of 83 degrees."

"Ha!" Cornelius's smirk defied the dark. "So you *have* been listening, Morgan."

"He's always listenin'," Hascal put in. "He just don't say much."

"So I've gathered," Cornelius replied.

Nate chuckled. "My guess is that we're better off findin' the Moonbow Inn than the Swift silver mines."

Cornelius made a scornful sound. "What? An ordinary? In the wilderness?" His contempt knew no bounds. "And just where would this bastion of civility happen to be?"

Nate bristled. "I ain't sayin' it's real or anything better'n a fleasy station. I just recollect somethin' Daniel—that's *Captain Boone* to you—said about a place near the falls of the Shawnee River. A mighty big falls, bigger'n any waterfalls you ever saw, I'd wager."

"We'll soon be crossing the Shawnee." Cornelius pocketed the compass and withdrew his pipe, its white clay a beacon in the last of daylight. "By heaven, what I'd give for a tavern and smoke and a pint."

Nate saved Sion from cautioning. "Best save your vices for the hearth's fire at the Moonbow Inn."

"And why, pray tell, is it called the Moonbow?"

"On account of some magic that occurs at night beneath a full moon. A sort of rainbow in the mist of the falls." At Cornelius's second snort, Nate shrugged. "Since Dan'l said it, I'd be inclined to believe it."

Spencer and Hascal were chuckling and elbowing again nonetheless. Ignoring them, Sion stroked Smokey's velvety ear absently as the collie stretched out beside him, warming his buckskin-clad thigh. The appeal of an inn, however paltry, seemed more woolgathering. But buried in the back of Sion's conscience was hazy confirmation. "I recollect something about a woman innkeeper and her daughter being a part of Boone's first try at Kentucke in '73."

The chuckling ceased.

"You mean that time when Boone's son was killed just shy of the Gap?" Nate's face looked as gray as his hair in the twilight. "That was a mournful time, to hear tell of it."

"Aye. Somehow a few people in their party made it into Kentucke later on and ended up along the *Wasioto*—the Shawnee River—and started being hospitable." Sion paused, dredging his memory for details. "Likely this so-called inn is no more than a fortified cabin or blockhouse with a few pickets and loopholes, something along the lines of Boone's and Harrod's stations."

"A woman innkeeper and her daughter?" Cornelius made a sour face. "Surely you jest, Morgan."

"Likely there are some menfolk around too," Nate speculated, "if only trappers and traders and the like. More settlers are coming over the Gap than you think."

"Sounds like a curious operation to me." Cornelius stuck his pipe between his teeth as if pretending to smoke. "Though I would warm to a pretty petticoat if one should materialize."

"Best shut your yap and hie you to bed, then." Nate stood slowly, retreating stiffly to a pile of dry leaves he'd gathered beneath a rocky overhang. "The sooner we see sunrise, the sooner we'll be downriver and mebbe learn if there's somethin' to this whole moonbow affair."

"I'll take first watch," Sion said, shouldering his rifle as the dogs about them bristled and the wolves' hair-raising howling began anew.

2

There is nothing which has yet been contrived by man, by which so much happiness is produced as by a good tavern or inn.

—SAMUEL JOHNSON

At first light this bright April morn, the low-beamed kitchen was humming with life and spirit. The spicy-sweet scent of sassafras clung to the air, competing with the sizzle of sausage seasoned with sage and red pepper.

Giving a last poke to the meat, Tempe Tucker sat back on her heels, studying the axe near the fire. Russell kept it there on cold mornings, warming the steel before cutting wood. She listened for his ungainly step on the dogtrot, but all she heard was the burst of birdsong beyond the open door. Its piercing sweetness did little to dispel her uneasiness. Once she had been her brother's worry; now he was hers.

The back door creaked open to admit the bound girl, Paige, toting a piggin of new milk. She poured it into a shallow keeler to cool whilst Tempe's mother, Aylee, parched coffee in a skillet. When the sausage was fried and the eggs were set, Russell appeared, studying Tempe and murmuring a greeting to their mother but avoiding Paige. She seemed not to mind, though a telling flush rode her cheekbones beneath her pale cap.

Taking a stool, Russell dipped his head in a silent prayer as Tempe placed breakfast before him. "Best set a few more dinner plates," he murmured. "Some men from Harrod's Fort are headed back to the settlements."

Aylee gave a nod, returning to her biscuit dough. "Raven told you that, I reckon."

When Russell didn't respond, Paige filled the silence. "Raven, aye. He's always on the prowl. For a little powder and bullet lead he'll share just about anything."

Tempe nearly sighed aloud. When her brother's half-blood friend came near, she cut a wide swath around him, though he'd done them no ill. In truth, he often made their lives easier, spelling out who was coming and going, the where and why of it. Still, she felt uneasy in his presence, his dark eyes and long silences unsettling.

By the time Russell had finished eating and gone outside to split wood, they were playing the "here's what I miss" game again. Though it had been four years since they'd fled Virginia, the yearning for safety and civility still lingered.

"Here's what I miss." Aylee began to pound the mound of beaten biscuit dough with the stock of a broken musket. Looking on, Tempe wondered if her mother relished the chance to vent her pent-up frustrations. Three hundred licks and the dough would be ready to cut into rounds, prick with a fork, and bake. "I miss hearing Squire Boone preach Sundays on the Clinch." Aylee paused and waved a floured hand. "He had a way about him that always left you pondering till the next Sabbath."

Nodding, Paige returned scrubbed pewter plates to a shelf. "Here's what I miss." She hesitated, tongue between her teeth. "I miss market days—and Punch and Judy shows in town that made me laugh till my sides hurt."

There was a long pause. Both women looked at Tempe. She poured herself a splash of sassafras tea, weighing her answer. Truth be told, her heart was so full of the here and now there wasn't room for any woolgathering.

Taking a pinch of sausage from the skillet, she finally said, "We'll soon have a mort of men to feed tonight. Best ponder that."

Aylee began rolling out dough. "We can fix those squirrels you caught and salted down in barrels. They'll make a fine dinner with cornmeal dumplings and leather-britches beans. We're a mite short of flour, but Paige can turn out ginger cake and custard with what's left." She set the rolling pin aside and began cutting out biscuits. "Temperance Grace . . ."

Tempe's gaze, fixed on Russell beyond the kitchen window as he chopped wood, returned to her mother.

"Mind the time as you go about your business." Aylee's words held a warning. "Take care to stay clear of the main trails."

With a dutiful *aye*, Tempe downed the dregs of her sassafras tea before slipping out the open door.

Tempe took to the higher ridges where snow and ice held sway, the cold polishing every rock and speck of grass like barley sugar. Scraggly pines clung to barren, rocky places, their seeds a bounty for winter-starved birds. Below, in the warmer hollows, the dogwood's riotous flowering spelled corn-planting time, but winter whispered *wait*. It was cold for spring, bitter cold, the chill hurrying her on. Dogwood winter, some said, with the snow on the blossoms.

It didn't take long to reach her father's rockhouse fronting the Shawnee River, but a world of danger lay in the distance. Spring was a chancy time to be about, with the Indians taking to the trails and traces, resuming their wandering and warring sure as spring's stirring. Only in winter did the Shawnee keep to their camps on the upper Ohio or the Cherokee to their southern villages, the troublesome Chickamauga down along Chickamauga Creek. But with the war on between the British and Americans, the Indians' habits seemed uncertain too.

She led two packhorses, one particularly mulish. Herod always behaved better when weighted down with flour and provisions. He tugged at the rope, snorting his complaint at leaving their warm barn-shed.

"Pa'll soon have you in hand," she murmured, thinking of the perilous journey to come and wishing she could go too. When Pa left, it seemed she held her breath for weeks till he returned, so worried was she he'd not come back.

Yet no matter how chancy, her father's treks west to trade were vital. West was best despite the ongoing Indian threat. He dare not go east, not with the trouble that had thrust them from the settlements to begin with. The crime that had sent them fleeing their shabby cabin on Virginia's Clinch River was ever fresh. 'Twas in another cold spring that her beloved father had snapped like a fiddle string, flying into the deadly rage that further uprooted them. 'Twas this that made them watch their backs.

Bending, she hobbled both horses behind a thicket of ivy, then straightened to give a last look about. The only sounds were the chatter of a squirrel and the faint piping of birds.

Satisfied no one else was near, Tempe gave a sparrow's simple but expected call. There was the customary pause before her father let down the ladder. It descended with a hiss, a curious concoction of whang leather and tough hickory, strong enough to bear her weight and the pack of provisions strapped to her back.

His sinewy hand shot out, gripping her outstretched fingers till her feet were planted firmly on the cliff's ledge. He then pulled the ladder up after her. The river's spring rush rumbled far below, muting their voices.

August Tucker's gaze cut to the rockhouse entrance and the woods beyond. "See any sign?"

It was the first question he always asked her. "None," she answered, "be it red man or white."

Pa had wintered with them at the inn, but now, whilst the woods were full of travelers, this hidden cave, one of a number of rockhouses fronting the river, would be his home. She looked about, getting her bearings. The dwelling bore a buffalo robe bed, a lantern on a ledge, some cooking vessels, and a fire pit. All familiar, even beloved. His custom before retiring each night was priming his two flintlock rifles and setting them and his sharpened axe beside his bed.

"Looks like you don't need any sweetening." She shot him a half smile. Crock after crock of maple syrup lined one stony wall. Her pa, for all his peculiar ways, was never idle. "I brought salt. Meal. Some needful things for your journey." She handed him the shoepacks Aylee had made.

August took them, examining the work of his wife's hands, his expression pronouncing them adequate. "Tell me again what she has need of."

"Flour. Ink and paper. Straight pins. Maybe a trinket for Paige." She wrinkled her nose at the bounty ready for market at the back of the rockhouse. Such a wealth of skins he had, a whole winter's cache, feral smelling but perfectly tanned.

Much could be gotten from French traders farther down the Shawnee River, even comely things that turned a woman's head. "Russell needs a new file for his gun mending, some powder and bullet lead."

"I'm considering making powder right here. There's a saltpeter cave near Piney Creek." He began pulling on the shoepacks, his feet like two canoe paddles they were so large. "Any news I should know about?"

She studied her much smaller moccasins, the elk skin worn smooth and dark, and resurrected the talk that swirled thick as smoke at the inn. Longhunters, trappers, and traders all carried tittle-tattle, some of it reliable, all of it dark. "There's been some trouble at Boonesborough."

"Shawnee raiders, like as not." He paced about, trying out his new shoes. At a raven's cry he moved back from the ledge. "But I misdoubt men like Boone and Harrod and Kenton will tuck tail and run."

Nay, not even the death of his son had curbed Boone's zeal. Despite her heartache, Tempe felt a pride in them all, these unflinching frontiersmen who stood their ground. "What with Kentucke being part of Virginia now, more settlers will be coming over the Gap. There's no stopping the wilderness fever, as Ma calls it."

He frowned, the deep creases in his forehead reminding her of plowed furrows in a field. "If folks can make it to the forts, they'll help defend the settlements till the end. They aim to win, come what may."

Stooping, he began riffling through the pack, provocation giving way to pleasure as he unearthed a clay pipe and a twist of tobacco. "Your ma's a good woman, always thinking of what I need." He fingered the pipe's smooth stem, clearly anticipating a smoke. "How's Russell? Paige?"

"His leg's ailing him some with all the cold and damp. He and Paige—" She left off, frustration gnawing at her. "They're no cozier than when you left."

He shook his head. "Russell lets his lame leg get in the way of his lovemaking." He closed the pack and straightened to his full height, nearly scraping the smoke-blackened ceiling. Tempe felt small as a meadow mouse in his lengthy shadow. His eyes were eagle sharp. "And you? Any man come by who takes your fancy?" When she hesitated, he added, "I should send you to Boonesborough or Fort Harrod. They're in need of able women—wives—though you're liable to shame half the men with your marksmanship."

"No man wants a woman who can outshine him."

"The right kind of man won't care. Mighten even be proud of such." His gaze narrowed. "I misdoubt it's your way with a rifle that keeps callers at bay. You can't get past what happened in Powell Valley."

She stared at him. Never did he speak of the valley. The shock of it sent all the coldness out of her. "Pa, I—"

"You can't keep grieving a dead man any more than Russell can keep grieving a lame leg."

The heat in his words matched the heat in her face. Setting her jaw, she looked to the back of the dwelling where, to occupy himself, he'd etched a battle scene with charcoal. She made out swivels and clouds of smoke, tumbled men strewn upon the ground like broken twigs. His stint in the French and Indian War haunted him still. Who was he to take her to task about the past?

"It's not been four years yet," she said, ever mindful it was approaching May, James's birthday month. May had ever been melancholy for her since. "Maybe in time . . ."

He shook his head, his unbound hair a mass of pewter

strands about corded shoulders. "Time enough to bury the dead and get on with living."

The rockhouse was suddenly stifling. Breathless. She nearly swayed from a suffocating sense of loss. With a lightning-like gesture, she unfurled the ladder. Down she went with nary a goodbye, looking up just once to see him peering over the cavern's lip, watching her descent, his face a stew of displeasure.

"I should be back by month's end," he called down after her.

"I hope you live to see it," she shot back. Just last May they'd stumbled upon a slain party in a thicket near the trace he'd soon travel. Bedding slashed open, feathers strewn far and wide. The ground had been white as snow . . . and red as sarvis berries.

"A right terrible waste," Pa had said.

They'd wrapped the bodies in sheets they couldn't spare and buried them, covering the graves with logs lest wolves dig them up. Just like the burial party had done with James back in Powell Valley.

Her James.

Blinking back tears, she shivered and darted a searching look about. Lightened of her load, she took a familiar path, traveling east straight as the crow flies, reluctant to return to the inn just yet. The ground was thawing now, the sun strengthening in a sky that was that startling shade of blue owned by early spring.

At the foot of the ridge she came to a swollen creek, its muddy banks buried by a tangle of laurel. Here a number of horses had forded, all iron shod and heading north toward Crab Orchard and the Kentucke settlements.

Numbed by sadness, she followed their trail for a time, distracted by showy blossoms and countless awakening things. Every minute or so she stopped to listen. But the sough of the wind overhead in the newly leafed trees kept her from hearing all but the mournful cry of an oriole. The woods were full of shifting shapes, the play of light and shadow unsettling.

The mounted party she pursued led into a heavy growth of hardwoods—giant chestnut and oak and elm—letting in so little light the forest floor looked swept clean of undergrowth. Here travel was easier, the threat of Indian ambush less likely.

In time she gained a favorite meadow and a little hollow, lacy ferns curling round a mossy spring rimmed with lichen-clad rock. Soft grass cushioned her feet and the light grew brighter. She could see several rods ahead, the beloved glade a sort of refuge after the heavy gloom. Could the horsemen feel it too?

She walked on with a tightening in her chest that was not all tiredness. A few paces more and she stopped cold. To the left of the trail, in a shaft of sunlight, a hatchet had blazed the smooth, silvery-gray bark of beech after beech, the initials cut plain.

SM.

Beneath it was the date.

8th April.

Two days past.

Tempe bristled. This was no man's woods. Beautiful. Hallowed. Prime bottomland. The soil was rich and unredeemed. Now the trees were disfigured. The land claimed. Desecrated.

She took a step back, disgust and dismay adance inside her.

Surveyors.

The Indians bore a particular hatred for such men. This she understood. They came. They took. Often they indulged in the wanton slaughter of game, leaving a litter of wasted meat in their wake. Frederick Ice, one of Virginia's Crown surveyors, leapt to mind, and his and Pa's deadly tussle. She shoved it aside with effort, folding the memory up like a tattered package, where it took up uneasy residence beside her beloved James.

Since Daniel Boone had been sent into the Kentucke territory to recall all surveyors two years prior due to Indian hostilities, few had been brave enough to venture over the Gap. She'd not come across a surveying party since. Maybe the strength of her reaction lay in this. She'd thought them gone. The woods theirs. Her father safe.

Till now.

❦

Still sore from her father's scolding, Tempe was more mindful than ever of the diners crowding the Moonbow Inn that night. Betimes it seemed her life was made up of wary men smelling of sweat and horseflesh, their long rifles leaning against log walls, their hunting shirts begrimed with grease and black powder. Rawboned and awkward, whittled down by weather and danger, most approached Aylee Tucker's table with an awe and gratitude that bordered on reverence.

Tempe's mother tolerated no spitting of tobacco, no profaneness or drunkenness or tussling. She was quick to dump a steaming trencher into the laps of any who dared defy the posted rules. Word traveled fast along the frontier. Best scrub your face and mind your manners at the Moonbow Inn where the Virginia widow held sway. Only a shilling for dinner and seven pence for lodging, and the fare was plentiful, the bedding clean, the serving girls among the fairest flowers of the frontier, it was said.

Tempe chuckled at the latter but secretly fretted that Ma was counted a widow. No good could come of that. At mid-century, Aylee Tucker was still a handsome woman. As for her part, Tempe kept her eyes down, her smiles sparse. But Paige—Paige was a wonderment, always sashaying, flitting, smiling. Did she mean to rile Russell? Goad him into some sort of heartfelt declaration?

As she thought it, her brother took up the tobacco jar and filled his pipe. He usually kept watch in one corner, overseeing meals and then the customary card playing and talk. Often Ma shed her apron and turned her hand to doctoring, dispensing tonics for those in need of her herbs and simples. Tonight there was naught but a gash brought on by a hunting knife gone awry.

Ma had bathed and bound the foot of one of Harrod's men with wild cherry bark. Its distinctive scent threaded the smoky air as Tempe passed in and out of the keeping room, first clearing the table and then sweeping alongside Paige as men moved nearer the hearth or bedded down in the loft overhead.

"Tempe Grace, fetch me the Reckoning."

The Reckoning.

At Aylee's request, Tempe felt chilled. The Reckoning. How she hated that book.

James's name was written there.

Her gaze flew to a little board shelf near the door joining kitchen to keeping room. In seconds she brought the ledger to her mother as requested, judging from Aylee's somber tone that the newest entry wasn't simply a notation about who had just come over the Gap but another tragedy. Another death.

Aylee sat by her patient, his expression gathered in a grimace of pain that had little to do with his wound. Her mother's slender hands were cutting a pen from a goose quill. Without waiting to be told, Tempe brought her the ink they'd made from pokeberries, kept in a smallish soapstone bottle.

The man heaved a sigh. "'Twas the first of February along the Rockcastle River . . ."

Picking up a trio of hickory cups, Tempe moved out of hearing and into the kitchen, her throat tight with unshed tears.

3

The Cumberland was called the Shawnee River and
the Tennessee was called the Cherokee.

—Josiah Collins

In three weeks' time they'd chained out of April and into
a May thick with peavine and clover, the dogwood and
redbud shattering and scattering their colorful blossoms
in a warming wind.

Sion had never seen such a wilderness. Such wildness. He
was at home in the backcountry and borders of Virginia
and the Carolinas and Pennsylvania, knew their rugged,
ragged edges by heart. Accustomed to danger, he'd roamed
the Alleghenies and the Ohio Valley, pitting himself against
earth and sky, his sense of discovery quickened at every
turn. But this . . . this vast, unbroken forest was a force to
be reckoned with but never tamed. Never counted a friend.
Never trusted.

They'd bid goodbye to the snug half-faced shelter they'd
made near a secluded spring. Their horses and provisions were
sheltered there, Lucian standing guard. The rest of their party

was following the curvaceous Shawnee River, encumbered with the surveying gear that was the heart of their work.

Sion could hear the river's steady roar as it boiled over endless, boulder-strewn banks. Not far from the riverbed they came upon dense cane land. The shiny new stalks gave him the shivers. A man could easily lose himself amid the choking reeds—or hide from Indians. Come summer the woody growth, now shoulder high, would shoot six to fifteen feet.

He felt a peculiar pleasure as the Gunter's chain was laid out on ground the axemen had cleared, all twenty-two yards of it. Whilst Cornelius oversaw the chain men, Sion led out. They crossed a nameless creek at three miles twenty-five chains, and a lightning-split elm at three miles forty-nine chains. Spencer and Hascal, glad to stow their axes, kept the chain tight and flat to the ground while Nate marked off with chaining arrows.

Sion paused every few rods to take a reckoning by the sun or the polestar. As their party pushed forward, he felt more and more chary. Time and time again he sensed someone was near at hand, intent on their every footfall.

Indians . . . or something else?

The suspicion lodged in his brain like a pebble in a brook. Nate and the others seemed blind to any danger, intent on the work. Sion took care to hide any fretfulness, continuing on at the front of the column in his usual thorough, measured way, talking little and observing much.

Soon the air would be heavy with the whirr and tick of cicadas and mosquitos and mayflies. He purposed to be well done with the work by midsummer, all the surveys mapped and platted, computations made. They'd made a tentative start.

It was the forenoon when Cornelius gave a howl. The sound

sent up the hackles on Sion's neck. Even Smokey bristled, ears and tail at attention, posture stout. Turning, Sion spied the barely masked mirth of the chain men a few rods back, Nate included. The Englishman's britches were unbuttoned and he was gesticulating wildly at a near cane thicket.

"Cursed cane!" Cornelius was staring at Sion as if he were to blame. "A man can't even make water in this country without some mischief!"

Sion slid his hatchet from his belt and blazed the nearest beech tree before backtracking, his soundless steps eating up the greening ground.

"Yonder comes Morgan," Sion heard Nate say.

Cornelius jabbed a finger toward the thicket, a sure spot for privacy but full of menace nonetheless. "How by heaven am I to run the line with a brutal gash to my foot?"

Sion looked to the ground where a swell of red was seeping beneath a flayed moccasin. The growth of cane was young but sharp, and Cornelius's cane-stobbed foot was proof. "We're a ways from camp and you'll not make it." Frustration flared but Sion stayed stoic, glad for the river's proximity. "If we raft down—"

"Raft?" Cornelius looked at him like he'd announced a hanging.

"Aye, raft. I'll not carry you." Sion's calm was a stark contrast to the Englishman's agitation. "Now seems a fine time to learn the lay of the river. Hasten back to camp." He started down the bank, calling for the equipment to be packed up.

Cornelius drew himself up like an injured rooster. "And what, pray tell, do we intend to float upon?"

"Hide and watch," Sion replied with a wicked wink.

"You sure about this?" Nate queried, hat in hand. When Sion didn't answer, he lowered his voice. "Cornelius Lyon is one of them mush-and-molasses sort of fellers. I don't think he'll take too kindly to this . . . er . . . pleasurable excursion."

Sion glanced at the roiling river. "It just might get his mind off his cut foot."

"I misdoubt it. He'll likely be howlin' all the way." Nate jammed his hat back on his head. "The river's got its big britches on now that it's spring. If you were a murderin' sort of feller I'd be a mite more worried than I am."

"I don't aim to hurt him, just ferry him back to camp. You and Hascal can go by land with the equipment and the dogs. I'll take Spencer. And Smokey." Beside him, the collie thumped a muddy tail, eyeing his work with almost human intelligence.

"Maybe we'd best be sayin' our goodbyes . . . just in case. Offer up a prayer or two."

Sion brushed aside Nate's mournful words. "I'm more in need of hickory," he said with quiet determination, bent on lashing the tree's tough innards around the frame they were making of elm bark. Glad he was that the bark slipped easy in spring.

Farther down the bank sat Cornelius, whey-faced, whether from his torn foot or the ordeal before him, Sion didn't know and didn't care.

Aware they were an easy mark, he looked to the opposite shore and then back to the axemen as they brought both hickory and elm. Nate stood watch, his rifle ready. Sion's own flintlock, Annie, was near at hand, leaning against a rock.

In another hour they had the vessel at the water's edge, testing it for leaks. Once Sion deemed it worthy, Nate removed his hat again, his voice a near shout over the water's tumult, his Quaker roots coming to bear. "Heavenly Father, hold these men in the light. Thee alone control the wind and the waves. We beseech Thee for safe passage."

They chorused amen, all but Sion, and Nate and Hascal helped launch the vessel before disappearing into the woods. Watching them go, Sion was sure of only two things. The swift, swollen Shawnee guaranteed no Indian could draw a bead on them from the bank, and they'd reach camp long before the others, slowed by equipment as they were.

He felt a final, fatal misgiving as he took position at the rear of the raft, bracing himself for the ride. Immediately, like a strong man tossing quoits, the current grabbed hold of them and flung the raft into the center of the river. There the water was a peculiar pale green, foaming white around rocks and snags.

Trepidation gave way to exhilaration. The river itself stretched seventy yards wide and was crooked as a dog's hind leg. Some of the riverbank was choked with cane, but even this was dwarfed by staggering chestnut, oak, and maple. In front of him, nearly between his knees, sat Smokey, ears forward and expression lively. The rigid set of Cornelius's thin shoulders was next, and then the broad, fleshy back of Spencer filled the bow.

They hit a rock, the force of it nearly spilling them sideways. Sion jammed the forked branch he held onto the boulder's slick surface and thrust them back on course. Breathless now and bewitched by the changing landscape, he barely noticed a slight shift as the riverbed began a gradual drop.

"Morgan!" Cornelius's bellow was swallowed in a storm of cold spray. "By heaven—"

They were picking up speed, sweeping over massive sandstone ledges that were narrowing and propelling them toward a high-walled gorge. The river had altered suddenly from a southwesterly to a northerly course. Sion was unprepared for such a turn and felt oddly out of touch with the careening world around them. In the bow, Cornelius was still shouting but Sion only heard his panic, not words. And then . . .

The falls.

Nothing else could account for that unearthly roar, nor the veil of mist that rose like a wall before them.

"Save yourselves!" Sion shouted.

He dove right. The water was like ice and he was sucked under, pinned between two jagged rocks. He came up gasping, his breath like a knife in his heaving lungs, his sodden hair hugging his scalp and stealing his vision. It had all happened so fast—the launch, the upset, the near drowning.

Summoning strength, he fought his way toward the south bank, moccasins full of sand, finally breaking free of the brawling river. Stumbling ashore, he pulled himself to his full height and took in the spectacle before him.

A deluge of water, a full hundred thirty feet across, spewed greenish-white in a foamy seventy-foot fall.

No man or animal could survive such a torrent. Could they? Mayhap Nate had been right about the river's spring rush. Sion felt murderous. A quiver of relief coursed through him that Nate hadn't been in the boat. If he'd sent men to their deaths, he hated that he felt more of a loss over Smokey than Cornelius or Spencer.

Since Harper had stormed into his life and sent him unraveling, he'd felt little at all.

His bleary gaze fastened on the river as it clawed and chewed its way north. Best work his way down and scour the bank for a body . . . the remains of the raft. His head spun and refused to settle.

Even the weather seemed put out with him. Clouds lay

like waves overlapping, black upon gray, heavy with rain. The day was almost spent. An hour of searching turned up nothing but smoke.

An Indian campfire, likely. The plume of gray hung low amid some distant trees, a promise of stormy weather. He'd sensed rain was coming with the rise of the wind and myriad swallows flying near the ground.

Heart still a-gallop, he stood poised on an outcropping of dry rock, his hunting shirt chill against his skin, his buckskins black. His hands rested on his blackened belt that still held both hatchet and hunting knife. Exposed here on the riverbank, he sensed every instinct tug him to the hiddenness of the woods.

Nate had told him that the Cherokee considered the falls sacred. That they sent their dead into the river, believing the path to the spirit world lay in the mist. The irony of the situation bit into him. He'd likely sent two men to their deaths—and his dog. Where their spirits had gone, he didn't know.

His gaze fastened on a precipice clear of the smoke and spray. Dizzy, he shut his eyes. He'd hit his head on a rock in the spill. A touch to his forehead came away red.

Was he seeing things?

A figure stood on a lofty ledge above as if carved from the sandstone cliff. He squinted. Blinked. The image stayed steadfast.

The woman was clad in the colors of the woods, her dark hair snaking over one shoulder and hanging braided to her hips. Like Harper. The rifle at her side told him she was smallish. Again like Harper. The muzzle, the very tip, of the upturned barrel shadowed her shoulder. He felt an uncharacteristic shiver. And then, with an ease that belied the gun's heft, as if she'd had her fill of the sight of him, she took her weapon and vanished from sight.

The warm pressure of Tempe's hand stayed Paige's stirring. They both looked up from the boiling kettle of wash to take in the dark shadow moving haltingly among the trees toward the back of the inn. Tempe said nothing, but her thoughts ran wild.

A white man.

But not much of one. His shoes were missing, his clothes torn and muddy. He wore no hat, neither felt nor fur, and looked in sore need of the lye soap they washed with.

Tempe cast a glance at the woodshed where the honey-hued dog lay, broken leg splinted. The collie gnawed contentedly on a ham bone and swished its pluming tail when Tempe spoke a few low words to it.

She'd watched the bark boat bearing both dog and men come hurtling down the river, witnessed every detail of their spill the day before. Whoever had decided on such a venture was a bold soul. She sensed it wasn't the man now struggling uphill. He looked to be puny. No match for the woods. Nor was he the flaxen-headed boy in the bow who'd finally crawled onto the opposite shore, heaving greenish water. Their untimely river journey was the doing of the dark-haired man she'd seen searching the bank long into the twilight.

Why this odd disappointment that the stranger coming toward them wasn't him?

Tempe had told no one what she'd seen. Not even Russell. Paige stood at the kettle, clearly curious.

When the man was a few feet from them, he offered a stiff

35

bow. "Pardon me, ladies. Cornelius Lyon of Williamsburg, Virginia. And you are . . . ?"

Recovering her manners, Paige dropped a little curtsey. "Paige Shaw." When Tempe made no move toward introductions, she added, "And this here is the daughter of the mistress of the Moonbow Inn."

The stranger smiled a white smile, revealing no snuff-yellowed or rotten teeth, his gaze lifting to the inn's far rafters. "Well, Mistress Moonbow and Shaw, might I beg your assistance?" He looked down at his shabby state of dress, clearly embarrassed. "I seem to have had a falling out with the river. The river won."

To Tempe's dismay, Paige giggled just as Russell rounded the corner, half a dozen dogs at his heels. At the sight of the newcomer the lot of them set up snarling and wagging all at once.

Her brother's eyes narrowed as he surveyed the Englishman in silent appraisal whilst Tempe fixed her attention on the stranger's head. He might have passed for handsome if not for the goose egg swelling his brow, though it was his limp, grievesome as Russell's own, that first caught her notice.

"A porch chair, Russell, if you will." Tempe took the wash paddle and resumed stirring. "And some metheglin, Paige, please." Left alone with the stranger for a few moments, Tempe dared, "You're one of the surveyors." His eyes flashed surprise. She'd not tell him she'd watched every detail of their watery ordeal. "What exactly brings you to these parts?"

"What indeed." His gaze shifted to the inn and outbuildings, lingering on the May blossoms crowding the back steps as if the knot on his noggin—or the mere mention of metheglin—was conjuring up comely scenes. "The better question is, what brings *you*?"

Paige saved her from answering, bringing him the requested

cup. Cornelius Lyon murmured his appreciation and downed the drink in two thirsty swallows. Russell returned, bearing a chair he'd recently finished, of stout hickory with a cane seat.

Tempe spoke with care. "My brother's got some britches and a shirt you can have, and some shoes." Russell was still regarding the stranger with a shrewd eye, never one to let his guard down. Tempe struck a deal. "Maybe in exchange you can tell us why you've come and how long you aim to stay."

4

There was nobody in the wilderness but God and us.
—Simon Kenton

J ust where do you think you're goin'?" Nate stood by,
pulling on a fleshy earlobe in agitation. "You ain't hardly
dried out yet."

"I'm going on a little sashay thataway." With a westerly tilt
of his head, Sion began stuffing a few essentials in a knapsack, mainly jerk and a flint box. "I'd be lying if I told you
it's Cornelius I'm after."

"It's Smokey, ain't it? You can hardly rest for thinkin' about
that dog."

Sion sidestepped the question. "We're not running any
line, and I'm getting camp fever."

"Wilderness fever is more like it. I'll come with you."

"Nay, you hunker down here with Lucian and Hascal and
Spencer."

Nate shook his head mournfully. "Spencer ain't been right
since he swallowed all that river water."

Truly, the stoutest of his chain carriers looked puny even
two days hence. With a last look at the lad, Sion flung the

bridle over his stallion's head. Prime Virginia horse stock, Beck nickered softly, nuzzling his hand. He felt a swell of pleasure at Beck's sure-footedness on the trace and how willing the animal was to please him. Next to Smokey, Beck was nearly as essential as his rifle. He eased his flintlock into its saddle holster, wondering if he'd have call to use it. He needed to fire Annie to clear her of damp powder after the storm, but an uneasy feeling kept him from it.

"Maybe you can sashay down to a salt lick and bring back a buffalo. We could use fresh meat." Nate scratched his whiskery jaw and began to chuckle. "Remember that time along the upper Ohio when—" He couldn't speak for laughing, hand slapping his thigh.

"When you ate all those marrow bones and like to have died?" Sion grinned beneath the brim of his felt hat. "I'll never forget it."

Nate snorted. "Sick as I was, I still crave 'em." He sobered all at once, his gaze turning fretful. "You'd best tell me why you're takin' to the trail. If somethin' happens to you—or us . . ." He left the thought unfinished as Sion swung himself into the saddle.

"I won't be away but a couple of days. Mayhap Cornelius will turn up. If not, I might have to ride to the settlements and see about more help. Jim Harrod is a fine one to run the line, so it's said. There's bound to be others like him around Logan's Station or Boonesborough."

"Watch your back," Nate told him. "I got an unlikely feeling about all this, Corny bein' gone and now you ridin' away."

"No call to fret." The words were calm. Confident. But nudging the stallion's flanks with his heels, Sion wondered if and when he'd see Nate again.

The way was little more than a deer trail, but it penetrated the dense backwoods, leading Sion past windfalls and ivy thickets and strange rock formations peculiar to river country. Gaze never settling, ears open to the slightest sound, Sion pressed west, mapping every feature of unfamiliar ground in his head.

No Indian sign. No game to distract him. Just an aggravation of noisy red-billed, green-bodied parakeets that seemed to resent his presence. And yet . . . he sensed someone at his back, ever shadowing him. Mayhap this wild, unsettled country was just like that, a-haunted. Else it was the shadows in his own conscience he felt so keenly.

He commenced climbing a long, woodsy slope till he came to the ledge on which the woman had stood watching him. Worn to bare rock and free of grass, it appeared to be a favorite lookout. Had she been here many a time? Drinking in the falls and river as it snaked southwest?

If not for the distant mountains crowding the northeast horizon, he could glimpse the Great Meadow, as Boone called it, the place where the first Kentucke settlements were struggling to stand. He longed to push free of these steep draws and ridges that tried his breath and his patience, but he had a job to do, and he couldn't do it without Cornelius.

He blew out a breath, his empty belly gnawing a hole to his backbone. Again that uneasy feeling hovered, that certainty he was conspicuous as a fly in new milk. He scanned the ridge just ahead, Annie close, Beck following.

The snap of a twig sent him spinning. He whirled, gun to his shoulder, and saw a flash of indigo blue. A lissome figure shot away from him like an arrow launched from a bow.

Abandoning Beck, Sion gave chase. Over windfalls and creeks, around boulders and laurel thickets he trailed her, determined to catch her yet unsure what he would do or say if he did. Even in a skirt she flew over the unforgiving ground in such a way that told him she knew it well, every inch. He, the outlander, was at a distinct disadvantage.

Lungs crying for air, sweat damping his hairline, he gained speed when she started downhill. She cut away from him round a protrusion of limestone, and he spied a flash of white stocking. Her moccasined feet hardly seemed to touch the ground.

They were on a thread of muddy trail now. The roar of the river was to his left, a wall of rock to his right. On and on he ran, slipping and stumbling, the recent rain wreaking havoc with his sure-footedness. And then, without warning, he found himself in a clearing, his senses scrambled by an unaccountably domestic scene.

The sun, six hours high, slanted down, casting everything in a golden glow. The indigo-clad figure had disappeared. Sion stood in back of what looked to be a sizable dwelling place. Raising a frayed sleeve, he slicked the sweat from his brow and willed his breathing to settle.

Nearest him was a stone springhouse situated on the hillside, set in the deep shade of twin sycamores. Water cascaded from beneath one rock wall, spilling like a waterfall into a cedar trough before turning into a trickle as it ran off down the hill into the river far below.

Cleanly folks, whoever they were.

Setting Annie aside, he plunged his hands into the trough and splashed his heated face. A clean tow linen towel hung on a nearby buttonbush. Ignoring it, he swung his gaze wide, taking in the usual necessities of living. Ash hopper. Hominy block. Smokehouse. Woodshed. Kettles and piggins and tubs rested atop an abundance of stumps. Barrows and sleds held river rock and firewood.

Cleanly, aye, and industrious.

Twin cabins claimed his attention—and respect. South facing and connected by a dogtrot, they were as stout as a station even without pickets and loopholes. A thick column of smoke curled from one chimney. Sion caught the savory odor of baked bread and meat, and his stomach cramped in empty protest.

Taking rifle in hand, he started toward the buildings, where half a dozen mongrels stood guard. Growling. One old gray-muzzled cur lounged idly and didn't even lift his head. The thought of Smokey brought a pang. His gaze roamed log walls hung with traps, bridles, and tools as two of the dogs sniffed his leggings. Halfway down the dogtrot the door to the east cabin was open wide, enticing him.

Where had the woman gone?

He meant to find out.

Tempe returned to the kitchen, her legs atremble from running, her heated face the shade of the pickled beets Aylee was spearing into a bowl.

"Mercy, but you're tardy," her mother admonished. "Tie you on an apron and make ready to serve some hungry folk."

"There'll be one more, likely," Tempe said.

Aylee stopped her spearing and Paige her frying, both of them looking at her in expectation. Tempe tied on the apron with nary an explanation and sailed into the keeping room as if she'd not run two miles through thick woods and a blaze of danger.

She sensed her pursuer would come and stay. The excited bark of the dogs along the dogtrot needn't announce him. Going to the shelf that hugged the west wall, she took down a shiny pewter plate. The room was empty but would soon fill. Harrod's men were gone. In their place was a party of longhunters headed downriver into the French Broad territory of Tennessee—and Cornelius Lyon.

Aylee didn't open the door to the dining room till noon. All comers were free to loiter in the yard in fair weather or seek the shelter of the dogtrot in foul. Setting down the plate atop the puncheon table, Tempe was glad to the heart she'd ironed a linen cloth and picked some phlox and Jacob's ladder early that morning. Such care had a gentling effect on the roughest men.

Once the door opened, Russell appeared, Cornelius Lyon after him. Tempe nearly chuckled. He brought to mind a banty rooster, strutting and proud. Somehow he'd managed to wheedle a scrap of red cloth from Paige, which he wore around his neck. It brightened up the dull homespun Russell had lent him, giving him a jaunty air.

The fish she'd caught that morning—fat catfish and carp—had been fried to succulent, brown perfection alongside crusty slabs of venison steak. A mound of hominy seasoned with bacon filled a wooden bowl, and there were enough corn cakes to rival the miracle of the loaves and fishes. The Englishman's eyes lit with pleasure.

"Ah, Mistress Moonbow. Another extraordinary meal, I see."

Tempe smiled at Cornelius's flatter. His air of refinement hinted he'd known far better fare. In the brief time he'd been with them, she'd grown used to his gushing ways.

The longhunters came in, resting rifles against a sidewall before claiming the benches. The empty chair at table's end, once reserved for Pa, yawned empty.

And the stranger in the woods? Would he not come? After chasing her such a distance?

Maybe he'd gone back for his horse. She'd hate to part with a mount with so fetching a blaze down its muzzle.

Russell shot her a querying look from his end of the table. She was alarmed now—and more than a little dismayed. Had her plan to reunite the banty rooster with the rest of his surveying party gone awry? Not only that, the longhunters looked famished. If her pursuer didn't come quick, nary a crumb would remain.

Lord, please. I asked Your help to find this man, and now I need You to usher him in.

Before she'd mumbled amen, a figure darkened the doorway. Aylee came out of the kitchen right then, bearing a bowl of sallet. With her usual courtesy, she simply said, "Bide awhile."

With nary a word, the stranger ducked beneath the door's lintel before parting with his rifle, hanging his hat from the barrel's tip.

Standing unseen beneath the loft stair by the kitchen door, Tempe felt a flicker of triumph. It took little time to size him up. She was used to men like Simon Kenton and Daniel Boone. This man was their caliber, right down to his fine weapon with its silver mountings. He had that same air of intense quietness, that inbred strength and stealth that marked an able woodsman.

But that was not all.

His hair was so black it had a blue sheen to it, so raggety on the ends it seemed like scissors had gone awry. It lay like a mane across his broad shoulders, broken free of its tie. Had he lost the tie in the chase? He wore the typical garb of the woods, a linsey hunting shirt and deerskin leggings, every seam fringed to repel water, all a pleasing nutmeg hue. Her gaze dropped. His moccasins and his hands were immense, nearly as large as Pa's. Hatchet and knife hung at his sides.

She dug deep for some imperfection. Some flaw. But this man, at least outwardly, was as fine a one as the Almighty ever made.

After James.

44

His eyes seemed to be everywhere at once, sorting, sifting, weighing, missing nothing. When he turned her way she expected to feel dissected by that gaze. As if he could see clear through to the heart. To the hurts and thwarted hopes secreted there. But he hadn't seen her. Not yet. She'd stepped behind the loft stair out of sight.

And then Cornelius murmured a stiff greeting, stealing the frontiersman's attention. With a sigh of relief, Tempe turned into the kitchen, leaving the reunited men to their dinner and their talk.

The lure of the open cabin door and his empty belly proved too much. Sion ducked inside the west cabin, unsure of his welcome. A spare, sandy-haired woman greeted him. "Bide awhile," she said. Neat and tidy as a well-kept cupboard, she led him to a table at which sat half a dozen men—and Cornelius Lyon.

Sion staunched his dislike as best he could. But Cornelius was not so stoic. Animosity sprawled across his bruised face, checked only by a serving girl offering him something to drink.

The only open seat was at table's end. Sion sat, head swimming with a great many things at once. Ash floors scoured a lighter shade. Stout oak walls and walnut shutters. No cat-and-clay chimney but one of sturdy river rock, a carved sunburst on the mantel. He surveyed the burgeoning table. He'd not seen such an abundance of food since—his throat knotted and he forced himself to finish the thought—since he'd first met Harper amid the opulence of Oakwood. Walnut trenchers and buckeye bowls held cheese, pickled vegetables, conserves, even a mound of butter with a dogwood flower molded on top.

His pewter plate was soon heaped with fried fish and more.

Along with all the bounty he felt a queer emptiness that he'd not yet sighted that indigo skirt. It was on account of her being like Harper that moved him so. Fleet of foot. Cider-haired. Bosomy yet spare-waisted.

Here he sat at a strange table bearing heaven's bounty, when all he wanted was to ride home to Virginia and fall headlong into Harper's arms.

"Sweet milk or buttermilk?" The serving girl was at his elbow, holding two pitchers.

He swallowed a bite of cornbread drenched with butter, nearly speechless at its goodness. "Sweet."

What he needed was a staunch mug of applejack or ale, but this establishment might be dry. And in the face of such abundance he'd not ask for it. The woman who'd greeted him upon entering had disappeared through a door below the loft stair. The kitchen? The only sounds in the keeping room were utensils scraping plates, grunts of approval, and some ill-bred belching. Men generally made little conversation at meals, and Sion felt at ease with the silence.

Through the open door to the dogtrot he heard a familiar neighing. *Beck.* He'd been foolish to leave his horse. What was the matter with him? He'd hardly had room to think of Beck, what with his sprint through the woods and finding Cornelius and his ongoing angst over Smokey. He felt nigh addlepated.

When the kitchen door creaked open again he felt an odd twist of excitement. The indigo skirt came in. She rounded the table, refilling drinks and bringing more butter. Eyes down, she didn't look at him, just made a dance of her work, leaning and pouring and sashaying in and out.

She came to a sudden stop at his elbow. "Be you a surveyor?"

Clearing his throat with a swig of milk, he said, "Aye. Sion Morgan. And you?"

"A tavern wench."

"Tavern wenches have names."

A slight hesitation. "Tempe."

"Tempe . . ." He waited for a surname.

"Just Tempe," she returned quietly.

"Well, Just Tempe, what business do you have with me?"

"Only this—your horse is outside . . . and your dog."

"My dog?" he said, forking a last bite of fish.

"Her leg's broke and splinted but she'll mend." She poured him more milk without his asking. "If you carry her across your saddle careful-like, you and your partner can be on your way."

He didn't miss the meaning buried in her hushed words. Had Cornelius overstayed his welcome? He could believe it. But Cornelius, finished with his meal, showed no sign of departing. With a lingering scowl at Sion, he got up and wandered to the rack on the wall that bore a collection of clay pipes. A tobacco box rested on the mantel.

"As I have no ha'pence to pay," Cornelius announced, "you can charge Mister Morgan the amount."

Sion said nothing, just raised his gaze to look into the woman's, a query in their blueness. His gladness over her news about Smokey curbed his ire over Cornelius's arrogance. "You saved my dog."

She lowered her eyes, flicking away a crumb on the linen cloth while the longhunters got up from the table. "Nay, just mended her."

He sat back as she stole away his empty plate. "What do I owe you?"

"Naught for the dog, but your friend there . . ." Her eyes rounded as she cast a glance Cornelius's way. "He's a mite more troublesome, being a gentleman."

Sion couldn't hide a rueful smile. *Mite* was an understatement, as was *friend*, even *gentleman*. "I'll settle up with you before I go."

Cornelius was lounging now, occupying the best chair by the hearth. He took up smoking tongs and snagged a live coal from the dwindling fire to light the tobacco Sion now owed.

The kitchen door swung open again and the other serving girl, the flaxen-haired one, brought in a tankard. "Your metheglin, sir."

Cornelius smiled his ingratiating smile. "Miss Shaw, you anticipate my every need."

She gave a little curtsey and produced a pack of playing cards. "The mistress will see to your injury shortly."

Sion studied the exchange, remembering Cornelius's cane-stobbed foot. Foot encased in a moccasin, he still bore a limp. But it was nothing compared to the man sitting opposite him who took up a fiddle, his bow sliding across the strings with a finesse that belied both his quiet and his crippling. The French Broad men and Cornelius listened. The other longhunters had gone outside.

Sion judged the man to be shy of thirty, the leg he dragged behind him turning him older still. He had seated himself with difficulty, though no pain marred his face. An old injury, mayhap. His hair was cider-brown, like the indigo-skirted girl. Were they kin? Both bore the markings of the older woman who'd first greeted him, owning her intense blue eyes and that wary watchfulness.

Cornelius looked his way and said above the music, "Care to join us, Morgan?"

Though he wanted to bow out, he knew Cornelius was in no mood to leave, and short of hauling him back to camp, he'd wait till the metheglin had done its mellowing work.

"I'd best see to my horse and dog first." With that, Sion passed outside to the dogtrot. Beck had been hobbled in back, and Smokey's tail was waving wildly from beneath the low eave of a woodshed. Relieved, he knelt beside her, running a hand over her silken coat, wishing he had no more to do than pack her back to camp.

She licked his hand, nuzzling the fringe of his hunting shirt as he took in her splinted leg. "You're but a little worse for wear, tackling the falls like you did. At least you bear me no grudge, like some."

Returning inside, he selected a pipe, leaving money enough for his and Cornelius's expenses. Ignoring the smoking tongs, he snatched a glowing coal between thumb and forefinger, his calluses shielding him from its heat. The heady blend of tobacco riffled through his senses as he settled down to play a round of All Fours.

If he tipped back in his chair he could see outside and keep an eye on both Smokey and Beck, a far better prospect than watching the bewhiskered, bruised face of Cornelius across from him.

The man with the lame leg was dealing. He hadn't said his name and Sion wondered. Just who were these people surviving—nay, thriving—along a remote river in the howling wilderness? He supposed it didn't matter. He had a job to do. The sooner he returned his mapmaker to base camp, the better. They were expected back at Fort Henry by August.

"Another drink, if you will." Cornelius was almost comical in his condescension, but the serving girl hastened to do his bidding, clearly charmed.

Soon all the men were sipping and smoking, earning points and playing tricks in order to reach the winning score. The game intensified, the tension mounting. When Sion won the first round, Cornelius began to tap his foot, a sure sign of his agitation.

"We agreed the score was to be fifteen," he murmured.

"Eleven," Sion corrected, leading another trick.

Cornelius studied his hand coldly. "I didn't doubt you'd be good at this, Morgan. 'Tis known as a game of low repute."

The table stilled. Sion digested the words in teeth-gritted silence.

"If you're so high and mighty, what the devil are you playing it for?" One of the longhunters clapped Cornelius on the shoulder and gained a slim smile.

"I do prefer whist or faro," Cornelius said.

"Them's for fancy pants. You ain't a Tory, are ye?"

Cornelius snorted. "Best ask that of the man next to you. He's with the Loyal Land Company as a Crown surveyor. I'm merely his mapmaker."

The man pulled on his unkempt beard, eyes narrowing to suspicious slits. "The Loyal, eh?"

Sion played another card. "Running the line for the Loyal makes me no more a Tory than being in the wilderness makes you an Indian."

All chuckled but Cornelius. He sat in broody silence, holding up the game till more metheglin was served. Sion eyed his hand, sorry he'd followed the woman here in a dose of rashness he now regretted. A sense of foreboding hovered, pungent as the swirling smoke. Sion knew what Cornelius was capable of. And he didn't want these hospitable people, whoever they were, privy to the Englishman's outbursts.

"There's been more than a few surveyors in these parts, but most don't make it back to the settlements." The lame man spoke, tone thoughtful. "'Tis a dangerous time to be carrying a compass."

"There's nowhere safe, be it east or west," Sion said slowly, thoughts full of General Washington's ragtag army. "I'm against the king's proclamation prohibiting settlers from western lands. Seems like a man can move when and where he pleases. Surveying Kentucke may be the best way to fight the British in the end."

"You turncoat." The slur slid off Cornelius's tongue all too easily. "I wonder what the Loyal would say about that, Morgan. No doubt you'd lose your precious pay—"

"Or yer scalp." The longhunter's throaty chuckle was unnerving. "Best heed them musket-totin' red men. Word is the Redcoats are givin' guns to the tribes and aimin' to fight a war right here in the woods, or soon will be."

"Muskets are hardly needed when knives and tomahawks suffice. I'd be more worried if the Redcoats supplied the redskins with fatal Pennsylvania rifles like these." Setting his cup aside, Cornelius leaned toward the wall where Sion's rifle rested and took Annie in hand.

Sion went white-hot at his impudence. His tilted chair came down. Loose-limbed, Cornelius swung the gun to his shoulder like a careless child with a toy, the barrel leveled at Sion's chest. The trigger clicked. Primed and loaded, the rifle exploded in a storm of fiery sparks. Sion lunged right, his chair tumbling backwards.

Every man was on his feet, their startled faces obscured by a cloud of dense, choking smoke. The acrid burn of powder soured the air as Sion wrested the gun away, sending Cornelius against the log wall, the pipe collection shattering.

The lame man's shout for order was lost as the rest of the longhunters rushed in from the dogtrot to join the melee, a dozen snarling, riled dogs on their heels.

5

In going up the Cumberland River, I saw the highest and stoutest cane I ever saw.

—JACOB LAWSON

While she swept the kitchen floor, Tempe kept one ear tuned to the keeping room. Would the men stay on? Bed down in the loft? Her step lightened as she listened to them playing cards. Though the dark-haired stranger's low tones were new to her, she could have easily distinguished it from a roomful of other masculine voices.

Who *was* this Sion Morgan?

A borderman, likely. One of those hardy souls from back of the settlements, more at home in the woods than a cabin. Maybe kin to the sharpshooter Daniel Morgan or one of his revered riflemen. How such a man came to be tied to the banty rooster was a downright riddle. Necessity, she guessed. Cornelius Lyon would be easy prey for Indians. A meadow mouse to a hawk. But this man Morgan . . .

As she thought it, a harsh laugh shattered her reverie. And

then, a heartbeat after, came rifle fire. Like her bad dream that morning she'd waited for James and he never came. It had been her marrying day, but there'd been a burying. It had come swiftly. Without warning.

Would her entire life be marked by bursts of powder and lead?

Dropping her broom, she made for the kitchen door and rushed into the keeping room. Smoke seared her senses. A bench had been overturned, and brawling dogs and men were hither and yon. Paige was cowering beneath the loft steps, and Ma—Tempe looked wildly about—Ma had likely gone to work in the corn patch, sparing herself the spectacle.

Tempe startled as Russell fired his pistol into the floorboards at his feet, the angry jut of his jaw carrying further warning. The floor was more easily mended than the roof, rafters crowded with herbs and strings of beans and other sundry things. Russell yelled for order as he reloaded with shaking hands, hardly able to manage the task.

Hurt took hold of her. Hurt that her brother was broken in body and spirit, scarred beyond telling. Hurt that such a ruckus had been raised when they took such pains to be peaceable. Hurt that she'd thought well of a man who seemed ready to tear the heart out of his friend.

Cornelius now had more than his cane-stobbed foot to trouble him. He'd been pinned to the wall by the surveyor she'd just served, his arrogant nose bloodied, perhaps broken.

If Cornelius Lyon was a banty rooster, Sion Morgan was a wolf.

❧

Half crazed with fury, Sion jerked the red neckerchief from Cornelius's throat and proceeded to tie his hands in an unforgiving knot. The ring of men looked on, the lame man's pistol trained on whomever cared to court more trouble.

Crowning Sion's humiliation, the indigo-clad girl had just come in, and he felt a fresh flare of aggravation that he didn't know her full name. She stood, hands on hips, looking at him warily, almost accusingly, as if he was to blame for the mess—or should have stopped it from the start.

Sion pulled Cornelius to his feet and shoved him out the door to the dogtrot. The coin he owed was uppermost, though he was too riled to take account of all the damage. He removed a small pouch from the bosom of his hunting shirt and tossed it to the lame man, who caught it midair. The merry jingle of money added to Sion's aggravation as he ducked beneath the door's lintel, never so glad for fresh air.

With a last, regretful look at Smokey, he slung the bound, inebriated Cornelius onto Beck's saddle and began an ignoble retreat, intent on their camp downriver.

Tempe attacked a clump of weeds crowding the corn patch, cleaving the green intruders with a vicious jab of her hoe. She'd helped clean the keeping room, sweeping up scattered shards of pipe, even picking the spent rifle ball from the log wall, but her emotions still ran high. Before it sank into the wood, the bullet had burrowed clean through a beloved book, the very heart of Robert Herrick's *Poems*. She felt the loss keenly, though she'd committed most of the verse to memory.

Down the row, Aylee bent and watered plant after plant, her comely frame with its cambric apron and cap out of place amid the dirt and stumps. Despite the recent rain, the May sun was hot, the soil crusted dry. She glanced Tempe's way. "Tell me again what happened to get you het up so."

Whack. Another weed fell. Tempe leaned on her hoe, gaze roaming the narrow field's shadowed borders. She'd explained the fracas once, but her mother dug deeper, beyond spent rifle balls and overturned benches.

When Tempe said nothing, Aylee filled the silence. "There's bad blood betwixt those two strangers. What has that to do with you?"

Tempe uprooted another weed. "Nothing . . . everything." She swallowed, the words sour. With all her heart she wanted to spare her mother more trouble. "They're with the Loyal Land Company, Mama. The *Loyal.*"

Aylee's watering ceased. "Says who?"

"Says Paige. Then Russell heard it from Cornelius Lyon himself when they were playing cards after supper."

Rarely did Aylee show alarm, but now stark vulnerability etched her face. "They've not come for your father? Or is it land they're after?"

"Both, maybe."

Aylee resumed her pouring gourdful by gourdful, again the picture of composure. "How are they to tie us to the past? Your pa hides hisself. We take care never to say we're Tuckers. Most ask few questions and are just glad for bed and board."

"Most aren't the Loyal Land Company." Despite the heat of the day, Tempe shivered. Standing on the dogtrot an hour earlier, she'd seen the way Morgan had hog-tied Lyon and slung him atop his horse. It brought to bear Pa's words when they'd fled Virginia after his deadly scuffle.

I'll not stay and be hung from a crossbeam or even branded on the cheek.

Sion Morgan could do either with ease. There was something smoldering inside him, some fire that threatened to reduce him to ashes. Despite his stoic demeanor, Tempe sensed the rattler's bite beneath. Anyone who'd set foot on the frontier held tight to something that haunted them. What haunted Morgan?

"All that matters is that your father's out of harm's way." Aylee began moving toward the creek that skirted the cornfield to refill her bucket. "Misters Morgan and Lyon won't stay long in the Kentucke territory, to my way of thinking. They're liable to be gone before your pa returns from trading, and we'll be none the worse for it."

Tempe opened her mouth then shut it, not wanting to naysay her mother. Let Aylee live with the hope there'd be no payment, no reckoning, for Pa's crime. But Tempe knew better. Killing a man cast a long shadow, be it in settled Virginia or the savage woods.

∽

The short path between cornfield and inn was well trod, wending through dense forest and overlooking the river far below. Most days it held a bit of enchantment, wooing Tempe with a clump of May strawberries or wild honeysuckle or the oak's gauzy tasseling. Such things crowded out care, allowing her to lose herself in the pure beauty and lonesomeness of her surroundings. But today, as twilight set in, she was still full of the noon fracas and what the coming of these men meant.

She stood at the entry to the barn-shed, eyes adjusting to the dimness, breathing in the rich scent of wood, recalling the sweat and pleasure she and her brother had shared cutting cedar in the fall when the sap was down. Now stacked along one wall and dried, the wood would become all manner of things. Tubs. Rolling pins. Piggins. Farm implements. This was her brother's domain, the tools on the walls made by his hands, his companionable presence felt.

56

"Russell."

He looked up at her soft call—she knew better than to surprise him—then returned to the wood he was perusing by the light of a fat pine notch.

Putting away her hoe, Tempe eyed the dog lying in a bed of cedar shavings near a worktable. How the hurt creature had managed to make its way from the woodshed befuddled her. On sight of her, it thumped its pale, plumy tail, eyes eager.

Stooping, Tempe ran a hand down the downy back, careful to avoid the splinted leg. Why hadn't she asked Sion Morgan more about his dog? "Would that I knew your name." Weary, she sat down, her fingers sinking into the dog's fur, the cedar shavings beneath them, and looked up at Russell. "What are you making?"

He began splitting cedar into staves, hands steady as he managed the froe. "Ma said Paige needs a new churn."

Nay, Russell. Paige needs you.

Would he attempt to woo her with wood? Tempe felt a bit of Pa's exasperation. Weary of being the go-between, Tempe sighed, a sign he easily read.

"You still nettled about Morgan and Lyon?"

She nodded. "I told Mama. She thinks they'll soon move on."

"The tall one, Morgan . . ." Russell cast a look her way. "He'll be back for his dog."

"I wonder . . ." Could such a man have any tenderness inside him? Waste time on a wounded creature?

At her tense silence, he said, "You misjudge the man. It's Lyon you need to be chary of."

The banty rooster? Tempe held her tongue. *Or the wolf?*

"Lyon's the one who fired the gun, remember, and made a mort of trouble over cards. He lit into Morgan like a bear cub after a bee's nest while playing All Fours, even before the bullet went awry." He hissed out a breath. "Mishandling a man's rifle is akin to mishandling a man's woman. You know that."

She understood. Not even her own flintlock, given her by an ague-ridden Pennsylvanian who'd died in their care, was so finely wrought. But it was Sion Morgan's hands that left her pondering. At the base of his fingers were fleshy indentions made by keeping extra balls in hand, a sure sign of an experienced rifleman, a sharpshooter. "I've never seen such a gun."

"I favored his engraved powder horn myself." Russell set the froe aside. "Reckon you could manage Morgan's rifle?"

Tempe bit her lip. "I wouldn't try lest he shackle me like he did Cornelius Lyon."

Russell frowned when she'd rather he chuckle. "I'd like to see you outshoot him."

"He'd likely not warm to that either." Her thoughts swung to more troubling matters. "Paige wheedled all sorts of talk out of Lyon, waiting on him hand and foot. Seems like they're to meet up with a guide come Crab Orchard just shy of the settlements. They mean to map the Great Meadow—"

Russell's countenance darkened. "The land around the Kentucke forts?"

"My guess is, given the danger there, they'll head south, toward the Cherokee in Tennessee, the very trail Pa is taking. I fear—" She wrestled with her thoughts, barely able to corral them into words. "I fear they'll meet up with Pa either coming or going."

Russell hung his head, broody. A-shiver again, Tempe got up and went to stand by the barn-shed door. Through the wind's gentle soughing she could hear Ma in the distance, driving the belled cattle home. "These men—the Loyal—put me in mind of the past, how Pa might have done things differently."

"How so?"

"Mighten Pa have turned the other cheek, as Scripture said, let the Crown surveyor have his way? Saved himself from becoming embroiled in a lethal boundary dispute? Even though Frederick Ice started the trouble, Pa could have walked away. They were mismatched. Pa doesn't know his own strength. He took the man's life meaning only to warn him."

"'Twas more than about the land, Tempe. Ice was a Tory who had it in for Pa from the start, protesting all Patriot claims."

She fell silent, the details fuzzy. Still reeling from James's death, she'd recalled little but their hasty flight months later over the Gap. Late spring it had been. They were continually wet. Hungry. They'd lived in a cave all the while they'd built this place. For a year or better they'd expended their strength carving something civilized from soil and rock and river, always on the lookout for Virginia authorities or those intent on collecting a bounty. Fugitives, all of them. Or so it seemed.

"You forget that Pa would have been tried by Tories in those parts and hung more for his politics," Russell said. "Even though Ice started the trouble and stole Pa's claim, few would oppose him. He was a man of means with ties to Williamsburg, thus the generous bounty."

The bounty. One thousand British pounds for Pa's capture. Was a man's life worth so little?

"I'm in agreement with Ma." Russell continued on in a rare burst of verbosity. "We should have stayed on the Yadkin back in Carolina where we were born. Stayed on where the Tuckers and Bryants and Boones had roots."

The longing in his voice wrenched her. "You could go back, Russell. You could leave here—"

"And what would a lame man do, Temperance? Farm? I—"

"You needn't farm. You've no call to set foot in a field." She waved a hand about the shed. "You're a cooper and black-smith and gunsmith and more. Let folks come to you. Take Paige and go back—"

"There's no going back." He began examining the staves, his hands beset with a slight tremor and drawing her notice. "Powell Valley was the turning point. Seems like little has been right since."

She stared at him, stunned he'd even mouthed the words. Like Pa, Russell never spoke of the valley or that chill October morning. Nor could he bear the mention. For weeks after, he'd uttered nothing, nor responded to anything asked of him, and it seemed his mind struggled to heal alongside his shattered leg.

She returned her attention to the woods beyond the barn-shed, to the little dip in the trail where Ma would soon drive the livestock past trees and blossom bushes, her willow switch swishing this way and that.

Dare she speak of it? "I keep thinking of that haunted day, what James's father said . . ." She swallowed, summoning the words beneath a swell of still-tender feelings. "When the men went back to say words over the graves . . ."

James was a good son, and I looked forward to a long and useful life for him, but it is not to be . . . Sometimes I feel like a leaf carried on a stream. It may whirl about and turn and twist, but it is always carried forward . . .

She felt the want of Russell's presence before she'd finished speaking and turned and saw that he had gone. Where to, she didn't know. Remorse flooded her. She knew better than to speak of the past. He'd lived through the horror she'd only heard about secondhand. She had no right to the mention. He'd carry the scars, seen and unseen, to his grave.

6

Only a few white men were ever as good as the Indians at the Indian game. Boone and Kenton were.

—FREDERICK PALMER

Fog rolled in, spreading a gauzy white blanket over the river bottoms, as thick and bewildering as the surrounding cane land. Such weather made surveying work impossible. The fact chafed like a burr as Sion pondered what little land they'd laid off, looking over the documents he carried. Encased in hog bladders to protect them from the damp, the Virginia land warrants looked as new as when they'd arrived by express at Fort Henry three months before.

Was he the only one who minded the delay?

Around him his party was almost comical in their Sabbath rest. Across the low fire—their one comfort as its smoke if not its scent was masked by the weather—sat Nate, humming a hymn as he repaired a moccasin with awl and whang leather. Beside him, sunk into *Gulliver's Travels*, was Spencer, still looking a mite green from all that river water. Hascal kept himself occupied checking and polishing all the equipment while Lucian, ever obliging but silent, concocted something in a kettle that bore no resemblance whatsoever to the fare at the Moonbow Inn.

Had he and Cornelius only recently left the inn amid such an uproar?

As riled as the memory made him, Sion felt powerless to halt the pictures the place had painted in his head. Pewter plates burgeoning with crusty corn cakes. Slabs of steak. Chill mugs of sweet milk. Deep dishes of pie . . .

An indigo skirt.

As if to taunt him, Cornelius sat across the fire, partaking of some edible. Sion reckoned the serving girl—Paige—had supplied him. As he thought it, Spencer looked up from his book and whined, "What's that you got?"

Cornelius ceased chewing. "A culinary wonder from the Moonbow Inn. A delicacy known as a beaten biscuit."

With a chuckle, Nate looked up from his moccasin mending. "I was beginnin' to believe you boys had dreamed this Moonbow business up, but that there's proof. Got any to spare?"

"Nay."

"You lyin' Redcoat!" Spencer tossed aside his book in a rare show of temper. "Here we be, unable to lay any chain or hardly stir a foot for the fog, and you fill your greedy belly with such."

"Easy," Sion warned, knowing hunger and boredom were one step away from mutiny. "The weather will clear and we'll soon be at Crab Orchard. There'll be more to eat then."

"Guess we'll have to make do only hearin' about beaten biscuits, then." Nate took up his awl again, not one to make trouble. "So is this here inn run by the same folks we heard tried to come over the Gap with Boone in '73?"

"Not sure about their tie to Boone." Sion spoke carefully, certain Cornelius was wiser to the situation than he, given the time he'd lodged there. "Looks to be a woman with a grown son and daughter, aye."

"No other man about the place?"

When Sion hesitated, Cornelius launched in. "There's a steady stream of longhunters and settlers in due season, or so the serving girl told me. For all their hospitality, the tenants are a close-mouthed bunch."

For once, he and Cornelius agreed. The Moonbow Inn's occupants were an odd clan, tight-lipped if cordial. But it was a cordiality that bordered on coldness if a man raised too many questions. Fiercely knit, all of them. And bold, camped so close to the Warrior's Path.

"Seems like we could sashay over thataway given the weather's so chancy." Nate examined his work. "It ain't but a bit southwest of here, you said. I'd give my eyeteeth for some hot coffee. Cornbread."

Sion stirred the fire with a stick, watching the thin column of smoke vanish into the fog. "We're no longer welcome."

Cornelius snorted, no mirth in it, eyeing Sion as he gave the fire another poke.

Nate was looking from him to Cornelius, bewhiskered face full of questions. "Not welcome, you say?"

Since they'd returned to base camp, Sion had said little, leaving Cornelius to sleep off the spirits the serving girl had given him. All Nate knew was that Smokey remained at the inn, an enviable position given their own damp, fog-bound state.

Sion changed course. "We'll leave out at first light for Crab Orchard, weather permitting. There'll be no backtracking." Even as he said it, he envisioned the flash of displeasure in the eyes of the young woman whose full name he didn't know. Just Tempe, a winsome wisp of a lass if there ever was one.

Would she follow them again like she had at first, raising the hair on the back of his neck because he thought her Cherokee or Shawnee? Or was her interest limited to their trespassing on her territory? He sensed she'd wanted to be rid of them but was content to keep Smokey. He'd rather it be the reverse.

"So we're to meet up with a guide?" Cornelius glanced at him, sulkiness replaced by curiosity. "Someone from one of the three Kentucke stations, I suppose."

"Aye, it'll likely be Boonesborough depending on any trouble and which gun can be spared."

Cornelius looked to his supplies, the paints and brushes carefully packed alongside rolled blank paper. "This Crab Orchard, the rendezvous point . . . might there be a cabin there? A dry place to resume my maps?"

Sion lifted his shoulders in a shrug. "We could set about building one, if needs be."

Surprise washed Cornelius's face. Catering to the man's maps was the one route to appeasement. If Sion could keep Cornelius away from spirits, allow plenty of room for his detailed work, they'd likely stay out of further trouble, personal and otherwise.

For all Cornelius's faults, Sion could find no quarrel with his skills. He was known for the excellence of his maps, some of which had been engraved and printed in Williamsburg and Philadelphia. This was what had first caught Sion's eye. Well, not entirely.

He felt a chill, thinking of Harper. Always Harper. With effort he shifted his thoughts toward safer ground.

On this particular journey, Cornelius's intricate work

would be based on Sion's surveys. Sion's other preoccupation was creating a guidebook of the region, detailing trails, mountains, settlements, and countless rivers that lay between the Gap and the Falls of Ohio. But he'd not reckoned with the depth of all that wildness, the dearth of knowledge he had with the land, how difficult it was to master or make peace with.

Ambitious. Treacherous. Laborious.

Insane.

But for the injured dog and the hole in her poetry book, Tempe could almost believe Sion Morgan and Cornelius Lyon were naught but a bad dream. She went about kitchen and woods for days after, expecting more passersby, but none came. The lull unsettled her. She didn't dare venture far with the fog. It seemed to take the land captive whilst scrambling her usually sound sense of direction. Without the sun or North Star as her guide, she felt adrift.

'Twas full spring. All the wilderness seemed to be holding its breath, pining for summer's start.

Was Pa sitting by in some distant rockhouse or cave till the weather righted itself? She prayed not, though it bemused her to think of the strapping Sion Morgan fog-bound and befuddled. Maybe a spell of bad weather would send the surveyors back over the Gap to Virginia. *That* she welcomed.

Pondering it, she helped Paige finish hetcheling the flax. It was tedious, smelly work breaking the molding, dried straws and dancing with the flax, as Ma called it, once they got the rhythm of the hetchels. Their reward was silken strands fit for Aylee's spinning and weaving.

It seemed she ran between the flax and sheep, helping

Russell with the shearing. Tempe stood by with baskets as her brother wrestled with their small, predator-harried flock. It was her job to wash the filthy fleeces in the sudsy lye kettle, then tease them clean once dry. Tempe warmed to the plushness of the fleece, the softening of the lanolin on her workworn hands.

All of this was a prelude to the task she loved best, the assembling of dye pots. Ma said she was a hand at concocting colors. The pleasing beige of sassafras bark. Madder reds and browns. Oakish yellows. It was a joy to scour the woods for what was needful, though they had a small dye garden that her mother tended like a baby. Of all the fabric they made, wool was the best to work. She shut her mind to the notion of Tidewater finery to the east, savoring both the challenge and the joy of making much of little, reassuring herself they had no need of the life they'd left behind. But Paige wasn't so easily persuaded.

"Here's what I miss." Paige held up a handful of shining flax, full as a horse's tail. "I miss apple trees and pies and such. That's nearly the first thing the Englishman said to me. 'Have you any cider?'"

"Cornelius Lyon?"

"Aye. I told him orchards grow slow here or the savages hack them down like happened at Boonesborough." She looked a trifle dreamy as they hung sacks of wool near Aylee's spinning wheel in a cabin corner. "He asked me to go with him."

"He—what?"

"That he did. 'We're in need of a camp cook,' says he. He promised me wages, safe passage to the settlements."

Tempe's grip on the wool tightened. "When he was full of spirits, likely."

"Nay, 'twas said sober."

"Wages, maybe, but no one is sure of safe passage."

Paige studied her, a rare rebuke in her colorless eyes. "Mister Morgan is of Boone's ilk. If there ever was safe passage, 'twould be with him."

This Tempe couldn't deny, but she was unwilling to dwell on Sion Morgan's merits. "And what would you do once you reach the settlements? You'd create quite a stir arriving with so many men."

"Sully myself, you mean? Nay. With women so scarce, I could have my pick of any man I pleased." Wonder teased her face into a smile. "Fancy that!"

Bemused, Tempe began to dress the distaff of Aylee's great wheel, glad Ma was in the kitchen away from their silly prattle. "I misdoubt forting up is what you make it out to be. Most say settlement life is naught but a pigsty with pickets."

"My brother's in the middle ground. I might see him."

Elisha? Was he even alive? They'd had no word . . .

Tempe amended, "I wouldn't blame you if you were to go. Betimes I'm tempted myself."

Wistful, Paige looked toward the open door, voice dropping a notch. "You reckon Russell would miss me?"

The hope in her words twisted Tempe's heart. "Oh, he would, but he'd never likely say. Russell holds tight to what hurts."

"Here lately I been thinkin' about Russell and me . . ." She lifted slim shoulders in a shrug. "I ain't so sure about the two of us. Betimes life only gives you so many chances. I don't want to reach the grave full of whethers and what-ifs."

Tempe straightened, struck by the words. Paige, for all her simple ways, could turn profound. "Maybe your leaving will stir Russell into action." Why did she taste betrayal in the words? If she encouraged the girl to go . . . "But I'm not sure I'd trust Cornelius Lyon. He's a rascal if there ever was one. I haven't made up my mind about Sion Morgan."

Aylee came in, wiping her hands on her apron. Her eyes lit with pleasure at the sight of the readied flax and wool. "What with the foul weather, no one's coming or going here lately. I just might get some spinning done, and I'd welcome some company. Fetch you a chair, Paige, and commence knitting. Russell will be here shortly."

Russell? Tempe halted on the loft stair. It was unusual for Russell to come in so early. He kept to shed and stable, sleeping in the loft there all but the coldest nights. Hope ignited as she climbed upward, gaining the top step when his voice met her ears.

Below, filling the doorway, stood a freshly shaved Russell in clean linsey-woolsey shirt and breeches. He looked up at her as if as surprised to find her there as she was him. Fair enough. She was usually out on a ramble.

Stepping around Paige's bed and then her own, the two separated by a blanket chest, she found her moccasins and a shawl spun by her mother's hand and dyed a deep butternut.

Aylee resumed work again. The wheel bore a familiar rhythm, Russell's voice overriding it as he read. Ma had gotten hold of a newspaper, probably months old, her hunger for the East never satisfied. She had kin in Carolina, all Patriots. Unable to read or write, she relied on Russell. Like Aylee, Paige had never learned her letters. She regarded Russell and Tempe with a sort of awe. Russell had begun to teach Paige in spare moments, but their work often got in the way.

Pondering it, Tempe reached for a tiny book of Psalms, the print so fine it seemed made for a fairy or some small-sighted creature. It fit easily into her pocket, best read in a glare of sunlight.

Once free of the cabin, she cast a glance skyward. The heavens had cracked open, patches of blue amid gauzy tendrils of fog. Thankful, she took the river path, wishing Sion Morgan's crippled collie could follow.

"Soon," she told the doe-eyed dog.

The other curs, always loath to leave Russell's side except to chase a fox or wildcat, lazily watched her going.

The woods were an unending palette, its unearthly hues evidence of a Master's hand. Spring always renewed her sense of wonder. Soon the fireflies would flare along the riverbank, tiny lights against the endless rush of green. The air would turn sticky and summer sweet. Garden and inn would steal all her time. But today the afternoon was hers till the twilight.

She moved freely, unencumbered by her rifle. Yet she was enough like Pa to stay alert to the slightest sound, the barest intrusion. She stood on the overlook where she'd first spotted Sion, the very place that inspired their forest chase. Below, the river heaved and foamed, a reminder of his wild ride. She'd spied a ragged scratch along his jawline, evidence he'd not escaped unscathed, though his dog and Cornelius bore the brunt of it.

She pushed deeper into the woods, wondering where the surveyors camped. In time she forgot them too in her climb to what she called Fairy Rock. Smothered with the softest, plumiest moss, the throne-like stone made a fine seat ringed with blooming haw shrubs. Fit for royalty. The Lady of the Woods, as James once called her.

She walked on, book tucked to her chest. The solitude, the shift in weather, brought about an almost unbearable sweetness of soul. She'd heard that Boone, caught up in an ecstasy of aloneness, would sometimes burst into song, heedless of any danger. She longed to do the same.

A hymn stirred in her spirit. Her mouth opened, then shut. She sensed the meadow wasn't entirely hers. Like a cloud passing over the sun, she felt a cloudiness. Not fear, just a foreboding, a heightening tension. She stepped behind a chestnut, its bulk broad as two men.

Raven.

He crossed the clearing, moving with an easy grace, gaze turned toward her as if telling her she was plain as a parakeet with its noisy chatter and brilliant plumage. She looked down at her showy skirt, dyed pumpkin orange. She'd have to take care. Only she didn't care.

Her attention returned to Raven. Half Chickamauga Cherokee, Raven seemed rootless, restless, living between two worlds, never quite at home in either. Whenever she saw him he was on the move, usually on the Warrior's Path. But today he was in this very meadow, near her beloved Fairy Rock.

She felt . . . wronged.

Chafing at her resistance, she stepped from behind the tree as if to banish any territorial thoughts. This was Indian ground be it anyone's. She had no special claim, no preemption here. 'Twas more Raven's than hers. The Almighty had made the Indians same as she, determined the bounds of their habitations, as Scripture said. Who was she to name him an intrusion? Not once had she ever spoken to him, only tipped her head in silent greeting.

Raven's gait never slowed, and in seconds it seemed she'd dreamed him up. He headed east in the direction of the inn. Like as not he was hungry for the white man's bread, as he called it. Though he never set foot inside the keeping room, he was a frequent visitor to the barn-shed. Russell always gave him food or performed some task Raven wanted done. In exchange, Raven brought him some trinket or needful thing like seed or black powder. Usually all he had for Tempe was a small smile, though he bore no smile this day.

Sunlight blanketed her shoulders, warm as a quilt, as she moved into the meadow. The giant rock was heated too, and she settled in, her gaze landing on a fitting Psalm. By chance? Or was the Lord taking her to task? *The mountains shall bring peace to the people, and the little hills, by righteousness.* She pondered the words. Committed them to memory.

The still, sunlit moment shattered. A cry rent the air, animal-like in its intensity. Dropping the Psalms, she shot to her feet, gaze swinging wide. She half expected an ambush, her beloved meadow overrun with screaming, writhing red men. But nothing had changed save that anguished cry.

She started in its direction, past spicebush and yellow poplar, down a gravelly slope, her moccasins nearly sliding out from under her at her rapid descent.

Below, Raven lay on the ground amid a scattering of faded redbud flowers. Pain and panic chased all stoicism away. He looked at her like a trapped creature, his dark eyes communicating a great many things, one foremost. He was unsure of her. Unsure if she would help him—or forsake him.

Her knees hit the hard ground near his imprisoned foot. 'Twas a leghold trap, the length of rusty chain anchored to a towering hickory. Intended for spring beaver, the vicious device cut off the blood and could break bones. Desperate animals would eat their own limbs to free themselves, the main reason Pa shunned such.

Sickened, Tempe took in the carved jaws and foot plate, the powerful springs. Made by a blacksmith, its iron teeth called to mind a bear's mouth. Grabbing a near stick, she tried to pry the contraption open with all her might.

Raven groaned as the jaws eased then clamped shut again. His moccasin was mangled, blood staining the worn elk-skin seams. She fought back her own rising panic and stood, eyeing the iron teeth with gritty determination. And then, overriding all, came a chilling reminder.

It's been said Raven was with the war party in Powell Valley.

Among all the ale-soaked speculations and rumors that swirled at the inn, this had stuck to her like pitch. But would Russell be helping him if Raven had been a part of that terrible time? Would Russell even remember the attack through the haze of pain and war paint?

Another glance at the half-blood left her torn. She had every right to leave him, let him die of thirst, fall prey to hungry wolves. A fitting end to the misery of Powell Valley, where unspeakable things had been done to James and his party. Things too dark to mention. Russell kept what he'd witnessed to himself, leaving her to fester, forever wondering.

She stood, her slim shadow cutting across Raven's dusky figure as he lay vulnerable and exposed on the unforgiving ground. His bare chest rose and fell in shuddering waves, his sinewy right leg tensed so tight every cord and fiber bulged above the trap's iron teeth.

She choked out a breathless command. "Pray to God I can get you sprung."

His lips were moving, making her wonder. Was the Cherokee god her God? Raven spoke English, Russell said. She caught a few strained words.

"Free . . . me."

She swallowed, the bile backing up in her throat. "Give me your hand."

Dark fingers shot out, cool and firm. She held on to him for balance, placing her feet over the trap's jaws and pushing down with her weight. The contraption creaked and gave way but slightly, not enough to free him but unleashing another spasm of pain.

Breathless with dismay, she startled when he gritted his teeth and swung his body nearer the trap. With his free hand he pressed downward on the jaws alongside her feet, throwing both his weight and hers behind the effort. Together, tethered hand and foot, they felt the trap give way. At last the bloody teeth released his tortured limb. He lay back spent as she flung the offender into the brush.

Dropping to her knees again, she removed his moccasin and began examining the torn flesh. If he hadn't cried out . . . If she hadn't come . . .

"Stay still," she told him. She felt his eyes on her as she ran off, fleet as a deer, toward a rushing creek. There, she tore off the hem of her petticoat and plunged it into the cold water, not bothering to wring it out.

Returning to him, she smoothed the blood away, wishing for some of Aylee's herbs. His coppery skin disguised the worst of it, but the gashes went deep. Bruising and swelling would follow, maybe blood poisoning. She prayed not.

"Keep the wound clean with comfrey or witch hazel. It'll knit your skin back together." She looked up and found understanding in his gaze. Tearing free more of her petticoat, she began wrapping the foot as best she could, forcing her next words past her reluctance. "Best come to the inn and lodge with Russell whilst you mend."

Could he even walk? As if in answer to her unspoken question, he got to his feet with none of the grace of before. The makeshift bandage was already dark with blood and in need of replacing. Without thinking, she untied the string of her petticoat and let it fall to the ground beneath her shortgown.

"You need it worse than me." Fighting immodesty, she gathered her remaining garment around her even as she held out the petticoat to him.

He took it, clutching it beneath one silver-banded arm, the glint of the metal catching the setting sun. Without a word in either Cherokee or English, he gathered his remaining dignity and began a slow walk away in the direction that he'd come. Toward home? She didn't even know where he lived. She'd heard he wintered with the Chickamauga but roamed other times.

Feeling weak-legged herself, she forgot about Fairy Rock. As Raven limped away, the meadow changed, resuming its pleasant, peaceful lines. Her thoughts swung from the half-blood to James. She examined her heart for the slightest stain of hate.

She couldn't shut her mind to the notion that the Boones had been hospitable to at least one of the Indians who'd killed James. Though several Cherokee had been pursued and punished by British authorities, one named Big Jim, a Shawnee, had eluded capture. He was later found in possession of some books and farming tools carried by James's party.

Relief and resistance warred inside her. *The mountains shall bring peace to the people, and the little hills, by righteousness.* Despite her feelings, how glad she was to have done a righteous thing. The trap might well have ensnared her instead. Would Raven have heeded her cry?

Or left her to die?

Slowly, she began walking in the direction she had come. Her gaze lit on a dirt dobber's nest and her heavy spirits began to lift. She saw God in so many earthbound things. A spider's delicate web. An abundance of silver bells and bush honeysuckle. The warm, scented wind. If this be a fallen, half-forsaken world, what wonders lay in the next?

She had a large hope for what waited on the other side of death. She was sure James was there. If God be love and light, then death itself must be full of splendor. A gateway sure as the Gap.

Betimes in the stillness and sunlight James seemed only a handbreadth away. Wordless. Invisible. Ever present. She fancied she nearly felt the reach of his hand. His going had taken all fear of the wilderness away. She no longer cared what became of her.

Death was the door that led to James.

7

It came over me, then, that any woman who ever loves more than one man must carry forever with her, in her heart, a ghost.

—Janice Holt Giles

Sion felt he'd walked the entire length of the Shawnee River, every league convincing him that it was as much a foe as its namesake. The fog had lifted, but two more days had been lost. He stood along the river's banks at its narrowest point thus far, scalp prickling. The greenish water still held an icy grip, and its ferocious rush was no match for the strongest raft, the ablest swimmer. Other rivers sluiced through his mind, yet unknown. The mighty Cherokee lay to the south, the Rockcastle, Muddy, Green, Pigeon, and Chenoa all writhing in other directions. Was the Chenoa as touchy? It stretched between them and Boonesborough. For now they needed only to ford the Shawnee to reach Crab Orchard, the rendezvous point.

He still felt a tad bewildered. Like he didn't know if he was afoot or on horseback. The clear weather was no doubt an answer to Nate's prayer, or so he claimed. Mayhap a fording place needed praying for too. But Sion sought an answer on his own, leaving the rest of his party at base camp.

Thirsty, he knelt at a willow-shaded spring and tasted the cold, sweet water, the hair on his neck still a-prickle. He retreated farther into the trees, glad for the covering, careful to keep moving. He tarried but once when he found a slight imprint along a creek bank. A lone Indian? The toes were pointed inward, the tread light. A lone Indian he could handle. A war party he could not.

Betimes the wilderness held an overpowering sense of aloneness. He longed to put names to nameless things. The only places he was now sure of were the Gap and the Moonbow Inn. Mayhap his uneasiness had to do with that.

Was *she* shadowing him again? He stifled the urge to call out. *Tempe.*

Temptation got the best of him. He had blazed in his head a hundred times the trail he now took. Keeping clear of the thickets and windfalls and overgrown places in case of ambush, he walked on. Wrestling with himself all the way, he soon stood in back of the inn in deep twilight. Lights shone from a few shuttered windows, high enough off the ground to add safety in time of attack. Aglow like fireflies, the narrow loopholes winked at him in a sort of halfhearted welcome.

He'd forgotten what it was like to feel a bond, kinship. To come home. To be greeted, open-armed and openhearted . . .

On sight of him, the dogs began a chorus of discontent. Was Smokey among them? Sion's gaze ranged from the dogtrot to a shadow filling a far doorway. The lame man? Sion helloed and saw a hand raise in welcome. Once again the air held the aroma of cornbread. Hot and crusty and thick with butter, if memory served.

Shouldering Annie, he bypassed the kitchen with its savory smells and rattle of crockery, aiming for the hay-scented expanse of the barn-shed. A pigeon cooed from a high rafter. He'd never seen so many pigeons as in Kentucke. Sometimes the sun was snuffed from their hurried flight.

The young man extended a hand, his eyes on the trees in back of Sion. "Welcome, Morgan . . . if you've no Englishman trailing."

"None today, nay," Sion said quietly. "You know my name. I would have yours."

"Russell." That guardedness flared again then quickly mellowed. "You're not too late for supper."

Sion shot a look toward the open keeping room door. "I wouldn't brave it."

"The womenfolk, you mean." Unsmiling, Russell pointed to a stool. "I could serve you out here."

"I'm more in need of directions." The words belied the surly growl of Sion's belly.

"Directions?" Russell's brows peaked slightly. "Best ask my sister, then."

How easily he said it. As if this little bit of a woman had taken up the slack of all that he couldn't do, lamed as he was.

Russell began a slow walk to the dogtrot, gaining Sion's sympathy with every labored step. It was akin to being shackled, dragging that leg like a ball and chain, ever shy of the liberating key.

In seconds Tempe stood before him. She cocked her head to one side, her braid swinging free and brushing her hips. Sion found himself wishing Russell would return.

She studied him, a hint of distrust in her eyes—or mayhap dislike. "You don't seem the sort of man to be bewildered, Morgan."

Was that a compliment—or a subtle dig to his pride? "I'm in search of a fording place."

"You mean to cross the Shawnee?"

"Aye. We're to rendezvous in Crab Orchard just shy of the settlements. Meet up with a guide."

She bit her lip, thoughtful. He liked that she took her time and didn't spit out a hasty answer. "There's but one fording place this time of year." She reached for a stick and cut a wide swath in the dirt—indicating the river, no doubt—next marking an X where they now stood. He swallowed as her stick moved to the east. "You'll find passage along Boone's Trace, in the shadow of Pine Mountain. Look for a sandstone boulder. If it rides high in the water it's safe to cross, else you'll have to camp a spell."

He digested the details, dwelling on the distance. With a flick of her wrist she sent the stick into the woodpile and left him looking into her eyes. An unabashed blue. As blue as the chicory crowding the door stone in back of her.

"How far?" he murmured.

"Fifty miles straight as the crow flies."

Sion hid his dismay. "How wide the fording place?"

"Shoal water, some two hundred yards."

"Obliged." He took a step back, his odd desire to linger mingling with his wish to be gone. His mouth watered as the wind teased him, this time carrying the scent of roasting meat. Venison.

Russell reappeared, a tied bundle in hand. The drag of his leg along the dogtrot raised the same nettlesome question. How had he come by his injury? "You're likely in need of meat. I've not heard any gunfire your way, lessen you load light like an Indian."

Sion took the offering, and the greasy covering gave way,

revealing a flitch of bacon and—lo and behold—cornbread. He nearly chuckled, anticipating Nate's glee. "We've taken no shots, lit no cookfires."

"All the better," Tempe said. "The Warrior's Path cuts across where you're headed." With that, she turned and made for the barn-shed, taking up a hoe in her journey.

He'd rather she have a gun. The sign he'd seen, even though it looked to be a lone Indian, was uppermost in his mind. Something was building inside him, something sinister in his spirit hinting that the inn's inhabitants were one step away from ruination. Living like this, acting as if they weren't planted smack in the middle of a yellow jacket's nest but somewhere safe like parts East, was bound to stir up a mort of trouble.

With a biddable goodbye, Russell moved away, clearly expecting Sion to go. Into the barn-shed Tempe's brother disappeared, the ensuing ring of his hammer on the anvil jarring in the sudden hush.

There, just inside the workplace, lay Smokey on a bed of cedar shavings. She gave a little yip of welcome. He could take her, carry her across his shoulders, but she was still not fit for travel. For the moment, Tempe crowded his thoughts, little more now than a swish of indigo skirts as the trees swallowed her from sight.

Where would a contrary woman with a hoe go in the purple twilight?

❧

"You'd best take heed."

Sion Morgan's voice reached out to Tempe like a restraining hand as she stepped from shade to waning sunlight. She whirled, unsuspecting. Boone and Kenton were the onliest men she knew to creep quiet as an Indian. This man had just joined them.

She sensed his surprise at the corn as it spread behind her, the remaining flax a coverlet of blue blossoms. The toil it had taken was not lost on him. Stump after stump spoke of blistering days and sore nights, the constant fight to keep the forest at bay. She read appreciation—even admiration—in his slate gaze. And then it shifted to subtle concern.

He gestured north. "There's Indian sign along the creek below."

"It's likely Raven, a Cherokee half-blood." Her shoulders lifted. "He's injured and liable to limp."

"But it could be any unkindly Cherokee or Shawnee—and you arm yourself with a hoe."

His quiet rebuke stung. "And you think your rifle would answer a volley of arrows?"

"Mayhap better than your hoe."

"I'm not scared of death, Mister Morgan."

His face flashed a question, but she turned toward the field, the glare of sunset making her squint. For a moment she lost herself in the lovely sight, tugged backwards to another time and place. The sky was just that shade of rose that long-ago day, pretty as a party dress. Her eyes smarted and she set her jaw.

James, James . . . Are there sunsets in heaven? Or is the Lord's glory so great there's nary a need for them?

Her thoughts tumbled one after another, resurrecting snatches of that day. The chill dawn. The stir of camp. Hope snuffed by fear.

Hearsay from the settlements brought a new ache. James's kin were now busy marrying and settling out, then forting up as needs be. Time moved on, each beat never to be taken back.

"Take care, Tempe."

The stranger's ease with her name turned her round again. She felt a bristling at such familiarity, but in his defense, he couldn't say *Miss Tucker*, as he didn't know it. She, in turn, had begun to think of him as simply Sion.

Soundlessly he moved away, square shouldered and limber legged, rifle in hand. She watched him go gladly.

She pitied the Indian in Sion's sights.

Backtracking fifty miles was no small task. There was no such thing as "straight as the crow flies." Mosquitos and chiggers hatched amid a spell of sweat-stained weather. The bacon and corn cakes Russell had generously given over had run out long ago. Sion braved a shot and brought down a buffalo, jerking the meat and feasting on marrow bones over a chancy fire. Nearer the Warrior's Path they stood double watch when they camped.

All was an unearthly quiet save the scampering of a squirrel or birdsong or the burble of an occasional creek. And then, like the strike of flint on steel, Boone's Trace turned dusty, burdened by folks fleeing over the Gap.

"Lord have mercy . . ." Nate removed his hat and swiped at his damp forehead. "What's come over all them people?"

The men crouched on a lip of limestone above the thin slip of trail leading back over the mountains. A party of harried settlers—men, women, and children—struggled back toward civilization. Safety. Single file they went, working upward in a line, the front and rear guard ever cautious.

"I smell blood in the air." Cornelius's voice was subdued, mayhap out of respect for the graves they'd just passed, the earth stacked high with stones just off the trace. "You'd best go down and see what the trouble is, Morgan."

"The trouble is Indians, and it has little to do with us."

"I beg to differ." Cornelius let out his breath in a gust of disgust. "From what I've heard, the red men are none too particular about whose feet they heap burning coals upon or which fingernails they stick flaming pine splinters under. They—"

"Enough." Sion's hiss, though hatchet sharp, was more whisper. He didn't want Spencer and Hascal and Lucian to hear. They stood farther back in a sheltered cove with the horses, awaiting directions. "There's no call to alarm. We'll take care to stay off the trace like we have the past three days. We should make the fording place by dusk and then Crab Orchard."

Uttering an oath, Cornelius stalked off, leaving Sion and Nate alone.

Nate turned beleaguered eyes on him. "I fear all this land grabbing has got into your soul."

The words hung between them, full of angst. Next Nate would spout Scripture. Sion knew the very verse. *For what shall it profit a man, if he shall gain the whole world, and lose his own soul?*

"I've got a job to do and you signed on for that. We've lost time and needs be pressing toward the rendezvous point."

Nate snapped free a sassafras twig from a nearby bush. "What's drivin' you? Greed or regret?"

Sion stifled a hasty retort. "Mayhap both," he finally admitted. No sense turning surly with Nate. Nate had seen Sion's misfortunes unroll like a map, knew every hill and valley. The last valley was all too fresh. Betimes he felt marked by misfortune, albeit blazed with a hatchet.

"You don't want to add to your burden exposin' men to unnecessary risk." Nate chewed on the twig, pensive. "You don't want that markin' your conscience too."

The woods were settling now, the last of the settlers fading from sight. Would they reach the Gap in safety? Sion turned his back to Nate, his voice rising above the spill of a waterfall. He took in the waiting men in his party below.

"There's your last chance." Every eye was on him as he jabbed a hand east. "Go. Leave if you must. There's other chain men and markers to be had in the settlements. I'm headed toward Crab Orchard come what may."

Tempe plied her needle, having let out her marrying dress. Tongue between her teeth, she worked as the candle at her side sputtered low in its pewter holder. She was not the girl she'd been in Powell Valley, neither in body nor in spirit. If only she could ease the strained seams of her mind, snip out all the tattered places, and sew in unsullied cloth. The fabric of her thoughts seemed bunched and knotted. Try as she might, she could not iron them out. Sion was mostly to blame, he and the Loyal Land Company. When he'd left her in the field, carrying his bacon and bread a few days past, she'd thought of little else.

And then there was Raven. They'd seen no sign of him, leaving Tempe to wonder if his foot had festered and crippled him sorely—or worse.

"Where'd you get such a fancy?" Paige was at her elbow, returning her to the present.

"It's my marrying dress."

A surprised pause.

Tempe filled the silence. "I expect I'll have no need of it. I thought you might wear it."

"Me?" Wide-eyed, Paige regarded the dress as if it might bite her. "I—well, I misdoubt—it wouldn't look well on me."

Ever chary, a tad superstitious, Paige trod as cautiously as she could. She'd take no hand-me-down with heartache attached.

"Never you mind, then," Tempe whispered.

Appearing mollified, Paige pulled up a stool and wrapped her arms around her knees, the freckles riding her cheekbones reminding Tempe of a fawn's spots. "If you don that pretty dress, some woodsman might walk out with you."

Tempe grasped at a bit of whimsy. "And who would you choose for me?"

"Well, there's Captain Holder from Boonesborough or Ezra Mason from Logan's or Joshua Bryant from Harrod's. Any one of them would be glad of your hand, though you pay them no mind when they pass by here."

Tempe lowered her head to better see her stiches, such talk usually setting her cheekbones afire. "If they pay me any mind, it's because there be so few of us and so many of them."

"All the better." Smiling, Paige reached for her knitting basket, a soft pile of yarn within. "I'm still ponderin' women-folk doin' the choosin' . . ."

A burst of masculine laughter snuffed their words, as if the longhunters on the dogtrot were privy to their talk.

"They mean to overnight with us and leave at first light," Paige murmured. "The trace is chancy, I heard them say, with the settlements bein' under siege. Captain Boone took a ball to the ankle and is laid up hisself."

Tempe cast a look toward the open cabin door. Betimes the inn seemed the safest place with so many guns present. Still, they always barred the cabin doors at sundown, a customary caution.

"I'm not fretful for your pa." Paige worked her needles expertly, a stocking taking shape. "Not with the Indians afeared of him like they are, callin' him an Azgen ghost. But I do wonder about those surveyors headin' into the very heart of the trouble."

Tempe straightened, placing a hand to the small of her back to ease the ache of weeding all the forenoon. Had the surveyors reached the fording place? Would they? Her stitch slipped and she reworked it, glad her wondering kept her thoughts off the bittersweet task at hand. The wedding gown had long haunted. Now it would serve a purpose.

Paige's whisper stopped her cold. "Your ma spent a heap of time tonight after supper writing in the book of the dead."

"The Reckoning?"

Paige's needles lagged. "Aye, seems every man here has a sad story to tell."

Tempe checked a sigh. The book was near to bursting lately. She could see Ma in her mind's eye, sharpening her quill and snuffing out lives with the scratch of her pen.

Would she next scrawl the name of Sion Morgan?

Try as she might, she couldn't rid her mind of him. Rarely did a man garner her attention as he did. Though she didn't know him, she already rued his loss if the wilderness claimed him. Men of his ilk were needed on the frontier. To fight for the land. Farm it. Raise a family.

She felt a tad flushed. She even liked his name, the way it felt on her lips. Melodious. Strong. His voice matched the height and breadth of him. She remembered that too.

And rued it as well.

Aylee entered the cabin right then, leaving Russell to oversee the lodgers, their weary packhorses corralled in a brush fence of Russell's making. Her mother's spare form moved to each window, fastening the shutters.

Abandoning her work, Tempe tucked the half-finished dress away. "There's a full moon tonight."

Paige smiled. "A moonbow, reckon?"

"Likely. Care to come? The moonflower's fixing to bloom."

"I'm too tuckered out from servin'." Her eyes turned beseeching. "Mighten you want to stay here with us? Given all the trouble?"

"Nay." Glad to go alone, Tempe moved to the door before Aylee dropped the bar in place. A wordless look passed between them. Aylee had long stopped asking her, "Be you back by morning?"

Yet Tempe felt she owed her some explanation. "It's a fine night for a moonbow with the river running so high and an abundance of mist."

At Aylee's reluctant nod, Tempe went out into velvety darkness, the night air like a breath from the bake-oven door. With so generous a moon, her steps were sure even in the dark. Lush light silvered the woods and river, rivaling any silversmith's finest work.

Downriver a quarter of a mile or so was a ledge of rock aglow with fireflies, the sandstone surface adorned with lichen puddles, a delicate tracery of fern rimming each. The nearer she came to the watching place, the more her wonder bloomed.

There was magic here. A hallowed, heavenly magic. Aside from a star shower, those white bursts that streaked across a moonless midnight, the delight of the moonbow went deep.

The great slab of rock was cool, as cool as Fairy Rock had been warm. She sat down at the edge, her skirts a tangle of worn linen around her, feet dangling. Far below, the river settled into a stretch of pools. Mist cooled her face and bare arms, rising like a white veil about the falls.

She watched, breath held, snagged by a sudden movement to the left where the brush hugged the riverbank. A figure emerged, straight and narrow, the glass beads amid dark hair glistening. Shirtless and in leggings and loincloth, Raven moved with an easy grace.

A chill took hold of her. Had Raven been with Russell tonight? All her questions were snatched away when he stepped onto the ledge. She wished Russell—or anyone—would come. But Russell's leg rarely let him wander.

Raven lowered himself to sit a stone's throw from her. His expression was unreadable, inclined to severity. The tomahawk in his belt glinted sharp and hard in the moonlight. Unsure of his intent, Tempe studied him longer than she wanted, aware of a great many fearsome things. He had only to extend a hard hand and send her over the rock ledge. Her cry would be lost in the thunder of the falls.

And yet . . .

Why did she always think ill of him? Had her time in the valley—Powell Valley—so scarred her?

Raven was, she reminded herself, half white. It was the other half that fretted her. Word was he was the son of Oconostota, a Cherokee chief, and a white captive taken along the Watauga. Save the lightening of his skin, he looked full Cherokee. His English was nigh flawless, better than many a white man. She recalled his pain-laced plea.

Free . . . me.

Tonight he did not speak. She couldn't have heard him over the fall's torrent if he had. He simply extended an arm made bright with silver bangles. In his fingers was her forgotten book of Psalms. She'd dropped it that day at Fairy Rock and forgotten about it in the busyness since.

She took the little book, glad to the heart. Could he read? The assumption seemed silly. Tucking the Psalms away in her pocket, she nodded her thanks.

He lifted a hand, his forked fingers eye level and pointing toward the falls. *Look.*

She looked, awe unseating all distrust.

The moonbow spanned the river in a gentle arc, its ends resting on far limestone banks, the sight most vivid against the froth of the falls. As if it were a seam of brightly colored clay the Indians used for war paint, Tempe could make out rich red hues that melded to a fetching bluish purple and then pale green, the very green of the river itself.

The moon floated free of gauzy clouds, as bright as she'd ever seen it.

Betimes when the river ran fullest and seemed about to burst its banks, she feared all that water would tear down the cliffs and boulders and sweep them all away. But the falls seemed as enduring as the hills, the heavens.

Raven's hands were moving fluidly, even eloquently, making the gesture for *good*, expressing his pleasure in the night. She knew some Indian sign. When the danger peaked and they couldn't risk the silence of the woods, she and Pa talked with their hands. In answer, she passed her right palm downward over her face to denote *beautiful*. He nodded, a half smile softening his stern features.

Easing, she looked again at the moonbow, a sudden catch in her spirit as it began to break apart. Like a mist clearing, the colors were no longer gathered in wide bands but scattered bits, and soon the moon was swallowed by the clouds altogether, leaving her and Raven smothered in darkness.

Her body tensed as he made a move. But it was away from her, not toward her, and then he too vanished from sight, the glint of his weapons a grim goodbye.

8

Reached the Crab Orchard, and lodged under a tree
... very feverish and unwell; a poor beginning this.

—Francis Asbury

Sion sat with Annie, his back against a black walnut,
Smokey's absence a widening ache inside him. One
by one the party's other dogs had begun dying on the
trace, poisoned by some plant or victim of some mishap
or malady. The two curs left were an aggravation, always
underfoot and distracted by so much game. But they were
good at sensing trouble, and that was why he put up with
them. Thankfully he'd seen no sign. His relief at reaching the
rendezvous point after another grueling week and a chafing
wait at the fording place Tempe had told him about made
him a mite reckless.

Aye, Tempe seemed to have followed him here, at least in
spirit. Somehow she'd snuck into his head if not his heart.
All too easily he recalled something she'd said or done. Her
terse way with words. The far-off look in her eyes. The maddening swish of her indigo skirt. She was an uncommon

woman, graced with a man's habits. The why of it teased at him, embedding her further in his overfull thoughts. If Cornelius had half her gumption and woods sense, they'd be farther along on this foray than they were.

Pluming steam from the mineral springs wafted over him in unsavory waves, carrying the taint of rotten eggs, at odds with the sighs and groans of delight around him. He stood guard while the others bathed, pondering what a fine ambush was to be had with five unclothed men.

Though he sat stone still, his eyes made a tireless sweep of their surroundings. Crab Orchard was a comely place, long favored by whites and Indians alike. Thick clusters of wild crab apple trees were no longer in bloom but full-leafed now in early June. Farther back in dense brush were the springs, the green ground steaming like a kettle. He could hear the hobbled horses chewing on peavine and clover near a pretty little lick where buffalo had made deep grooves in the salty clay.

Nate was the first to emerge from the stinking water, dripping wet and red as a piece of flannel. Sion handed him a tin cup, gesturing to a smaller, shallower spring seeping from a ledge. "Best cleanse your innards as well."

With a chuckle, Nate did as Sion bid, filling the cup and swigging a mouthful. One swallow was followed by a spasm of coughing, and then Nate slapped his knee as if to quell the outburst. "Anything that tastes that vile must be good for you. Here, you drink it down. Maybe it'll cure body *and* spirit."

Sion took the cup and finished it off, determined not to cough. Failing. A far cry from Ratafia or Perry, Nate's preferred pear cider. Whistling softly, the old man sat down in a clump of sun-warmed grass to dry himself.

The springs made a fine laundry. They hardly needed soft

soap, the heat working with the minerals to strip the grime from their garments.

"Your turn." With a playful punch, Nate unseated Sion's battered hat, exposing a mass of lank, black hair in dire need of washing.

Sion got to his feet, leaving his hat where it lay, though it was in need of a soaking too. Having no desire to bathe with Cornelius or the other men, he sought a secluded sinkhole, a deep blue-green pool rimmed with sedges and cattails.

Pulling his shirt over his head, he shed his moccasins, Annie within reach. His thoughts tumbled forward, toward settlement. Civilization. So much water would make a fine source for a gunpowder mill—even a distillery once the country was finally settled.

Taking a breath, he went under, the tepid pool more agreeable on so warm a day than the hotter holes. When his head cleared water, a song sparrow piped three short notes. He held his breath and listened past an army of shrill cicadas, detecting a new sound. A new voice.

By the time he emerged from his bath, fully dressed and clutching his soiled clothes and rifle, a stranger stood in their midst. Nate was nearly dressed, and the other men save Lucian ringed the newcomer.

"Yonder comes Morgan," Hascal said.

The stranger looking at Sion was so shriveled and bent it seemed the wilderness had whipped all vitality out of him. But the clasp of his hand was strong, his gaze a direct if beleaguered blue.

"I'm Levi Todd from Logan's Fort."

"Sion Morgan of the Loyal Land Company."

"So your men tell me. What I mean to tell you is this—best clear out of Kentucke whilst you can. All the forts north of here are under siege, and I was barely able to get out last night to go for gunpowder. I'm headed over the Gap, and pray I get there."

"You expect no reinforcements from Virginia?"

Todd shook his head in disgust and disappointment. "We sent word awhile back, begging for militia, powder, and bullet lead. But nothing's forthcoming, not that we know of. It's a poor time to be wandering about this country."

Dropping his dirty clothes, Sion retrieved his hat. "I'm supposed to meet up with a guide from Harrod's here, but from the lay of things that looks to be wishful thinking."

"Aye." Todd accepted a cup of water from Nate's hand. "There's but one hundred twenty guns in the whole of Kentucke, and you ain't likely to get any one of them."

Ignoring Cornelius's growl of protest, Sion weighed his options. "With the Indians fixated on the forts, our party could push west instead, survey the Barrens. Green River country."

"I don't know if that's any safer, but you daren't come near the settlements. If you're dead set on pushin' west, you'll need an able guide."

"Are guides any easier to get than guns?"

Todd shouldered his rifle, looking thoughtful. "Down along the Shawnee River I've heard tell of a fine woodsman and marksman. The folks at the Moonbow Inn mighten direct you."

Sion's interest piqued. "His name?"

All the men were quiet as if their fate hinged on his answer. "I recollect he goes by Tucker . . . Tim Tucker."

Sion rolled the name over in his mind before storing it for safekeeping. "Obliged."

Cornelius spoke, looking to Sion as he did so. "We could accompany Todd to the fording place, then part ways at the Shawnee. There's safety in numbers, as they say."

"Aye, if he's willing."

Todd smiled, his lined face easing. "I'd welcome the company, boys. What say you we take to the trace before the red men are any the wiser?"

Alone in the kitchen, Tempe pulled on a wide floorboard in front of the fireplace, revealing narrow steps leading down to the cellar. Pa had created the dim, dank space as a caution in times of Indian unrest. She felt her way through the darkness, fingering papery-skinned onions and shriveled potatoes and pitted turnips. With the garden not yet in, they made do with last year's bounty.

Apron full, she climbed the steps and deposited the wizened vegetables on the trestle table, eyes on the back window and ears attuned to the venison haunch sizzling on a spit, its juices trapped in the dripping tray beneath. To this she'd add the cut-up vegetables to create a savory stew. Though there'd been few at their table of late, they were always prepared.

Beyond the open window came Paige's high, lilting laugh. It reminded Tempe of a song sparrow. Paige and Russell were at the hominy block, pounding away, cracking the corn to fill the open meal barrel. Paige had no need of help, but Russell had burned out a new bowl and crafted a new pestle for grinding and was overseeing its first use.

Tempe saw Paige move nearer Russell, her bare brown arm brushing his loose linsey sleeve. There was the slightest pulling away as Russell maintained the distance between them. Paige looked up at him, gaze fixed on his sun-browned face, the dark hair along his temples sweat-damp and curling. He paid her little mind, intent on determining if the wood was too soft for repeated pounding.

Tempe's frustration flared. Why wouldn't Russell just let Paige love him?

Never had she seen a woman so besotted with a man. To her credit, Paige cared not a whit about Russell's limp. It had been that way since they'd taken her in when her owners succumbed to fever along the trace. Paige's older brother, Elisha, also indentured, had gone on to Boonesborough whilst Paige, fevered herself and too sick to go another step, stayed behind with them.

Back then, Russell had regarded her as little more than another sister, whittling puzzles and games for her out of wood, even crafting a cage for a wounded robin to keep her company as she healed. Did he still regard her as a child? Bosomy and tall as she was three years since, how could he? Might Russell's reserve make him more appealing in turn?

Thinking it, Tempe whacked at a potato with such force, half flew across the tidy kitchen.

Aylee entered, fanning her heated face with her apron. She stooped to pick up the wayward tuber. "Mercy! Be you splitting wood or cutting vegetables?"

"Mama, maybe it's time to give Russell a talking to."

Aylee's dark brows arched. "What for?"

"Don't you want some grandchildren?"

"I'd like a wedding first." Aylee uncovered a piggin of cream, careful of insects. "But there's no preacher to be had."

"There's no *couple* to be had either." Tempe resumed her frenzied chopping. "I've never seen such a predicament. Paige is a peach ripe for picking, and Russell treats her like a green persimmon."

With a sigh, Aylee stared out the window. "Love won't be forced."

Nay, it would not. Love would be denied, rebuffed, cut

down. Nipped in the bud long before the blossom. But never forced.

"Best tend your own orchard, Tempe Grace, and stay out of your brother's." Aylee turned toward her. "I did not tell you, but last time John Holder was by here he asked if he could court you."

"Captain Holder?" Disgust doubled Tempe's aggravation. "Seems like a man of courting mind could ask himself."

"You give him no room." Aylee's retort was swift, as if she'd been seeking such a confrontation. "Nary a warm word passes your lips, nor a kindly glance."

"Would you have me make free with him, then?" Tempe's tone sharpened. "The last time I smiled at a longhunter, he pinched me a blue place through my petticoat." Her thoughts traveled backwards, unhappily, at the half-truth. Nay, the last man she'd spoken to had been Sion, and he'd been respectful, as guarded as she.

"John Holder would be a good provider. He aims to operate a ferry and tavern along the Chenoa downriver from Boone's Fort."

"John Holder is sweet on Fanny Callaway and has sired a child by Margaret Drake, both of them at Boonesborough. I scarce think he has time to walk out with me."

Aylee began fanning herself again, whether from the heat of the kitchen or the shameful news, Tempe didn't know. "Where'd you get such?"

"There's advantages to keeping your mouth shut. You hear a heap better."

Letting go of her apron, Aylee chuckled. "I may have the gift of gab, but you're just like your pa. Slow to speak . . . if not slow to anger."

The weight in Aylee's words struck Tempe hard. She'd

tried to tame her temper. It had gone easier given what Pa
had done in Virginia. His crime was an everlasting reproach,
the repercussions from an unbridled spirit ever before her.

Desperate to turn the tide of conversation, she was relieved
when Aylee said, "I've been some worried about Paige. I
overheard that Cornelius Lyon fella sweet-talking her when
he was here."

"Maybe she simply means to get a rise out of Russell."
Tempe wiped her hands on her apron, gaze straying to the
window again. "Like as not she's missing her brother. It's
been a year or better since he's come by from Harrod's
Fort."

"I pray the surveyors won't be back thisaway."

"Then we've another dog to tend." Tempe's thoughts swung
to Smokey. At last count they had nine curs. But Smokey could
hardly be called a mongrel. Fine collie-bred she was, and sweet-
tempered. Tempe had grown attached to the creature, sneaking
it scraps and spending time she didn't have, its shaggy head
in her lap, its expressive eyes asking questions she couldn't
answer. It seemed Sion's dog missed him. Would he be back
to claim her?

"Morgan's party'll fare no better than Harrod's surveyors,
truth be told. I've not forgot all those names in the Reckoning." Aylee bent over a barrel of kraut. Tempe smelled the
potent brine as the lid was lifted. "I misdoubt Paige has the
gumption to go with the surveyors. She's a mite fearful. You
know how skittish she is around Raven. The others."

"The others?"

"Aye. Some of Nancy Ward's kin."

"Nanyehi?" The name slid easily off Tempe's tongue. Pa
spoke of this beloved woman of the Cherokee often enough.
He was familiar with the Overhill sect, trading with them

and on friendly terms with their Indian agent. He was likely there now, taking advantage of British trade goods.

"They've been passing by here lately when you're not near at hand. Peaceable, seems like."

Tempe stared at her mother, nearly forgetting to crank the spit and baste the smoking venison. "Why do they come?"

"To hear tell of the trouble between the settlements and Shawnee and such. Betimes Russell fixes something for them or makes a trade."

Truly, Russell was never idle. A wonder with iron and anvil, crafting everything from fishhooks to horseshoes to knives. Word had spread about what a hand he was. But . . .

"And Russell—he's at peace with it?" The thought of her brother dealing with the very Indians who would have killed him in Powell Valley gave her pause.

"So long as they're amiable, like Raven . . ." Aylee left off, uncertainty in her voice. "Maybe it's best you keep to home. Curtail your rambles. You can never be sure of Indians, what with the fresh trouble in the settlements and the change of weather."

Curtail her rambles? The very thought made Tempe itch. Granted, spring to Indian summer was always a chancy spell. Smoothing her irritation as best she could, she said meekly, "All right, Ma. I will."

9

How love came in, I do not know, whether by the eye,
or ear, or no: Or whether with the soul it came.

—ROBERT HERRICK

The rolling water was up to the horse's hocks now. In two steps it licked the stallion's belly, darkening the underside of the saddlebags. Sion pressed on, the reins in his left hand, his rifle held high in his right, out of harm's way.

The fording place spanning the Shawnee was still a challenge even in June, the rock marker barely visible above the river's relentless rush. First to cross, Beck climbed the gravelly bank with unsteady legs as if the current had stripped all the strength out of him.

Levi Todd came next, bobbing along in the current woodenly, used to the rigors of the frontier. The others followed without mishap, Nate giving a resounding *amen* when all reached the south shore.

They soon parted ways, Todd bent on the Virginia settlements and what help he could garner there for the struggling

Kentucke stations. No sooner had his buckskin-clad back disappeared than Cornelius started in.

"We've yet to see an Indian, Morgan, and still this everlasting caution. 'No talk. Walk in water. Shun soft ground. Backtrack now and again to throw any trackers off the trail.' Ad nauseam."

Sion looked up the rocky trace the frontiersman had taken. "You aren't shackled, Cornelius. Follow Todd if you must."

For a tense second, indecision warred on the Englishman's flushed face. He slapped at a mosquito but said nothing more, and Sion faced forward again, leading.

'Twas the hottest day yet. Nary a breath of wind stirred. It took concentrated effort to breathe. The sultry air hung thick and sticky, ripe for a storm. Cicadas unreeled their raggety tunes, but the birdsong was muted as it tended to be in the heat of summer, the forest a crush of vivid greens. Sion felt more aggravation than admiration, ignoring the asters with their bewitching butterflies and the clumps of blood-colored phlox that begged a second look.

They were heading west along the Shawnee, away from danger, back toward the Moonbow Inn. Toward Tempe and her lame brother and widowed mother and serving girl, an odd assortment in the wilderness.

His mission was twofold. Reclaim his dog and learn the whereabouts of the guide Todd had told him about. Then their surveying could begin in earnest. What they'd accomplished thus far was barely passable, hindered by a bout of foggy weather and Cornelius's temper.

He felt fresh disgust they couldn't survey the Great Meadow where the Kentucke settlements stood. Mayhap the unclaimed land along the Green River would bear fruit. Once they secured a guide, they could construct a base camp, giving Cornelius a place to make his maps. Sion's own field notes and diagrams were becoming quite complex and needed organizing.

They journeyed on, past dense canebrakes and breathless bottoms, massive sandstone cliffs on every side. His eye lingered on the caves—rockhouses—etched into the cliff's face, a perfect cover in time of danger or storm. They overnighted in one, leaving the horses to graze in a secluded cove. The next morning they continued into denser wilderness, most of it uphill. Nary a blaze mark on a tree, no sign of a claim anywhere. The country was theirs for the taking.

"Just think, Morgan. Virginia law says four hundred acres can be yours if you build an improvement and raise a crop of corn."

There was mocking in Cornelius's voice. For a poor settler, this might seem a dream, but to surveyors paid in vast tracts of land, it was a pittance.

Ignoring Cornelius's arrogance, Sion looked over his shoulder down the line. The horses were merely plodding now. Beck's saddle sore had returned, and another packhorse had thrown a shoe. They were all struggling, every man, fighting brush and fallen timber and swarms of insects, sick to death of meat and in need of bread. Hascal's feet were scalded on account of walking with wet moccasins, the bane of the frontier. They all were in want of another soaking, a clean shirt.

All held fast to the promise of the Moonbow Inn, a phantasm or fancy. Sion felt an odd anticipation. A small hope. Trouble was, he'd begun to question his own motives. Why was he not more aggravated by all their backtracking to the inn? The pleasure he felt had more to do with burgeoning pewter plates. Yet he'd deny it to his dying day.

When at last they saw and smelled the inn's wood smoke, Sion's breathing eased. Lifting a sleeve, he slicked the sweat from his brow, nearly toppling his hat. Next he gave the signal to stop. The halted packhorses waited wearily beneath their loads, snorting and huffing, tails swishing at flies. Taking Annie from the saddle holster, Sion walked to the rear of the line where Cornelius stood, their last ugly encounter firmly in mind.

"If you make any trouble for these people"—Sion canted his head toward the inn—"I'll exact a stiff penalty."

"Stiff, aye?" Cornelius's smirk was wide. "I merely mis-fired—"

"You'll act the gentleman you pretend to be." With one hand, Sion maneuvered his rifle so that the barrel's tip rested against Cornelius's chest. "You'll mind your thirst—"

"The metheglin, you mean."

"You'll take care with the ladies."

Cornelius snorted. "*Ladies* is generous. They're naught but a bunch of ill-bred, backwoods hussies—"

The barrel pressed harder, level with his heart. Sion continued evenly, "And you'll mind your tongue lest you lose it alongside your scalp."

Lucian spoke up, clearly spent. "Should I see about supper, Mister Morgan?"

"Aye, if they'll have us." Sion looked toward the inn, seeing little through the trees but detecting something savory. The feast they'd had at first, nearly wiped away by their fracas in the keeping room, was joyfully resurrected in his memory. Butter molded with a dogwood flower. Steaming catfish. Potatoes and hominy. Rich cream gravy.

When they finally cleared the trees, anticipation faded to dismay. In back of the inn was a great many people. Two dingy tents had been pitched in the yard. Horses were hobbled to the side, ripping at the grass and undergrowth. It had been a while since he'd seen so many folks in one place. There was safety in numbers. Likely they had gathered here because they'd heard of the trouble in the settlements and were going to wait it out before braving riskier ground.

He made his way to the dogtrot whilst Nate and the others managed the horses. He wagered they'd get no supper, his party at least. The best he could do was find out about the guide.

The dogs had been expelled from the dogtrot. There was simply no room. Several men sprawled about, no doubt waiting to be fed. Seasoned woodsmen, from the look of them, who might have what he was in need of. They regarded him in broody silence.

Sion cleared his throat and came straight to the point. "I'm looking for a man by the name of Tucker. Tim Tucker."

A stream of tobacco juice flew past as a low ripple of laughter washed across the porch.

"What you askin' for?" This from a one-eyed monstrosity of a man who'd clearly tangled with a bear and lost.

Sion eased his rifle to the ground. "I'm in need of a guide."

"You ain't from around here, are ye?"

"Nay," Sion answered. "Fort Patrick Henry."

The man spat again, his face scrunched in thought. "You come to the right place. Who sent ye?"

"Levi Todd from Logan's."

"Standing Fort? St. Asaph's they once called it." The mauled man got up from his stump of a chair, outright amusement on his face. Cracking open the door to the keeping room, he bellowed, "Tem Tucker in there?"

Sion sensed something amiss, some private jest, long before the door opened wider and Tempe stepped onto the dogtrot.

"Here's yer guide," another man drawled. "And ain't she a pretty one?"

Laughter split the air, great, gaping guffaws that made a fool of Sion if not Tempe.

Sion took a step back, heat filling every pore, every crevice. "My mistake," he said, taking his rifle in hand again.

Tempe looked hard at him, a flash of something he couldn't name in her eyes. He turned to go, wishing the ground would open up and swallow him.

"Now just you wait," the man called. "Todd told no lie. Tem Tucker's the best shot along the Shawnee, mebbe even farther. We'll have us a little target practice and show ye—"

"A shooting match, McRae?" came her soft voice. "Or your supper?"

Sion turned back around to see Tempe wipe doughy hands on her grease-speckled apron. "I don't hardly have time for the both of them."

"Sup first. Shoot later," McRae returned gruffly.

Without another look at Sion, Tempe slipped inside, shutting the door forcefully behind her.

$\mathcal{D}$

A crowd had gathered, the sun casting russet fingers of light through the trees as it slid slowly from sight. Sion stood along a rail fence, watching Russell limp toward a gate at a distance of one hundred yards. In his hands was a tanned deerskin that he affixed to the wood, carefully marking a circle at the center with a piece of charcoal.

A number of men had gathered, but Tempe kept back, sweeping the empty dogtrot with a brisk broom as if she wasn't part and parcel of the drama unfolding around her. Her temper had cooled from being called onto the porch, which cost her a burnt skillet of potatoes. Thankfully, the men had eaten them with nary a complaint as if aware their tomfoolery was the cause.

She was dog-tired, her plan for a bath below the falls tucked away. A mosquito had bitten her, raising an itchy lesion on her neck, and she felt sore and unattractive in the midst of so many men. Her nettled thoughts spun back to that twilight in Powell Valley along the creek with James. Despite the grime of the trace, he'd made her feel giddy, pretty, exquisitely alive. Now she just felt worn and soiled as an old moccasin.

The men kept looking to the porch, all but Sion. She still didn't understand their amused talk, why she'd been mixed up with a guide and Levi Todd. Todd and McRae were among the few who knew their name. The ensuing laughter hadn't bothered her, as it was directed at Sion. Though he'd stayed stoic, she sensed his deep discomfiture. And hers. He now knew they were Tuckers. What would he make of that?

She took her time sweeping the dogtrot, swinging the broom this way and that, till there was no more dust left to settle. In the field bordering the corn, the men had formed a line as if weary of waiting for her. One by one they began proving their marksmanship, filling the far field with noise and smoke.

Reluctantly, she put the broom aside and went to get her gun. Pa had taught her to shoot after Powell Valley when they'd lived at Blackmore's Fort, before the terrible trouble with the Loyal. Back then hunger had honed whatever innate ability she had. She took a quiet pride in it but shunned any matches or contests.

"A right terrible waste of powder," she said without rancor as she took her place at the end of the line. No one could dispute the words. Powder was a precious commodity. There never seemed enough.

Sion was two men ahead of her. The broad set of his shoulders was a fine distraction, so wide it would take two skins to make him a shirt. He wore one of linsey once dyed a rich indigo but now faded to pale blue with so much use. She knew he was a good marksman just as she knew the sun would set and the moonbow would appear. Cornelius and the rest of their party she was less sure of. The older, silver-haired man with them simply leaned against the fence, smoking a pipe and talking with Russell between bouts of gunfire.

There were grunts and grimaces as men shot wide of the mark. Tempe's breath grew shallow as the intense heat of dusk pressed down, casting long shadows that made shooting more chancy.

She watched as Sion stepped into place and took aim. No matter how she felt about the man and this silly match, his rifle was a work of art. Of beautifully grained maple, the stock was decorated in brass, as was the butt plate and patch box and trigger guard. A stallion among geldings. He raised it to his shoulder and sighted. The crowd quieted when he paused ever so briefly before squeezing the trigger. The rifle roared.

Dead center.

There were whistles of admiration and a few glances tossed her way. She couldn't best him. She could only match him. How would he feel about that? Not all men took kindly to soldierly women.

The man ahead of her shot second best. He swaggered away in marked contrast to Sion's handsome reserve. A tendril of admiration grew for this borderman, but she brushed it away before it took root.

"Best shot takes all the lead dug out of the target," Russell called.

Tempe tamped down a queer excitement. There were worse tasks than splitting lead with this stranger, but given the strain of the moment, could she match him?

Her rifle felt heavy, and she took her time getting her bearings whilst the men around her reloaded. Bracing herself for the kick since she was not a stout woman, she squinted and sighted. A trickle of sweat made an itchy trail down her back. Taking a steadying breath, she sighted a second time. The shot rang out, choking and blinding her with burnt powder, but it was true.

"Nary a hair's width off!" a man shouted.

To the left of the target, Russell gave her a long look. Even at a distance she read his admiration. She couldn't bring herself to look at Sion. Rather than a bonnet full of bullets, she'd rather have the why of his coming and this strange talk of a guide.

To his credit, he approached her, offering her his share of bullet lead. "Nay," she told him a trifle pridefully. "You'll be needing it more than I."

He said nothing to this, just gave a nod.

She turned aside, declining a second round. All the men but Sion continued until dark. Last she looked he was leaning against the fence with the silver-haired smoker, deep in conversation. She slipped away without another glance.

Maybe she'd get that bath after all.

Clutching a moss sponge and a dab of hair wash made from chestnut leaves and skins, she took her bath. Under cover of darkness, in a placid pool far below the falls, she felt the heat of the day and the grease of the kitchen melt away. The moon was full but fickle, only hinting of a moonbow. She was cast back to her time with Raven a fortnight past, when the moonbow had appeared and bewitched them both.

Pulling free of the refreshing water, she sat on a rock and untangled her hair with a comb of Russell's making, the teeth wide and smooth. The clean shift she'd brought settled over her like a caress.

Here in the quiet she was better able to sort through the demands of the day. The tumult of the falls was more a whisper this far downriver, allowing for unhindered thought. Deep in her spirit she sensed Pa was on his way back to them. Two months he'd been gone. Tomorrow she would go to the rock-house, tidy things there, and see if any critters had made mischief, though Ma couldn't spare her long with so many clamoring to be fed. Provisions were running thin. Pa was never so needed as now. Russell was busy night and day shoeing horses and making repairs, running low on iron. A smithy so far from civilization was a difficult endeavor. Her brother was a master at making do.

Hair almost dry, she gathered up her soiled clothes and started toward home reluctantly, the ground warm beneath her bare feet. Heading uphill, she followed a willow-skirted creek. A few steps more and she heard whistling. Low and musical, it gave her pause. Few chanced the woods at night, yet there in the path not a rod away stood a man. But not just any man.

Sion.

He sought her out for a purpose, she knew. And kindly gave her notice by making noise. A sliver of moonlight pierced the gloom, laying a skim of silver light upon his features and blue-black hair.

Save an owl's hooting, silence fell between them. She hugged her comb and clothes closer, wondering if her state of undress bothered him. But why would it? The worn linen was like a tent, disguising every hill and valley of her. She minded her hair the most, hanging free with a will of its own, buckling and curling in the damp heat of a summer's night.

"Seems like we should make proper introductions." His eyes seemed to dance. "Your brother calls you Temperance. Your ma calls you Tempe Grace. Levi Todd referred to you as Tem Tucker. I'm not sure what a borderman like myself would say."

"Just Tempe."

His chuckle returned her to their first meeting when she'd told him the same. It dawned on her with another fearsome pang that he knew her last name. But it was common enough in the colonies. There were as many Tuckers as Boones and Callaways. Pa was . . . safe.

"And you?" She well knew his name but wanted to hear it outright as if it would take away the remaining awkwardness between them. She would have her clamoring questions answered, Lord willing.

"Sion Silvanus Morgan."

Her nose nearly wrinkled. An odd name, Sion.

As if reading her thoughts he said quietly, "It's Welsh." He rested his gun on the ground. "Means 'God is gracious.'"

Oh? Not just a comely name but a godly one. She'd not belabor the meaning of hers. She'd always thought Temperance plain, as parsimonious as its origin. Her middle name, Grace, suited her fancy far better.

"Well, Temperance Grace Tucker . . . I had no inkling you were so fine a shot."

The compliment begged explanation. She couldn't tell him about their sojourn at Blackmore's Fort. It would lead like a trail of bread crumbs to Pa's misdeed. A chill spilled over her, raising gooseflesh. Maybe Sion already knew and was drawing closer, using her to reach her father. The bounty was ample, his for the taking. Far easier gotten than surveyor's pay.

The comb's teeth bit into her palm. Other settlement women

sprang to mind. "There's more than Jane Menifee and Esther Whitley who are good with a gun. Some can stand up to a loophole as well as any man. Better betimes."

"Can you reload on the run?"

"No call to."

"Pray you never will." He looked away. "What do you know of the Green River country?"

The Green. The name brought a strange wistfulness. She thought of all her tramping to the west with Pa, their favorite haunts, the forbidden places. "There's a nest of rivers that way. Caves and canebrakes. A few rogue Cherokee roam—"

"Chickamaugas, you mean?"

She gave a nod. "But no settlers to speak of."

"I'm in need of a guide." He was looking at her again, weighing, studying, sifting. Awaiting her reaction. "That would be you."

"I'm a good many things on any given day, but I'm no guide." She nearly squirmed beneath his scrutiny . . . and her in her shift. What would it be like on the trail with him and a passel of men, day in and day out? What respectable woman would bend to such a task?

His gaze never wavered. "If a woman can stand up to a loophole as good as a man, what would hinder her from being a guide?"

"I've never heard of such."

"Be the first."

She nearly rolled her eyes. Yet he made it sound so doable . . . almost tempting. Stubbornness took hold. She'd heard of camp followers and cooks with the army in the East, most of them slatternly, it was said. She raised her chin. "And besmirch my reputation . . ."

"I can promise your reputation would never be besmirched.

No man would lay a hand on you—or an errant look. You'd be addressed however you wish. Draw fair wages."

"What need have I of wages?"

He lifted his shoulders in a shrug. "You might go over mountain and want a pretty dress. A bit of lace." He looked to her feet. "Some shoes."

She laughed at this flight of fancy. "I have all three right here. And a moonbow besides." Stepping around him, she started up the trail only to stop again at the sound of his voice.

"A moonbow?"

She faced him again, drawn by his earnest query. "It's a wonderment, I'll give you that, if the signs are right."

"The signs?"

"A full moon . . . ample mist . . . patience."

He studied the sky. "Patience I have. The moon looks fair enough. I don't know about the mist."

She smiled without wanting to. He'd removed his hat and angled it over his heart. Whether deliberately or without guile she didn't know. The effect was the same. For a few light-headed seconds she forgot her shift. Her tumbled hair. Her resistance.

"You could tarry awhile," he said.

Was he asking her to walk out with him? Or sway her into accepting his offer to be a guide?

"I misdoubt you need a guide, be it for the moonbow or the wilderness." She meant it as a compliment, but he might not take it as such.

His face, so plain before, was cast in darkness as the clouds shifted. She took a last hard look at him before continuing up the trail to home. When she reached the top of the rise she turned round again. But he was gone, the slip of trail bereft.

And she felt oddly bereft herself.

10

Behold, I Myself have created the smith who blows the
fires of coals and brings out a weapon for its work.

ISAIAH 54:16 NASB

Sion had watched many blacksmiths, but few with the art
and skill of Tempe's brother. Russell stood in the barn-
shed turned smithy the next morning, leather apron
hugging his narrow waist. The small stone furnace glowed
when a bellows belched air at necessary intervals, stoking
the flames. Sweat ran in shiny rivulets down his half-bearded
face as he hammered and turned an orangey morass of ore
into a horseshoe. He was a forge master, such a melding of
muscle and intensity that one soon forgot his lameness.

Russell didn't look up, just kept to the task in that almost
effortless, unfailing way that made Sion want to try his hand
at it too. He seemed unaware of Sion's entrance, or mayhap
rued the interruption. Or had overlooked Sion entirely.

There was a queer vacancy about Russell sometimes, a
sort of otherworldliness, of not being fully present. Sion
had seen that same blankness in other men, those marked

by bloodshed and tragedy. His thoughts spun back to '73 when Boone and a large party had failed to gain Kentucke and Boone lost his son. He recalled newspaper accounts of the day. Others besides James Boone had died. Had Russell somehow been a part of that?

"Where do you get your ore?" Sion asked, eyes roaming the rough walls adorned with the work of Russell's blackened hands. Clearly, material was not a hindrance to Russell's industry. Sion took in all the means necessary to subdue the wilderness. Hammers and hoes. Axes and plowshares and pot hooks. Hinges and rims and harness fittings. Cowbells and froes.

"Ore? I dig it out of the mountainside. Plenty of wood handy to make charcoal too."

"You'd do well in the settlements."

"Someday this'll be one." Finishing the shoe, Russell began work on a link on the Gunter's chain Sion had brought in.

Sion risked another question. "No other men about the place?"

"Mayhap in time. With two unwed women . . ."

Two? Tempe and the serving girl, Paige, Sion reckoned. But what about Russell's own mother?

"Shouldn't take too long." Russell's odd half smile was as crooked as his gait. "We need some least'uns running about."

Sion's thoughts clung to Aylee. Nate sure sat at attention when she came round. The widow Tucker, folks called her in hushed tones. Sion sensed it unwise to press the matter about what had happened to Mister Tucker. He'd heard of men walking off and never coming back, leaving their womenfolk ever wondering what happened to them. Harper had expressed such a fear, all but begged him to stay. A sharpness stitched across his chest. He'd not heeded her.

"And you?" Russell looked up briefly, startling Sion with his sudden affability. "Looking to settle out somewhere?"

"Nay. I've work to do. As soon as you mend that chain we'll be on our way west."

"West?" Raising a heavy hand, Russell swiped back a damp hank of hair. "That country's a mite formidable. It's big, barren. Some of those canebrakes are so thick you can wander for days. Best take a guide."

"I tried. She refused me."

Another crooked half smile. "Levi Todd had a bit of tomfoolery sending you to Tempe. But he was right about her knowing that part of Kentucke as well as any man who ever made a study of it. Maybe better."

"I expect she's needed here."

"Ma would likely never forgive you if you took her away. Tempe lends her hand to just about everything."

The prospect made Sion want to risk Aylee's displeasure. Tempe could cook. Forage. Shoot. Track. Hunt. *Run.* Their forest chase was never far from his thoughts. The memory kept him on a short tether, always circling back to amuse him. Taunt him. Tempt him.

"What makes you so bent on the Green River country?"

"The Great Meadow's been overrun with British-backed Indians. That leaves the land west of here. It's ripe for settlement, or will be."

"You might tussle with a Chickamauga or two."

"What of their Scots Tory agent, Alexander Cameron? Doesn't he keep the peace?"

"Scotchie? The redheaded Indian? He lives among the Cherokee, but the Chickamauga are beyond controlling."

"You've not had any trouble here?"

Russell shook his head, eyes on his work. "None to speak of.

There's superstitions that come with these hills, this river. It's sacred ground, a burial place. The ghosts of Azgens and such."

Sion had heard the legends. The Azgens were a light-skinned, blue-eyed people from across the eastern sea. The Shawnee claimed Kentucke belonged to the white Azgen spirits, a murdered race. The Indians were a superstitious lot, mostly fearless yet easily frightened in terms of the supernatural and entirely committed to the British cause, which included driving the settlers back over the mountains.

Sion didn't share Russell's calm or confidence. A wilderness war was coming that made the war to the east look like child's play. The trouble with the Kentucke settlements was just a foretaste. No doubt the Shawnee and Cherokee and their allies would strike here, at this very inn, hallowed ground or no. Sion intended to finish his work and be well out of the way before then.

The Gunter's chain was finished, the conversation stalled. Sion caught a flash of movement pass by the barn-shed. Just Tempe armed with her hoe. On her way to the cornfield? He watched her a second longer than he should have.

Russell was studying him, understanding in his gaze. He gave a sly wink. "Careful, Morgan, lest you be inclined to stay."

❦

The large party of settlers encamped in their loft had decided to return to North Carolina and wait for a safer time to trespass into Kentucke's heart. In their wake were abandoned belongings, a broken tool and misplaced knife, a forgotten cornhusk doll. Paige picked through the offerings beneath the stifling sun, gleeful over a lost shilling glinting in the tamped-down grass.

All morning they'd cleaned, scouring the scuffed keeping room floor with river sand to free it from tobacco stains and spills, washing the loft's soiled bedding and airing the mattresses, finally beating the rugs. By suppertime it was only the four of them. Tempe took advantage of the long summer's eve when the heat of the woods settled a bit and a coolness drifted up from the river, weariness slowing her steps as she made her way to the rockhouse.

The surveying party had come this way earlier in the day. It was Sion's footprints she saw—nay, sought—among the dust and horse droppings. She fancied she could distinguish between Cornelius Lyon's light, trifling gait and the deeper, slower tread of the silver-haired man. Indians toed inward but a white man walked wide, outward. Broken brush and tamped-down undergrowth showed their passing. She guessed they couldn't help it, burdened by the surveying equipment as they were.

She might have been among them.

Sion's startling offer still gnawed at her. Bestirred her sleep. What manner of person made such an unfitting proposal, exposing her to untold dangers and the attentions of too many men? Yet something indefinable filled her, a strange yearning she hadn't experienced since James. It felt good to be wanted even if it was for mercenary means, to do a job usually done by a man.

Now she half regretted sending him away. Mayhap it would have been best if she'd softened her stance and taken in the moonbow with him at least. Only there'd been no moonbow. Not since the night she'd spent watching with Raven.

Half a mile more and her thoughts took a dangerous turn. What if . . . ? She frowned and fingered the knife in her pocket. What if Sion met up with Pa coming and going?

Lord, please . . . nay.

But the possibility stood. The Loyal Land Company surveyors couldn't have picked a better time to intersect with August Tucker, who was heavily laden with trade goods and slow to return. Sion and his men were on the main westerly trace.

She veered off the deer path toward the rockhouse, empty as Lazarus's tomb. How glad she would have been to find Pa here, trade goods scattered about, a feast for the eyes and heart.

A bat flew low, nearly skimming her head as it winged farther back into the cavern. Nothing was disturbed in the fortnight she'd been gone. All was as Pa had left it. Another worry took hold of her that had little to do with Sion's men.

Might Pa have been delayed by something else?

The wilderness offered many ways of dying. Wild animals. Accident. Disease. Indians. Ruffians. It wasn't herself that she feared for but those she loved, Pa foremost.

As for her own death, she prayed it would be swift. A sudden fever. A fall from a cliff. A flint-tipped arrow straight to the heart.

Not slow and agonizing like James's.

❦

Forsaking the main trace, Sion followed a buffalo trail to a lick. Cane rimmed the outer edges, a sort of reedy prison offering temporary refuge but no liberating escape. They'd come thirty foot-scalding miles since daybreak by Sion's calculations. Well beyond the Moonbow Inn.

And they were being followed.

No one seemed the wiser, though Nate was watching Sion hawk-like as if reading his consternation. With a low word to stand guard after herding the horses and equipment behind a canebrake, Sion doubled back off the trail.

He was glad to keep moving. When he stood still, gnats and biting flies swarmed him. His linsey-woolsey shirt was damp from exertion, and his hat had made a sticky mass of his hair. He started to climb, Annie in hand, three rifle balls in his mouth to keep it from drying out completely.

He gained a ridge and kept to the tree line, gaze never settling. When he saw what he sought, he expelled a relieved breath. A lone Indian. Young. Fleet of foot. An expert tracker. Fully exposed on the riverbank below and within rifle range.

If he sighted . . . fired . . .

It would be justice. Retribution. Revenge.

For Harper. For all that had been lost. For all that could never be regained.

He raised Annie, drawing a bead on the Indian's bare back. His heart beat in his ears like the rush of birds' wings. *Vengeance is mine; I will repay, saith the Lord.*

His hands shook. Emotion clouded his vision. The moment was lost.

Or mayhap redeemed in light of eternity.

※

A week passed. A tense, breathless week when the heat heralded late June and the garden slowly came into its own. Rotund melons and deep green cucumbers. Golden potatoes and pungent onions. Crookneck squash and gourds of all shapes and sizes. Climbing beans entwining leafy arms around everything.

Whilst Paige and Aylee tended the garden and helped Russell in the corn, Tempe was let loose in the woods. From now till Indian summer she'd be gathering, her most beloved task of all. With the sap running high beneath the new July moon, she fashioned her berry baskets. The bark of tulip trees was best, laced together with hickory.

For a brief spell she almost fancied she was in Eden, taking a special delight in her Maker's garden. As she wandered, she felt the Lord's pleasure in the things He had made. Did He too take pleasure in the ways she put His bounty to use?

"Gather you some blackberries," Aylee called after her. "I'll be needing some leaves for the summer complaint."

Tempe began gathering thimbleberries in cool mountain ravines and gooseberries atop rocky outcrops and ledges. Raspberries, huckleberries, and blackberries filled her baskets and her belly. Once dried they'd hang in sacks from the rafters. But first their kitchen would turn out an abundance of pies and cobblers brimming purple, with sweet, rich cream poured atop them.

Thoughts as full of Pa as her baskets were of berries, she had little room left for Sion. He and his party might have reached the Green River by now or the white sulphur springs on the east fork of the Little Barren River. With the Shawnee River sinking lower by midsummer, he'd be wise to raft to the farthest reaches.

She tarried late in the woods, stumbling home by the stars, having waited at the rockhouse without reward. No light issued from the inn. Ma and Paige were early to bed, early to rise. The door was barred and she'd need to sleep in the loft of the barn-shed.

Opening the springhouse, she left her berry baskets till morning, tarrying long enough to drink some rich sweet milk, the cream at the top unstirred. Thirst slaked, she quietly shut the heavy door.

Was Russell abed?

The barn-shed loomed empty as she passed through to the loft. The hay gave beneath her weight, and she was spared its prickles by lying atop a saddle blanket. The familiar smells and sounds settled around her. Worn leather and wood shavings. Burnt ashes from the forge. Aging rafters. The cooing of doves. Through the shrunken timbers she could see the stars, great white spangles of them flung out across the heavens.

Russell usually slept in a near corner. Tonight no one seemed to be lodging with them. The few hobbled horses at the woods' edge were their own.

She fell asleep missing her feather tick, then stirred awake at the sound of someone below. Raven? His striking silhouette was before her. The supple upper body, bare in summer. The ragged outline of fletched arrows at his back. The graceful arch of his bow. Three hawk feathers in his hair.

She rolled to one side to better see him and realized her mistake. Not Raven. This man was taller. Stouter. The hay gave a faint rustle as she moved for a better look. He looked up, and she held her breath till he turned his face away.

Hiskyteehee. Five Killer.

An icy finger trailed down her spine. She'd last seen Five Killer a year or so ago when Pa took her south to trade with the Cherokee. She'd not forgotten him. On his jawline was a ragged scar that told of a hard-won victory over five white men in the settlements, hence his name. He was young. A leader among the new Chickamauga sect. He had a special hatred for settlers coming over the Gap. She'd heard worse . . .

The moon bespoke midnight. 'Twas light enough for her to see a rolled paper leave his hand. As soon as he placed it on Russell's worktable he left, moving beyond her line of sight to the midnight woods.

She waited for several long minutes before going below

and lighting a wick from the forge's dying coals. Holding the taper aloft, she perused the paper. A handbill from the British? Since the war began she'd seen her share. This one was meant for the tribes, and not only the Cherokee. Sent by the Cherokees' agent, Alexander Cameron, one boldface line particularly chilled her.

Your father, the great King George, who lives in the lands where the sun rises, says the time has now come to feast on settlers and drink their blood.

Sickened, she let the paper go as if her fingers were soiled. It landed on the worktable, but she was of a mind to burn it. Taking it up again, she turned to feed it to the forge's embers when the sound of horse hooves stopped her.

Russell rode into view just outside the barn-shed, looking just as she remembered him before Powell Valley. Unmaimed. Whole. In control. Where had he been? His stallion snorted, further jarring her. A look of pure suspicion marred his face.

"Temperance, what is that you're holding?"

She faced him, torn between destroying the missive and handing it over. "Somebody just brought this by. Some Indian other than Raven."

Dare she say it was Five Killer?

He dismounted and walked toward her as fast as he could. Taking the paper from her hand, he read it. Stoic, he turned his back on her and surrendered it to the forge's embers. "It doesn't concern us."

Stunned, she stared at him. "Are we not settlers?"

"Aye. But we're peaceable folk—"

"Peaceable? This inn sits on unpeaceable ground near the Warrior's Path. An Indian delivered this very handbill. Do you think it some courtesy on his part?"

"He might have tomahawked the lot of us instead."

"What are you going to do about it?"

"Do? What can I do?" He thrust his bad leg forward and locked eyes with her. "I can do nothing but keep the peace."

"Peace? There is no peace!" She thrust her hands into her pockets to still their shaking. "The Indian that came—Hisky-teehee—was one of the party that killed James and the others that day, or so I heard tell of it. They meant to kill you—"

The words died in her throat as she took in Russell's expression. His haunted gaze left her and fixed itself on a far corner. She'd seen that look. Feared it. It bespoke a terrible wound, one she couldn't see. His silence was sudden and full of reproach. Twice now she had mentioned what happened in Powell Valley. What had made her blurt it again?

"Take care, Russell." She gentled her tone, carefulness with him taking hold. "When Pa comes back he might bring news. He never says where he's going, but I sense he's in the thick of trouble traveling south into Cherokee country."

Russell blew out a breath. "This is hallowed ground, remember. You know that Raven's full of talk about how the tribes give us a wide berth because this is a burial place." He took down a large wooden hetchel from a beam, its bed of nails coarse. The flax harvest was over, but the gathering of green corn was nearly upon them. "The Indians are shy of Pa, Raven says. They think he's naught but an Azgen spirit."

"What about the rest of us? We're flesh and blood, living right here in the way of danger. This handbill is naught but a flaming arrow. We need to prepare, lay up provisions, and bar our doors. You need to arm yourself, sleep inside the cabin of a night with us women." At his indifference her anger simmered and boiled over again. "You need to quit jabbering with Raven and mending Indian muskets and whatnot—"

"Mending those muskets and whatnot is what keeps your hair attached to your scalp." He turned on her, hetchel in hand. "How else do you account for my jabbering and fixing? I aim to keep things calm, to stop any bloodshed. You, Ma, and Paige are my responsibility. With Pa in hiding, what else am I to do?" He threw the hetchel into a spidery corner. "I keep the peace to keep you safe."

She fell silent, torn in two. Wasn't Russell's logic twisted? Could one wounded man keep danger at bay by mending a few Indian guns or fixing what they brought his way? Living unharmed by the falls but a few years was no promise of continued safety. They'd once thought that those first settlers would scatter the tribes and quash the danger. They'd been wrong. Something terrible was coming, mayhap a hundredfold of what had happened in Powell Valley.

Russell was regarding her with a haggard look, clearly spent from her outburst—and his. "Say nothing of this to Ma or Paige, nor Pa when he comes back."

If he came back.

With that, he turned his back on her and staggered off into the shadows.

11

Our way is over mountains, steep hills, deep rivers, and muddy creeks; a thick growth of reeds for miles together; and no inhabitants but wild beasts and savage men.

—Francis Asbury

A giant chestnut and laurel thicket shut out Sion's view of Nate at the rear of the column, but he could hear Lucian's exclamation of alarm followed by the dull thud of a hatchet.

"Lord have mercy!" Nate's voice, rarely aggrieved, had the capacity to chill Sion to the bone.

Alarmed, Sion pushed past Cornelius and the chain carriers and the skittish pack train through a swarm of chiggers to reach Nate. He sat on a downed hickory, clutching his leg, abject apology on his grizzled face.

"Lucian here—he nearly saved me."

Nearly. Cornelius's manservant stood by, hatchet in hand, near the coiled, cleaved body of a copperhead. Thick as Sion's forearm and still writhing, it had done its ugly work. Deep in Nate's calf two scarlet gashes were sunk.

Kneeling, Sion examined the leg, soon to swell.

"By heaven, it burns," Nate moaned.

Sion looked up at Lucian. "Get some whiskey." Out of his budget Sion took a dried root and thrust it at Nate. "Chew this hard then spit it out."

Nate stuffed the gnarled root in his mouth and chewed, making a disagreeable face.

"It's campion," Sion explained. "Rattlesnake's master, some call it."

Nate jabbed a dirty finger toward the copperhead. "*That* ain't no rattlesnake."

Sion shrugged. "No matter. Poison's poison."

Lucian brought the flask of whiskey and Sion poured a bit over the wound. "Now drink some down."

Nate spit the chewed root into Sion's hand and took the flask with far more glee, sipping and watching as Sion applied the mashed campion, tying it in place with a strip of clean linen.

"Best get you to the Moonbow Inn. It's not more than a few miles south by my memory." He couldn't recall how much time had passed since he'd last seen those rock chimneys. A blur of humid days dazed his brain. But there was no disguising the glimmer of pleasure the prospect of returning once again wrought. On account of the victuals, not that indigo skirt. "Want to ride?"

Lucian had brought Nate's horse, which nickered at the sight of his fallen master. "If I'd been ridin' to begin with, I'd not be in this predicament." With a sigh, Nate handed Lucian the flask. "'Behold, I give unto you power to tread on serpents and scorpions, and over all the power of the enemy: and nothing shall by any means hurt you.'"

Standing, he tottered toward the waiting gelding, and Sion helped him into the saddle. The other men ringed round, concern on all their faces. Nate, for all his Scripture spouting, was a favorite. Sion took the reins, leading him toward the front of the line where he could keep an eye on him. Surprisingly, Cornelius took his place at the rear without comment, and they started off again as the forenoon faded and the real heat of midday spiked, the Moonbow Inn ever in their sights.

❧

"Well, I'll be . . ."

Aylee's wonderstruck tone turned Tempe round before she set foot in the keeping room.

Her mother was looking out the kitchen window, suspended in a rare idle moment. "Here comes Sion Morgan—and a string of men and horses. *Again.*"

"Looks like they've lost all but one dog," Paige mused.

They'd last seen Sion's party at planting time. Were they now back? This was the last thing she'd expected. Her insides somersaulted, betraying her outward calm. Why this unbridled excitement at the mere mention of him—*them?* Aye, it was *them* that addled her. Fear of another fracas left her half winded and nervy.

The dogs began to howl, and Tempe could hear Smokey's excited yip. Clutching a bowl of new peas, as supper was about to commence, she stood stone still till the flutter inside her settled. Only it didn't settle.

Did the inn have enough to feed them? Maybe they weren't after a meal. But why else would they come? There was so much trouble brewing she'd expected them to head back to Virginia till things quieted down, if they ever did.

But Sion was a man who defied expectations. She could only guess the gist of his thoughts. *Make a stand, stake a claim, come what may.* Like Boone, he probably reasoned the land would never be settled by running back over the Gap at every whiff of trouble. This was why he was at their door. He was about his business, passing through, or in need of something. This she knew.

Russell entered the kitchen, looking no less worn down than when she'd confronted him about the handbill. Their heated words seemed to leave a bitter aftertaste, tainting their every exchange.

Yet here lately she'd begun to feel a new understanding for her brother beyond the usual pangs of pity. She needed to say she was sorry, that she'd spoken out of fear. She now saw Russell in a kinder light. Not the lame, haunted survivor but a man who made the most of what he had, not striking out in anger and hatred but attempting to secure their safety by keeping the peace. Even if he was misguided. Even if it seduced him into believing they were safe.

If it be possible, as much as lieth in you, live peaceably with all men.

The Scripture had come to mind a dozen times since. But she wasn't sure how it fit into their life on the frontier, when it was settler against Indian and sides must be taken.

"You have plenty to feed Morgan and his men?"

She stared at Russell. What did it matter if they did? Russell, shy of most newcomers, seemed to take a shine to this particular surveyor. But Tempe couldn't move past the fact that having them at the inn was like firing a powder keg. Explosive. Dangerous. If the Indians knew they were cavorting with land stealers—feeding and hosting them—there'd be a price to pay.

⁂

When he could see and smell the inn's wood smoke, Sion's breathing eased. But another quick glance at Nate ratcheted his fears. The exposed, bitten leg looked like a water-soaked log, half again its normal size. Nate's face was fevered. He was having trouble sitting on his horse, listing slightly to the left. Sion expected him to fall to the ground any second.

Heavyhearted, he called for Spencer and Hascal to take Nate on up to the inn.

Tempe's mother had come off the porch and was making a beeline toward Nate. Sion watched as she motioned for the chain carriers to bring him into the west cabin, not the keeping room. Curious, Sion followed, leaving Cornelius and Lucian to see to the horses. His spirits rose on sight of Smokey, who hobbled to him despite her splint. Her fur was like lamb's wool against his weathered hand, her tail a-swish. The dogtrot curs quieted as Russell emerged and stood in the keeping room doorway.

Nate was moaning now. Was delirium setting in? Once inside the west cabin, Sion swept the room in a glance. As tidy and spare as its mistress, the room held a charm and warmth that only came from a woman's hand. At Aylee's bidding, a cornhusk tick was brought down from the loft and placed beneath a far window.

Sion removed his hat and ran a hand through his damp hair, glad for the shade. The cabin was blessedly cool and smelled of sassafras. Clumps of herbs hung from rafters overhead. Nate was in good hands. Sion stood by silently as Tempe's mother brought a basin, seating herself on a low stool to bathe Nate's flushed face.

Aylee shot a glance at his departing chain men intent on a meal before settling her gaze on Sion. "Get you into the keeping room and see to your supper. I'll tend to your friend, but I don't know his name."

"Nate. Nathaniel Stoner."

In time Sion went out, wondering if any supper could be had given the number of horses tethered about the place. He crossed the dog-infested dogtrot, disgusted at the sight of Hascal's and Spencer's bad manners at table. He could only see the tops of their heads bent over their trenchers.

Cornelius and Lucian had yet to enter, and the main table was full. A man and two women occupied one end, two small children between them. Russell motioned Sion to the cold hearth, fireless on so warm a day, where an empty chair beckoned.

No sooner had he sat down than the door to the kitchen swung open and his meal was served. He'd expected Tempe, but it was the flaxen-haired girl who came, two plates in hand, her long braid swishing like a pendulum as she walked. He tucked away his disappointment, refusing to glance about for a glimpse of Tempe.

His own table was a checkerboard that the girl soon crowded with ham and new potatoes and peas, fried hominy and cornbread. A mug of cold sweet milk hovered precariously on the board's edge.

Saying little, Russell had taken up a pipe that turned the air rich and spicy. Sion paused before he took a bite of meat, almost missing Nate's mealtime prayers. The hearty mouthful tasted like ashes. A few more halfhearted swallows and he pushed away from the table.

He felt he owed some explanation but had no words. Russell looked unconcerned, puffing quietly on his pipe, eye on the main table. Across the dogtrot Sion tread, enveloped again by the sweet scent of sassafras. Tempe's mother hadn't left her stool, and Nate was still thrashing, murmuring a string of fevered words that made no sense. Sion stopped in his tracks at two unmistakable, aggrieved mumblings.

Harper . . . Sion.

A rush of emotion poured over him like scalding water. He took a cane-bottomed chair at the foot of Nate's pallet, trying to stay atop his fractured feelings. They frothed and bubbled over, stinging his eyes and tightening his throat till it seemed a hot stone lodged there.

Somehow Tempe's mother had peeled off Nate's shirt. It hung from a peg on the wall Sion leaned against. Nate's worn moccasins lay beneath, nearly soleless from all their tramping. She didn't look Sion's way, her ministrations never ceasing. To his amazement, she was parroting Nate himself, Scripture flowing from her lips like a song. As if she knew Nate. Knew that he needed the Word as much as any tonic.

At last she looked over her shoulder. "Fetch me some spring water."

He took the empty piggin from her hand and returned outside, trying to shut Harper's memory away. He kept to the shade, moving toward the spring and the big water trough that emptied down the hillside in a noisy trickle.

The springhouse door opened and Tempe stepped out, nearly in his path. He looked briefly at the ground and then back at her. He felt as addlepated as Nate. Her eyes communicated a quick compassion, and her hand shot out to take the piggin and fill it to the brim for him.

Smokey came between them, wagging tail brushing his leggings. The collie looked from Tempe to Sion, loyalties torn, or so it seemed.

Tempe stroked Smokey's head, but her words were for Sion. "Sit here beneath the sycamore if you like—or return to table."

"Nay," he replied quietly, taking the piggin and returning to the west cabin.

Was Nate asleep? His body was motionless atop the pallet, no rise and fall to his rib cage. Sion looked to Aylee, who simply put a finger to her lips. Bewildered, Sion looked back at Nate, willing him to breathe, holding his own breath till he did. A slight shudder of the sunken chest foretold Nate's breathing was simply shallow, not absent.

Smokey had settled in the open doorway as if trained not to enter in. Feeling the need to be near her, Sion traded the chair for the floor, her answering delight a solace as she pressed into him, her nose damp and cold on his hand. Bone weary, he let his guard down and closed his eyes, fading into the hazy oblivion of sleep.

Tempe surveyed the food Paige had served that was now growing cold, trepidation ticking inside her. Russell pulled the pipe from his mouth, face grim. "His friend's snakebit and doing poorly. Like as not that's the trouble."

Should she leave his meal be? Wait for his return? Russell's noncommittal shrug gave her no answers. "Raven's out back needful of something done at the forge. I'll leave the keeping room to you."

Raven? Was he fully healed? She glanced through the open door and saw his supple form half hidden behind the barn-shed door. Yet there wasn't one but two Indians. Curiosity spiked. When she looked again they had vanished from sight as if aware of her scrutiny.

The other boarders were finished, the women and children ready to bed down in the loft. Though the summer night stretched on, full dark hours distant, the travelers were tired, anxious to be on their way at daybreak.

Paige and Tempe returned the kitchen to order while Russell

retreated to the barn-shed. Sion's party sprawled across the dogtrot, some smoking, all silent and preoccupied.

"Mister Lyon ain't even asked for any spirits," Paige whispered as she returned her broom to a corner. "I overheard Mister Morgan tell the rest of his party to set out at first light and start whacking their way west a few miles from here. They're to join up again when Mister Stoner's some better."

Pondering it, Tempe threw out the dishwater before rinsing the basin clean and leaving it to dry.

The usual night noises were setting in—the burry chirruping of katydids and frogs and the lilting call of the whippoorwill. On such a peaceful eve it was hard to fret about Indian unrest and snakebites or the sobering handbill left in the barn-shed. Tempe felt in her pocket for her Psalms. Maybe she'd spell Ma. Tempe's concern for the stranger in their private quarters was on par with her curiosity. Was he Sion's kin?

Avoiding the dogtrot, she reached the cabin another way, bypassing the stares of too many men. It was the door her father took when he crept in and out, a small square of an opening more like a fort's sally port, a tangle of laurel hiding it. The bushes scratched and tugged at her as she finally gained entry, her bare feet cool against the cabin's pine floor.

Aylee had brewed a tonic. Tempe pieced together the ingredients from the fragrant air, milkwort and fleabane foremost. With a start she drew up short in the shadows, spying Sion by the door with Smokey. His head was tilted back against the log wall, eyes shut. He made a comely picture sitting there, the strength and heft of him undiminished in sleep. One large hand with its odd pockets from rifle balls was sunk into Smokey's fur, his lean, muscled legs folded Indian-fashion.

Asleep . . . or only pretending to be?

She touched her mother's elbow, communicating a wordless wish. With a nod, Aylee let Tempe spell her. Paige came in, eyes wide at the sight of Sion before she scampered to the loft ahead of Aylee.

Tempe took the vacant stool, the candle on the sill offering ample light to study their patient. One look assured her he was neither father nor brother to Sion. This stranger looked tough as whang leather but was smallish and silver-haired. Beneath the scruff of beard his features were well drawn, even handsome, despite the pockmarks pitting his skin. Was he valuable as a member of the surveying party—or merely close as kin? Both, she reckoned, had made Sion shun his meal.

As if sensing Aylee had gone, the stranger began to toss and mumble, rustling the cornhusk pallet. It bore the hiss of a snake and set Tempe a-shiver.

Taking up a cloth, she began to swipe the sweat from the man's face. It beaded again as soon as she wiped it clean, kindling a deeper worry. She longed for a full name. Then she could say it soothing-like, granting her a familiarity that befit the moment. She wasn't used to tending half-clad men on the cabin floor—or having one behind her, even fully dressed, that rattled the daylights out of her.

Despite Ma's tonic, a fierce battle was brewing inside the man beneath her hands. If she failed to calm him, comfort him, she would feel she'd failed the man at her back.

She set the cloth and basin aside and took out the Psalms. Pa said she had a soothing voice. She turned to the 139th chapter, her most beloved. Maybe it would bring this feverish stranger solace too.

Sion came awake to the mellifluous voice of . . . Harper? Nay, Tempe.

That she was spouting Scripture didn't distance him like Nate sometimes did, with his preacherish, holier-than-thou ways.

Sion opened an eye, not bothering to resettle his stiff limbs. No need to announce he was awake. She might stop reading and . . .

He swallowed, tracing the candlelit line of her profile. Through sleepy eyes he noticed the delicate line of her cheekbones and the generous slant of her mouth—and that aggravating dimple made more pronounced when she spoke or, more rarely, smiled.

He nearly wished he was Nate, the sole object of her attentions. Every so often she would stop her reading and brush his lined face gently with a damp cloth.

"'Search me, O God, and know my heart: try me, and know my thoughts.'"

Shutting his eyes, he bent his thoughts toward what she said. Unwillingly. Even grudgingly.

Did the Almighty search him? Know his heart? Try his thoughts?

If so, He then knew the wretched state of things. His past. His present. His future.

If only Tempe's tending could mend not only body but soul and spirit.

Not Nate's. *His.*

She finished reading. He opened an eye again to watch as she laid her Psalms aside and silently got to her feet. Nate shifted and then moaned as if protesting her going. But go she did, slipping soundlessly out the cabin door to who knows where, Sion's curious gaze trailing after her.

"About time, Daughter." August Tucker's gravelly voice filled the whole rockhouse. "What's kept you?"

What's kept me? A slew of responses flew to her lips. And then a joyful relief swept through her as she leapt from ladder to ledge. When her feet touched the rockhouse floor he swept her up in a hug, and she was overcome with the sweating, filthy mass of him, his raggety beard scraping her heated cheek.

"You'll be a sight better to welcome once you bathe," she chided, wrinkling her nose.

Chuckling, he took her in, a rough hand stroking a tendril of hair that had escaped her braid. "I only just got here. Had to hide the horses and trade goods, as there's strangers about." When she gave a sorrowful nod his levity faded. "A small party, mayhap. They've been a thorn to me, coming so close. I nearly plowed right into them along Greasy Creek."

"Surveyors, Pa . . ." She drew a breath. There was no sweetening the news. "They're with the Loyal Land Company."

He swore, a rare utterance, and stood at the mouth of the rockhouse, his view obscured by a great many trees. "Who exactly?"

"Six of them, all told." She hesitated, momentarily frozen. Betimes Sion defied words. "Aside from the lead surveyor, there's an older man and then an English mapmaker. Two axemen serve as chain carriers."

His brow knotted. "How long they been here? Mayhap the better question is, how long do they aim to stay?"

"They came again a week ago, but we first met up with them in May. They planned to survey up Boone's way around the settlements, but with the trouble in the middle ground they now mean to chain the Green."

"They've come by the inn, then."

"Two of their party are there now. The rest are camped near here—"

"Why have they divided?"

"One man's snakebit. The lead surveyor, Sion Morgan, brought him in. Ma's tending him as best she can."

A medley of emotions played across his face. She stayed stoic despite her sympathies, torn between Nate Stoner's plight and her father's predicament.

"What do they know of you?"

"They ask few questions. They know our name." Alarm leapt into his eyes. She hurried on, serving him the paltry pieces that would not satisfy. "I heard one refer to Ma as the widow Tucker."

"They have no guide?"

She hesitated a tad too long, earning his sharp scrutiny. "They've been asking for one."

He hunkered down, hands fisted, and peered through the screen of trees as if fearful the men had followed her. All talk of Virginia, the Loyal, turned him almost feral. Irrational. "Get rid of them."

She stared at him, mouth open. "Get—*what?*"

"I said, get rid of them."

Light-headed from thirst, she stooped beside him and un-corked a canteen of spring water, hoping she'd misheard. "They'll likely be on their way as soon as the one man heals."

Or dies.

"Go tell him—this Morgan—you'll act as their guide. With you along they won't tarry long. Send them upriver by way of the falls when you're through. There'll be no call to pass by here again."

She nearly choked on her swig of water. "But Pa—me alone—with so many men?"

He snorted. "You fancy a chaperone in the wilderness?"

She flushed. The rockhouse turned sweltering. She tried a different tack. "And you would send me knowing the Indians mean so much trouble? Knowing the British have rallied them to feast on surveyors and drink their blood?" The ugly wording in Alexander Cameron's handbill was bitter to the taste. Desperation crept into her voice. "These land stealers are shown no mercy but are drawn and quartered or burned at the stake—"

"And what of me? Rotting in a Tory prison? Hanging by the neck from the nearest tree?" With a hard hand he struck her, the searing pain lightning quick. Her head was jarred by the force of it.

Never had he hit her. Not even in her childhood had he lashed or switched her. Her fingers went to her mouth, the bottom lip split and bloody. Tears blurred her vision and she struggled to stand.

"Tell your ma to come here tonight. In the meantime, do what you have to do."

She grabbed the rope and began her descent, unable to speak past her throbbing lip. He would not apologize. She knew him too well for that. He was hell-bent on ridding the land of the Loyal. He would make her obey, come what may.

And she? Would she do his bidding? Trembling, half sick, she nearly stumbled as her feet touched solid ground. Embarrassment flushed her from head to toe at the prospect of returning to the inn with such a blow. There was no disguising, no explaining her torn lip.

But the stain on her spirit was worse.

12

When she I loved looked every day
Fresh as a rose in June,
I to her cottage bent my way,
Beneath an evening-moon.

—William Wordsworth

It was the forenoon when Sion realized Tempe was missing. The sounds of crockery and the steady banter of Aylee's and Paige's voices issuing from the kitchen told him she was gone. Every half hour or so Aylee would cross the dogtrot and see about Nate.

"He's resting easier," she'd sometimes say, or, "Once his fever breaks he'll take some nourishment."

Sion kept occupied splitting wood for the cookfires, creating a hill of hickory and oak in back of the woodshed where the roosters strutted cockily and the hens preened.

Farther back in a little meadow was Tempe's makeshift kingdom. For a week or better he'd surveyed her comings and goings, half amused and half admiring. Slabs of chestnut bark lay across sawhorses, laden with a staggering abundance of berries, some he couldn't name. Clover, bee balm, and mountain mint were strewn about in baskets, ready to be strung up for drying or brewed for tea.

He was reminded of his mother's quiet industry those peaceful days along the Watauga. There she'd gather her bounty beneath the noon sun when the dried blooms would have the most potency. Did Tempe believe the same?

She'd paid him no mind other than to ask about Nate. Sometimes she bypassed him altogether, disappearing inside the west cabin to see the patient for herself.

Today he'd seen no sign of her. Her absence added to his angst. When he wasn't helping with some needed task, he appointed himself guardian of her workplace, shooing off birds and other critters that swooped to steal her berries.

Bedeviled past the point of sense, he took cover in the shade of a chestnut, knapsack beside him. Removing a cedar pencil and scrap of paper, he gave vent to his thoughts. A line there. A curve here. Some shading. The face of a woman soon took shape, not the quality of Cornelius's artwork but telling nonetheless. Anyone who knew her would recognize it was she. Just Tempe of the indigo skirt. He even drew her dimple and the line of her brow that made her face so expressive. Studying it, satisfied, he thrust the paper among his field notes to better stay hidden. Somehow it solaced him that her likeness would go with him once he left.

Near noon the midday meal was partaken of by Sion, Russell, and two longhunters passing through. Paige served blackberry cobbler, no doubt made from Tempe's forays. It sat rich and heavy as he listened to the men talk about an alternate route to Virginia in light of the unrest.

"Boone and Harrod sent word to Patrick Henry in Virginia they need reinforcements if they're to stand . . . and survive."

"I misdoubt any men'll be spared what with Washington's war."

"There's war, war everywhere. What say you we head west where the French and Spanish ain't fightin'?"

The kitchen door opened and Tempe appeared at long last, murmuring something to Russell, who regarded her with concern before clearing away their empty dishes. Sion's attention left the longhunters.

Her eyes were down, chin tucked in low, but there was no disguising her lip. Busted open, looked like. He'd seen tamer in a tavern fight.

He leaned back in his chair, clenching and unclenching one fist as he watched her. She seemed . . . wilted. As if somebody had knocked all the fire out of her.

Uneasy, he went out onto the dogtrot, where Smokey waited. He bent and rubbed her ears, thoughts elsewhere.

Who had struck her?

He felt a bit queasy pondering it. A human hand had left that mark. It wouldn't have been Russell or the women. The longhunters had only just arrived, with no time to make mischief.

He took a step off the dogtrot. The sun was at one o'clock, the cicadas shrill. He wondered how his party was taking the heat. Nigh blistering, the sun had leached the last of the indigo from his shirt and baked his exposed skin a deep russet.

A great many gourds were growing along the rail fence where they'd held their shooting match. The vines climbed the weathered wood, a tendril threaded through. Reaching out, he stripped some briar leaves and crushed them. So used, they made a fine tonic for swelling. Or so his mother always said.

When Tempe appeared to throw out the wash water, he was

waiting. She stood at the edge of the woods where the spring ran off down the mountainside, unaware of him. Shoulders bent, she stared dully into the trees.

Coming behind her, he stole the empty basin away and set it aside. She spun to face him, putting her hand to her mouth as if to hide it, her eyes holding his in question. Taking her idle hand, he pressed the briar leaves into her palm. Understanding dawned. When she looked up again, tears glazed her eyes.

His chest swelled tight. The leaves seemed a paltry offering. He took a step back, wanting to comfort her, touch her. He had no call to ask who had hurt her. He hardly knew her. But the small familiarity they shared made him want to do more.

Aylee appeared just then, offering him an escape. "Mister Stoner is asking after you."

Sion walked toward the cabin and didn't look at Tempe again.

Where was Russell? As night settled in, Tempe sought the solace of her brother. But the barn-shed was wanting, overwarm and empty. The heat was making Paige cross, so Tempe had fled the cabin, unable to countenance the girl's whipsaw moods. Usually she bore them gladly, teasing or talking Paige out of any sourness, but since she'd left the rockhouse she wanted to avoid any questions. She touched her tongue to her hurt lip, uglier now hours later.

Once in the barn-shed, she determined to wait for Russell. She took a stool by his worktable and rested her head on her folded arms, pressing the crushed leaves to the sore place. Tonight Smokey was keeping close to Sion, and Tempe missed her sweet presence.

Thankfully, Nate Stoner had taken a turn for the better, able to keep down some broth. Ma was nearly worn to a frazzle tending him and the kitchen too, though Tempe had noticed them talking together in Aylee's spare moments. Nate often had a Bible in hand. Sion had fetched it from a saddlebag once Nate was rid of fever.

Tonight Nate was moved to the keeping room loft, and Sion lodged there too. Glad she was Sion was out of sight if not out of mind. His unexpected sympathy touched her. Twice now he'd shown her a tender side. She much preferred his cool silences, his frugal way with words. It had taken all her will to hold herself together when he'd given her the tonic. It was nearly as jarring as Pa's slap. She who slighted Sion at nearly every turn, paying him no more attention than she would a bug on a branch.

A snort interrupted her reverie. She raised her head to look toward a far stall at the young colt Russell was raising to ride. Another pang shot through her at her brother's plight. On horseback was the only time he felt whole, free of his limp.

Lately he'd said little and toiled much. Summer always brought more work. She looked about, wanting to escape her misery by lightening his own. Leaving the briar leaves atop the worktable, she began tidying the shop, tucking a hammer away here and hanging a hoe there. Next she took a broom, sweeping up wood shavings from beneath a half-made chair.

A gourdful of nails had spilled. She got down and gathered them up, the ends sharp against her fingertips. The colt was bumping against the stall, tired of confinement or perhaps hungry.

She hung a lantern on a hook, took a handful of corn from a feed sack, and held out her open palm as her eyes roamed the stall. Farther back against the wall was a hide-wrapped bundle. Curious, she let herself in, unmindful of the colt nudging her for more feed. Cast in shadows, the bundle was larger than first appeared, hard and heavy. She took her penknife from her pocket and slit the leather tie.

The hide slipped open. Wooziness swept through her. Guns. Muskets. British-made.

Questions pummeled her like buckshot. Russell . . . was he repairing the Indians' guns? The very ones used to make war on the settlers?

Sore lip forgotten, she knelt and ran a hand over one weapon, marveling at the lack of quality. Dull walnut. A short barrel. Serpent side plates. The butt plate was simply a bent piece of flat brass. As clumsy and crude as Sion's rifle was remarkable. Yet still deadly.

If Boone or Harrod got wind of such treachery . . .

Her first impulse was to dump the guns over the falls. To do so meant taking them in batches. There looked to be two dozen. Her fingers shook as she retied the bundle.

Ma had made mention of the presence of more Indians. She'd thought it odd, then had quickly forgotten what with the summer gathering and this business with Pa and the surveyors.

Half sick, she shut the stall and went out into the still night, needing to talk to Ma. But Aylee was with Pa at the rockhouse and wouldn't return till morning. Paige was likely abed. And Russell? Something was very much amiss.

A loneliness she'd never known assailed her. She'd seen a side of Pa that frightened her—and now Russell. Suddenly he seemed distant, secretive, unreachable. Not her beloved brother. More stranger.

Having Sion and Nate Stoner across the dogtrot didn't

help. Though they were outsiders, she sensed to her everlasting hurt that they were better men, more to be counted on than blood kin.

"Russell can't be found." Paige's voice held a plaintive note.

Tempe stood just shy of the springhouse, full milk pails in hand. Dusk was settling in and supper was done. Other night chores awaited. Like Ma, Russell had been gone a full night and day. Odd, the both of them. She and Paige weren't often left alone.

"I'll see to Russell if you mind the milk."

"Take your gun," Paige cautioned.

"Nay."

Without another word, Tempe untied her apron and hung it from a peg. She wouldn't say she knew where Russell had gone. When he was most disturbed, most haunted, he went where he knew few would follow. Behind the waterfall. She was chilled to the marrow even thinking it.

Leaving her rifle untouched, she hurried through the woods toward the riverbank. Her gaze fell to the curtain of water hiding the secret passage behind the falls, still a roaring, writhing deluge. The hidden tunnel was best reached when the river was at its lowest lest the water sweep a body away. Few could say they'd been behind the waterfall. Few knew of it. Pa had shown her when they'd first settled on the Shawnee. He stored his valuables there, his cache of silver coin and the sword he'd worn in the last war.

Pausing, she removed her moccasins and tucked them away beneath a laurel bush. The back of the falls was best navigated on bare feet. Up and over boulders she climbed, squeezing through tight passages till she emerged on a harrowing slip of ledge that led to the inner chamber. Now at midsummer the river had only begun to ebb.

Mist drenched her. Tingling and chill, it lay against her heated skin. The waterfall's roar filled her ears. Her heart beat double time, not in terror but in awe. James was closest here. Where the danger was the thickest she felt him best. Near as a handbreadth. Watching. Waiting. Perhaps wondering if it was her time.

Slowly she edged, one foot after another, beyond the curtain of cold greenish water. The ledge widened. She was able to face forward. Her heart settled and then started up again upon sight of Russell. At the back of the cavern he sat, staring unseeing into the torrent. She had a terrible premonition that he was pondering leaping to his death. It was a worry she had carried with her since '73.

She stood between him and all that water as if her simple stance could sever the frightening possibility. But he continued to stare past her, through her, as if unaware she had risked life and limb to reach him.

He made no sign he'd heard her. Not a muscle twitched. Just that sad, vacant stare unlike anything she had ever known.

If he jumped, would she follow?

It was Powell Valley all over again and those long, lonely months after, when all was dark and unsettled. Russell had gone vacant, speechless, refusing to eat, only bodily present. Now she knew it for what it was. When he was most haunted he left them, his mind in a place far beyond their reach.

"Russell!" she called over the water's roar, extending a shaking hand.

She stepped away from the falls, toward him, her fingers extended.

Nearer.

Some impulse urged her closer when all she really wanted was to flee. But to flee meant certain death, or so she sensed. Russell was closer than he'd ever been to leaving them. The darkness inside him went deep. She must break it—or lose him completely.

Kneeling, the unforgiving rock beneath her, she put her arms around his legs, resting her head against his knees, as if she could prevent him from harm. He hunched over, fists clenched, his longish hair free of its usual tie.

He felt like stone. And then . . . the warmth and weight of his hand atop her head told her some part of him was present.

"Russell . . ." She raised her head. "Talk to me."

He didn't look at her but his hand stayed steadfast, slipping slightly to wrap around her braid as if it was an anchor for his turmoil.

She took advantage of their closeness. Mighten she break the power of the past by begging him to talk?

The words she thought she'd never say tumbled one after the other. "Please . . . tell me about that day." Yet something told her she'd get no answer. "Tell me . . . please."

Yet did she want to hear? When everything in her recoiled at the telling?

His hold on her braid tightened. He set his jaw, swallowed. Could she even hear him speak above all that water?

Lord, if it's meant for him to tell, if there's healing in the telling, please let him speak and enable me to bear it.

"I wanted to die that day."

His voice reached her ears, each painstaking word.

"I wanted to die so that James might live."

Tempe stayed rigid, as if she might halt his speech by even a flicker of movement or a word.

"He died hard. Try as I might, I can't cut out his cries . . . what he said . . . what they did."

She looked down to the damp rock beneath them, fighting the tide of emotion already welling inside her. She would not cry. She would not ask questions. She wanted to close her ears to the details. Let him talk if it would bring healing, but she had no heart to hear.

"We camped on the north bank of Wallen's Creek that last night. We were slowed some by tools and books . . . a drove of cattle . . . seed. Unbeknownst to us, you and the main party were three miles ahead."

Three meager miles?

"We'd slept little that night on account of the wolves howling. One of our party laughed and said we'd best get used to such come Kentucke." He hushed, leaving her on tenterhooks. "Now I think it wasn't wolves but Indians."

"They'd likely been trailing you ever since you left Castle's Woods."

"Dawn brought a heavy dew." His hand on her hair was heavy, like his voice. "At daybreak the Indians fired on us. They shot James through the hips straightaway. Me, I was hit in the leg but managed to run into the brush and hide. The Negro, Adam—he hid with me."

With every careful utterance, the harrowing scene was etched in her mind, never to be undone.

"James couldn't move, shot as he was. Some of the Indians were rounding up the horses and supplies whilst the others taunted James. I recognized one as Big Jim, the very Cherokee the Boones had befriended along the Yadkin. James called him by name, begged him to spare his life. But the Indians were beyond listening."

His hand clenched, tugging her hair so taut she nearly felt scalped.

"When the Indians ran up to stab James, he tried to fend them off with upraised hands . . . I've never seen such a sight, his skin slashed to red ribbons." His breathing grew labored, as if the exertion of the telling was taking a toll. "James called out, saying he suspected you and the main party were already dead, killed by these same Indians. He cried out again—this time for his ma."

Rebecca? Tempe knew of their close tie. Her heart, always bruised, broke anew. Did Rebecca know her boy had wanted her? Wanted the solace only a mother could give? It did not grieve her that it was Rebecca he needed at the last.

"At the end, they tore out the nails of his hands and feet."

She shut her eyes. Big Jim had done this? The very Shawnee who had shared the hospitality of James's father's house? Was there no mercy? Was heaven shut and silent that day? Could not the Lord have reached down and stayed the Indians' brutality?

"I've never seen a man so mangled. They shot James and another man full of arrows and left a war club beside them. But they did not scalp them."

Nay. This much she knew. When Daniel had sent Squire back to bury the dead, he had recognized James by his tangle of fair hair.

"I stayed low in the brush, bleeding heavy as I was, whilst the Indians made haste to leave. Charles, another slave, was taken prisoner. Another man escaped." He hung his head lower. "The war party wanted the horses and provisions more than anything."

Yet those very provisions—all the livestock and farming tools—must have ignited the Indians' fury. They were evidence of white encroachment, a foretelling of white settlement to come and a lost way of life to any Indian in their path.

She swallowed down the few questions he had not answered. Had James and Russell and their party not posted a watch that night? Why had they not pressed on in the dark to rejoin the main party? Had they thought them farther ahead than a mere three miles?

Would she ever know?

She looked up at Russell, who was still staring at the torrent of falls. He was done with the telling. And it had exacted a high price. Gooseflesh lined his bare arms, and his face was more gray than tanned. She still held on to him, her cheek pressed against his bony knees. She would not let go till he agreed to leave this place. Yet what if he threw himself off the ledge as they left? It was her ongoing fear.

Lord, please.

The short, beseeching prayer was as much for her as for him. She felt weighted—leaden—with the knowledge of what had happened in Powell Valley. The details crowded her brain, bloodstained and agonizing, carving a deeper hurt. Too much for heart and head to hold.

She felt Rebecca and Daniel's sorrow, the fears and tears of James's brothers and sisters. She recalled her own grief like a blow, fresh again from Russell's telling, their hurried, harried flight away from the Gap and Kentucke, every stunned, sweat-stained mile.

Jesus, heal us.

13

I was most afraid coming down the Cumberland Mountain. The place was narrow and rocky . . . woods more beautiful in Cumberland Valley than any other place.

—JANE GAY STEVENSON

That night Tempe had no memory of climbing into her loft bed, Russell's words had so upended her. She was cast back, mired, in '73. Just when she'd thought her brother's memories would send him over the edge of the falls, he'd snapped to, as if sensing the peril of the moment. And then he'd left the cavern ahead of her, taking her by the hand, his limp hardly slowing him, as if his unburdening had left him lighter, less lame.

Now she lay still, Paige's soft snoring hardly noticed. Her eyes fixed on the moon's slender crescent beyond the loft window. Where was the girl she'd been? The one she'd left behind in Powell Valley?

Dare she revisit her own memories, those last days of her girlhood before tragedy took hold? Could she even resurrect them, hidden away in the darkest corners of her conscience?

The recollections, dusty and bittersweet, seemed as fragile as Ma's chipped china from Virginia, the few pieces of porcelain that had survived their hasty flight over mountain after Pa's misdeed.

Sweat that had little to do with the searing heat limned her lip and brow.

What would the price of remembering be?

She recalled a timeworn thought . . . that sitting atop a horse sixteen hands high made a fine target for a flint-tipped arrow.

Tempe pushed the worry to the far reaches of her mind as the mare took a hairpin turn, hooves a-clatter on the steep, stony trace. The horse stumbled, sending Tempe's arms around the sleeping child astride the pommel in front of her and an avalanche of rock into the ravine below.

Danger was quickly followed by delight. A spider had spun some enchantment overhead, the gossamer web catching the sun as it slid across the forest floor. It was on this she focused. Not the dizzying heights. Not the mare's missteps. Nor the swelling stings of a yellow jacket's nest they'd encountered farther back. Though she was glad to have flung herself like a cape around little Lavina, taking the hurt instead, her bare arms and cheek throbbed a reminder.

Autumn had taken hold of the woods, creeping softly as if on moccasin feet. The whisper of falling leaves pierced her tiredness and reminded her it was her favorite season. Another hundred miles and the woods would be layered with gold. Shutting her eyes tight, she prayed they'd live to see it.

She sent her gaze to the head of the long, snaking column. The men led off, able woodsmen most of them, some forty guns, all told. Beneath their wide-brimmed, dark felt hats, Tempe read their consternation. While a man could cover thirty miles or more on foot a day, they'd gone but a hundred in two weeks, only as fast as the livestock would allow.

"Devilish rough," her pa called this new country. Devilish and dangerous.

Their party was mostly women and children, a great many curious dogs and skittish horses, unruly pigs and beeves and sheep. Such a ruckus they were raising!

Here we be, come get us, their passing seemed to shout.

Ahead of her rode several stoop-shouldered women, babies and small children tucked in hickory hampers slung across horses' backs, packsaddles bearing the brunt of feather beds, coverlets, and kettles. The older children walked along what was little more than a bridle path. All but Lavina, who shared Tempe's mare. Slightly feverish, Lavina slept, unmindful of their trek, her tiny chin tucked to her chest.

They made camp at dusk. Soon half a dozen fires, nearly smokeless from dry oak, lit the darkening woods. There were cows to milk and supper to fix, mostly cornbread and meat that tasted of wood smoke and ashes.

The music of some nameless creek called to her, wooing her away from the bustle of so many folks. Having eaten, Tempe sat atop a mossy log, her linsey skirt embroidered with briars and burrs. She allowed herself a moment of stillness before washing up plates and cups.

At the edge of camp, her pa stood guard whilst Ma busied herself with their bedding beneath a sugar tree. All around them men's voices rose and ebbed, their words flitting through Tempe's mind like fireflies. Moccasin Gap. The Narrows. Sand Gap. Shawnee River. The Great Meadow.

Kentucke.

She looked west, finding a break in the trees. The sun was sinking in a blaze of red and gold, the sky pretty as a party dress. So lost was she in the winsome sight she nearly missed the voice in back of her.

"Tempe."

James? She turned and took him in, the blue of his eyes like cold, quenching water. She felt a little start at his warm scrutiny. He leaned on the barrel of his rifle, and for a moment the busy encampment faded away.

"The sunset's better seen at the mouth of the creek." He angled his head west. "Care to walk out with me?"

With a glance at his family encamped near her own, she smiled her answer. But before she took a step in his direction, the least ones rushed him, hanging on to the hem of his worn homespun shirt.

"Mind if we come too?" The plea would have snapped the hardest heartstrings. Tiny Becky, barefoot and begrimed with trail dust, smiled up at him, little Daniel on her heels.

"Hush, sissy." Farther down the creek bank, James's sister Susannah paused from searching for wood ticks on Jemima's scalp. "Can't you see them two lovebirds want to be alone?"

Flushing, Tempe plucked at another briar embedded in her petticoat, wishing for a comb . . . a clean cambric apron . . . room to breathe. But privacy wasn't to be had in a busy camp.

"Best bring Livvy too." James leaned his rifle against a near tree and picked his sick sister off a pallet, her arms open wide, eyes still fever bright.

Tempe reached for his weapon.

"No need." His low words, even softened with a smile, failed to bring reassurance. "There's a guard, remember. Peace."

Peace? If peace could be had by treaty with the tribes—the

153

ever-warring Shawnee and roaming Cherokee. The settlers never relaxed their stance, all but James. He was more at home with a plow than a gun.

A burst of homesickness smothered her. She longed for wide-open spaces and acres of corn and the deep stillness of the Yadkin far from any Indian trails. Not the driving dream of a dangerous land, this everlasting pull toward the wilderness. Kentucke fever had infected her pa too. She stole a look at him as he hunkered down with a knot of men, drawing a map in the dirt.

Above the tree line the sunset had deepened, a smudge of crimson riding the horizon. She pushed aside her fretfulness, glad her tiredness didn't dim her pleasure. It was beautiful. Life was beautiful. Even weary beyond words and worried about Indians and Livvy, as James called his littlest sister, Tempe still felt full. Thankful.

Once they stepped free of the trees near the creek's sandy mouth, James set Livvy down and the children joined hands, thrusting bare, brown feet into the racing current, faces alive with delight.

Tempe watched them, all too aware of the man beside her. "Betimes I wish I was knee-high again."

"I thank the good Lord you're not." James passed a broad, work-hardened hand across his mouth as if to hide a smile.

Color high, she bent and picked up a large maple leaf to fan herself. "Do you recollect where we were September last?"

His pensive look told her he'd not forgotten. "On the upper Yadkin in Carolina, you mean. When my cousin wed yours."

She smiled, warmed by the memory. A sweet ceremony it had been, with his uncle Squire saying the words over the nervous couple, followed by a lively frolic. The encounter shone like a star in Tempe's memory. It was the night she'd become smitten with James. But most remembered the occasion as the day James's father was resurrected from the dead. Gone two years in the Kentucke territory, bearded and ragged beyond knowing, he'd returned and asked his estranged wife for a dance. She'd balked.

"You need not refuse me, for you have danced many a time with me," he'd told her.

She recalled Rebecca's joy. The tears and fears of the least ones who didn't know this bewhiskered, bearish stranger. Then and there Tempe had shut her heart to the notion of a wandering man, thankful James was as different from Daniel as daylight and dark.

"I'd rather think on where we'll be September next." The words came low and thoughtful. "Ever ponder marrying here and now?"

Eyes wide, she shed her shyness. "Right here on the trace?"

"It'll make the steeps and sinkholes a mite more bearable." When she stayed quiet, he added, "Uncle Squire is a preacher, remember."

Her heart hitched. *Temperance Tucker Boone.* It sounded big. Proud.

James looked down, the broken thong of his moccasin holding his attention.

Was he only fooling? He'd not once kissed her. He'd only lately touched her back or arm in spare seconds wrested from endless motion, in that sweet, possessive way a man touched a woman that made Tempe feel half his already.

Had he, like she, fashioned their cabin log by log in his mind's eye? Stout oak walls and walnut shutters and a river rock chimney with a carved sunburst on the mantel. She'd sprinkle flower seed, now stored in a dried gourd, about the door stone. Flaming bee balm and violet-blue spiderwort.

Trumpet flowers and silver bells. In time they'd have need of a cradle. She hoped for as many children as the Lord allowed. A quiver full, as Scripture said . . .

"I know how you want a place to call your own." He sat down and stretched his long legs out in front of him. "As for me, you know all about that too."

A whole year they'd danced around the prospect of settling down. "Too young," her ma said. "In time," said his father.

She held back a sigh and darted a look at the least ones wading now. "You oughten not speak of such, James Boone. I'm liable to say yes."

He made a motion to stand. "Then I'll talk to your folks—"

Her hand shot out and clasped his tanned wrist. It had the feel of knotted rope beneath her callused fingers. "Ma's still feeling dauncy. She says the trace is no place for a—" The word *honeymoon* hung in her throat. "For a man and woman to—to come together."

He laced his fingers through hers, whirling any concerns to the wind. "I ain't marrying your ma, Tempe."

She gave him a half smile. "I reckon not."

"On the Yadkin, farming and living apart, I could bide my time." He swallowed, the faint sun lines about his eyes creasing in concentration. "But here, within reach of you and your sweet talking, it's nearly beyond bearing—"

"Hush." She went pink at the confession. A sudden breeze lifted the damp hair along the nape of her neck. "You could talk a jaybird off a tree limb."

"I ain't full of flatter, Tempe." He turned solemn as the Sabbath. "Look at me."

She met his eyes. Trouble was, it went hard on her to look away from him. The wide set of his shoulders, the unflinching, sometimes fierce line of his jaw, his mane of flaxen hair, wove quite a spell. But he owned some of his ma's spirit too. He was a hand with children and animals. The land. Few could plow as straight a furrow as James. In their earthy, uncertain world, these were the things that mattered.

"You'd better ask your folks, same as mine." Tempe picked her way carefully, unused to tender talk. "With your pa wedded to the wilderness . . ."

"There's Israel, remember."

She bit her tongue. Two years younger, James's brother was often poorly and even now was healing from the slow fever. Middle-heighted and spare, Israel lacked James's heft and strength. He seemed more his brother's shadow. It was James who mattered most to the big Boone brood. Israel was hard-pressed to take up the slack of James leaving.

"Lookee here, Jamie!" Becky's lisp carried on the breeze, high as a bird's chirping. She held up a shiny stone treasure.

He smiled at her, thoughts clearly elsewhere. "I reckon our cabin will sit betwixt your people and mine."

"Best begin with that, then." She wiped the damp from her hairline with the heel of her hand. "When you're asking for my hand, I mean."

He stood, and this time she made no move to stay him.

꧁

The next morning Tempe watched both the sodden sky and James as he slid the bridle onto her mare. The scent of horseflesh, coupled with the musky smell of wet leather, stirred her senses like the man standing beside her. Next she knew, his warm hands had spanned her waist and he lifted her into the saddle.

"I should be walking," she said, touching her sore cheek. "Nothing wrong with me but being stung."

James leaned in to adjust the stirrups. "Seems like my bride should ride."

Bride? Joy took hold of her. "You mean . . ."

"We're to wed in Powell Valley."

She looked ahead at the long, sleepy procession, the blue haze of mountains beyond. Wedded. At last. She felt a wild, giddy rush. "How far?"

"We're fixing to climb the Clinch and pass through Moccasin Gap. Next comes Powell Mountain and a sightly river bottom some sixty miles."

She bit her lip and studied him. Would they say their vows at the beginning or end of it? She opened her mouth to ask.

The wind was blowing out of the southwest, slashing the wet sideways, stealing her words away. Rain was beginning to bead on James's low-crowned felt hat. Her bonnet began to sag. Her books—would they get wet? She'd seen the men packing their precious gunpowder in leather pokes coated with beeswax, safe from the damp. She wished she'd done the same with her beloved things.

She shifted self-consciously in the saddle. She could feel James's father's eyes on her when he passed, likely taking her measure as his firstborn's future wife. Daniel doffed his hat, a courtesy he had little time for, and she eased. When he took his position at the front of the line, she turned her attention back to James.

"Up you go." James lifted little Livvy, whose eyes were barely open, her cheeks still stained with fever. Tempe leaned into the girl as if to shelter her as James turned away.

Thunder shook the sky. It would be a long, rough climb in the rain. Far behind her, driving the stock and guarding the rear, were a dozen or so men and boys, her brother Russell among them. Mud sucked at their moccasins, turning the trail into a streambed. She had grown used to the tinkling of the belled horses and the muted lowing of the cows, the clang of a dangling kettle, and a babe's muffled cry.

By the time they set foot in Kentucke, would marriage feel as familiar too?

They came over Powell Mountain into the valley like beleaguered Israelites desperate for the Promised Land. But Kentucke still lay a world away. Rising up to the west were immense steep-walled cliffs, gleaming silvery white in the harsh afternoon light.

The White Rocks.

Somewhere in that forbidding, stone-studded wall of rock and pine lay a gate, a gap, a nest of rivers. Tempe braced herself for another hard climb . . . but first the wedding.

"When the time comes," her mother was saying, unpacking a saddlebag, "this'll do for your marrying dress."

Aylee's liver-spotted hands shook out a linen garment dyed a winsome indigo. A quilted cream petticoat and filmy lace kerchief broke up all that blue like clouds in a summer sky. Wrinkled as it was, it was clean, befitting a wedding. All but the kerchief had been worked by her ma's hands.

"Best hold off a mite." Behind them, Russell stood casting a long, damp shadow. She'd hardly seen her brother since they'd first set out. "We're running low on supplies. The men agree we'll lay by here and send a small party back to Castle's Woods for provisions."

Tempe pushed aside her dismay. "A small party?"

Russell tugged on his hat brim and looked apologetic. "Me, the Mendenhalls . . . James."

"Mister Boone will go with you, aye?" she asked, hopeful.

"Nay," he said, no hint of disquiet in his features. "Just us younger men."

"Well, I'll welcome a rest." Their mother began folding the wedding garb up again. "Lord knows the children need it."

This Tempe couldn't deny, but inwardly she wilted. Only Russell—her blood brother—could have seen past her stoicism. He answered her unspoken questions, as always.

"Castle's Woods is off the trail some twenty miles north of here. We'll be bringing back flour and farm tools and the like before leaving the settlements completely." He gave her a reassuring wink. "You'll be wanting provisions enough for an infare, likely."

The infare. Would there be a wedding feast, even in the wilderness? She doubted Russell would brandish his fiddle on account of attracting Indians. A silent frolic it would be. "You'll not be gone long . . ."

"A few days is all. Should be back by Saturday next. Daniel says a wedding would be a fine thing to bolster spirits before we head over White Rocks. Looks like you'll have your Sabbath ceremony after all, Sister."

Her heart lifted. Only a few days' time. Till then she'd be of help to James's mother and the children. She'd pray a speedy journey for the departing men. Looking across the busy encampment, she spied several of them outlined around a campfire, deep in conversation—James, his father, and his uncle Squire among them.

Russell took a step back as if already anxious to be on their way. "We leave at daybreak."

She shook off her chary feelings. Maybe by week's end the weather would dry out. Time enough to make James a new shirt. She could sew and ruffle one with the linen they'd brought. Her gaze fell to the chinkapins strewn across the forest floor, ready for gathering. She'd take the children nutting.

"Take care, Temperance. Stay close to camp." With another wink, Russell shifted his flintlock to his other roughened hand. "Come Saturday we'll be back. Mayhap I'll bring the bride a little trinket to sweeten her wedding day."

But it was not to be.

14

There are some things you learn best in calm, and some in storm.

—WILLA CATHER

The next morning, Tempe was alone in the kitchen when dawn lit the July sky. The morning stillness was broken by the sweet song of birds, piercing her hurt. Coffee needed making, but for the moment she was lost in the past, ushered down that lonesome road by Russell's unburdening the night before. And then her own heartrending recollections.

She shut her eyes like she'd wanted to shut her ears to his shattering words. But they were now a part of her, never to be undone. She tried to focus, staring at the scene before her. Tried to dispel her own lost hopes and heart dreams. Finally the kitchen resettled into familiar lines, no threatening shadows within.

Before her were a variety of tin jelly molds. Stars. Flowers. Half-moons. Sold by a Virginia tinker in a variety of shapes, they were relics from another life, another season.

James had given her one shaped like a shell. She'd tucked it in her marrying chest, but today, like the dress she wore, she'd brought it out. No sense keeping beloved things that begged use shut away. Maybe airing them would help take away the sting. Or, like her busted lip, might the wound heal but the pain remain?

Leaving the jelly tins, she swung a small copper kettle over the fire before making batter, listening for movement upstairs. Sion was an early riser. He took his breakfast on the dogtrot, preferred coffee to tea, and was partial to waffles. To sweeten them, she drizzled maple syrup and added a splash of cream atop the butter. It was her way of thanking him for the briar leaves. Thanking him, too, that he'd asked her no questions about how she'd come to need them.

The aroma of parched coffee beans threaded through the air when the doorway between kitchen and keeping room darkened. Her eyes went wide. Nate Stoner stood there. Dressed. Beard trimmed. Eyes a livelier green than she'd ever seen. Hardly the man they'd pulled back from the brink.

"Mornin', Miss Tempe. Where's Mistress Tucker? I want to thank her for her doctorin'."

"Morning, Mister Stoner." She swallowed. "Ma is . . ." Aylee had likely left the rockhouse by now and was on her way back to them. 'Twas Russell she was most sure of. The ring of the axe was sweet music indeed. "She'll be here shortly. Care for some coffee?"

"Obliged," Nate said in his easy way, eyeing the waffle iron. As if breakfast was the sole reason he'd risen from the dead.

Her disquiet deepened when Aylee appeared just then, flushed and winded as if she'd run all the way from the rockhouse. Unaware of Nate, she began, "Your pa—"

Tempe cringed. Noticing Nate, Aylee tied on an apron,

recovering her composure. "I never thought to see you standing there hale and hearty this soon, Mister Stoner."

"It's on account of your fine care," he replied, taking a steaming cup from Tempe's hands. "That and the Lord's resurrection power."

"Amen." Aylee took up the waffle iron whilst Tempe finished whisking the batter. "I'll serve you and Mister Morgan breakfast soon as I can."

With a nod Nate retreated to the dogtrot, and Aylee shut the kitchen door, her features a stew of concern as she faced Tempe. "You wouldn't lay the blame to your pa for your lip, so he told me himself. He's sorry as can be."

Tempe said nothing to this. What was done was done. She'd heal and hope it didn't leave a scar.

Aylee poured the batter into the greased iron with an expert hand. "I suppose you'll pay heed to his words."

Setting her jaw, Tempe shut the iron and thrust it into the fire by its long handles. She'd expected Pa to reconsider his rashness. She'd hoped to gain an ally in Ma, at least. "So you reckon I should go with these men, who are little more than strangers, into hostile territory at Pa's whim?"

Aylee looked hard at her. "Since when did you worry about what became of you?"

Unable to deny it, Tempe lapsed into silence.

Aylee continued in low tones. "You might be safer leaving out with these surveyors. There's an abundance of Indian sign here lately. Russell is acting queer, as if he knows something he's not telling, and your pa won't leave the rockhouse till these men with the Loyal are long gone."

Distracted, Tempe flipped the iron over, fearing she'd scorched the bottom half. "So my going will snuff the Indian sign and restore Russell and let Pa roam at will."

Hands on hips, Aylee regarded her with none of the sympathy of before. "Are you afeared of these surveyors?"

Tempe opened the iron and dumped the waffle on a waiting wooden platter, hardly noting the crisp edges and savory aroma. "Ma, it's you who raised me to act like a lady even if I'm not. And ladies don't go traipsing with men like common camp followers."

Hand unsteady, Aylee overfilled the iron, spilling batter onto the floor. "I trust this man Morgan. Mister Stoner too. Neither of them would make free with your virtue."

"There are four more men to consider." Cornelius Lyon flashed to mind, always with suspicion. She wouldn't broach the delicacy involved. What of her monthly? Endless trips to relieve herself? The need to bathe? Prudery had no place in their harsh lives, but modesty was another matter.

"I can talk to Mister Morgan."

"Talk, Mama? About what?" She was near tears, only her ire keeping them in check. "How are you to manage with me gone? Who will keep you in meat?"

"Your pa will see to that."

So all was settled, then. Cornered, flustered, lip throbbing, Tempe lashed out a final time. "You can tell Pa this, that he may as well mark a target on my back sending me into the wilds with a party of hapless surveyors."

Aylee refused to be daunted. "*Hapless* is a poor word for Sion Morgan. As for Mister Stoner . . ." She broke off, her rosy hue returning. "He's asked to stay on once the surveying's done, be an extra gun."

"Is that all, you reckon? The *widow* Tucker, he calls you." Tempe turned loose another waffle. "I suppose Pa expects me to unravel that too. Well, it's entirely his doing if folks are fooled into believing you've no man about the place save Russell."

"Shush!" Aylee cautioned, their sharpened voices in danger of carrying beyond the kitchen.

Aylee took the iron while Tempe made ready to serve, wishing she'd gone to milk in Paige's place. She was not of a mood to step on the dogtrot and pretend all was well. Yet when she walked onto the porch it seemed all was right in Sion's world, with Nate Stoner risen and a plate of savory waffles to boot.

"Thankee kindly," Nate said with a humility that moved her. He bent his head, murmuring the rambling grace that had been missing from their table since Pa went into hiding. Russell could but choke out a few thankful words in his absence.

"Father, we thank Thee for this food, for all the blessings Thou dost give. Strengthen our bodies and our souls, and let us for Thy service live. Amen."

Sion merely gave her a hint of a smile, eyes averted. Had he overheard what had just played out in the kitchen? She prayed not. Her words came calm and certain-like, belying the storm inside her. "I suppose the both of you will soon be on your way."

"Aye," he answered, taking the plate she offered.

Unwilling to return to the kitchen, she set the coffeepot between Sion and Nate and picked up an empty basket. But once she set foot in the woods she found she had no heart for her usual gathering.

It was the river's solace she sought, as if its roar and rush could carry her troubles away. At the bend in the trail she looked back. Ma stood on the dogtrot talking with Sion.

Confusion doused her. Pa's plan might well backfire. Sion was not likely to overlook her outright refusal at first. What would he now make of her *aye*, meek as a lamb?

She reached the river, abandoning her basket to walk out

on a rocky ledge nearest the falls. Mist cooled her face and neck, leaving tiny glistening beads over the indigo of her marrying dress.

How different her life would have been had she wed James. In the span of four years' time they'd have shared vows, a bed, babies. Settling out from a fort had been his plan. She'd never forgotten how he'd drawn her a replica of their cabin in the dust of the trail a fortnight before he died. How gleeful she had been back then. How heedless of the heartache to come.

She looked down as she stepped onto a flat boulder that led to other boulders lining the river. Her shoes felt strange. Rarely worn, they pinched her feet. Mindful of snakes after Nate's ordeal, she'd begun wearing them. Of all God's creatures, she had an everlasting fear of snakes.

She hovered on the mist-slicked ledge. One errant step and she would slide over. Away from Pa's befuddling plan. Away from Ma's meddling and Russell's melancholy.

Into James's arms.

15

A sweet disorder in the dress
Kindles in clothes a wantonness:
A lawn about the shoulders thrown
Into a fine distraction . . .
A careless shoe-string in whose tie
I see a wild civility,
Do more bewitch me, than when art
Is too precise in every part.

—Robert Herrick

Aylee's surprising words hardly had time to settle when Sion placed his unfinished breakfast on the dogtrot's planks and made for the river. Behind him Nate was talking—*courting*—with little notice of his leaving.

Sion had an uneasy feeling about Tempe. He didn't know what he'd say to her once he found her, though he'd rather lay it out plain.

You first refused me, and now your ma comes telling me you'll do as you denied.

Yet he sensed she was too tender, that for the moment

168

something had so undone her she'd fled to the river, and he'd best tease open the reasons with care.

He saw her long before he set foot on the boulder-strewn bank. Again her dress was a puzzle to him. Hardly a work dress, it was finely made as if for some special occasion. A lacy cap perched on the back of her head, beneath which she'd pinned her plaited hair. She wore shoes—another oddity. Mayhap Nate's calamity made her cautious.

He drew nearer, undetected. She was entirely too close to the waterfall, hovering on the very lip of the limestone cliff. Tendrils of her hair were tossed about in the damp, moving air. A corner of her apron lifted. Even the hem of her skirt was stirring.

"Tempe."

He wasn't sure she could hear him over the force of the falls, but she turned toward him too quickly, one foot failing her.

Fright darkened her face just as fear smacked all the breath from him. He lunged toward her. Nothing was sweeter than the feel of her wrist, soft and small in his leathery grip. He jerked her forward, out of harm's way.

"You shouldn't stand so close," he shouted.

Her face crumpled, her sore lip trembling. With a gentle hand he tightened his hold on her, not letting go till they'd backtracked to the sandy riverbank far from slippery rock.

Only then did he release her. He expected no thanks, but she gave him a small, sorrowful smile, glancing over her shoulder to the falls as if she'd only dreamed of such a close call. When she faced him again, her eyes were no longer damp but resolute.

"I'm considering going with you, Mister Morgan."

He made no reply, unwilling to tell her Aylee had just said the same.

She looked up at him, brows pensive. "But I'll only go if you'll take Raven too."

The Cherokee? This was the last thing he'd expected. He'd not met this man, but suddenly it seemed the most important thing to do.

"He knows the country better than I do. He speaks the Indian tongue more than Cherokee." She looked to the woods as if hoping he'd materialize. "He'll be . . . security."

Security? An Indian? By heaven, she was a bewilderment. A mass of contradictions. "What makes you think he'll go?"

Her chin came up. "He owes me a favor."

A favor. He could only make a wild conjecture as to what that entailed. Was she . . . partial to this Indian?

"It might take some time to find him." Her tone was unconcerned, and he felt an odd amusement. As if she could round up a red man at will in untold acres of wilderness. "He's usually not far."

"So be it," he said. "He'll be paid wages same as you. We leave as soon as you locate him."

He watched as she shed her clumsy shoes, then averted his eyes when she peeled off her stockings. She placed both in her empty basket.

Barefoot, she made quick work of the rocky shore, heading west as if she knew just where this Cherokee was. As for himself, he hardly minded staying on for another meal, another night's rest on a feather tick. But his gut churned as he thought of Cornelius and whatever mischief might have befallen the rest of his party in his absence. He'd been away for too long.

What would the next hours bring?

Tempe stood in the doorway of the barn-shed, relieved to find Russell at work on an unfinished chair. The fragrance of wood shavings sweetened the air, something she'd miss on the trace.

He looked up, chisel suspended. Her thoughts swung to the hidden muskets . . . Alexander Cameron's deadly words . . . Russell's increasing absences. But for the moment her love for her brother was uppermost.

"You leaving?" he asked when she didn't speak.

"Morgan's unwilling to wait any longer. Mister Stoner is well enough to travel." There was no complaint buried in her words, just stark urgency. "I wanted Raven to come, but he can't be found."

"It's Pa's doing, you going." Russell's low words were garbled, so soft only she could hear them. "Same as that mark on your lip."

She said nothing, just shifted the saddlebags in her arms. Her mare waited, stamping impatiently beyond the entrance. In the clearing Sion and Nate were saddling up. Aylee was dashing about with provisions, her usual calm decidedly stirred.

"You want me to tell Raven next time he comes?"

She nodded again, sick inside, so afflicted by all that was happening she didn't trust herself to speak.

"Should he decide to go, you'll be easy enough to follow." There was an underlying fretfulness in the words, an odd sheen in Russell's eyes that added to her angst.

Easy to follow, aye, with so many men and horses, and now a lone woman in the mix. "I'll miss you," she choked out, haunted by a wild worry she might never see him again. Maybe now was the time to settle her nettlesome questions. She'd best start with the guns in the barn-shed. "Russell, I know about the mus—"

"Tempe? You leavin' us?" Paige's alarmed words snuffed Tempe's query as the girl rounded the corner of the barn-shed. "And here you cautioned me not to ride off with a passel of men!"

What could she say to this? A deeper misery lined Tempe's insides. "There's much that you don't know. I'll leave it to Russell to tell the why of it. Truth be told, I'd rather join up with a war party of Chickamaugas."

In minutes she'd tied on her saddlebags, talking to the mare in coaxing tones if only to settle herself. Goodbyes were wrenching. They bled the heart right out of a person. But Russell had risen to the occasion, abandoning his wood-working to pat her on the shoulder at least.

Paige was crying now, head bent more from a missed op-portunity than Tempe's leaving, likely. Tempe ignored her, wishing she had wits enough to risk a farewell without break-ing down. Untethering her mare, she swung herself into the saddle as Sion and Nate mounted and bid Aylee goodbye.

Tempe took a hard look at her home place, lingering on the meadow bereft of all her gathering. The berries had been sacked and hung from the rafters amid aromatic herb bundles, enough to last through the long winter to come. She had a sudden, unassailable urge to climb the loft steps a final time and bid her feather bed and dower chest goodbye.

For a moment it seemed she hovered between two worlds, both dark. 'Twas 1777. The year of the bloody sevens, some were calling it, and it was but July. Was she the only one who sensed they were walking into the midst of an ordeal like '73?

✍

They rode single file, Sion ahead and Nate behind. Hem-ming her in. Respectful. Protective. *Suffocating*. Back rigid, she sat uncomfortably in the saddle, unsure of her free-spirited mare that was adept at snatching brush lining the trail without missing a step. Rarely did Tempe ride. She much preferred a soft, moccasined footfall.

They covered miles at a steady pace almost dulling in its regularity. She'd slept little the night before, tossed about by Pa's brutish behavior and being foisted upon a surveying party.

So weary was she that she barely noticed the wonders around her. She'd been this way before many times. But mounted on Dulcey, surrounded by two strange men—this was another world, and the woods seemed almost new.

Sion said not a word. He was tireless in his scrutiny. She fancied he had eyes in the back of his head. Nary a sound or sight escaped him. It seemed he hardly breathed. Once again a dozen questions begged answering. She'd bide her time and have them satisfied one by one. There was naught like the familiarity of a camp to spill secrets, though she intended to hold tight to her own.

Within eight miles, just as sweat made a damp patch on her bodice and her throat was chalked with dust, she heard a high, nervy whinny.

The camp.

A burst of color amid the crush of green woods made her think a parakeet was near, but it was simply Cornelius's head covering, a square of flaming red flannel.

His greeting was no less colorful. On sight of her he called out precariously loudly, "Well, who have we here?" Eyes alight, he came forward as she dismounted, making a little bow and kissing her hand. "Mistress Moonbow?"

She cracked a smile as her feet hit solid ground, finding his flair almost refreshing after Sion's stony reserve.

The other men got to their feet, gazes swinging between her and their leader and Nate, who had yet to dismount and still looked haggard. Ma had packed a bundle of medicine just in case. He'd have need of it, looked like.

Cornelius stared at Sion, expression hardening. "Is she camp cook?"

"No need," Sion replied, unbuckling her saddle's girth. "Lucian does ably."

"Laundress, then?"

Tempe's smile faded as Sion swung her saddle over a downed log. "She's here to keep you fools from being swallowed up by the cane or gored by a buffalo . . . or worse."

Cornelius stared at her unashamedly as if seeing her in a new light. His gaze traveled the length of her in a way that made her skin crawl. Or maybe it was the garb she wore, suited for the task at hand but unfit for civilized society. Skirts cut to mid-calf that revealed leggings and moccasins. A bodice that now seemed too tight though her stays were loose. She wore Russell's black felt hat in a childish token that made him seem nearer. Its broad brim shadowed her features but made her scalp itchy and hot. Her braid snaked to her hips, fraying and in need of smoothing.

"She has the look of a guide," Cornelius conceded. "But can she shoot?"

Sion snatched the red handkerchief from Cornelius's head, balling it in his fist. "Ask her."

"I matched Mister Morgan," she said quietly, removing Russell's hat and fanning her face.

"Would that you had *bested* him," Cornelius muttered, scowling at Sion. The tension between them seemed hatchet-sharp, like that brawling day at the inn.

As Lucian led her horse away, Tempe turned to Nate, who

dismounted slowly as if weighted with stone. Pity lanced her. It was unbearably hot, and the evening promised no respite. She spied a mosquito on Nate's grizzled cheek. Was he too weary to lift a hand and bat it away? An unnatural lethargy glazed his eyes. Fever? Was he failing again? It would be a sorry journey without Nate Stoner, this she knew.

"Well then, we shall remember our manners." With a wave of his hand, Cornelius made proper introductions. "Here is my manservant, Lucian, and our two axemen and chain carriers, Hascal and Spencer."

She smiled at the two youngest men, who were regarding her with mingled curiosity and interest. "If you'll help me cut some pine we'll make a bough bed. Mister Stoner is still ailing and needs to be off that leg."

Feeling Sion's eyes on her, she retreated to the nearest pine. She slipped her hatchet free and began chopping at the lower limbs. Making a bough bed was something Pa had taught her early on, a way to make peace with the wilderness. Now the memory brought a little pang. The men began hacking, mimicking her as she used her hatchet as a carrying pole, draping a great many branches over the handle. Rather than tell them what to do, she began planting the rough ends in the ground, laying the boughs in one direction. They followed suit and soon had a thick, fragrant bed beneath a sugar tree.

Sion approached as she unrolled a deerskin and then a saddle blanket atop the branches. "We should have left Nate at the inn."

The inn? When we need every gun we can get?

She continued to smooth the bedding, casting a concerned look over her shoulder at Nate . . . who was nowhere to be found. "Where is he?"

Sion checked a smile. "He . . . um . . . has business."

Business. Her attention returned to the task at hand, her face heating the color of Cornelius's handkerchief. She'd soon get used to such things, outnumbered by so many men.

Nate returned, seemingly relieved and touched by her efforts. "Think I'll lay down a spell. Wake me for some supper, if you please. I don't care to miss your ma's fixin's."

Aylee had indeed packed a feast, filling a saddlebag and sparing them a cookfire. Chunks of smoked ham and cheese. Cornbread now beginning to crumble. Dried corn and assorted nuts. After supper, Tempe made a pretense of picking berries in order to have a moment of privacy.

When she returned to camp the men were still seated, all but Lucian, who was washing tin cups at the creek, and Nate, who lay on his bough bed. She knelt beside him, wishing for a little of her mother's poise. "Best take a look at that leg, Mister Stoner."

"That's just plain Nate to you." He gave her a wink. "It's a sight better'n it was, thanks to your ma. She has a way about her, she does."

Still a worrisome color, the wound was healing slowly, the swelling gone.

"Tell me if it pains you." She glanced at her open saddlebag. "I have a secret stash—a bit of gooseberry wine to hasten you back to health, or at least help you sleep."

"This here bough bed you fixed for me is help enough." He leaned in conspiratorially. "Best keep that stash hidden. One of our party is powerful fond of spirits."

"I know just the one," she whispered, remembering Cornelius, the metheglin, and the lead ball burrowed in her book. She'd brought the poems along with her Psalms but misdoubted she'd have time for either.

Nate settled back, seemingly restored after a meal. "'I will both lay me down in peace, and sleep . . .'"

"'For thou, Lord, only makest me dwell in safety,'" she finished.

He regarded her through half-shut eyes. "Yer ma ever get lonesome with no other menfolk about the place save Russell?"

She hesitated, wanting to blurt out the truth about Pa. "I reckon she does," she replied as honestly as she could. Ma saw Pa so seldom, betimes she seemed more widow. "But Ma isn't one to complain about her lot."

"She's missin' you 'bout now, I figure."

"And you, Nate?" She turned the question around gently. "Surely there are folks missing you."

"Me? Nary a one." He shifted on the bed, resting his head on the curve of his saddle. "My wife, my one daughter—they passed some time ago. We were livin' at Fort Henry when it was called Fort Fincastle. Met Sion there a few years back when he was actin' as scout."

Scout? She'd figured him for a borderman. He'd honed his skills along the upper Ohio River, then. Fort Henry was nearly as treacherous as Kentucke, continually harassed by Indian unrest.

Her heart wrenched. "I'm sorry about your kin." How many times had she mouthed such? How long must she keep saying it?

He stayed stoic. "Everybody's got a sad tale to tell." His eyes fluttered closed, perhaps to spare her his scrutiny. "I hear you come into Kentucke with Boone—or tried to—back in '73."

Had Ma told him this? Tempe focused on Sion's broad back as if it were ballast that could keep her from sinking.

How different he was from James. Her ongoing angst, held at bay by the events of the day, came rushing back. She felt weighted with misery.

"Mistress Moonbow." Cornelius stood before her, returning her to the present. "Our fearless leader, the mighty Morgan, is in need of your expertise." He cast Nate a baleful glance. "If Methuselah here can do without you."

"Go ahead, steal her away," Nate answered. "Just you be respectful whilst you're doin' it."

Cornelius offered her his arm. When she refused him he made a contrary face. "I insist. How else are we to tame the wilderness without a show of civility?"

Nate snorted and rolled over, his loaded rifle his bedfellow. Tempe lay her hand on Cornelius's arm reluctantly, the slender limb beneath the fine linen almost skeletal compared to Sion's burly forearm.

Lucian stood guard at the outer edge of the camp. Was he a hand with a gun? She and her escort navigated the brushy ground to the circle where Sion held sway, a pointed stick in hand. In the dirt he'd drawn a map. To the east he'd denoted the wall of mountains and the Gap. Tempe noted the inn marked on the hillside fronting the falls. Now he worked his way west, the stick never settling, surprising her with what he knew.

He handed her the stick, wordlessly communicating his wish. The other men looked on as if this was some sort of test.

Impressed, she studied the curves and bends he'd made of the Shawnee. "We'll need to ford the river here"—she marked an X and moved on—"then head northwest toward the Green River, cutting a wide swath around Logan's Fort where the trouble lies." Even as she said it she felt a pull toward those pickets, be it Harrod's or Boonesborough. Never had she seen the three Kentucke forts, though she'd heard aplenty, forever wondering if the pictures painted in her mind of the Great Meadow were merely that—fanciful pictures.

"Overland some thirty miles north lies the easternmost end of the Green." She left off, recalling the canoe she and Pa had filled full of stones and sunk for future use along its banks. "We'll have no need of boats. We'll simply chain our way west till . . ." She shot Sion a questioning look. "Till you tire of surveying or run up against the Sault River."

"The Ohio—Belle-Rivière?" Cornelius looked up from the crude map. "Shall we go all the way to the falls?"

She gave a nod and handed Sion the stick, torn between sitting among them or retreating. Weary, mindful of her glaring lip, she chose retreat.

Tossing the stick aside, Sion stood, gaze sweeping the woods, which were finally cooling. In a few terse words he relieved Lucian of his watch, and one of the axemen was posted.

Tempe felt a girlish shyness as Sion turned to her. He had a fierce energy about him even as night crawled in. Was he all business, this borderman? Had he no more room for kindly conversation? Once again she sensed she'd missed her chance there on the riverbank when he'd first asked her, with a stark unguardedness, to show him the moonbow. Now his tanned face, slightly stern, invited no talk.

She focused on the sky beyond his shadow, an intense golden-orange, the color of the squash and pumpkins in their garden. They were in a heavy growth of hardwood trees and bushy windfalls, the first step from home.

He shouldered his rifle. "We sleep in a circle. One of us stands watch."

"My turn is coming, you mean."

"Aye. For now we'll bed down around Nate."

Spencer, the youngest chain carrier, was already on the ground atop saddle blankets, feet to an imaginary fire. Sion began to unroll his bedding while she awkwardly filled the space between him and Nate, well away from Cornelius. Across the way he was still regarding her like buttered bread. She shivered. Though she was being paid wages, no amount of coin could make up for his unwanted attention.

Mistress Moonbow, indeed.

Nate was soon snoring, reminding her uncomfortably of Pa. Was he bedding down in the rockhouse, ruing he'd struck her and sent her off with these men? No matter. The memory of his fury was growing smaller, much like her hurt lip. It was Russell she was most fretful about and the cache of British-made muskets, the bloodshed to come.

She made herself small, curling up in a ball. Why did everything remind her of that first try at Kentucke? Of James? She'd lain on hard ground like this that last night in Powell Valley, waiting for him, dreaming of her wedding day.

If she could have but one wish, it would be to reverse time. Return to the girl she'd been. Have the man nearest her be not Sion but him.

Her James.

※

Was it any wonder she dreamed of being on the trail again, this time in '73?

That last, expectant morning had dawned dry, warmed by a southwest wind that sent gold-tipped leaves shaking down like rain. The horses had been hobbled in a meadowy place downstream from camp, the clover thick. It was there Tempe and James's littlest sister, Livvy, walked to bid the small party bound for Castle's Woods farewell. Though she'd dreamed of a few private moments alone with James, it wasn't to be. Time enough for that when he returned, she reckoned.

For now she took in his sun-streaked hair, worn loose, and his sure, steady movements as he strapped on his powder horn and bullet pouch. Beside him was her brother. Russell was counted a good woodsman, considered one of the best shots in the backcountry. James himself was no stranger to the wilds. His father had bred that into him, taking him out as a boy on long hunts in the fall and winter, wrapping him in his own hunting shirt when the weather turned bitter.

Their hatchets hung at their waists, their skinning knives whetted and sheathed. They looked fit for anything. Fleet of foot. Fearless.

Tempe tried not to think of snakes. Sinkholes. Brush to fight. Galled feet. Worse.

James looked up and smiled, scattering her fears, nearly making her forget the provisions she'd brought him. Tempe passed him a packet of rockahominy sweetened with maple syrup. Their fingers touched. Tingled. At that moment Livvy let loose of Tempe's hand, flinging herself against James, her small head a dark stain upon his linsey shirt.

How she wanted to do the same. Tempe's throat clenched as he stroked his sister's tumbled hair, unkempt from sleep. They drew apart reluctantly, Livvy's chin a-wobble.

Russell came to the rescue. "What? No 'fare thee well' for me?" He grabbed hold of the little girl and began spinning her around till he'd gained a reluctant giggle, giving James and Tempe a quiet moment.

Shyness engulfed her. Tempe was struck right then by how chancy life was. Like a spider's web or an eggshell or a butterfly's wings. Their world seemed made of little losses. She was always having to say goodbye, part with something. A brilliant sunset. A blossom. A sweet feeling.

James's eyes sought hers, saying more than words ever could. Precious seconds ticked by, and then practicality rushed in. Pulling a string of whang leather from her pocket, she came behind him, gathered up strands of his sandy hair, and tied it back. It was a wife's privilege, and she gave herself up to the delight of it.

"Stay safe," she whispered over his hard shoulder. "Keep your powder dry."

He bent, picked a flaming maple leaf off the ground, and tucked it behind her ear. "Aye, Lady of the Woods."

Her heart felt swollen, too big for her chest. Did he know she was undone in little moments like these? When he turned fanciful? Poetic? Betimes he nearly made her forget just who she was. Poor. Plain. Besotted.

"Tempe . . ." He leaned in, brushing her flushed cheek with his lips, tarrying so near only she could hear. "I wish you could go with me."

Her very bones seemed to melt. She balled her hands into fists beneath her apron lest she reach for him. Try to hold on.

The Mendenhalls appeared just then. The rising sun burst through the trees, sending spokes of light across the waiting horses' flanks. James's father came next, wanting to say a few parting words. Soon the small party faded into the forest.

Heartsore, Tempe stood looking after them till little Livvy tugged on her hand.

16

The further we went the richer the land became . . .
amazing blue grass, white clover, buffalo grass, and reed
pines waist high . . . in cultivated meadows, and such
was its appearance without end in little dells.

—James Nourse

Sion couldn't rid himself of the notion that Tempe might
do their party more harm than good. Every one of them
to a man seemed distracted by her presence, himself
included. With her beside him the previous night, he'd slept
little, acutely aware of every turn and sleepy sigh she made,
reminding him of Harper again and again.

She'd awakened slightly red-eyed, as if she'd been crying
or had gotten little sleep. He had a notion to ask her if she
was having second thoughts, then tossed aside any softness.

At the moment she was modestly rubbing pennyroyal on
her bare arms and neck to keep away seed ticks. Leering like
loons, Cornelius and crew were doing the same a few feet
away, giving her little privacy.

They were in for a long march, and thunder grumbled

in the distance like a disgruntled tyrant. Dawn broke. The woods were dark since the skies were a pitted pewter, ripe with rain. Glad for a reprieve from the heat, Sion led off, Tempe behind him.

They came to the fording place she'd chosen, and she went ahead of him, her skittish mare soon swayed by Tempe's calm. She held her gun high in her right hand, the reins in her left. Mid-river she was up to her waist, never showing a hint of disquiet. His own chest seemed to thunder with the tension of the moment. He followed close behind, jaw set at the Shawnee's tricky currents. Was the Green River as cold?

The ensuing rain was far warmer, running over him in refreshing trails, easing the taint of sweat and unwashed garments. His horse found its footing on the rocky sand the very second Cornelius gave a howl. Precious supplies—maps and paints and more—were embedded in that cry, all in danger of being swept away.

Be calm.

Sion didn't dare shout the words, lest they unravel Cornelius completely. The man was terrified of water, and this was water at its worst, a seething, foaming mass of green between impossibly wide banks. But Tempe had chosen well. No other fording place was half so agreeable, yet Cornelius still wrestled, panic in his strained face. His bay, every bit as high-tempered as its rider, sensed that fear and began to give way to the current.

"Hold your ground!" Sion yelled as Tempe watched alongside him, riveted to the struggle and clearly anxious to intervene.

She turned on him, blame in her gaze. "You best help him."

"If I do I'll be coming to his rescue the rest of the trip."

She kneed her horse forward, but his hand shot out and stayed her. "Nay."

It was Lucian who came to his master's aid, swimming out to grab the bridle and lead horse and rider in. Once his feet gained solid ground, Cornelius began rummaging through dripping saddlebags, his expression answering to the sorry state within. He'd not heeded Sion's advice to wrap his supplies in protective gear, yet he was all too willing to place the blame.

He flung out an epithet, hands full of sodden papers. "I suppose we're to cross another river after this?"

Rain was pelting down, and the sparse woods they were heading into offered no reprieve from the damp.

"There are Indian mounds ahead," Tempe told them. "Some rock shelters. I say we find one and dry out, maybe build a small fire to help save those papers. The smoke won't be seen in a rockhouse—"

"Just smelled," Sion cut in, relaying his caution. "We've come but eight miles. We need another five or more before making camp."

"In this damp?"

Their eyes met, his disdainful. "Are you a fair-weather guide, then?"

"Nay, I am not. Just wise to the signs." She glanced at the swollen sky. "Another few miles and we'll walk into lightning on a stretch with little cover. It's the start of the Barrens. It isn't named such for naught."

Her words were lost as thunder burst around them and lightning lit the woods. A packhorse began a mulish dance as Sion turned toward the men. "Be alert for a rockhouse to overnight in. The Barrens are just beyond."

Cornelius scoffed. "Acquiescing, Morgan? To a woman?"

The sarcastic jibe rose above the punishing rain. "That's not like you. If only you'd been so attentive to my—"

Sion swung round. "Don't dredge up the past."

"The past?" A thoroughly soaked Cornelius faced him, fists full of damp maps bleeding color. "Is that all it is to you—*the past*? All but forgotten? By heaven, but you're a hard man, Morgan."

"Better than soft." The slur, quietly stated, carried the force of a fist.

Flinging his ruined maps aside, Cornelius charged Sion, ramming him squarely in the stomach and catching him off guard. Like a pair of wind-toppled trees they tumbled, Sion easily gaining the upper hand but for Cornelius's fury.

Nearly snarling, likely knowing he could never best him, Cornelius bit Sion on the forearm. His teeth sank through the thin linen of Sion's shirt, deep enough to tear fabric and draw blood. Grinding his jaw to keep from hollering, Sion threw him off, springing to his feet before Cornelius lunged at him again.

Tempe and the chain carriers ringed them, leaving only Lucian paying any attention to the dripping woods and danger.

Sion wanted to ignore his arm but sensed it might cause him grief. He'd known a man in a fight whose bite proved fatal. Dead within days he was, the puncture wound worse than that of any animal.

"I'd rather be bit by a rattler," Nate said, backing off from the both of them. "'Be not hasty in thy spirit to be angry: for anger resteth in the bosom of fools.'"

Tempe was staring at them both like she'd witnessed a cock fight. Hascal and Spencer knew better than to say a word. They understood how things stood between Sion and Cornelius even if they didn't know the root of all the trouble.

"See to the horses," Sion told them in an attempt to restore order. He gestured to a wall of limestone fronting the north bank of the river, in which he hoped was a rockhouse. "Find some shelter. I'll see about supper." With that he stuck out a hand to help Cornelius up, but Cornelius was having none of it.

Spitting into the dirt just shy of Sion's outstretched hand, Cornelius glowered at him before getting to his feet and retrieving his ruined maps, leaving him alone with the too-silent Tempe.

Face full of questions, she implored him with a look, but he simply shouldered his gun and took to the woods.

Sion risked two shots, the gunfire rising above the storm. Turkeys, Tempe wagered. The birds liked to flee into the open when it rained and were easy prey. Lucian had made a small fire, and Cornelius's maps were gathered round, a marvel of artistry even half ruined. She'd not thought there was much to the man till now, but some artistic thread ran deep, giving rise to such giftedness. Drawn with pen and ink and painted with watercolors, the maps bespoke hours of painstaking labor.

She no longer blamed him for panicking fording a cantankerous river or being put out about his maps, but she didn't care for the petulance marring his face when Sion was near or that he'd bitten their leader, a rash and unmanly act if there ever was one.

Stepping widely around him, she helped Lucian tend the fire and gathered wood before it became too sodden to burn, ever alert for Sion's return as the others huddled in the rockhouse. She needed to see to his arm without any onlookers and ask her burning question.

The rain had quieted when he returned at dusk, soaked to the skin, his buckskins as black as his shaggy mane of hair, two plump turkeys dangling at his side. He came from the west, framed by a crack of yellow light riding the horizon— and looking no more inclined to talk than he had after the tussle.

Wordlessly she approached and took a bird from him. Finding a spot on which to work, she laid the turkey on its back and began plucking some of the breast feathers before taking the meat. Sion did the same beside her, their quiet movements muted by the dripping all around them. Her newly sharpened knife made the task quick.

Eyes on the bird in hand, she finally broached her clamoring question. "Before we go another step, I would know about this bad blood between you and—" She worried her tender lip with her teeth, nearly saying "the banty rooster."

"Cornelius?" Beside her, Sion cleaned his knife in the rain-slicked grass. "He's my"—he swallowed as if the word was distasteful—"brother-in-law."

Her heart stilled. Near kin? *This* was the last thing she expected to hear. She found her voice. "He wed your sister?"

"Nay . . . I wed his." Picking up both birds, he made for the rockhouse, leaving her standing slack-jawed beneath a sprawling chestnut tree. She began cleaning her own knife, barely aware of what she did.

Sion . . . married.

The vicious bite on his arm was no match for the vicious bite of his words.

⁂

A pile of stripped turkey bones left Tempe longing for bread. Or maybe it was simply a longing for home, for a time before she knew too much. Suddenly the tenor of the journey had changed and she felt uprooted again. She'd asked her bold question expecting an altogether different answer, and now she looked at the dark stranger across the smoky haze of the campfire, adjusting her sights.

Sion Morgan. Scout. Surveyor. Borderman. Virginian. Tightly wed.

It cut her to the quick, it did. But why? Many frontiersmen had wives back of the settlements. But his shocking revelation spurred more questions.

What kind of woman was Mistress Morgan?

A quick glance at Cornelius playing cards left Tempe hoping Sion's wife was nothing like her brother. This tenuous tie was why the two men had been tossed together like flint and steel. There could be no other answer.

As night deepened, her gaze wandered to Sion's sleeve. Cornelius had bitten the fleshy forearm, which was now swelling. Tempe went to Aylee's stores and took out the healing herbs while the chain carriers and Cornelius began another round of cards and Lucian stood watch. Nate was bedded down already, snoring softly.

Matter-of-factly, Tempe met Sion's gaze through the dwindling smoke. "You're fixing to ask me another question," he said coolly. "I can feel it."

She took a breath. Was she so easily read? "Your wound may fester. Best let me look."

He shrugged, another off-putting gesture she was coming to know. "If it doesn't worry me, why should it you?"

"I can doctor a bite, but I can't mend a lost limb."

He chuckled. "You think Cornelius packs that much venom?"

"For a brother-in-law, he's frightful kin."

He said nothing to this, rising from his seat to circle the

fire and sit down beside her. Pulling his linen sleeve to his elbow, he offered her his muscled forearm. But for the moment it was a scar that took her notice. Running from wrist to elbow in a seamless line, it posed yet another question.

Setting curiosity aside, she began applying the healing salve made from the ground roots of butterfly weed. He was patient as she worked, his other hand encircling his rifle, attention fixed on their surroundings beyond the golden rim of firelight.

Other than the inn, she felt safest in a rockhouse and was glad for the rain. Raiding parties didn't like the damp any better than they. Sitting back on her heels, she considered what else she might try if festering set in. Witch hazel? She wanted moonflower, if she could leave the rockhouse and take a nightly tramp when it bloomed.

"You're an able hand with your doctoring," he said quietly when she began binding the arm with a strip of linen. "Anything you can't do?"

"Aye, a great many things. I can't make peace between men nor bring them back from the dead." James hovered in her thoughts, but here in the rockhouse he seemed to have stepped aside. Sion lapsed into a pensive silence, leaving Tempe's mind to roam. Her thoughts kept returning to a festering question . . .

How had Sion laid hold of a woman's heart?

Little wonder. It was likely the way he carried himself, not cocky but sure, and the sight of all that blue-black hair rivaling Raven's own. Or the fullness of his shoulders as they turned a worn linen shirt in need of washing into something that sank into the heart and stayed there.

She stole another look at Cornelius as he played cards. Fair of hair, this sister of his? As sweet and amiable as he was surly? Oh, he had moments of charm, but they were when he turned butter tongued and wanted something. She had a hankering Sion's wife was all her brother was not. She longed to know her name.

As she pondered it he stood and unrolled his sleeve so that it covered her patching. There was just enough light to read by, and she dug for her Psalms, surprised when he produced a book himself. So he could read. Many men couldn't. Once again she longed to know the whys and wherefores of his past. Boone oft read the Bible and was known for his fondness for *Gulliver's Travels*. She'd seen him peruse both at their very inn.

Sitting across from her again, Sion set the slim volume aside and stirred the fire with a stick, then added another chunk of smokeless dogwood.

As the dry wood caught she ventured another question. "What have you there?"

"Herrick."

She couldn't hide a rueful smile. "Once I had some poems by him . . . till a bit of lead tore the heart right out of them."

He was quick to catch on. "I owe you." Extending a hand around the flames, he offered her his battered volume.

She waved a hand. "Say some verse aloud."

"Which do you favor?"

She was partial to them all, full of love and loss. Glancing at the card players who were too taken with their game to pay them any attention, she summoned some beginning lines that had been a favorite of James's. "'I dare not ask to kiss, I dare not beg a smile . . .'"

Surprise lit his eyes—and an undeniable amusement. "'Lest having that, or this, I might grow proud the while.'" His gaze fell to the flames. "'No, no, the utmost share of my desire shall be only to kiss the air that lately kissed thee.'"

Wonder bloomed as he finished with nary a misplaced word. She said, "I never figured you for a man who spouts poetry."

"Who did you figure me for?" He looked at her with such purposefulness every reply flew out of her head. When she failed to answer, he said, "What have you in hand?"

She opened her forgotten Psalms. "Scripture."

"Say any by heart?"

"Some. But I'd rather live it by heart." Isn't that what Nate had told Aylee whilst he was at the inn? Overhearing them, Tempe had tucked the wise words away, touched that an old snakebitten borderman would speak of such.

"There's plenty who only pay it lip service." Sion's gaze strayed to the rockhouse's entrance again, but he seemed to be waiting for her to say something. Do something.

She took a breath. One particular Psalm had wended its way around her heart. She was drawn to the mournful, Ma said. Ever since Powell Valley. Its darkness had gone deep. "'Man is like to vanity; his days are as a shadow that passeth away.'"

"You and Nate kin?" He looked askance at her. "Churched and all that?"

"Churched?" She took his teasing with a smile. "Are you?"

"Nay."

She wanted more than *nay*. Why was she so hungry for talk? Sion wasn't a man given to it, eluding her with his long silences and one-word answers. She'd best content herself with that.

Lucian loomed over them, sleepy-eyed. It was her turn to stand watch and relieve him. But before she did she passed Sion her Psalms.

17

One man's life is worth a hundred horses.
—Daniel Trabue

The next morning Sion halted on a buffalo trail, holding up a hand as the party reined in their horses in back of him. Up ahead, just out of rifle range, was Raven. A little trill of delight coursed through Tempe. Raven looked down at them from his position on a low ridge. She sensed he'd been watching their progress and that Sion had been aware of him for some time but had said nothing. The closer they drew, the more each man sized the other up.

Sion tossed a few terse words over his shoulder. "Is that your Indian, Miss Tucker?"

"He's not mine, Mister Morgan," she replied carefully. "But his name is Raven."

Kicking her mare's flanks, she maneuvered around Sion, pondering this sudden turn of events. Russell had obviously given Raven word he was needed. The timing was nigh perfect. They were on the edge of the Barrens, that treeless stretch between the Sault and Green Rivers that in no way resembled the Kentucke she loved.

She pushed off the buffalo trace to meet him as he came down from his perch, sweat trickling beneath her arms and between her thighs. Summer had returned with a vengeance after the rain, so sultry it stole her breath.

Raven was mounted on a feisty pony. Chickamauga stock, she guessed. All the tribes were wild about horses and plundered with that in mind more than scalps. It had been the same in Powell Valley, all the horses stolen. Sion's fine stallion would make a coveted prize.

She reached Raven, the dust already stirring despite the damp. "Hello, *oginalii*."

He shunned her friendly greeting. "So you follow the Long Knife?"

She nodded, aware of his gaze on her slow-to-heal lip. "My father—he wants them out of the country."

Raven looked toward the waiting party. "Not only your father."

So they were of one purpose, then.

Raven turned half-amused eyes on her as she shifted uneasily in the saddle. "Should we run them into the ground?"

"You'll not succeed with this Long Knife. We'll likely eat his dust."

"And the others?"

She hesitated. "One of them—the yellow hair—can't be trusted. Another is old but tough as whang leather. The black man is a keen shot—and unafraid. The others are mere boys. Bear cubs."

"I'll take them as far as the Falls of Ohio."

She nearly sighed with relief. It was more than she bargained for. "You'll be paid for your trouble."

"White man's money?" He shrugged, reminding her of Sion. "You should know the Shawnee have taken up the hatchet. Our white father—"

"The English king?"

He gave a nod. "He pays for settlers' scalps. I can earn more from my British brothers than this man Morgan."

Other than from the handbill in the barn-shed, it was the first time she'd heard the truth so bluntly. Mad George, known for his raving fits across the sea, had turned on his colonial subjects in a most uncivilized fashion. The cache of British-made muskets in Russell's keeping was proof. And Raven, she sensed, was alarmingly close to siding with the British. Had she done wrong by asking him here?

She took a breath. "These men—these surveyors—are loyal to the king—"

Raven's eyes narrowed. "They are not land stealers?"

"They survey under Virginia's authority as a crown colony."

His tight smile became a smirk. "They are still land stealers."

This she couldn't deny. What *was* Virginia doing sending surveyors into territory forbidden by the king's proclamation? And what of Virginia's bold claim on Kentucke as its westernmost county?

Raven studied her, the sleek feathers in his hair stirring in a sudden wind. "The king makes war on the colonies. The Shawnee and Cherokee and their allies make war on Kentucke's settlers and surveyors. All is madness, as Scotchie says."

Madness. The Scottish Indian agent had pegged it properly. "So long as we stay clear of the settlements, the Great Meadow, we should be safe."

"No, *oginalii*. Nothing is safe." He looked past her toward Sion again, his grim expression a burr. "Go talk to the Long Knife. Tell him to turn back."

Stubborn, she resisted. "There is no talk. No turning back. Morgan is as impatient as a goat tied to a stake."

Raven gave a rare chuckle. "His would make a prized scalp . . . two hundred pounds sterling."

Tempe shuddered openly. Though death itself held no terror, she did not warm to the ways it was done.

Wheeling her horse around, she pondered what to say, how to say it. By the time she'd returned to the party, all the men had dismounted save Sion, who sat on his horse with a simple heightened guardedness. The others were studying Raven as if a war party lay in wait, unsure of his intentions.

There was a grudging respect in Sion's expression that had been missing before. Though he wasn't privy to her and Raven's talk, he no doubt sensed the emotion of the moment.

"All right, Miss Tucker. Just say it."

In one breath she let loose her angst. "You're liable to lose your scalp for all your surveying."

There was a prolonged pause. Sion's eyes—such an uncanny, calm silver—showed no more emotion than a pond's reflective face. As if they were on some mission to pick posies from here to the Falls of Ohio, not dodge hostile war parties with every step.

"So be it," he said.

"*So be it?*" Tempe nearly started as Cornelius voiced an ugly echo.

She herself was full of unspoken concerns. *What of your wife, Sion? Least ones?* The latter struck her cold. Did he have sons and daughters? She knew what happened to widows, their children apprenticed or bound out or worse . . .

"I'll not stray another step if a savage himself"—Cornelius gestured to Raven—"advises otherwise."

Sion's voice was ice cold. "If you turn back now you'll have farther to go than where we're headed. The falls will take you upriver to Fort Henry."

"*Safely* upriver?"

"Upriver," Sion stated flatly.

Cornelius tugged at his linen collar, more agitated. "And the Indian?" He was eyeing Raven again with heightened suspicion. "Is he friend or foe?"

"That depends on your stance," Sion returned. His gaze swung from Cornelius to Tempe. "Bring him in."

Tempe returned to Raven halfheartedly, feeling foolish, knowing he wanted little to do with them. But he was regarding her kindly, reminding her of their tie, and no doubt wishing it was just the two of them heading west without a noisy, heavily laden string of packhorses and equipment sure to draw notice.

Only Raven, being of two worlds, could lead them. He was a rogue, a half-blood, whose allegiance was somewhat misty. Being kin to Alexander Cameron—Scotchie—he enjoyed certain privileges full-bloods did not.

Facing him, Tempe could not push any words past her throat, overcome with a dire foreboding that held the taint of Powell Valley.

"Come, *oginalii,* and show me this *onaka,* this Long Knife." With that, Raven maneuvered around her, heading toward the waiting white men.

※

With Raven among them, Sion pushed hard toward the Green River, going in a northwesterly line till darkness denied them another punishing step. Just shy of a dense canebrake they made camp, and Tempe noted a few familiar landmarks. Spared any signs of settlement and the hatchet marks of surveyors, the Green River country was untrammeled.

The next day was the Sabbath.

"The white man's rest?" Raven queried her when dawn broke and no one stirred.

"Aye, the Sabbath." She smiled and reached for her pocketed Psalms, only to remember she'd lent them to Sion. His bedding empty, he stood watch. She could see his shadowy outline, a tan smudge against a world of green.

Lucian stirred, rolling up his bedding before serving breakfast. "Mornin', Miss Tempe. Mornin', friend," he said genially to Raven as if an Indian encamped with them was a usual occurrence.

Raven looked up from the arrow he was fletching to hear Lucian mumble about misplacing his fire-making tools. Reaching for her gun, Tempe mimicked something she'd seen Sion do in place of flint and steel, using a bit of char for powder and pulling the trigger so that the flint sparked and made a flame. Clever, that Sion.

"You is a quick study, Miss Tempe." Smiling, Lucian took over, using some of the coffee Aylee had packed to brew a full pot. Raven sniffed, his stoicism softening as Lucian served him first.

Opening another pouch, Lucian produced a handful of sugar. "Sweetenin'?" With a half smile, Raven indicated he drop the entire amount into the cup. Lucian did as he bade, stirring it with a twig. Shunning coffee, Tempe longed for a cold glass of buttermilk, as it was so hot.

The woods were already a-shimmer, the dew drying fast. A westerly wind scattered the coffee's fragrance, teasing the remaining men awake. Hascal soon relieved Sion of watch, and Lucian was quick to hand him a steaming tin cup. Sleeves rolled up, he extended an arm, and Tempe had a clear look at the bite wound. Frustration flared anew at Cornelius's orneriness. Witch hazel was called for. But not now, and not till Sion had his breakfast.

In the brief time they'd been together, she'd begun to take notice of his personal habits. Camp conditions allowed her a closer if not entirely comfortable look. Uncommonly tidy, Sion picked up after himself in such a fashion that one hardly knew he'd been there. Bordermen were ever cautious, never leaving a trace but always looking for one.

She bit back a smile to find his dark hair once again in need of combing. Often when he first roused it was a bit wild, sticking up in odd black patches that turned him boyish. This morning, like most mornings, he was quiet. She liked that he took care with his words and yet could recite poetry all the same.

But there was a heap of things she didn't like.

She went to her own saddlebags and retrieved a sack of beaten biscuits. A smile surfaced as she pictured Ma armed with a broken musket, pummeling the dough into submission.

Holding open the sack, she urged Sion to partake. Was his wife a fine cook? The thought was snatched away by the pure pleasure on his bewhiskered face. Never had she seen him so delighted. As if a beaten biscuit was a wondrous thing.

Soon they all were chewing and sipping, a rare contentment between them. Tempe took Hascal's share to him as he stood watch. By the time she'd returned the men were readying to throw hatchets at a mark—hardly a Sabbath-worthy pursuit, but about to commence nonetheless.

"Is it true," Cornelius began, addressing Raven from a safe distance, "that a warrior can launch six or seven arrows for every one to two rifle shots?"

Raven shrugged, eyes narrowing.

"I've heard tell one white man is worth one hundred horses," Hascal said.

Uneasy, Tempe turned her thoughts toward summer Sabbaths when they'd gather with any passersby on the dogtrot and have a little praise. Betimes a traveling preacher would say some words, something to chew on in the week ahead. Here Nate would have to suffice.

He looked askance at the gathering men. "I never could abide any hatchet throwing on the Lord's Day. As the Good Book says, 'Honor the Sabbath and keep it holy.'" He winked at Tempe as she poured him more coffee. "You don't aim to join in, do ye?"

"Nay. Let the men prove themselves. I was never a hand at such."

"You're a worthy shot."

She warmed to the praise. "I hope to be better with bow and arrow."

Nate's brows shot upward into silver peaks. "On account of that Raven fellow?"

She nodded. "He's promised to show me how. A bow is far lighter and quieter than a gun, and nary so dependent on hard-won powder and lead."

"I'll bet he's a fine hand with a hatchet besides." He gave an exaggerated shudder. "The thought of a tomahawk in the hand of a less-than-friendly Indian sure sets my scalp atingle."

"Raven's not one to trade in scalps," she assured him with a confidence she was far from feeling. "He's kin to Scotchie, remember." Yet even as she said it she nearly choked on the words. The Indian agent was as much a scalp taker as the warriors he roused, was he not? Sending dire, bloody messages as a king's man? Raven's smidgen of white blood was no guarantee of peace.

Nate was studying her as if sensing her troubled spirit, so she busied herself redding up the camp, the dull thud of the hatchet an onerous backdrop. She didn't have to turn around to witness who was besting who. It would be a draw between Sion and Raven no matter how long they sported.

"Why don't we have us a little praise," Nate was saying. "I lost my Bible when we took a tumble and first come over the Gap. But you have some Psalms, you said."

"Did have." Tempe shook out a saddle blanket. "Till I lent them to Mister Morgan."

Nate's brows peaked again. "And he ain't give 'em back?" At her "nay," a slow grin lit his face. "Well, I'll be. Mebbe you're on this here mission for more than your woods skills. If we was to find ourselves sorely tested, to the point of . . . um . . . expiration, I'd rest a heap easier knowing we're headed in the same direction, Sion and I."

"You believe in heaven, Mister Stoner?"

"More than I believe in here, aye."

She smoothed a corner of the folded blanket. "Out here in the quiet heaven seems near, nearer than the inn where it's all bustle and noise."

"You can hear the Almighty speak in the silences, you mean. See His hand most clear. I believe so too, but you got to want to see Him. Hear Him." He looked toward the hatchet throwers. "Not turn a blind eye and ride right over what He's put in your path, nor try to outrun Him. Mebbe it's up to you and me to slow some folks down so they get quiet enough to hear Him."

"That's a hard-sounding task." She took a seat, her back to the men. "Something's driving your Mister Morgan, you mean."

"Nothing that the Almighty can't cure."

She waited, ready to take in whatever crumbs might be shared regarding Sion, but impatience flared at Nate's sudden silence. Her longing to know more loosed her tongue. "Mister Morgan tells me Mister Lyon is kin by marriage."

Nate nodded, sipping his coffee. "On account of Harper, you mean."

Harper? Her heart flipped. A pretty name if there ever was one. She swallowed down the hunger to know more. Nate was regarding her as if her belly growled and exposed her.

"Aye, Harper Lyon Morgan." Raising a hand, he dried the sweat beading his upper lip. "But that's Sion's story to tell."

And Harper? What would she say herself? Back at Fort Henry, or wherever she was, Harper waited for a man in buckskins, an obstinate surveyor, to finish his rambles and return to her.

If she was Harper . . . Tempe's hands curled round the log on which she sat, nails biting deep into the hickory's shaggy bark. She forced the thought to a finish.

If she was Harper she'd never let such a one go, just as she shouldn't have let James go at the last. A thousand times in her mind's eye she'd taken back the day, rearranged it to suit her fancy and spare herself the heartache.

She dared another question. "Any least'uns?"

For a moment Nate's faded eyes turned a watery gray. "There was a one, aye."

Tempe lowered her gaze. A man-child? Or a girl? Gone like a breath, then. Never to be seen or touched again shy of eternity. She studied her moccasins, one in need of mending.

Nate's words when they came were soft. "You're speaking out of your own need, your own loss."

Was she? She seldom mentioned James. Maybe she could confide in Nate, a man whose hurts didn't seem to hinder him but turned him rich and reflective instead.

"You and Sion ain't so unlikely a pair. You could learn something from the other. Turn all this wilderness wanderin' into a promised land."

She smiled through her sadness. She liked this old man. Not so old, truly. Just in sore need of a razor and a comb to tame the pewter strands in his hair.

Leaning forward, he rested his elbows on his knees and folded his hands. "Let's have us a word to honor the day."

She bowed her head. The hatchet throwing ceased. Birdsong and a trifling breeze were all that were heard and felt. Had the men paused out of respect? She daren't look up and find out. It was a hallowed, holy moment, made more so by the earnestness in Nate's gravelly voice.

"Wherein we have done amiss, we humbly crave Thy forgiveness, O Father in heaven. Draw near to us now and overshadow us with Thy great goodness, for Jesus's sake. Amen."

She tried to be still, to sink herself into the words, the wonder. For a few moments the heaviness of Powell Valley lessened. The journey ahead of them loomed large, but there was a sweetness woven within, a thread of promise and discovery.

Lord, let it be.

18

The heart of another is a dark forest, always, no matter how close it has been to one's own.

—WILLA CATHER

The woods were putting on a show, distractions at every turn. A fetching blossom. A dislodged bird's nest. A berry bush. Sion tamped down his impatience, equally snagged by Tempe's movements. She'd even found a parakeet's feather and worked the plume into the band of her hat, a burst of lime green amid the black felt— another distraction. He opened his mouth to caution her, but sensing what was coming, she plucked it free. She clutched the colorful feather in a grimy fist.

Raven was leading, she and Sion just behind. Rather than bring all their party, the three of them decamped at dawn on foot, bent on backtracking after locating a suitable survey site. Finding it, Sion sank his hatchet deep into the biggest elm, itching to begin but unable to go farther without his chain carriers and equipment.

Horses tiring, they began retreating. They'd entered a

glade knee-high in peavine. It was there that Raven tossed up a cautionary hand, bringing his mount to a standstill. Through the endless chanting of cicadas came the barest indication of movement. Sliding off his horse, Raven crouched behind a bank of brush, and Sion and Tempe quickly followed, leaving their horses, on the razor's edge of fear lest their mounts give out a fatal nicker.

Past a screen of leafy green Sion peered, aware of Tempe on her knees beside him, her chin tucked low, eyes closed as if locked in silent prayer. Beside her, Raven's wary features sent a message that chilled Sion to the marrow. He blinked, sweat staining his temples, the sunlight near blinding where it cut through the trees like a golden scythe. When it faded behind a cloud, his vision sharpened.

Just below, a line of Indians made a near-silent passage along a creek bank, the very watercourse they themselves had followed at dawn, wading to better hide their presence.

The lead brave—nearly naked save for loincloth and leggings, his tuft of charcoal hair befeathered, neck and forearms flashing silver—was painted for war. Black and red ochre smeared the Indians' lean, muscled bodies. Not a one wore the white of peace or mourning.

Sion had slipped his rifle out of its saddle holster on his way to the forest floor. Annie was primed and loaded. Tempe's small, callused hand encircled her gun barrel, the butt of it on the ground. He was glad to the heart she was an able shot. Raven, deadly with a hatchet as he'd proved in yesterday's Sabbath challenge, was equally intimidating with bow and arrow.

The braves were pausing now, their attention fixed on the ground. By heaven, had he and Tempe left any earlier sign? The beating of his heart seemed outside his chest. He'd had

Russell unshod Beck before leaving the inn. Now the horses were blessedly quiet, sated on clover from a brief rest, hides aquiver and tails noiselessly swishing against the ever-present insects.

Yet anything might change in a heartbeat.

He waited for that first chilling whoop, that deep guttural cry sounded by the lead scout that told them the enemy had been sighted . . . or perhaps exposed by Raven himself. Sion stemmed the traitorous thought with effort, but the suspicion remained. How many in this party were known to the half-blood?

His mind turned another fearful corner. He rarely let himself linger on that bloody day three years past. It was always like an echo in his conscience, muted by day but loudest in the long, silent nights. This was how it had been that final, fatal afternoon—the unsuspecting intrusion, the fatal pounce. His own life, his mistakes, seemed to parade themselves through his tautly stretched thoughts.

A slight movement to his left brought him round. Tempe looked up, took in the war party below, her lovely face calm. Nay, *haunted*.

He wanted to reach out and shield her as he'd been unable to do when his whole world was torn asunder. It hadn't righted yet. It might never. All his wilderness wandering had taken him far from the tragedy, but somehow the tragedy had followed. He swallowed back the bile the memory always wrought. He focused. Fixed his hate.

Raven seemed cast in stone, frozen by that uncanny stealth that few white men, ever twitchy, seemed to master. The war party finished their searching and with silent looks communicated it was time to continue on. They swept upward and away from the creek bed onto higher ground.

Straight toward the surveyors' camp.

Like a bird flushed from a bush, Tempe passed Sion her gun and lit out, still half crouched. She was quick, ever so quick. Words of caution gathered and died in Sion's throat. He gauged Raven's reaction, startled to see his half smile.

Sion could vouch for her being fleet of foot. The day she'd led him on a chase through the woods was never far from his thoughts. Bold she'd been, giving him a hint of her courage. If anyone could run undetected through the wilds, it was she.

Raven moved next, a flick of his fingers indicating they were to follow the war party. They hobbled the horses in a patch of clover and matched their pace to the Indians', beginning a precarious pursuit. One wrong move, the slightest sound, would mean the Indians descending on them like a host of yellow jackets. Or . . .

Sion tried to dislodge the other unsavory possibility. They might detect Tempe even before she reached the camp. Depending on their mood, they'd either kill her outright or take her captive. Death was often the better choice.

Either prospect taunted him. He felt a-simmer, his energy renewed as he kept to Raven's heels. As the sun tilted west and baked the woods brown as bread, Sion fought for breath. Parched, cramped, he kept on. Somehow, despite carrying Tempe's rifle and his, he managed to extract a ginseng root from his budget, bit it in two, and passed half to Raven.

The half-blood's eyes communicated gratitude, though ginseng was hardly needed. Raven was a marvel of endurance. There was precious little time to pause. To think. Keeping moving consumed Sion, his gaze never leaving the line of Indians, the rear scout sometimes swinging round like a weather vane as if he detected them.

God, help. Help Tempe.

But for her name, it was nearly the same prayer he'd prayed for Harper.

To no avail.

※

Tempe's every step was a silent prayer, words enough to fill the wilderness. In half a mile she'd gained on the war party and in another half had outdistanced them altogether. Off the trail on the ridge above them were frightful risks. The woods were dry again. Bone dry. If a twig snapped beneath her feet or a leaf rustled, might the Indians think her a deer?

When the rockhouse came into view she could hear Cornelius.

Singing.

Had he nary a care for where he was? A bawdy song spilled from his lips. For the moment "Let's Be Jovial, Fill Our Glasses" resounded through the woods, when it was a hymn she craved. Something befitting the moment, like "Lord, Be Thou Merciful."

Lucian was the first to see her though she had long since seen and heard them. Their camp proclaimed it washday. Cornelius's red handkerchief hung in brazen defiance of Sion's everlasting caution. It was the first thing Tempe snatched, stuffing it out of sight down her bodice beneath her stays. She scoured the bushes clean of men's smallclothes, nearly mowing Hascal down in her haste. Where was Spencer?

Wordless, she looked at Nate and Cornelius and thrust a hand back, hoping the frantic gesture conveyed what she could not say. *Into the rockhouse. Without so much as a whimper.* Cornelius's mouth opened, but her dagger's glance cut off any questions. Lungs crying for air, she couldn't talk if she wanted to. She herself was a mess, hairline wet beneath her hat brim, eyes burning with salty sweat.

Lucian began rounding up stray items. A wash kettle by the creek. Lye soap. A beater. Nate was stamping out the fire that Sion had forbidden, throwing handfuls of dirt to smother the flames. She couldn't account for the axemen. Were they with the horses? It was Cornelius who first scrambled up the cliff's scrubby side to the rockhouse, Lucian close behind. Tempe was next since Nate stubbornly held his ground, spurred by some gentlemanly courtesy she couldn't fathom.

She recalled the prayer he'd prayed. Was it just yesterday? He'd asked for a hedge about them. Peace. Maybe this was his answer. She herded the men to the back of the rockhouse and crept back to the ledge, belly flat against the rough stone as she lay prostrate and looked out, Nate's loaded rifle alongside her.

In the span of a few more ragged breaths the war party appeared, single file and no less fierce than at first. Her chest heaved, her breath frozen in place. On the belt of the lead scout dangled two scalps.

Nay . . . oh, nay.

Dropping her head, she swiped sweat from stinging eyes before studying that dangling hair. One scalp flaxen. So like James's. Another a pleasing russet no longer. Not Raven's. Not Sion's.

One of the warriors left the column. Riveted, Tempe watched his every move, mesmerized by all his silver. He came nearer their abandoned washing, the doused fire and tumbled kettle in the brush.

Lord, have mercy.

The scent of wood smoke lingered. She wanted to kick Cornelius. No doubt he had deemed it washday. His fussy habits would be the death of him.

Catlike, the warrior crept closer, so close she could see the hammered indentions in his necklace and the bangles about his arms.

Her breath held tight in her lungs. She daren't twitch. Death was but a few steps away. If she was of a mind, she could draw a bead on the Indian's tawny chest. But that would bring the other warriors down on them, and what good was Cornelius cowering in the back of the rockhouse? She'd have a furious fight on her hands with only Lucian and Nate for help.

She nearly groaned when the warrior knelt and examined the hastily extinguished fire. The warrior's wary gaze swept upward, to the mouth of the rockhouse.

Their only hope was heaven itself.

But heaven, she remembered, had stayed silent for James. Would her life end the same way? Was she truly ready to die? Her one solace was that Sion wasn't present. And Raven. Both men were safe, or so she hoped . . .

Straightening to his full height, the Indian paused for a brief moment before backtracking. With his every step away from them, Tempe's own breathing eased. He rejoined his party, befuddling her.

Weak as water, Tempe let the ledge cradle her till they'd passed out of sight, counting to one hundred before drinking from the canteen strung around her neck. Emptying it, eyes never leaving the woods, she gained some relief.

Nate had dropped down beside her, lowering his old bones to ask one worrisome question. "Sion and your Indian fella all right?"

"I don't know any better than you," she whispered back.

Her anguished mind played out one scenario after another. Both men tomahawked, the horses taken. Raven turning on Sion and joining the war party.

Nay. She wouldn't think less of Raven.

Below, rustling in the brush, Hascal returned with Spencer. Whey-faced. Shaken. The both of them darting furtive glances at the rockhouse and then the trail the Indians had taken. She motioned them up, wondering where they'd been but unwilling to risk any talk. Sometimes an Indian doubled back . . .

Scrambling upward, clutching brush and rock to gain a hand- or toehold, they came over the ledge and nearly ran to the back of the rockhouse. She wouldn't risk so much as a chuckle, though relief bubbled up inside her like a new-found spring.

Nate's whisper, riddled with thankfulness, captured her attention. "There they be."

Sion approached in the brush just below while Raven continued on, no doubt to discover just where the war party was headed.

Another fear flared. Unless the Indians changed course and forded the river, the inn lay directly in their path. A thick resignation took hold, overriding any gladness.

Sion entered the rockhouse, stared at the wad of clean clothes she'd tossed along one rock wall, then sank down on the other side of her. Wedged between him and Nate, she suddenly felt as safe as if she stood behind a fort's pickets.

Her mind veered to Raven again, but Sion quickly claimed her next thought. She could feel the heft and strength of him this close, smell the exertion the summer's heat always wrought. His hat was off, his chiseled features plain. Whiskers stubbled his jaw, a shade lighter than his shaggy mane. The woods claimed his attention, his gaze never settling.

For all the notice he paid her, she might have been one of the axemen. She hoped he was more attentive to Harper. The mystery of their marital tie consumed her. She misdoubted Harper Lyon Morgan would be lying here on jagged rock, sweaty and stinking and disheveled. Tem Tucker was no better than the men.

She shrank inside herself, wishing she could be as small as the spider working its way along the rock floor. For some reason she'd packed her marrying dress. Her hope had been that they'd make it to a fort. There she'd shed her woods garb and make herself presentable again. Fort frolics were known far and wide for their revelry, full of feasting and dancing come a marrying or a holiday. Could Sion dance? Could Nate? Cornelius likely outshone them both.

Disgusted, she bent her thoughts to the danger at hand. For what seemed an eternity they stayed flat on their bellies, till Raven returned near dusk. Hardly winded, he scaled the cliff face effortlessly, his terse words unwelcome but hardly surprising. "They go to make war on the settlements. Boone's Fort."

"You're sure?" Tempe queried.

"When they stopped to rest I got ahead of them and circled back, saying I was moving west." His half smile was for her. "No lie."

Nate motioned to his belt. "Just whose scalps are they parading?"

A slight pause. "Two land stealers along the French Broad."

Tempe went cold. Though quietly spoken, the slur seemed more epithet. Nate winced but Sion stayed stoic, slipping his next words in beneath the jarring beat of Tempe's heart.

"It's a small war party headed to Boone's," he said, easing into a sitting position. "Virginia militia might be inside Kentucke, mayhap at the settlements by now, with enough powder and bullet lead to last."

Raven shrugged. "It matters little. More Cherokee are gathering to fight. Shawnee come from the Ohio with their allies—and swivels."

Cannon? A combined force, then, determined to oust the settlers once and for all. Could it be done? Tempe began fanning her face with her hat. The stoutest pickets couldn't withstand cannon fire, nor were the keenest sharpshooters a match for a three-pound cannonball.

Raven was full of grim news. "This war party plans to burn the settlers' crops. Butcher their livestock."

Tempe longed to put a hand to Raven's lips and staunch the words. Cornelius and the chain carriers emerged from the back of the rockhouse to listen. Still whey-faced. Still wary.

"We'll leave out again at dawn." Sion looked around the circle, indicating all of them, taking in every face but Tempe's own. Could he sense her resistance? "We've but a few miles more to survey prime ripe bottomland before crossing the Barrens. Tempe and Raven will scout while we run the line."

Her chin came up. He'd called her by her given name with surprising ease. No more Miss Tucker? She longed to crawl inside his head and account for the switch. Should she call him Sion in return? Pondering this was far more pleasant than leaving the relative safety of the rockhouse. Or fretting over the Indians passing too near the inn.

As the men began talking about the equipment, Tempe got to her feet and gathered up the clean clothes. Raven shadowed her, his back to the others.

"You are worried?"

Straightening, she took another look out the rockhouse at the woods. "I'm thinking of Russell. Ma and Paige."

"You think the war party will make trouble for them." At

her nod, he said, "Your *adadoda* has come back. He casts a long shadow."

Yes, her father had returned. Somehow this failed to bring the comfort of before. She cast a glance at Sion, wondering if the men could hear them. Her tongue worried her lip, still slightly tender. "I saw who was leading the war party." The knowledge sat like a stone inside her, plummeting ever deeper.

"Hiskyteehee?"

She could only nod, swallowed up by the memory of the scalps on Five Killer's belt. Despite the glare of war paint and tattoos, she knew it was he.

"Five Killer is a hard enemy," Raven admitted.

She began folding strange breeches and shirts and stockings she'd torn from the bushes earlier, needing a distraction, unmindful of any immodesty. "He came to us late one night at the inn . . . left a handbill of war." She darted another glance at Sion and lowered her voice. What would he make of their talk? "Russell has a cache of British muskets. I don't know how he came by them."

She felt certain the Chickamaugas would force Russell into mending their muskets, maybe use the inn as a way station for supplies like powder and bullet lead. If so, Ma and Paige would be at their mercy.

Raven studied her. "Are you loyal to the king, *oginalii*?"

Was she? Or did she unwillingly harbor her father's hatred of anything British, given his near hanging at Tory hands? If Pa found out Russell was siding with the Tories and Indians in their fight . . . If Boone and his kinsmen discovered the same . . .

She turned Raven's question around. "Are you?"

"For now I am your friend." His kindly eyes held hers. "I have not forgotten what you did for me."

"Only what a body should do—"

"No. Not everyone." His intensity returned, raising his voice a notch. "Since that day you freed me from the mantrap, you see past the color of my skin. My clan. This war. You are goodness to the bone."

Self-conscious, she dropped her gaze to his beaded neck, the oiled skin almost iridescent, his shoulders tattooed with twin crescent moons in blue. He was of the Anikawi, the blue clan. Five Killer belonged to the Aniwayi, the war or wolf clan. She shoved the reminder to the back of her conscience, taking in Raven's solid, less threatening form. He shunned the split ears of most of his clansmen, wearing strands of trade beads about his neck instead. Chevrons of cobalt blue. Red whitehearts. White rattlesnake beads. She was most appreciative of the garters that held up his leggings. The blue and white design of interlocking crosses appeared to be loomed they were so finely finger woven.

Aylee's loom leapt to mind with a heartfelt pang, followed next by a niggling question. Did Raven have a woman? Or was this beadwork by his hand? In asking him on this perilous journey, had Tempe deprived him of his love?

Her gaze fell to his worn moccasins. Of buffalo hide, they looked much sturdier than her own and far more artful.

The rockhouse quieted. She'd missed the gist of Sion's conversation by indulging in her own. Leaning into Raven, she mouthed near his ear, "Say nothing of my father."

Later, when the others weren't so near, she'd tell him why.

19

All you need for happiness is a good gun, a good horse, and a good wife.

—Daniel Boone

They ate a cold supper, unwilling to risk a fire even in a rockhouse. Stringy jerked meat, dried corn, and the few remaining beaten biscuits filled their tense bellies, and then Sion watched Tempe leave the shelter without her rifle. Though both Hascal and Raven were at watch, Sion's every nerve stood on end and left him wishing he could accompany her himself. But she needed privacy. It went hard on a woman being with so many men. Just that morning he'd nearly laid Cornelius out for staring at her so blatantly with a misplaced longing. For now Cornelius was farther back in the cavern along with Spencer and Lucian.

Beside Sion sat Nate, patching his moccasins with deerskin nearer the rockhouse entrance. Fireflies flared in the woods, drawing Sion's notice, but it was Tempe he looked for. Minutes stretched long and lonesome. When she didn't return in the time he reckoned she needed, he could hardly sit still.

Nate seemed not to notice, working his awl and sinew with patient deliberation, squinting in the fast-fading light. "You remember the Cherokee word for *father*?"

"Easy enough. Sounds like *daddy*." Sion leaned a shoulder into the rock wall, Annie across his lap. "*Adadoda*."

"Well, our little miss was talking with Mister Raven about her daddy, then."

Sion pulled his gaze from the woods to look at him. "What do you mean?"

"And here I thought Ayl—Mistress Tucker"—Nate cleared his throat—"was a widow woman. But I'm beginning to believe . . ."

"What makes you think they weren't talking about Raven's pa?"

"'Cuz she was doin' most of the talkin'."

Sion resumed his watching. "Learn anything else?"

"A few words here and there. Seems they were most het up about the war party more'n anything—that lead Indian who goes by the name of Five Killer."

Sion held his peace, mulling the words till memory served. "Isn't that one of the Cherokee who lit into Boone's party in '73 and killed his son?"

Nate exhaled. "I disremember exactly."

Tired of waiting, Sion pushed himself to his feet.

Nate abandoned his mending. "You goin' after little miss?"

"Mayhap."

"Just you remember she may be in need of some solitude."

"It's too chancy for solitude."

This Nate couldn't argue. Over the ledge Sion went, landing soundlessly on a tuft of springy moss. A blackberry vine wended a thorny arm within reach. He picked a tendril clean and ate a few overripe berries, gaze swinging wide. The late-July lushness hid Tempe. Standing watch, Hascal and Raven saw him pass, but he didn't ask them where Tempe had gone nor tell them he was looking for her.

☙

The sturdy, sleek bodies of the horses surrounded her, their moods and quirks plain. Even at rest, Cornelius's mount was wound tight as a fiddle string, amusing her with its eye rolling and sidestepping. Sion's horse was much like him. Quietly powerful. Able minded. Controlled. Whilst her own mare, Dulcey, was sweet if feather headed, tearing away at the clover in a state of unparalleled bliss, Tempe was most drawn to Raven's mount.

Lowering his shaggy head, the pony nuzzled her as she stroked his muzzle before picking the burrs from his coat. A curry comb was needed but not near at hand. She spied a hoof pick in the grass, abandoned. One of the tasks of the chain men was to see to the horses, but Hascal and Spencer were too nervy from the Indian scare to be of much use. Glad for the solitude, she was of a mind to bed down right here and shun the men. One in particular was like a bee in her bonnet. It wasn't Cornelius Lyon.

The twilight deepened. At home the milking would be done and the supper dishes washed. Russell would take up his fiddle or retire to the barn-shed, depending on their lodgers. Paige would flirt and cajole, be it with Russell or a stranger. At a distance their familiar ways were more endearing. Near at hand they rubbed her raw.

Her nimble fingers swept Raven's pony clean of tangles. He nuzzled her again, catching her under an upraised arm so that it tickled and she nearly laughed.

"You rascal," she whispered, laying her cheek against his

sturdy neck and taking in his herby breath. Of all God's creatures, horses seemed the most needful yet the cleverest.

"Tempe."

She whirled, aggravation trumping surprise.

Sion stood behind her as if out on a Sabbath stroll. "Would you rather I call you Miss Tucker?"

"Tempe'll do." She let go a breath. "My name's no matter. It's your being here so sudden-like—"

"On account of your leaving without your gun." He held out her weapon.

"I won't use it. It's merely for show. A bluff." At the quirk of his brow she said, "I could never kill another human being—"

"Not even one intent on killing you?"

"Nay." She took hold of the flintlock reluctantly, avoiding his gaze.

"You've been away from camp a mite too long, besides."

She gave another pat to Raven's pony. "I was thinking about bedding down here with the horses."

He grinned, then covered it by rubbing his whiskered jaw. "I'm liable to come out here of a morning and find the horses took. You too."

"There's worse things."

His brows peaked. "Worse things than being took?"

Far worse. There's heartache. Regret. Lost chances. Shattered dreams . . .

His gaze was combing the woods again, as if sure Five Killer would reappear. In another surprising move he took her hand. Shock skittered through her. Mercy, how long it had been since she'd felt the touch of a man's hand. He led her beyond the horses to a secluded cove even farther away from the rockhouse. Away even from the guard.

Her heart began a little jig. She tried not to look at him.

Tried to remember just who he was. Harper's own. Yet something had tripped inside her, some thawing, some warmth. When he let go of her hand she missed his strength, that sense of purposefulness about him. James had had that same quality. Aye, it was James she missed.

"Sit back to back with me."

She did as he bid, understanding the need for extra vigilance, relieved to be facing outward. Thus situated, their backs touched where their hands once had. She took in the night sky riddled with stars like she'd heard decorated the new rebel flag. Flintlock forgotten, she leaned into him and he her, albeit ever so slightly.

His low words carried over his shoulder as he turned his head. "I'm of a mind to send you back."

She inclined her ear to catch every syllable. They were nearly cheek to cheek. "Back?" she echoed.

"Aye. To the inn."

She knew what he meant but wanted to prolong this moment. The sweetness. The stillness. Yet time pulsed on, drawing them ever toward a deeper danger.

"No woman should be outside log walls." The sudden heat in his voice was like the heat of the woods. Unrelenting. Searing. "At first light you need to set out toward home. Once we reach the Barrens, it'll be too late."

"And Raven?"

"I'll give him double wages to see you safely there, enough to trump the scalp bounties I hear the British are paying."

How had he come by this? Had Raven revealed such? "What if I want to keep on to the Ohio?"

"Then you're more a fool than I reckoned."

"What does that make you?"

"Twice the fool you are."

220

She smiled, but it was a sad smile, quickly fading. "Tomorrow doesn't affright me."

"And that's what affrights me." The honest edge to his voice seemed to belong to someone else entirely. The Sion she knew was no more. This borderman was almost . . . gabby. "I think you court death. Court it in ways I can't reckon."

She cocked her head, listening for anything ominous through the blackness. "I reckon we have little to do with it, this living and dying." She said the words slowly, examining her timeworn grief in a new light. If God called James home in His perfect time, shouldn't that speak peace to her harassed heart? "God only gives a man so much time, so many breaths. It's written in His book."

"You believe that?" he queried.

"And you don't?" she hissed back.

"Nay. There's been too much lost." He swallowed, seemed to stumble. "You'll understand better once you lose something irreplaceable. Some piece of yourself."

"I have." She hugged her knees closer, forgetting to keep her gaze outward.

Five Killer cut across her conscience. Seeing him again, wanting to give in to her hate, left her feeling further from James. Five Killer had not been brought to justice, but God was just. And God had seen fit to take James. Her greater woe was that James's death had been so unmerciful. No matter how she worked it, there had been nothing redeeming about that day shy of eternity.

She said, "Back in '73 it seems I left my very soul in Powell Valley."

"Powell Valley?" His voice was so low it was nearly lost to her. "Boone's first try at settling Kentucke. When his son was killed . . ."

There had been others lost that day. But for the moment she forgot them, adjusting to Sion's knowing.

"What was he to you, Tempe?"

An oriole flushed from a bush, rapid in its wing beat. Startled, she looked up, weighing her answer. What had James been to her? What had been lost? Her girlhood. The first flush of youth. The purest sort of love. A man who wanted to stand by her. Share his name. His days.

"What was he to me?" she echoed. "I was to be Tempe Tucker Boone."

A long silence fell betwixt them, broken by a mockingbird's cry. Should she tell him all the rest? That instead she'd reaped a barrenness of heart, her mind eaten up by angst. That Pa had foundered and lived on the run, haunted. That Russell was still not right. That Ma was forced to live a lie as widowed innkeeper. Was there no end to Powell Valley?

"You love him still."

It was not a question, thus she did not answer. Could not. Sorrow took hold of her, making a mess of thought and emotion.

I will always love him.

The Indians had taken much. But they couldn't kill love. Love, unlike many things, never failed. Love endured.

"In light of all that, why would you go another step?" The question was softly, even respectfully worded, no hint of exasperation within.

Because death is the door that leads to James.

She got to her feet, the weariness of spending too many nights on the ground with too many men catching up with her. Without another word she started away from him, her rifle a reminder of what awaited should she push west.

"You need to think hard on turning back," Sion repeated.

To the east, Ma's table and her own feather tick beckoned. She missed Paige's chatter, Russell's moody silences, every leather hinge and dusty corner of the inn. And Smokey. She missed Sion's dog, not the ill-bred mongrels crowding the dogtrot.

Night had overtaken them, the rising moon shiny as a newly minted copper shilling.

Stay or flee?

She'd have her answer come morning. First it needed praying for.

Sleep would not come. Yet it wasn't Sion's offer to return to the inn that consumed her but the last of her memories from '73. She'd lain on hard ground like this back then, but there'd been hope in her heart. And love. Always love.

Those final October days in Powell Valley, Tempe and the other women and children gathered grapes and pawpaws and nuts, nearly hooting with glee over the beloved chinkapins, whilst the men dug a pit to roast a whole beef. Out of pouches spilled meal and dried corn, beans and fruit, even coveted herbs and spices. Tempe smelled something akin to cake, quite a feat without a familiar fireplace and proper cooking vessels.

Their clever skill at making do with whatever was at hand was both a delight and a befuddlement. A reminder that they'd let go of everything. Farms. Fields. Possessions. Once James and Russell and the Mendenhalls returned, they'd all break camp and press on toward distant, unknown places they'd call their own, crossing into the land beyond to reach the unclaimed Kentucke meadowlands. For now hearts were high from several days' rest and the coming nuptials.

She'd soon be a married woman. Beloved. Changed. Wiser

to the ways of the world. For now twilight was creeping closer, filling in the forest's nooks and crannies as Saturday ebbed. Tempe listened past the call of a whippoorwill and the fading shuffle of a busy camp to hear the sounds she craved above all else. An excited whinny. A careful halloo.

Full dark had come on when the wolves began to howl. Would James and the men not come? They'd promised to return by Saturday eve. Something kept them at Castle's Woods, or with a full load of seed and farm tools and such, they'd been slowed.

She lay down on her pallet, the forest floor chill and uneven beneath her. A snaking root stabbed her back, and she felt the ticklish trail of an ant across her bare arm. Russell usually slept an arm's reach away on the outside, his rifle slung across upright sticks, ever ready. Across the embers of a dwindling cookfire, her mother lay, eyes closed, lips parted. And Pa? She didn't know.

Tempe stared heavenward, eyes on the full moon floating free of the sugar trees.

Blind to the beauty, she sent three words into the stillness. *Lord, please . . . James.*

When she finally slept, she'd dreamed of thunder.

The distant thunder of guns? Uneasiness smothered her heart. Her head came free of the pallet, her body poised for flight. Her sleepy gaze was drawn to the Boones, an assortment of lumps beneath unkempt bedding a few families away. Maybe James had come in during the night. The moon had been full, good for travel.

But it wasn't James she saw.

Standing a few feet from her was the young man—Isaac Simmons—nobody seemed particularly fond of. He'd earned a brand for cowardice and thieving and had left their party earlier on the trace. Now his face stood out in the wan morning light, pale as frost, eyes wild.

The guard gathered round him, a trio of buckskin-clad men who seemed more aggravated than alarmed by his presence. Hastily, Tempe stood and ran callused hands down her dress to smooth out the wrinkles before plucking a shawl, damp with dew, from a laurel bush. She hardly felt its chill as it draped her.

The camp was astir. Bedrolls needed to be strapped to packsaddles and children fed. But Tempe kept her gaze on Isaac, who'd finally begun to talk. She moved nearer, reading his lips, his gestures and grimaces. He turned and spat into a clump of weeds, looking sick enough to retch.

Tempe hardly noticed Mary Mendenhall's approach. Mary was sixteen and newly wed, her face holding a question. Her husband had gone with James and Russell to Castle's Woods.

Next came Jane Mendenhall, carrying the least of her children. Her face was still pinched with fatigue despite several days' rest. "You bring word of my Richard?"

For a split second, Isaac just stared back at them before starting up again with a choking stutter.

"It—it's bad—I come upon an ambush some three miles back along Wallen's Creek—Cherokee and Shawnee—from the look of it. The stock's all scattered—the horses took. Both Mendenhalls killed outright." The young man spoke in breathless spurts, sweat slicking his brow despite the morning's chill. "Three more are shot full of arrows, so torn up I could hardly make 'em out. I believe one's Boone—maybe Tucker."

Tempe took a step back, blood singing in her ears.

A wall of folks were behind her now, hemming her in, leaving no room to run or cry or collapse. She looked about wildly, the ragged trees fading to gray then black, cutting off light and air. If she'd been high atop a knob, she'd have flung herself off it, so deep went her hurt.

James . . . dead . . . on their wedding day?

What of Russell? Was her beloved brother dead too?

James's father appeared then, gun in hand, striding toward them. Daniel held himself ramrod-straight at the news, his weathered features showing neither surprise nor sorrow. He asked a few low questions as if weighing all the facts before calling his brother and a small party of men to go back and bury the dead. James's mother took out linen sheets from their precious stores to wrap the bodies in.

Stoic, the men began herding the women and children toward a large hollow beneath a beech tree, throwing up a rude defense of brush and fallen timber. The scene was one of chaos and near panic.

Shaking from the storm of her emotions, Tempe fisted her apron, the linen wadded in trembling hands. Beside her, Mary Mendenhall cried quietly, but Jane Mendenhall—a widow minutes old with eight fatherless children—stood stricken, the forgotten baby in her arms fretful.

Across the way was Tempe's mother, also bereft of a son. Aylee Tucker put an arm about James's mother, leading her to the shelter of the beech tree, seven younger Boones trailing. Little Livvy was crying, her small chest working like a blacksmith's bellows as she clasped her older sisters' hands.

Unable to look at her, Tempe turned her face to the sky. Seeking answers. Trying to stay standing. Desperate to recall what James had said to her at the last.

I wish you could go with me.

With all her being, she wished she had.

Sion took the night watch till the moon foretold three o'clock and Lucian roused. Expecting to fall into a dead slumber, he lay on his scant bedding in the rockhouse, dreaming of softer ground. Between him and Nate was Tempe, but he couldn't tell if she was asleep or awake. And then when the silence and blackness of the night was deepest, she mumbled a few sleep-slurred words. He could make out but one.

James.

It was enough to keep him wide-eyed till daylight. After that she'd quieted. Was her time on the trace stirring up old heartaches like trail dust? If she turned back, headed to the inn . . . What a hole she'd leave should she retreat. And he had no guess as to whether Raven would accompany her for double wages or fly.

It was clear the half-blood was partial to her. Sion watched Raven craft a bow and a quiver of arrows for her. They bounced on her back, making her abandon her rifle altogether at times. Raven was teaching her how to use them, and being Tempe, she warmed to the task. Sion had yet to tease apart the reasons for their tie, and the wondering gnawed at him like a mouse finding a shed deer antler on the forest floor.

Turning on his side, he rested his head on his forearm and allowed himself an unguarded look at her. The moon was obliging, at such a slant that silver light spilled into the rockhouse and soaked every ridge and hollow of her. She lay on her back, her comely profile at rest, hands folded atop her middle.

If she left . . . what would he miss?

The flash in her eyes when he riled her? The deep-set dimple in her cheek? Her amiable self-possession? Her surprising, slow-to-speak ways? Tending to any complaint with her herbs and simples? The fall of hair to the small of her back, an untamed coil of too many colors to count?

She stirred then, turning toward him. A handbreadth away. Nate's raucous snoring didn't dent the enchantment or even earn the customary nudge to quiet down. Moonlight limned her cheekbones and fringe of lashes. Sion clenched his free hand, the temptation to brush back a stray wisp of her hair nigh impossible to resist.

She had nearly been James's bride. A worthy bride for a Boone. What had Daniel once told him?

All you need for happiness is a good gun, a good horse, and a good wife.

A true-hearted woman, Daniel had concluded. Sion had heeded that advice. Had all a man could ask for. Then as now the knife's edge of sorrow descended and cut short the faint stirrings of awe he'd begun to feel.

"Sion?" Tempe looked over at him. Her voice was like a caress in the darkness. "Is it time yet?"

He swallowed. Rolled onto his back. "Time?"

"To leave out?"

Would he lose her? He forced more words past a too-tight throat. "Which direction?"

She chuckled, a sweet, throaty sound, nearly drawing his eyes back to her. He focused on the rockhouse ceiling, a gnarled, smoke-blackened overhang he'd be glad to part with come daybreak.

"Time'll tell," she whispered, turning her back to him.

⁂

Tempe was aware of Sion's eyes on her as they decamped. She sent him several sidelong glances, enjoying his attention. Maybe a smidgen of Paige's flirtatiousness had rubbed off.

Though Sion was clearly in charge, she had the upper hand, at least for the moment.

The horses were saddled and loaded, the camp picked clean of belongings. A breakfast of spring water and parched corn sufficed, and then she saw to Sion's arm, pleased the bite was fading from an ugly red to a mottled purplish black, though her anger at Cornelius still burned bright.

This very morning Cornelius began to whine, pestering Sion about the particulars of their march. Sion wasn't in a garrulous mood, annoying Cornelius with belated, one-word answers. Tempe tensed. Would another fight erupt?

Cornelius stood over Lucian as the manservant tightened his saddle's girth. "I have decided that the fatal flaw of the wilderness is the dearth of daily bread. Had we some beeves, wheaten flour, and maccobean sugar, I'd be more inclined to suffer your tyranny." This he leveled at Sion, who stood inspecting the Jacob's staff, the crown jewel of surveying.

To Tempe's delight, Sion ignored him.

"I call for a change of order in the column," Cornelius droned on. "I shall lead out and set the pace, the Chero-kee and Miss Tucker scouting ahead, and the rest following behind, with you, Morgan, bringing up the rear. When we reach the survey site—"

"*When?*" Nate burst out. "*If* is more likely. Yer liable to lead us straight off a cliff. You might make pretty maps, but you ain't got no internal compass."

The chain men snickered as they awaited Sion's orders. And Sion—Sion was awaiting her, unwilling to make a move till she declared her intentions. She'd put him off long enough, though the lure of home was like the scent of baked bread. Nigh irresistible.

She swung herself into the saddle, facing west, still a bit

sleepy-headed. She'd dreamed of James again. Sifted through the last of her memories. Glad she was of dawn's light. Now her stomach, hardly content with her handful of corn, made noisy protest.

Mounted beside her, Raven turned to her with a sympathetic aside. "Fish enough to fill your belly once we reach the Green."

She smiled, having withheld from him Sion's tempting offer to turn back. The promise of catfish or carp, a favorite, seemed subtle confirmation to press on. Kneeing Dulcey, she moved past Sion to the front of the column.

Was he hoping she would turn back? Or had his dire words last night merely masked his feeling that he found her more hindrance than help? Then and there she purposed to prove herself.

Dawn bespoke another blazing day. A redbird sang from the topmost branches of a poplar, its sweet whistle one of the first songs of morning. Sweat began a slow trickle down her back. Her stays would soon be soaked through. She'd laced them less tight, leaving room to breathe as the heat ratcheted. She longed to be as unclad and free as Raven.

Turning to look over her shoulder, she found Sion watching her so intently she wished she could climb inside his head and try his thoughts. Squaring her shoulders, refusing homesickness, she steeled herself against the demands of the day, trying to stay forward thinking.

She remembered that along the Green was a series of waterfalls, a cool, misting place rife with shade. Privacy. On one of her forays with Pa they'd camped along the largest falls, naming it after Aylee. It had been late autumn and Pa was hunting buffalo. The cold turned so intense Tempe stayed wrapped in a buffalo robe the entire journey.

Now she followed Raven a ways and then they parted, he taking to the ridge above and she keeping to the humid bottoms, the surveyors trailing or between them.

Sion wasted little time laying the line, the sun soon striking the equipment and creating a fearful shine. Tempe kept alert to the line marks for the next direction west, their noisy work even bringing a halt to the birdsong. Though talk was minimal there was no doubt surveying was an intrusion to the untrammeled woods. The axemen never ceased their chopping. With Nate and Lucian as chain carriers, Cornelius grudgingly was made marker. Sion rebuked them for short-chaining—failing to pull the chain tight—making a mockery of his accuracy.

When Raven rejoined her at noon, his expression held a hint of disgust. Each foot forward thrust the Indians back. No doubt he was thinking it too.

"It's a wide sweep of world." Raising a hand, Tempe pushed back her hat to ease her damp hairline. "Can't we all just abide together in harmony?"

"No, *oginalii*." He flicked a mosquito from a silver-banded forearm. "The land stealers are here to stay."

"Where then will you go?"

His shrug held resignation. "Maybe it will not matter. I may join my Tsalagi brothers and fight."

Alarmed anew, she looked at him. "You would make war?"

Raven studied her, more grim. "This Morgan, the Long Knife, he is a wolf."

Wolf? Once she had thought the same. Now she wasn't sure. She cast a look over her shoulder as the main party caught up with them at the rendezvous point, a grove of stately maples near a sulphur spring. "Every man is part wolf, part lamb. The stronger depends on which you feed, remember?"

"You borrow the words of the holy man Asbury."

She nodded, the memory convicting if distant. The preacher had come but once, then gone back over the Gap. Raven happened to be at the inn when he held them spellbound on the dogtrot, planting biblical seeds. Was she watering them in his wake?

"I pray for peace," she said.

"To your holy Father?"

"God is your Father too," she returned quietly. "He makes a place for us in heaven, forever."

Still grim-faced, Raven reined his horse around to face the rest of their party. "I am not sure of this heaven you speak of. But I think the hell the holy man spoke of is here."

Her heart sank. Sion approached slowly as if gauging the intensity of their talk. With another push to her hat, Tempe sent it dangling down her back.

She was unsure of Raven. Unsure of Sion. Unsure of taking another step. And still missing James.

For now they rested, the axemen spent. Looking back over the ground they'd come, Tempe took in the destruction. Broken twigs and branches. Crushed undergrowth. The telling marks of men's tracks. Blaze marks on tree after tree. All the tools were finally idle—the red-tipped chaining arrows, the tally belt to track them, one too many felling axes and fascine knives.

Cornelius was bent over his plane table, a drawing board with paper and rule, a sight at each end. Sion kept slightly apart, jotting in his field book. At day's end they would gather and compare notes and sketches, astonishing her with their mathematical and artistic prowess. But at the moment they seemed subdued, overcome by the vastness they claimed by metal chains.

Cornelius looked up from his work, his fair hair hanging in damp wisps about his face. "There was a time we surveyed nine tracts totaling twenty thousand acres in seventeen days."

"Fincastle County is not the frontier," Sion replied without looking up.

"No, it ain't," Nate sputtered between a mouthful of jerky. "Most of Virginia seems naught but Yankee Doodle land from here."

"Yankee Doodle land, indeed." Laying his quill aside, Cornelius reached for a canteen. "The Kentucke guidebook you're writing shall be as formidable a weapon as these axes and knives, enticing settlers far and wide to venture into the wilderness, or so I hope. I'm confident my publisher in Philadelphia will print the guide along with my maps. Once that happens I shan't stoop to a field survey again."

Tempe uncorked her own canteen as Sion looked up at her over his notes. "How far to the Barrens, Miss Tucker?"

So he'd forsaken *Tempe*, had he? A stilted formality had crept between them again. So be it. "Another ten miles by my reckoning, Mister Morgan, though Raven might be of a different mind."

At that Sion tucked his field book beneath one arm and walked toward Raven, who stood beneath a sugar tree, leaving her to puzzle out Cornelius's lofty talk. A guidebook? Such a farfetched notion! Settlement was coming, but she rued its violent advance. Ink and paper, a guidebook, had little bearing on conquering the wilderness, surely.

Yet in her heart of hearts lived a longing for peaceful times. Neighbors. Acres of corn and rail fence. A lessening of danger. Caught on the cusp of change, she squirmed.

Her beloved wilderness was vast and unfettered. Free.

She was with the very men who would bring all that untrammeled beauty to an end.

And she had lent her hand to help them.

20

We had hoped that the white men would not be willing
to travel beyond the mountains. Now that hope is gone.
—CHIEF DRAGGING CANOE,
CHICKAMAUGA TSALAGI (CHEROKEE)

Cornelius was lost in the cane.

"Suppose we let him stay thataway," Nate said.

As Sion chuckled, Nate shifted in the saddle and
spat a stream of tobacco juice in the direction Cornelius had
taken. Ten feet high in places and thick as turkey feathers,
the reedy stalks seemed without end. Somewhere beyond the
mess of rustling green lay the Barrens, that treeless sweep of
grasses stretching as far as the eye could see.

Tempe's mare began foraging, mouth so full of cane Tempe
feared she might choke.

On his mount beside her, Raven waved a hand to the north.
"Keep to the tulip trees along the water. I will find the *dila*."

Both Sion and Nate looked from Raven to Tempe as if
wanting her to translate. She lifted her shoulders. "Cherokee
for *skunk*, likely." Or *fool*.

Sion cracked another smile as Nate dissolved in silent laughter. Raven frowned. He thought as little of Cornelius as Sion, though Sion had earned Raven's grudging respect, at least. Tempe could see it. Feel it. But Raven seemed especially contemptuous of Cornelius, who had charged into the cane in pursuit of a rare ivory-billed woodpecker.

Without waiting for any agreement, Raven plunged into the reeds atop his pony, a bone whistle in his mouth. In minutes, Tempe could hear the throaty trill of it, their main hope of locating the wayward mapmaker.

Lord forgive her, but she wished he'd stay gone. Last night when it was her turn to stand watch and relieve him, he'd come entirely too close. With Sion asleep and no one to intervene, Cornelius had slipped a possessive arm about her before she could shake him loose. Revulsion turned her sick inside. Had he no decency? Would he see his sister, Harper, so manhandled?

Aware of Sion beside her, she squinted beneath the brim of her hat and wished for a little shade. Cold water. Lightheaded, she followed him as he turned his stallion in the direction Raven had gestured.

In a few miles they were well beyond the cane on the cusp of the long-anticipated, luxurious grassland. Her grateful eyes took in flame-colored berries and flowers, their names unknown to her, alongside beloved violets and trilliums. In their season, wild strawberries grew in such abundance they stained the horses' hooves a deep red.

"The beginning of the Barrens," she said. "So called because the Indians set fire to the land each spring."

Nate angled his hat lower. "Why exactly?"

"To better chase the game. Buffalo, mostly."

The buffalo meat they'd jerked two nights before was heavy

in their packs, the memory of roasted marrow bones sweet. She uncapped her canteen and took a swig of lukewarm water.

"How far to cross?" Sion was studying her, awaiting her answer.

What had Pa said? "The Barrens are some sixty miles long and nearly as broad. The moon is full. We'd best travel by night lest we be easy prey."

"It'll be a tiresome meadow, day or night," Nate predicted, looking over his shoulder at the lagging chain carriers.

"North of here is the Green River," she told them. "Northwest are the caves." Cold. Strange. Unforgettable.

"I'll lead out at full dark," Sion said. "Best keep fifty paces between each man."

Nate was already looking weary. "How far you reckon we'll get in a night?"

"All the way through, mayhap, if a full moon." Tempe wanted to flinch, but Sion was suffused with a palpable enthusiasm. "We'll keep to an agreed-upon rendezvous point in case of attack or separation." His gaze swung to a ridge, another danger. Tempe pushed down any thought of ambush.

Nate followed close behind them as they moved toward the tulip trees. "I misdoubt we'll be long in findin' Corny. Not with his powder horn clinkin' on the hilt of his knife for all to hear."

Truly, it was a wonderment they'd not been ambushed yet. Cornelius made an infernal noise wherever he went, be it with his mouth or his gear. Someone was always trying to shush him. She'd rid the camp of his scarlet handkerchief a ways back by stuffing it in the hollow of a tree, bemused when he hunted high and low for it like a sulky child.

Lucian was more the man. She'd taken a liking to Lucian,

who was an able hand with any task put to him, his mood ever amiable, his patience with his irascible master biblical.

For now they sought the refuge of the shade, Lucian and Sion standing watch whilst she slipped off her moccasins and waded in the creek. One hour passed, then two. Occasionally she heard Raven's whistle. She imagined Cornelius in that maze of cane, bewildered and sweating, going in dizzying circles. She'd heard tell of men wearing themselves out and never being found. If anyone could ferret out the Englishman, it would be Raven.

By dusk her confidence began to wane. Full dark brought an end to the fleeting whistling. She studied the wall of cane, sorry she'd hidden the red handkerchief. A little color might help Raven's search. Weariness and worry tugged at her. While she stewed, the chain carriers bedded down in the brush, Nate and Lucian with them.

It was just her and Sion standing watch at opposite ends of camp, she keenly aware of his silhouette. She gnawed on a strip of jerky, craving bread . . . honey. She'd had no honey since leaving Virginia. Bees from the colonies were hard to come by. White man's flies, Raven called them.

She felt like a wild creature herself in her worn garments. What man would think her worth pondering even cleaned up? Again that sweet craving for a pretty petticoat or ribbon took root. Bloomed. And then the memory of Cornelius's unwanted attentions at their change of watch returned, banished only by Sion's reassuring presence some hundred yards distant. Their last private talk was never far from her thoughts, nor that confident way he'd taken her hand. She'd felt giddy as a girl at his touch. And then the shame of it washed all exhilaration away.

Maybe it wasn't counted a sin to feel something for a man,

even a married man. A body couldn't help that, could it? She reckoned it was only wrong if you fed, or acted on, those misplaced feelings.

And that she would never do.

⚬

Once Sion had looked at Tempe like he would a fetching flower or a striking sunset. Impartial. A thing to be momentarily admired then forgotten. But here lately . . .

His remedy was to push harder, to be so preoccupied with the task at hand and the danger that they drove out any notice of her. But the magic of the night had snuck up on him. Here she was, off watch, studying the sky like she'd never seen it before, open wonder in her face. Hardened as he was, he wanted to chuckle at her being so childlike, and then he found himself rummaging through his haversack like the moon had worked some spell.

In minutes his field glasses were in hand. Likely she'd never seen such. Removed from their leather case, their old-style workmanship seemed heavy. Sion took care not to startle her, but he'd noticed she'd begun to be a bit upended in his presence. Because of his being so quiet, he reckoned, both in movement and in speech.

Coming up behind her, he murmured her name and she half turned. He reached for her rifle and traded it for the field glasses. When she simply turned them over like they were little more than a Gunter's chain, he set both their guns aside. Enclosing her fingers in his, he positioned the glasses and raised them to her eyes, aiming for the North Star.

Her smile was his reward. "Such a fearsome sight. These spectacles put me there so close it seems like the stars might cut me if I were to reach out and grab hold."

"What do you see?"

"Star showers . . . and that long sweep of lights that has the look of a gourd. Two of them."

"Ursa Major . . . the plough."

The field glasses came down. "Why are they called such?"

"You'd rather they be the Two Gourds?" His voice was husky with mirth.

"Maybe."

He circled behind her, pointing. "Notice the seven stars in each. Two outer stars—Dubhe and Merak—point to the North Star, or Polaris. All together they form a pattern. Like a bear."

"A bear? Now that's fanciful."

Another chuckle rose inside him, followed by a bittersweet twinge when she said, "I never knew the stars had names till you surveyors came round. You're besotted with the stars."

"Aye." They were speaking in unwise whispers when any talk was risky. He was violating his own rule for quiet, yet the need to speak, to break the everlasting monotony, gnawed at him. Or was it merely the sound of her lilting voice?

And then, as abruptly as he'd handed her the field glasses, she returned them to him, taking up her gun in such a way he knew she was alarmed. Silently cursing his negligence, he reached for Annie and they took cover. But it was only a southwesterly wind kicking up, rustling the summer-dry grasses.

"You expect Mister Lyon will ever show himself?"

Sion mulled his answer. "I suspect Raven is befuddling him in that cane, teaching him a lesson he won't soon forget."

Her profile turned thoughtful, the dimple in her cheek more pronounced when she wasn't smiling. "A cane field at night can be a fearsome thing. Once Pa—"

He cocked his head toward her as she stuttered then righted herself.

"People tell of coming through the Barrens and sleeping in the cane to hide themselves," she finished.

"There's no call to sleep. We'll just cut straight through."

"You'll go on without Raven and Mister Lyon?"

"If they're not here soon, aye. Raven's a master tracker. He'll catch up to us." He read resistance in her sudden silence. "Mind telling me why he agreed to come on this jaunt when he's so all-fired opposed to surveyors?"

"He owes me a good deed, is all."

A mighty big one, likely. He wouldn't press her for particulars, but the question wouldn't let him be. Might her heart be tied up in it? For all his Indian-ness, Raven was a tolerable-looking fellow, his stamina staggering. Sometimes Sion was hard put to keep up with him. He felt a queer churning. Of all emotions, jealousy was hardest to stomach.

Sudden misery led him to ask, "Are you partial to him, Tempe?"

"Me?" She turned the full force of her gaze his way, her eyes a bold black in the moonlight. "He's my friend, if that's what you mean."

He listened hard, expecting her to say no more. But she continued, surprising him with her candor. "I never expected his owing me a favor would gain you a guide."

"He's partial to you."

"Partial?" She all but chuckled. "You've pegged Raven wrong if you're saying what I think you're saying."

Was she that blind? He felt both aggrieved and relieved. Raven did favor her, whether she owned it or not. What he couldn't pin down were her feelings for him.

Her voice came so soft he wasn't sure he heard her right. "Does it matter?"

She had him there. Did it?

He leaned into his rifle, wishing Raven and Cornelius back. It was nigh on midnight now, his fretfulness rising. They should be pushing farther west when the moon was most obliging.

She looked at the ground, the wind tugging at her braid. "I've been wondering about Ma and Russell. Paige. Whether the inn's still standing or little more than ashes."

The melancholy in her tone nicked him. He wanted to reach out and pull her hat free to better see her face. "You're still thinking of the war party headed that way."

"I can think of little else." There was no blame in her tone, but he felt as guilty as if she'd pointed her finger at him.

Her uncertainty about the inn rattled him. He doubted it would fall, having stood this long, but who knew? Again he wrestled with the thought of sending her back. "You should see home again by fodder-pulling time." At her uneasy silence he said, "A fortnight's surveying and then we aim for the Falls of Ohio. There we part."

It sounded sensible. Practical. Mournful. Again came that odd, unwelcome sensation that she mattered more than she should, that she'd somehow gained a foothold when his guard was down. Emotions long buried thrust through the hardened soil of his heart and head and turned him tender.

He fisted his hand lest he reach for her. Tempe gave him much to admire. Much to question. The matter of her father, what brought her family into Kentucke, remained a riddle. Time would tell, Nate always said. But for the moment, with the moonlight pouring down, calling out every fetching feature . . .

He was no longer just besotted with the stars.

21

I don't believe that grief passes away. It has its time and place forever. More time is added to it; it becomes a story within a story. But grief and griever alike endure.

—WENDELL BERRY, *JAYBER CROW*

Sion was as good as his word. Once Cornelius emerged from the cane—panting and near mad with thirst, Raven on his heels—they made their midnight trek through the Barrens' thigh-high grasses. And now, with the Green River wending west like a signpost to guide them, the surveying could resume.

"Fetching country," Nate said, encompassing in two words the sum of many admiring glances.

Tempe's chest swelled with bittersweet memories. Pa had first shown her this lush country when they'd come into Kentucke and were deciding where to settle. Green River country lay as big and rolling as when they'd first seen it, a sweet tangle of water and timber and foliage with none of the fierce rockiness of Shawnee River country.

"Prime bottomland for farming," Nate mused as if envisioning fields and fences as far as the Ohio. He glanced at Tempe. "No forts or settlers to speak of?"

"None yet," she answered, looking to Raven for confirmation.

"This is sacred hunting ground. It will not be easily lost or won."

Yet there was no hostile sign that she could see, almost as if the ever-present wind erased all evidence of anyone's passing, unbending the grasses, covering the dusty tracks of all who passed.

They camped on the edge of the Barrens that night. Though she was weary in body, Tempe's thoughts refused to settle. The farther west they chained, the more lax their party became. All but she, Sion, and Raven. The three of them eased not a whit. Negligence was the end of many a traveler.

"Well, missy. I got me a little pain." A bit shamefaced, Lucian stood before her after supper, his ebony eyes entreating.

Tempe tore her gaze from Sion and Raven, who'd just ridden off with nary a goodbye. "A *little* pain, Lucian?" She'd noticed him limping around as they made camp.

He looked to his leg. "Here we is, aimin' to ride farther west, and no saddle'll hold me."

Compassion stirred inside her as he raised the left leg of his breeches, revealing a carbuncle on his inner thigh. She nearly flinched. Chafed by constant movement, the boil looked about to burst. Pondering it, she worried her lower lip with her teeth. "It needs lancing."

Once again she wished Aylee was near. Ma always knew what a body was in need of, even to soul and spirit. "I'll get my awl and some clean linen and medicine." She took a breath. "It would help if you were to get wet all over first." None of the men save Sion had bathed. Weary of staying downwind of them, she fetched soft soap for Lucian, which entailed passing by the awning where Cornelius worked.

"Ah, Mistress Moonbow . . ." The lure in his voice set her further on edge. "Might you have a bit of brandy in your provisions?"

She looked at him. How had he known? Had he pilfered her belongings in her absence?

"Mister Morgan has forbidden any spirits."

His smile was oily. "But Mister Morgan is not here."

Painfully aware of this, she looked in the direction he had taken, an uneasy feeling nearly swallowing her. He and Raven had gone to scout out the best fording place along the Green. She wasn't needed, Sion said. Hurt by what felt like a rebuff, she'd been most touchy about him being with Raven alone. Always she'd accompanied them before. She sensed some tug-of-war within Raven, a turning. No longer the trusted guide she had counted on.

Just as Sion had a rarely seen lighter side, Raven had a dark one. She had never felt it before, and her hackles rose. Though Sion had earned his respect as a woodsman, Raven had no sympathy for surveyors. But his dislike went deeper. She could feel it, and it rattled her to her bones.

"Come, Miss Tucker, what would a wee dram hurt?"

"What would it help?" she answered, continuing on her way.

To her dismay, Cornelius followed her to where Lucian sat, his boil exposed. "What if I forbade you to treat my manservant till some brandy was dispensed?"

"What if I told you Lucian needs spirits worse than you?" she shot back, wanting to be done with him.

Cornelius chuckled, reaching out and fingering a lock of hair that had slipped free of her fraying braid. Startled, she moved away, glad to see Nate approaching. She said, "Lucian, go and see to your bath at the river's edge. Hascal's standing guard."

He went, leaving her alone with Cornelius save Nate. A rush of affection overcame her when Nate said, "Best keep your hands to yourself, Corny, or you'll have more than me to tussle with."

"Meaning?" All levity drained from Cornelius's voice.

"Ol' Sion yonder, he'll lay you out. Remember what happened in Williamsburg."

A marked pause. Whatever had happened was enough to return Cornelius to his awning. Never had she seen so slyboots a man. She hoped Harper was nothing like him.

By the time Lucian returned, looking considerably cleaner despite wearing the same shabby clothing, Cornelius had taken his turn at watch while Nate gathered firewood and the axemen saw to the horses.

"I'm fixing to make you a shirt," she told Lucian as she prepared to lance him. "Ma packed a right smart supply of linen. Thread and shears. I'll use your old shirt for a measure."

"You partial to sewin', Miss Tempe?"

"That I am." She wielded the awl, thorn sharp, and lanced away. Lucian stiffened and turned his head as if not watching could lessen the pain.

"I'll sew you on some bone buttons." Tempe rambled, hoping to distract him. "Stitch your initials inside."

"That sounds right fancy. One day, iffen we ever get back to Virginny, it'll bring to mind this trip."

"Where's home, Lucian?"

He looked east. "Home is Oakwood, where Mister Cornelius's people come from."

"Oakwood? Is it a fine place?"

"Finer than fine. Acres of tobacco and indigo far as the eye can see. Mister Sion deemed it worthy too. He came surveyin' for old Mister Lyon a few years back. Met Miss Harper . . ."

"That's a sightly name, Harper."

"Yes'm. She be—" He quieted as if groping for words. "Beautiful. Like you, Miss Tempe, with your dark hair and smilin' eyes."

Touched, she cleaned the sore place as gently as she could. "I'm a far cry from beautiful, Lucian."

"Well, if you ain't, I don't know what is." He batted at a mosquito. "Mister Sion, I reckon he never saw such a sight as Miss Harper, as good as she was pretty. And Miss Harper, she never saw the likes of a borderman before, bein' shut in and raised proper-like."

"So Miss Harper and Sion . . . met," Tempe said, not wanting the telling to end. Her fancies quickly filled in the gaps. A young, unhardened Sion. The lovely Harper, instantly smitten.

"Yes'm. Now, old Mister Lyon took a liking to Mister Sion, though Mister Cornelius was of a mind to run him off once the surveyin' was done. But Miss Harper had done worked her spell. You see, Mister Cornelius didn't care for a borderman courtin' his sister even if he did come out of William & Mary studyin' law—"

"Mister Morgan—a lawyer?" Surprise bloomed.

"Law, yes'm. But when he'd done with that, Doctor Walker at Castle Hill talked him into bein' a Crown surveyor."

Tempe listened hard, trying to keep up with so many facts and a lancing too.

"The Walkers were known to Mister Sion, you see, the good doctor bein' the first surveyor in Kentucke even before Boone." Lucian took a breath. "Well, Mister Sion, he leaves

Oakwood and rides off to Williamsburg to register the surveys in the land office there. And Miss Harper, bein' lovesick,
takes off after him. What was he to do but marry her lessen
she ruin herself runnin' after him?"

Nearly forgetting what she did, Tempe began applying
the salve. "So they wed?"

"Yes'm. Right then and there in Williamsburg, though
Mister Cornelius raised a ruckus and tried to stop it." Lucian chuckled, seeming to forget his sore leg. "Instead of a
weddin' feast there was a fight. Mister Cornelius got the
worst of it. It wasn't long before Mister Sion took his bride
well beyond his reach to Fort Henry."

Fort Henry was a far cry from Oakwood. Lucian had
reached the part that befuddled Tempe most. How had Cornelius and Sion come to make their peace in terms of working
together? And how had the mighty Morgan adjusted to his
genteel bride? Harper, despite her fancy ways, had begun to
sound a bit like her impassioned, impetuous brother.

"Fort Henry is in the wilds, nearly like here," she remarked.
"Quite a leap for a town-bred girl."

Lucian was studying the ground, suddenly quiet. "I ain't
never been there. Only heard talk. Some things is better not
knowin'."

There was a subtle thread of melancholy in Lucian's
story, suggesting Sion hadn't wanted to be married. Bordermen were often unwed, tethered to danger instead. What
sort of life would Harper lead in a rude, picketed fort
after Oakwood and Richmond? With a roaming husband
to boot?

Tying a bandage in place, she said, "I'd like to meet her."

Lucian all but squirmed on his stump seat. "Well, Miss
Tempe—"

Nate returned, arms full of deadwood, snuffing Lucian's next words. Finished with her doctoring, Tempe watched as Lucian stood, favoring his leg but helping Nate with the wood. Lord willing, they'd resume their talk in time, though she sensed an odd reluctance about Lucian at the end, as if he rued the rest of his story.

Nate dropped his load with a clatter, his stomach growling noticeably. "What's for supper?"

"Corn cakes. Fish." Tempe wished she could serve him some of Aylee's fare. "Maybe some red meat if Mister Morgan and Raven have their way."

"Some bear or buffalo would be welcome. I ain't partial to any more of them turkey eggs." Nate made a face, a wink following. "But I do favor your ma's corn cakes. And I confess to a right terrible hankerin' for a cold swallow of sweet milk . . . cheese."

"That'll have to wait till we come to a fort." In the back of her mind Tempe held on to the hope they'd spend time behind pickets. Boone's Fort in particular. It was besieged still, she wagered, Five Killer never far from her thoughts.

Remembering her promise of a shirt, she busied herself the rest of the afternoon on behalf of Lucian, working beneath the shade of a stout dogwood, the fabric soft beneath her callused hands.

Thoughts full of Harper and Sion's elopement, she watched anxiously for Sion's return, praying for a change of heart in Raven. When they rode in at dusk, her warm welcome had nothing to do with the buffalo they'd taken. She was glad to the heart to see them, one more than the other.

Sion's eyes found hers, and he seemed as glad of her as she was of him. Or was she only woolgathering? He made a clean sweep of camp in that canny way he had and, sensing nothing amiss, washed up before bedding down beside her.

She lay awake, listening to his even breathing, unsure if he slept or was awake. She longed to rouse him, have him tell her what he'd seen, how many steps they'd taken.

And he . . . did he lay awake, wondering the same of her?

22

Love is what carries you, for it is always there, even in the dark . . . shining out at times like gold stitches in a piece of embroidery.

—WENDELL BERRY, *HANNAH COULTER*

They reached the Green in a fever of heat on what Sion counted was the last day of July. Surveying was madness in such weather. Thinking it, he quashed a spasm of guilt. He was pushing the axemen too hard, so he called for a temporary base camp. An awning provided shade for Cornelius to work on his maps while Sion roamed with Raven and Tempe, scouting the next best survey site. The others were only too glad to rest from their labors, leaving Lucian to comb the woods for sallet, wild onions, and the disagreeable turkey eggs that made up their woods fare.

Now at midafternoon, Sion sat beneath the awning, refiguring calculations. Through the trees he had a dim view of Tempe and Raven on the Green's pebbly bank. Fishing, the both of them, and enjoying it too. Her airy laugh was in marked contrast to Raven's sobriety, though once Sion saw an approving smile light his features when Tempe caught a fat perch.

There was life in that laugh, lived to the brim. No matter her heartache, she'd begun to embrace whatever was handed her, shrugging aside a broody spirit to enter fully within. Some of that newfound joy threatened to spill over on him. He didn't even want to caution her for being chancy. She made him want to throw down his quill, spill his ink, and grind his pounce beneath his heel.

"Lookee here, Lucian," she crowed when she returned, glad as a girl. Her catch dangled from a long stick, the fishes' gaping mouths hooked.

Lucian took the offering, his dark features shining his pleasure. "We'll have us a fine fish supper with some to spare."

And so they did, Sion glad that Raven was on guard and not at the evening meal. Though Tempe, he noticed, set aside a large portion for him even before Nate said grace.

She sat between them, daintily eating her fish and picking out the bones. "Ma always said a body needs bread to wash down any fish bones. But this here'll have to do."

Baked in the coals of a near smokeless fire and salted, the catfish and perch soon disappeared. Sated, Hascal and Spencer burped their appreciation. Sion glared at them as they wiped their hands on their filthy shirts.

Mindful of his own unshaven, unwashed state, he pondered a good scrubbing. His hand found his jaw. He had soft soap enough in a gourd. His skin itched for a clean shirt. But what need had he of a clean shirt? He was not courting.

He glanced up. Tempe was looking at him during a lull in the scant conversation. Despite her trail-worn state and the hat she usually wore, she had a summer's glow about her, skin tan as a doe, a flush of pink riding her cheekbones. She glanced away, as did he.

Even saddle sore and shy of a wash, she had a natural tidiness and modesty about her. As he thought it, studying the dirt beneath his fingernails, she up and disappeared, the last of daylight with her.

To the necessary, likely.

Cornelius, served supper beneath his awning, paused in his work as she passed. The axemen began playing cards while waiting their turn at watch as Lucian cleaned tin cups and trenchers.

"What say you we have us a round of pokey?"

Pokey was Nate's name for any card game. Usually tempted, Sion shook his head. "If I don't see to this beard . . ." He left off, deciding to shave first. Tempe had told him of a pool of water rimmed by boulders farther downriver, deep enough for a bath.

Restless, still feverishly hot, he set out with Annie, a clean shirt rolled around a razor, shard of mirror, and comb. He nearly forgot the soft soap, but Nate reminded him at the last.

He'd be presentable again. Or bust.

Barefoot, Tempe hovered on a slab of rock, remembering. The pool was smaller than she recalled that time with Pa, shrunken now in summer but still beguiling, only hip deep when it had once been over her head. Her gaze cut clear to the bottom. High above in the cliff side a small falls was a frothing, twisting white as it tore free of its rocky spill, misting every rock and bit of moss, stirring the feathery ferns that gathered around the pool's rim.

She was torn between shedding her shift or not, but modesty won out. The worn linen pooled around her, then lay limp as water licked her ankles and rose to her neck. Holding her breath, she went under, the pool's cool embrace erasing every speck of heat.

When she finished her bath, skin tingling, every nerve enlivened, it was full dark. The camp was not far and the moon was new. Unsure when she'd next bathe, she stood behind the waterfall, missing her beloved moonbow and the Shawnee River country she called home.

It was now, as Sion said, too late to turn back. Once this bit of surveying was done, they'd ford the Green and chain west to the mammoth underground caves, a favorite haunt of her father. Just yesterday she'd slipped in the telling, nearly spilling her secret.

"There's saltpeter in the caves, so P—" She nearly choked on the word *Pa*, but recovered and changed course. "So people say."

Sion had looked hard at her but she'd hurried on, giving him no time to question.

A-shiver, she raised her eyes. The slant of the moon told her she'd overstayed her welcome, and the men might come looking for her. Her shift, wet to the skin, would be dry by morning. Reluctant to move from behind the watery curtain, she took a small step toward the bank. And froze.

Sion stood at the farthermost reaches of the pool, where the river had shoved boulders along the bank and hemmed the water in. Had he not seen her? The falls and her white shift hid her well. She stood still as stone to one side, winning an unrivaled look at him through the cascading curtain.

Never had she watched a man so intently. Modesty nearly made her turn her head. He bent, untying leather garters that held up deerskin leggings. His linen shirt, begrimed and torn in places, was in need of scouring—but first he raised his head and took another look at his rifle where it rested butt end to the ground and barrel to the sky, before stepping into the water, shirt and all. Unbelted, the garment nearly reached his knees, shining like a candle flame in the darkness, a perfect target.

Had she been his foe, a well-placed arrow would have met an easy mark, and his would have been a watery grave. But she was his friend, if that. More his guide. And if he discovered her here . . .

His beard was gone. Moonlight limned his clean-shaven features and illuminated his disgust as he pulled his dirty shirt overhead, smeared it with soft soap, and scrubbed it by hand. Waist-deep in water, he worked quickly. Amused, she watched as he rinsed free the soap and wrung the shirt out before he flung it atop a rock.

In another breath he was gone, disappearing beneath the water for so long she couldn't tell just where he was. Seconds ticked by and still he did not surface.

Her gasp seemed loud as a gunshot when one hard hand shackled her left ankle, and with a distinct jerk she was pitched forward into the pool.

Sputtering, still gasping, she came up out of the water and faced him, stung by his low laughter. "Do you oft lay in wait behind waterfalls, Miss Tucker?"

Her hands slicked back her hair. "I was here first. You left me little choice."

"And are you clean? Or do you need another ducking?"

Again she went under, held captive by his fierce grasp. He had her by the waist this time, so quick she didn't have time to dodge him or catch her breath. Water burned her nose and sparked her temper. Wrenching away, she slipped on a mossy stone and nearly went under again. Sure-footed at last, she whacked him with a spray of water, laughing when he shook his head from side to side to clear his vision.

"Truce," he said, teeth flashing white.

She eased then, savoring the feel of the water, this new side of him. The old Sion was no more. *This* was the man Harper had fallen in love with. She could understand that now. What she couldn't bridge was the change. The young, quick-to-smile Sion had gotten lost and then was found here tonight ever so briefly, before giving way to the hardened man he'd become.

Wonder crept in. And a telling awkwardness. She would have to retreat first because he . . . Flushing, she looked away and studied the falls. Because he had nothing on beneath all that water. The realization sent her out of the pool, more mindful of her own immodest state.

She'd best hasten back to camp the way she'd come. It wouldn't do to sashay in with him like a strumpet. Though she was a far cry from a lady according to Cornelius Lyon, her sense of decency was unshaken. Turning her back to Sion, she put on her moccasins and gathered up her few belongings, leaving him to the magic of the moonlight.

Lucian's leg was still ailing him, so she helped clean up after supper the next eve. "Obliged, Miss Tempe. I'm about to stand watch. Good thing my leg don't interfere with guard duty."

"You'd be a good hand in the middle ground at Boone's Fort or Harrod's."

"That I'd like to see," he murmured with a wistful smile. "That I would, aye."

The wind had finally gentled, rippling the surface of the river and the shirt she'd sewn him. He wore the walnut-dyed garment proudly, his shoulders a bit straighter. He squatted on the gravelly bank, washing out a kettle, while her gaze roamed, rifle by her side. The Green flowed mostly silent at midsummer, allowing her to hear any approach if one could hear a silent foe. She looked down, her moccasins worn beyond use. Nate, handy with an awl, was making her a new pair.

She and Lucian returned to camp to find the chain carriers at cards, Cornelius perusing his maps, and Sion checking equipment. Summer daylight meant less rest, and she felt it to her bones. How good a full meal would be. A new shift and stays.

She unrolled her bedding, nearly sighing at the memory of her feather tick. By now she was used to hard ground if not men on all sides of her. She knew their nighttime habits by heart. Sion never snored. Nate was one to make water from midnight to daylight. Cornelius thrashed and mumbled like a man possessed. Spencer and Hascal raised a ruckus between them, requiring those nearest to poke and prod them into quiet. Raven was so silent she wondered if he slept.

Once Sion had rolled too close, fitting his lengthy frame to hers in a breathless moment that left her weak all over. Was he thinking she was Harper? Needing his wife? No sooner had she thought it than he came awake and righted himself.

Since that night she was more aware of him. When he was near, all the other men faded to shadows. Somewhere along the trail she'd succumbed to the lure of him, that sweet pulsing that made her feel so . . . alive. She was too aware of him. Too tuned to him. Astute as he was, did he sense that?

Lately she had trouble looking him in the eye and answering any simple question he put to her, fearful he might see all that stirred beneath. Betimes the very air seemed to crackle. There was a new tie between them, thin as silk thread, invisible but heartfelt. Or was she only woolgathering?

Now he stood close by, holding a pocket compass in hand. "Tempe, what can you tell me about the caves?"

Best ask Raven.

The words died. She was aware of one thing. He'd started saying *Tempe* again. The elusive thread between them tightened. "The caves," she echoed, smoothing out her blanket. "We're nearly there."

He sat down on his bedroll, compass still in hand. "You've been before."

"Aye." Even now she felt its chill breath, dank and misty. "There's an entrance—a large one—near the Green. You can't miss it." And then she shivered, recalling the bones she and Pa had come across, bleached and dusty, near the entrance. "There's said to be an underground river. Fish without eyes. Saltpeter enough for gunpowder to hold all of Kentucke." She had his attention now. Men were rabid about the caves. Many a time she'd heard talk of their explorations at the inn. Mud in their blood, Ma said.

Sitting back on her heels, she admitted, "It's not for the faint of heart. There are bats by the hundreds. Sudden falls. Tight crawls and muddy tunnels."

"Light?"

She nearly chuckled at his terseness. He had a curious way of carrying on a conversation with a single word. "Cane torches last a good while."

"How far did you go?"

She hesitated, resurrecting that tense time. "I disremember." She had a bad feeling about the caves. All that dark. "Word is you can go for miles if your light lasts. We—" The word hung in her throat. She sighed, tired of hiding Pa. Big and ornery as he was, he could hide himself. "We didn't go far."

"We?"

"My pa and I." She could utter no more. She prayed he wouldn't dig deeper. To her surprise he changed course.

"We'll go on a little ramble. Canoe down the Green and have the rest of the party follow on foot. I need to get the lay of the land before laying any more line."

"And just where do you aim to get this canoe?" She stared at him, catching his half smile in the gathering shadows.

"What do you think Raven and I have been doing away from camp the last day or so?"

She'd wondered but guessed they'd gone on a scout whilst Cornelius colored his maps and the rest of them rested. How she'd chafed at Sion's absence.

Thrusting his compass in the bosom of his hunting shirt, he stood and took up his rifle. "At first light we'll set out."

"You and Raven?" she queried.

"Nay." A sly wink—or had she only imagined it? "You and me."

23

He had learned a long time ago, maybe been born with the knowledge that if you made a bold decision and followed it with bold action more often than not you could make it work for you.

—Janice Holt Giles, *Run Me a River*

Raven and Sion had fashioned a well-made bark canoe. Flat-bottomed and wide of beam, it was crafted of birch bark, now sunk beneath the Green by large rocks, the ash paddles hidden in a hollow log. She and Pa had done the same along the Shawnee River, but she never expected Sion to take the time to make one, especially with Raven.

With Sion at the stern as steersman and her at the bow, they crouched, sitting on their heels for better balance. Before they'd gone far they'd established a rhythm. The riverbanks became a blur of green. Should there be any enemy about, they couldn't aim at so fast a moving target, so she paddled with an easy indifference, free to savor her surroundings.

Springs that had burst forth from rocky bluffs in April had now withered to a trickle on both sides of them. Sandbars and small islands abounded, the Green feeding smaller rivers that seemed no wider than a hair ribbon. Her spirit expanded with a rush, the feel of the wind against her flushed cheek and the man in back of her a needed tonic.

She kept a close eye on her surroundings to gauge when to run ashore. If memory served, the Green ran fairly straight before taking a sharp southerly bend near the mouth of the caves. She'd been so wide-eyed that last trip she'd not forgotten. Pa lost a paddle at that very spot and nearly upset their canoe, the river high in late spring. It was half as mulish now and the paddling was easier, the only threat an occasional boulder or floating snag.

The sun beat down, reflecting so fiercely off the water Tempe squinted beneath the brim of her hat. An hour in, the sky darkened, snuffing the sun, but the gray clouds were simply a vast flock of pigeons, their wing beats like the distant roll of thunder.

The soft-sloping hills began to call out to her like an old acquaintance bidding her welcome. Beneath a flinty ridge were the caves. Their entrance. One of several, Pa said.

Did Sion mean to explore? She braced herself for bats and salamanders and the queer crickets that made no sound but jumped about, song starved in their honeycombed caverns.

They finally ran ashore near the spot she and Pa had grounded. Taking a long swig from her canteen, she waited as Sion gathered their rifles before helping him hide the canoe in a laurel thicket. Noon now, it seemed hotter here, the air thick with the whine and swirl of insects.

Yet nothing—not the heat nor the swarm—could dim her quiet delight in the moment. Sion could have come here with

Raven or Nate or any of the others, but he'd chosen her. Maybe he didn't disdain her after all.

They started away from ridge and river single file, she ten paces behind. The only thing wearisome about a scout was the utter quiet. Listening hard was essential. Tempe had learned to walk backwards silently, covering their trail when she had to.

She hadn't told Sion of her growing unease the nearer they came to the caves, or that, once tepid at the start of their journey, her unrest had reached a full boil this far west. Once Pa said she possessed an uncanny instinct about the woods. Did Sion share that same presentiment of danger?

Beneath the canopy of dense forest, they moved without bringing a halt to the forest sounds. Catbirds and robins sang and squirrels chattered undisturbed. A dull, distant roar bespoke tumbling waters.

So intent was she on their steps she left a thousand things unadmired. A fetching clump of maidenhair fern. The glint of the river through the trees. A vine-covered maple slightly tinted with the colors of the coming autumn.

They were closing in on the caves. Here the past winter's wind had done its work felling trees, which made their approach chancy. The windfall was ample enough to hide a whole band of Indians.

They stepped carefully, leaving no sign, hardly daring to breathe. She tensed tight as a fiddle string, half expecting the crack of a rifle or whoosh of an arrow. Her gun suddenly seemed heavy, her palms slick, the heat blistering. Sweat trickled into her eyes and set them afire despite a pennyroyal-lined cloth beneath her wide-brimmed hat.

Sion stopped. Knelt. She felt an overwhelming urge to cough. Reaching up, she yanked the cloth free and muffled the sound as he examined the ground. The faintest imprint had been left in the earth ahead of them, made by a moccasin toed inward. More than one.

She leveled her gaze on the surrounding woods, wiping the sheen from her face and neck with the cloth. Sion looked a mite cooler, one jaw swelled slightly from the lead balls he mouthed to keep thirst at bay. Beneath his felt hat his hair-line curled slightly but mostly lay damp against his skull. She longed to smooth the sweat from his brow. It reflected mightily, as much a signal as Cornelius's scarlet handkerchief.

In an odd about-face, she craved the coolness of the caves, that labyrinth of stone where the darkness was absolute. Just ahead, the shaded opening yawned at them through a small, sun-dappled meadow. Her focus narrowed to a nearby crab apple, the dusty bark marred by a handprint, the leaves bruised. When Sion looked at her she gestured to the subtle sign, and he thumbed downward, indicating the obvious.

Danger.

She crouched beside him, her gaze lifting to the forested ridge to the south where deep shadows stood. Slowly, like a mist settling, the shadows took shape. Cherokee . . . Shaw-nee. A whole slew of them. Frozen in place, they watched the Indians approach. The windfall would not hide the two of them much longer.

Rapt, she barely felt the touch of Sion's hand. It wasn't till he crawled away from her that she sensed emptiness and followed.

A hollow sycamore ten paces ahead was his aim. Big as it was, she'd noticed it when they'd first come into these woods. A grandpappy of a tree, past its prime, a massive shelter.

Stones and pine needles bit into her knees. Every thrust forward became a prayer. *Lord, help.* Fearful her canteen would clink and give them away, she abandoned it beneath some brush.

Though I walk in the midst of trouble, thou wilt revive me. Nate had read these very verses on the Sabbath. *I will give peace in the land, and ye shall lie down, and none shall make you afraid.*

The earthy smell of the sycamore, ancient and decayed, enveloped her as she crawled into its hollow center. Heart pulsing in her ears, she flexed her limbs and stood like Sion had a moment before, taking care to stay clear of the knothole at chin level. For the moment Sion was looking through the knothole from the side, back pressed against bark, Annie in hand.

Single file, the Indians continued their silent march. Like the first war party they'd encountered, these men were stripped nearly bare, their bodies agleam with paint and bear grease. They were a formidable, grim-faced foe, seemingly without end. Yet Tempe was aware of only one of them.

Just behind the lead Indian was Big Jim. She shut her eyes, her belly with its bit of jerky and parched corn beginning to roil. Sighting Five Killer with the previous war party had been grief enough. Bad to the bone he was, but Big Jim was worse. The Boones had opened their home to him on the Yadkin more than once, given him meat and bread, called him friend. In turn he'd joined Five Killer and others and led the ambush in Powell Valley. Or so it was said.

The memory was too much. Too raw. Would it never fade? Jerking her gaze from the Indians, she looked to Sion like he was the answer to her rising anguish.

At his most cautious, he stood perfectly still, ready to take action at a second's notice. They had powder and bullet lead enough, but what were two pitted against so many?

Eyes trained on the war party through the knothole, he was as calm as if encountering a herd of elk. She latched on to that look, that uncanny calm, lest she be swept away by the unforgiving onslaught of memory.

Unexpectedly, as if sensing her turmoil, he turned slightly toward her, easing his rifle to the ground. Her body was atremble. She felt a telling wetness on her cheeks.

He reached out a hand to circle her waist. The roughened fingers of his other hand, damp from her tears, trailed to her throat, giving rise to a shiver. In a heartbeat, she lost all thought of the enemy marching past, the danger of the moment blotted out as sweetness swept in.

The brims of their hats touched as Sion lowered his face to hers, unseating her black felt. It fell like a whisper down her back, dangling from its leather tie. He leaned into her, the burly, leathery heft of him so unfamiliar yet so . . . pleasing. She gave a little sigh as his hand cupped the back of her head, fingers tangling in her braid. The brush of his lips was warm.

No thought of James. Nor Harper. Just the two of them, here and now, pressed together in a hollow tree, whilst death stalked past.

He kissed her softly then soundly. She lost count of his kisses. Her arms went around his neck. The feel of his mouth on hers, feathery and brusque by turns, came to be as natural as breathing. Only she couldn't breathe. He stole all her air.

The hammering of a woodpecker farther up the tree restored all reason. She pushed at Sion's chest and he stepped back, attention returning to the woods. The Indians had gone, the forest sounds slowly resuming as if the Indians had never been there at all.

"What," she whispered, still breathless, "made you do *that*?"

His smile surfaced, turning her weak-kneed all over again. "I figured if this was the end of the trail I'd not leave any unfinished business betwixt us. But I misdoubt I'll have a killing need to repeat it."

The low words sparked her temper. So he dallied, did he? Then set her aside so easily? She simmered, unable to risk any more talk even whispered.

For half an hour they waited without touching, backs against the rough inner bark. Her heart settled but would never be the same. Sion seemed unchanged, giving no indication he'd nearly kissed her senseless, his tanned features composed and watchful.

"Harper," she finally whispered, a question in the word.

He looked at her again. "Harper's dead, Tempe." His slate gaze softened. "As dead as your James."

Expertly, the canoe shot into the jade water as if the very bank was aflame. Sion and Tempe paddled up the Green as they'd paddled down. Smoothly. Silently. Swiftly. Sion half expected to see the war party lined up along the bank, but the woods had absorbed them. They were likely en route to join the assault on the settlements in the middle ground.

Disappointment pooled in his chest that his hope of entering the caves had been thwarted. He felt it too chancy to remain. But nothing could contain the bubbling pleasure he felt having come away with those kisses, no war party intervening.

Death had come near, and he'd resolved to have no unsatisfied longings. No regrets. If his life was to end he'd go on a high note, in Tempe Tucker's arms.

His gaze left the high limestone gorge they'd entered to

take her in. Beneath her battered hat her fraying braid had unraveled completely. Like corn silk her hair had been, twined in his callused fingers. The color of maple sugar, it rippled to her waist, the very place he'd first set his hands in a tentative bid to gauge her reaction.

There were kisses . . . and there were kisses. He hadn't just kissed her. She'd kissed him. With the same unrighteous urgency he'd felt himself. The strength of her response hardly surprised him. She kissed as wholeheartedly as she did everything else. With abandon and a breathtaking thoroughness.

Aye, she'd been willing but emotional. The arrival of the Indians had shaken loose a memory, of James Boone, no doubt. Other than question him about Harper, she'd said no more. Now he only heard birdsong and the river's sweeping rush.

Everything had changed. Only it hadn't. They sat in camp that evening—every man present but Raven, who stood watch—partaking of their stale corn and tough meat, and listening as Sion told of their river ride and crossing paths with the war party. Tempe half expected him to recount the intimate details of their sycamore sojourn.

"So how long were you holed up in that hollow tree?" Nate wanted to know.

Long enough to make me forget I was sweat-stained and a hairbreadth away from harm.

Tempe bit her lip to keep a smile from forming as Sion murmured, "Half an hour or better."

Cornelius took out his pipe and began stuffing it with tobacco crumbles. "Cherokee and Shawnee, you say?"

"Aye. About fifty, to my reckoning."

At this Tempe stared at him. Did he have eyes in the back of his head whilst he kissed her? Or was fifty just a wild guess?

"Far too many." Cornelius gave a shudder as Lucian lit his pipe from a bit of flint and tinder. "We've seen no sign here. For all the talk back east, the country should be overrun with savages, but instead we only get an occasional glimpse."

"That's all the Indian I want," Spencer muttered, oddly irritable.

Hascal pulled a long face. "I wonder if the Kentucke forts are still standin'?"

"Time'll tell," Nate said, knocking the dottle out of his pipe. "Since that war party you saw was on the *other* side of the river, I reckon I'll have a smoke myself."

"It might just be your last," Spencer warned, glancing over his shoulder.

Looking to her lap, Tempe picked at a threadbare seam in her skirt, reliving in slow motion the breathless moments when Sion touched her and made her his, if kisses counted as claiming. On the heels of her wondering came Harper.

How had she died? When? Had her passing caused the festering wound between Sion and Cornelius?

Cornelius regarded Sion through the smoky haze of his pipe. The fragrant tobacco drifted to Tempe, a welcome mask for unwashed men. "Well, Morgan, my map work is progressing, but I believe your guidebook is . . . um . . . sorely lacking. You seem to have an inordinate fondness for going out on these scouts of yours and leaving your paperwork unfinished."

The slight seemed to have no effect. Sion studied his pocket compass with keen concentration, no change in his expression, but Tempe was coming to know that troublesome edge to his voice when he said, "I leave your maps to you. You'd best leave my work to me."

"I understand your surveyin' field book. But a guidebook?" Nate removed his hat and scratched his head. "Ain't that type of thing full of lies and exaggerations? Lurin' poor folks beyond the Gap to lose their scalps?"

Cornelius ignored him, firing another question at Sion. "If you plan to have one of my maps engraved and printed in Philadelphia to include in this guidebook of yours, I insist on the right to a title." He drew hard on his pipe, looking thoughtful. "*The Discovery, Settlement, and Present State of Kentucke* shall do nicely. I believe a first printing of fifteen hundred copies is adequate and two pounds per copy a fair price."

Nate gave a low whistle. "Two pounds?"

"And since General Washington is known to you, Morgan, I suggest you seek an endorsement from him."

"Anything else?" Sion queried, looking up at him with barely veiled disgust.

To Tempe's surprise, Cornelius said no more. They all fell silent as wolves began howling, chilling in their clarity and range. Hascal and Spencer exchanged troubled looks.

Without looking at Sion again, Tempe left their tight circle to take her turn at watch as the moon rose. Dark brought a blessed coolness, much like the caves. At her approach Raven's teeth flashed white as he smiled. Dog-tired she was, but she greeted him with quiet gladness.

"So the Long Knife wants to conquer the underground," he said beneath the wolves' noise.

"We came near the entrance . . ." She left off. Raven knew they'd had a close call with the war party. She'd overheard Sion tell him so. "We went no farther."

"The Long Knife won't leave the country till he returns there."

She'd suspected as much. Was Raven getting weary of their journey? Her own feelings were now in such disarray she felt knotted from head to toe. Mention of a guidebook, all this surveying, went against the grain. "The work's nearly done, Morgan says. He has his sights set on the Falls of Ohio, then they'll go upriver to Fort Henry."

"And you, *oginalii*?" Raven was standing back to back with her, speaking over his shoulder, his eyes ever roaming as the shadows overtook them.

She felt a loss she couldn't explain. Would Sion bid her goodbye? Or having kissed her, would he declare a change in future plans? Ask her to follow him? Her breath came shallow at the thought. If he asked, would she go?

"He is determined to take the land. To help others take it." She'd not heard Raven's voice so grieved, not since she'd found him in the leghold trap. "And then there is you. *Adageyudi*."

"*Adageyudi*?" she echoed.

"The Long Knife has taken you to heart . . . *adageyudi*."

The words sank into her restlessly. Hadn't she and Sion had this very same conversation about Raven? She couldn't deny Raven's claim, yet she wondered how he'd come by his knowledge. Was Raven jealous? Merciful days. If he tried to kiss her . . .

She stepped clear of him just in case. Here she'd been lamenting her loveless state, and now . . . The prospect of a romantic tie with any living man upended her. James held first place in her heart, no matter those heated, hollow-tree kisses. No matter Raven's shrewd observations.

She stared into the blackness, weary and wary. For all

269

she knew they were surrounded by the enemy, though the Indians usually struck at dawn. "Sion Morgan had a wife. He's still mourning."

'Twas grief that drove him, some unresolved matter over Harper. She didn't know what or why, but she sensed it plain.

Without another word, Raven returned to camp, leaving her in the lonesome dark. Lately he'd turned quieter, nearly as silent as Sion. That openness with her, being beholden to her, had passed.

Stroking her gun's stock, she shucked off any dark thoughts and got her bearings. Sion had posted her to the west of camp and Lucian to the east. Was Lucian as unnerved by the wolves as she?

She prayed silently as she stood watch, tracing the spread of stars with new appreciation. Sion seemed to be beside her in spirit, pointing out constellations whose names she didn't know. Till she'd met him she'd never felt the need to know, the need for more, but he enlarged her borders.

If she followed him, where would he lead?

24

A grand, gloomy, and peculiar place.

—Stephen Bishop,
early explorer and guide,
on Mammoth Cave

The next day was the Sabbath. Raven and Sion disappeared on another scout while the rest of them stood watch and minded the camp. Low-hung slate clouds seemed to press the heat down till sweat ran out of their every pore. Tempe could feel the coming rain even before the growl of thunder.

She heard the first spattering drops on the canopy of trees above before she felt them. Sion had left some papers out, a rock anchoring them, and she abandoned her mending to sweep them out of harm's way lest the ink spot and run. She stepped beneath a rock overhang and paused before securing them with his field papers in a saddlebag. The studious title on one page stretched her simple vocabulary. *A Topographical Description of the Western Territory of North America.* Despite being a borderman in buckskin, Sion seemed as much

a scholar as surveyor. He'd studied law, attended William &
Mary. She'd never known anybody to do the like.

Intrigued, she sat down, thumbing through the papers to
the title at the top of his notes. *The New Eden.* She'd always
wondered his thoughts about Kentucke, but he was like a
closed book, his expression unreadable.

> *3 June, 1777. Laurel rather growing worse. Moun-
> tains very bad, tops of the ridges so covered with Ivy
> and the sides so steep and stony, obliged to cut our way
> through with our Tomahawks. Creek so full of Laurel
> obliged to go up a Branch. Laurel thickest I have seen.*

She felt the sweat and toil of his journey, sensed the strain
on his endurance. The notes, more journal entries, were stern.
Severe. Was he blind to the beauty? What of the sunrise from
the crest of Pine Mountain? The laurel's flowering charms?
The tangle of rivers in the valleys below?

> *11 June, 1777. Came upon a queer inn near a bois-
> terous falls. Blazed a way from the inn to the River. A
> large elm cut down and barked about twenty feet. Two
> hundred yards below this is a white hickory barked
> about sixteen feet.*

She was reminded anew of his mission. Claiming land and
recording identifying marks. She read through the gathered
pages at random till a ragged-edged paper caught her eye.
Folded in half, it begged to be noticed. She opened it, stomach somersaulting as her eyes went wide. As though looking
into a mirror, she stared back at herself. The likeness was
not detailed but was true. Had Cornelius done such? Nay,
the paper bore Sion's initials in a crumpled corner.

His writing hand was like all the rest of him. Strong. Memorable. Steadfast. A strange whim assailed her. She longed to stumble upon her name written in his heavy hand.

Came across a doe-eyed girl, the prettiest I ever saw. Gave chase through the woods to a fine inn where I feasted to my heart's content.

But surely the drawing was enough. Yet what did it signify? That Sion was smitten? Bedeviled by her in some manner? She smiled at such fancy, earning a curious look from Nate. Off watch, he stood over her, surprising her. Last she knew he was seeing to the horses.

Cheeks pinking, she thrust the papers in the saddlebag, tying it shut for safekeeping. "Mister Morgan's papers were getting wet. I thought I might . . ."

"Read 'em?" There was no censure in Nate's query. He dropped to his haunches. Together they peered out of the rock haven. "You got a mighty big curiosity where Sion's concerned."

"Do you blame me?"

"Blame you? A pretty little gal like you? A big strappin' man like him?" He gave a decisive shake of his head. "I ain't so old I forget what it's like to be love struck."

Love struck? Was he talking about Sion? Or the both of them? An uncomfortable heat suffused her. Matters of the heart were hard to hide. Betimes they defied words, shining out bright as a lantern.

She took a breath. "Sion told me about Harper." At Nate's surprise, she said in low tones, "Only that she died. He didn't say when . . . how."

"And not knowin' is pesterin' your conscience."

She nodded. "I daren't ask him. This matter with Harper goes deep."

Nate removed his hat, scratching at his head with a grubby hand. "I'll make you a deal. I'll tell you about Harper . . . if you'll tell me about your pa."

A cold hand squeezed her heart. What exactly did he mean by that? Yet she sensed Nate's was a harmless curiosity. At the moment Harper Lyon Morgan was uppermost. Tempe stuffed any concerns about Pa to the back of her mind. "You don't reckon Mister Morgan would mind you telling?"

"Naw. I've rethunk the matter." Nate spoke with a confidence borne of a bone-deep tie. "Where'd you leave off last time?"

The thread was easily retrieved. She'd turned it over in her mind till it seemed woven into the very fabric of her being. "'Twas when Harper followed Sion to Williamsburg and they were wed. Then they went to Fort Henry, where he signed on as scout."

"Aye, Fort Henry." Nate took a breath, the rise of the wind rustling the leaves all around them. "Farther downriver, just a bit east, Sion built a little cabin on land he'd claimed. Built it snug and sweet, just right for his bride. But then the Indians started raidin' and settin' fires to fields, drivin' the settlers back into the fort. Harper hated bein' behind pickets. Never could get used to the frontier bein' so different than her home place."

"Oakwood?"

He gave a nod. "She'd sent word for her father and Cornelius to journey up and see her, meet her at the cabin. She wanted to return home with them for a spell. Sion knew nothin' about their comin'. He was away on a scout. So one summer's day Harper slipped out of the fort without tellin' anyone she was bent on the cabin. She was"—his voice deepened—"near her time."

With child? Tempe pondered this new wrinkle, watching the clouds scurry overhead. Nate needn't tell her the rest. From his mournful tone she sensed Harper's rashness was her and her child's undoing.

"Harper got to the cabin all right but left a plain trail. A war party, mostly Wyandot, were raidin' the farms thereabouts. They set fire to Sion's fine cabin—and tomahawked Harper on the threshold. It was this that old Mister Lyon and Cornelius come upon soon after. The old man was so overcome by the rigors of the journey and the sight of his daughter, he was dead by nightfall. Some said it was his heart . . ." Nate gave a painful grimace. "When Sion got back to Fort Henry, there sat Cornelius, fatherless and sisterless and blamin' Sion more than the Indians."

Tempe sat stunned, sensing the anguish on all sides. Nate painted so vivid a picture she felt its shadow. Harper had been unfit for the wilderness. Did Sion blame himself for her death? Her discontent? Tempe had seen but a few highborn women come through the inn. Most had slaves to do the tedious work for them, but nothing could protect a woman from the rigors of the frontier.

"There's more to be told." Nate reached inside his budget and extracted a plug of tobacco. Tempe waited, on tenterhooks till he stuffed it inside his cheek. "They buried Harper and the babe and her pa outside fort walls. Cornelius stayed on, too a-frighted to make the trip back to Oakwood. Since he wasn't the firstborn, his older brother inherited most everything, cuttin' him out."

So Cornelius's bitterness wasn't all Sion's doing but likely stemmed from being secondborn too. "He and Sion are an unlikely pair, working together as they do."

Nate talked around his tobacco. "One has what the other lacks, at least till this journey's done. Cornelius thinks he'll earn a heap off that guidebook. Truth be told, Sion bides Cornelius out of guilt, mebbe, more than a need of his maps. Sion has plenty of coin comin' from that stack of land warrants there." He thumped the saddlebag. "He plans to part with Cornelius soon as the work is done."

Would it ever be done? An expectant silence ensued. 'Twas her turn, her part of the bargain. She took a breath, unwilling to plunge into untried waters, unsure if she could trust Nate. Her tale was overdue for honesty's sake . . . but Pa would tan her hide if he heard her tell it. Removing her hat, she began to fan her face. The rain had turned the ground steamy as a hot spring.

"After the massacre in Powell Valley, nothing seemed to work in our favor." Her voice was low, so muted she wondered if the hard-of-hearing Nate would catch the gist of it. She paused, wrestling with the details. "We'd parted with everything we had to come into Kentucke with the Boones. Like a bunch of beggars we holed up at a fort along the Clinch."

Nate looked pensive. "Fort Blackmore?"

"Aye." Her voice thickened as emotion knotted her throat. "It was a mournful time. A lean time." If memory had a palette like Cornelius's prized watercolors, hers would be black. "We'd not been there long when my father decided to settle out on an abandoned claim along Stony Creek. A Crown surveyor happened by the fort about this time and took Pa to task about the land—"

"Did that surveyor go by the name of Frederick Ice?"

276

The bold question struck her as hard as Pa's hand. She opened her mouth to say aye. In doing so, would she help knot the rope around her father's neck?

"Mister Stoner, one of the horses needs lookin' after, as he's lamed."

So absorbed was she in the emotion of the moment, she'd failed to see Hascal's approach.

Nate stood. Stretched. "Excuse me, Miss Tucker."

Breathless with relief, she watched them go, Nate favoring his snakebit leg, as if their prior conversation was of no more consequence than discussing the weather. His limp drove home the memory of Russell, all the rest. She missed her brother and ma, even Paige's jabbering. She was undeniably sore about Pa. Her fingers moved to her lip, healed now and showing a slight scar. They all had scars, every one, seen and unseen.

Heavyhearted, she sat beneath the rock ledge till the rain eased quick as it had come, alone with her mournful memories of James.

And now Harper too.

#

Aye, something new had bloomed between her and Sion, only Tempe couldn't quite lay a finger to it. It was nothing spoken, for he seemed more taciturn than ever, igniting her impatience. 'Twas the unspoken that befuddled and lured her like a bee to a blossom. She was all too aware of him, all too conscious of that overwhelming pull betwixt them. Was it only a few days ago he'd kissed her breathless near the caves? It seemed far longer.

He was bent on returning there, but this time there would be no stolen intimacies, not in the company they were keeping.

Just as well. She was unsure of him. Unsure of his thoughts. His heart. His intentions.

Unsure of herself.

She followed along behind him, this time by land instead of river, amazed he could move so fast and so silently with a party of men behind him. Even Cornelius seemed unusually quiet. Soon they passed the hollow sycamore. She gazed at it, recalling every passionate second and the war party's passing. She looked at Sion, wondering if he thought of it at all.

No one could accuse Sion of being ill prepared. He stood at the cave's gaping mouth with haversack and coiled rope, a dozen unlit cane torches at his feet. He glanced at her as he tied on the rope. He'd hardly said a word to her since their treed tryst. Nate, on the other hand, had tried to corner her at every turn to learn the story of her pa, but she'd purposed to avoid him.

Sion finally spoke to her. "You coming?"

Her disquiet soared. Her gaze fell to the ground. She had no desire to go into that inky pit even with a thousand cane torches. She had a shattering sense that if Sion and Raven went into the labyrinth, Raven would emerge alone. Raven stood near, his sullenness forcing a contrary answer past her tight throat.

"Maybe," she mumbled, full of misgivings. "Aye."

At that Sion tossed her a length of rope. She caught it grudgingly, wishing he'd change his mind and push on toward the Falls of Ohio instead. None of the others showed any inclination to even approach the cave's chilly opening.

"Little more than an abysmal sinkhole." Cornelius strutted about, pronouncing it the black death. "I'd much rather stay above ground and see to my maps."

"We'll be waitin' for you right here," Nate said as the first of the cane torches was lit. "If you need a hand give a holler."

Tempe stared into the entrance, remembering the echoing. Voices carried far, wending down endless dripping passageways. Even a single drop of water sounded like a deluge. When they started down slick rocky steps into the first tunnel, she looked back to see Nate, hat in hand, eyes closed, locked in silent prayer. But she felt little peace.

Walking between Sion and Raven, she seemed the only buffer between them. Something troublesome was still brewing in Raven. She'd felt it for some time now but couldn't lay a finger to it.

As the passage narrowed, she felt like a ground squirrel in a burrow. Sion's stride was shorter, careful yet confident. Raven felt more shadow, at the mercy of their movements. The torches cast rich orange light over dry, dusty thoroughfares, the rock floor beneath their feet rough and uneven. And cold. So cold.

In another mile or so, dread gave way to awe as they entered a huge circular chamber with rock formations in the form of giant icicles. *This* had caught Pa's fancy with its queer otherworldliness. Like something out of *Gulliver's Travels*, he'd said.

Another qualm beset her. Shouldn't Raven be leading? She'd heard Sion ask him to go first, but she'd not witnessed Raven's response. Some Indians had a mortal fear of the caves and stayed clear of them, thinking spirits roamed within. Never had she seen Raven so distant. It shook her to her shoes.

They walked on, skirting a sheet of water cascading down a high wall and disappearing into a crevice. The cold spray turned the ground slippery, and she lost her footing. Raven's hands shot out and steadied her, though Sion, a few paces ahead, was none the wiser.

Beyond the remotest crags she could smell sulphur springs. Truly, the caves seemed little more than a series of sinkholes like Cornelius said, ready to swallow them at the slightest misstep. To his credit, Sion slowed, his gaze scouring the walls and ceiling and floor wherever they trod, making a study of the way they had come by turning round and scrutinizing the way back.

Tempe tried to sweep her mind clean of calamity as they stooped beneath a low place, nearly belly-crawling through a tight tunnel only to emerge into another grand, glorious cavern encrusted with lacy crystals and rocklike flowers.

Sion held his light high, running his free hand over a particularly odd mass of rock-flecked black. "Gypsum," he said. Their torches called out the shining specks like stars, a glittering mass of them that skewed her sense of time and place.

Enough, she wanted to say. But Sion clearly had cave fever. Mud in his blood.

She tried to gauge how far they'd gone. Three miles, four? Though the cave was cool and the pace careful, she felt strangely worn out.

"Wait here," Sion told them.

Ahead of them was a yawning hole of a pit with dark green, lifeless water at the bottom. Slightly dizzy, Tempe held on to a jutting crag, distrustful of her muddy moccasins. A few bats hung over the drop. Were these strange creatures as disturbed by her coming as she was by them?

Her cane light had nearly burned out. With a start she spoke over her shoulder to Raven, in need of another. When he did not answer, she whirled, walled in by blackness.

Raven . . . gone.

With a little cry she held her wan light higher. Had he fallen? Was he hurt? Backing away from the pit she gained solid ground. There she sank to her knees, tracing the retreating imprint of his moccasins.

She went cold then hot. Sick with confusion, she watched the last of her light sputter and fade. "Raven?"

Her answer was a rumble. Faint at first and then a fury. Rock began raining down, no bigger than acorns but stinging and sharp. Dropping her burnt torch, she raised her arms over her head, but nothing could be done to thwart the slide of mud and stone that swept her toward the open pit.

25

A wilderness condition is . . . a condition of straits,
wants, deep distresses, and most deadly dangers.

—Thomas Brooks

The hair on the back of his neck tingled, giving warning. Sion hadn't gone far past the pit when he heard a cry. Tempe? It held a desperation that betokened something dire. And then the rock rained down, snuffing the sound, the cave's stagnant air stirred into such a tempest it nearly snuffed his torch.

"Tempe!" His voice was more roar. It stretched endlessly once the rock slide stilled. He clambered over the muddy morass, the stench of decay turning his stomach. Sharp stones cut into the soles of his moccasins whilst mud oozed in all directions, threatening his balance.

"Tempe!" he shouted again.

Nary another sound was heard once his echo ended save the drip of water. Flinging his torch onto a ledge, he fought back that sick, irreversible sense that it was too late, that nothing could be done to help her.

He finally reached the portion of the cave where he'd last seen her. The slide had made a wide swath, bringing down an abundance of smaller rocks but no boulders.

Clad as she was, she blended in nearly seamlessly with the yellowish mass. It wasn't till the light flared and flickered that her braided hair offered a contrast, the plait half severed by a particularly jagged rock.

She lay on her side, mired from the waist down only inches from the pit. And Raven? Gone. Sion barely gave him a glancing thought as he took Tempe in. Her eyes opened then closed. She said nothing.

Couldn't she speak? On his knees now, he prayed as he dug.

"Tempe . . ." She looked so fragile lying there. He felt choked with the need to know nothing was broken beyond fixing. "Tempe, look at me."

Her head rested atop her flattened hat. It seemed to take her great effort to focus. "Raven's left . . . Get out whilst you can."

She turned her head toward the torch. Half burnt, it promised scant light, not nearly enough to see them to the cave's entrance. If he carried her and the torch too . . . The impossibility weighted him. With every second he tarried he lost more ground.

"Go, Sion." Her muddy fingers latched on to his sleeve. "Leave me be." With those few words all the life seemed to flow out of her.

He watched, wrung with anguish, as a bit of blood formed on her parted lips.

God Almighty. The broken plea resounded inside him as he used the edge of his sleeve to dab the red away. Was she broken inside, in places he couldn't see? He bent his head. The bold prayer was rusty. Desperate.

You raised the dead. Do it again.

Swiping the wetness from his eyes with a quick hand, he fought for his bearings. But the soreness was building. Unbearable. Unrelenting.

She moaned, eyes fluttering open and shut. More blood stained her lips. Moving her was chancy, but he couldn't let her lie there . . . die there . . . atop a pile of rock. Gently, he gathered her up in his arms and held her, his back to the cave wall.

"Tempe . . . I need you." The words came hard for one unused to tender things.

"Need . . . me?"

"Aye, here . . . beyond this cave. I—" He broke off, so full of feeling he was choked. "I've not yet told you—I want you with me—settled on a piece of land all our own . . ."

A fleeting smile, weak but full of wonder. "A dying man's pretty words."

"Nobody's dying, least of all you." He glanced at the torch, silently cursing Raven. "Pretty words, nay. More promise."

"You'd best go, then . . . get help."

"I'll not leave you."

"Then you're more fool than I took you for."

"Aye, a fool—over you." The admission flowed out of him, relieving some of the pain and panic. "Ever since I first saw you along the river that day, I never could wash my mind of you. You're a part of me, everything I do, everywhere I go."

"Pretty words."

"Promises." He had to keep her talking. He'd seen dying men slip across some irretrievable boundary when they fell silent, never to return. "You know where I stand. I would know about you."

Her head lay against his shoulder, her rent braid tearing

at him in fresh ways. A thousand times he'd longed to sink his hands into that glory of hair, savor its silk and scent once he'd freed the leather tie.

"Sion . . . I'm . . . not the least . . . afraid to die." The words came in breathless snatches, unwelcome and wrenching. She was thinking of James again, who was waiting for her in another world. A world that might well deny him.

Overcome, he let her be, a silent, open-eyed prayer of thanks overtaking him. No more blood spotted her lips. But he was far from easy. The light was nearly spent. He would not leave her. And Raven, their one hope of help, was long gone.

She came awake to a flickering light. The patter of rain nearly lulled her back to sleep, and then the sight of Sion's head canted forward in that familiar way held her fast. He had his rifle across his knees and seemed sunk in reflection. The both of them were in another rock shelter, and every inch of her felt bruised and broken, every breath bringing a new ache. The pain ushered in what was best forgotten. A long, dark wait followed by a frantic flight out of the caves. Everything blurred after that. Her world had shrunk from vivid color to shades of gray. It was the emotion of the moment that spoke loudest.

Urgency. Tension. Danger.

She reached for the cup nearest her, fumbled then raised it to her lips, smelling and tasting brandy when what she craved was water. She set it down clumsily. Her slight movement caused Sion to turn. Relief flooded his face—and something akin to heartache.

"Tempe." His tone, both tender and taut, shook her. He

uncorked a canteen, lifted her head, and let a trickle of water slide down her parched throat.

"How long have I been out?"

He studied her in a way he rarely did. "A few hours. You haven't been right since we brought you above ground."

That she believed. Her head felt full of cobwebs. She recalled little of what had happened in the caves, just mud and darkness and panic. "Where are we?" She felt a burning need to know. Were they going a new direction?

"We're headed east toward the settlements. You're in need of a doctor."

She almost smiled at the absurdity of such. "You think to find a doctor at Harrod's or Boone's?"

"I aim to, aye."

He dosed her with more water and cocked an eyebrow when she said, "Best take me to Logan's. It's closer."

"Logan's—St. Asaph's?"

She nodded. "But I'd rather see Boonesborough."

He looked hard at her, again the most vulnerable she'd ever seen him. Did he sense what was couched in those words? The hunger for James? Barring that, the hunger for James's kin? She thrust all thought of the past aside. How could she explain this insatiable need to reunite with James's sisters, see his ma and Daniel himself? As if seeing them could somehow return James to her, or convince her he was gone for good and the past needed burying too.

Taking a breath, or trying to, she looked down the length of herself, clothed in garments that had been hidden in her saddlebags. She had on her marrying dress.

"Your clothes were ruined in the slide," Sion said by way of explanation. "No sooner did Nate and Lucian haul us out of the caves than we crossed paths with another war party heading to the falls. There's sign everywhere. We've been traveling by night in the other direction."

They'd dosed her with brandy for most of it, enabling her to travel. The throbbing in her wrist was all too familiar. Splinted and bound with whang leather, her writing hand was swollen and nicked beyond recognition, a nail missing. For a moment she couldn't feel her feet. Wiggling her toes assured her she had on clean stockings and new moccasins. She wouldn't ask who had done the honors of cleaning and dressing her. Some matters were best left dangling.

She felt humbled. Gone over. Grateful.

"Your wrist is busted. I figured you were the same inside, as you were bleeding from the mouth right after the slide." He took a drink from the canteen. "But you'd only bit your tongue."

He set his jaw as if he would say more but couldn't. She saw stark worry flood his features. Anguish even. The mask was off. This was the true Sion. "Your leg is the worst of it."

"My leg?"

"You've got a gash that needs looking after."

She reached a hand to feel her left thigh swollen with linen wrapping. It formed a slight bulge beneath her petticoat. Strangely, it didn't pain her. "You've been carrying me atop your horse."

"You're not fit to ride solo. I'm thinking of making a sling, a litter between two horses, for you to ride on."

"That'll just slow us. You coddle me and I'll not be worth a continental." The firm words shot down the notion. "We've been moving fast. Where's the equipment?"

"Stashed in a cave."

"Nate and the others?"

"Readying the horses to ride again." He put the canteen

away. "The moon's full. We might make the middle ground before another day's gone if the forts aren't still besieged."

In that case they'd have to turn aside, take another way. She didn't dare dwell on this. The thought of riding right into the thick of bullet lead and smoke had the appeal of caves and mudslides.

The question that had dogged her since they'd gone underground could no longer be silenced. "What's become of Raven?"

He hesitated. "I can't answer that, Tempe."

Nay, he couldn't answer, but he'd obviously given it much thought.

He released a taut breath. "I suspect he joined a war party. He's a formidable foe."

She felt a crushing remorse. "I was wrong to ask him to scout."

"Misguided, mayhap. Raven's an able guide with questionable loyalties. I hardly blame him—or you. There's plenty of shifting sides with the war on."

"I thought—since I helped save his life—he'd be beholden enough to help us till the end." Such a hope seemed hopelessly naïve in hindsight. At Sion's querying look she continued. "I sprang him from a man-hold trap last spring. If I hadn't, he might have died . . ."

"Let it go, Tempe." The forthright words put an end to the matter.

Hascal brought Beck around, and Sion began gathering up their belongings. Tempe spied her book of Psalms lying open atop Herrick's poems. All the cobwebs left her head. "You've been reading to me. I thought I was dreaming."

He grinned. "What else was I supposed to do all the livelong day? Watch you sleep?"

The shadows about his eyes spoke of too much watching and too little rest. He tossed a saddlebag to Lucian, then bent and picked her up.

Despite his gentleness, she gritted her teeth. Without her asking, Lucian brought more brandy. She took two swallows unwillingly as Nate and Cornelius and the chain carriers looked at her apprehensively from atop their mounts. She was hurt worse than she realized. She could see it in their faces. Nate even had an odd sheen about his eyes—further confirmation.

Once she settled in the saddle she wasn't sure she could reach a fort, feeling swimmy headed and ailing. But Sion's arms went round her and she curled into him as best she could, his familiar bulk a blessed solace.

Sion knew the forts along the frontier's westernmost border like he knew his own name. Martin's Station. Blackmore. Glade Hollow. Elk Garden. Maiden Springs. But the Kentucke settlements were an altogether different matter. All the way along Otter Creek then halfway up the ridge to the south of Boone's Fort, Sion expected to find a sea of smoking rubble. Sign was everywhere, yet they'd not come across a single Indian. Heavily wooded, almost vertical in places, the climb was devilish rough, the gnats thick, the danger high. Every rod or so he and Lucian stopped to listen.

Early morn, the dew was heavy, wetting their moccasins. The land bore the overripe scent of late summer, the air shimmering like a cast-iron skillet. Sion longed for late autumn. The first frost.

The crest of the ridge was their reward. The rising sun poured pure gold into the chasm between bluff and outpost.

He narrowed his gaze to take in the scene some four hundred yards distant, hardly trusting his vision.

There, sitting on the south bank of the Chenoa River, was a sight for sore eyes. Four blockhouses with projecting second stories rose up, each made of round sugar-tree logs. Two gates were shut, the main north facing. Outside the fort were a small collection of cabins. Inside the pickets stood an impressive line of log structures, twenty-six by his count, their roofs sloped inward. The back of the fort ran parallel to the river.

Above the rugged slope of the riverbank were two springs and what looked to be a salt lick. An enormous elm shaded one side of the fort, its leafy richness a pleasing contrast to an abundance of ugly stumps. His eyes roamed, making judgments and calculations.

The fort looked too near the river and prone to flooding. No provision for water in times of siege had been made, as the springs were too far. The treed ridge to the west was fine cover for Indians firing directly into the fort. But it was a comely spot nonetheless. It bespoke ingenuity and endurance. Humble welcome.

At the foot of the hill along a small branch was a fine place for a gristmill. His mouth watered at the thought. Their cornmeal had run out long ago. He blinked. Inhaled. The river breeze carried the scent of roasting ears and cornbread. Was he delirious?

A hasty glance told him Lucian was just as dazzled. Sion even heard his stomach rumble. And then Lucian's silent chuckle gave way to a broad belly laugh of delight, his dark face shining.

"Makes me feel like one o' them Israelites finally gettin' some manna in the wilderness."

Sion's need to have Tempe near was keen. He'd left Nate

to look after her once he'd secured her in a little cove near a spring. She'd bid him a calm, clear-eyed goodbye, not giving in to the pain that beset her, but it did little to blunt his rising worry. Her leg needed care he couldn't give her, and that was why he was perched on this ridge, measuring their odds of traversing that muddy river to safety. Her heart needed some answers, and that was why he looked down on Boone's Fort and not Logan's. She needed to see Boonesborough, and he needed her to see it, though he wasn't sure just why.

He expelled a tense breath, his gaze never settling. The stump-littered clearing above the bank, absent of all foliage, was an antidote to ambush yet exposed any friendly approach just the same.

Impatience told him to venture in, but long experience urged restraint. They waited atop an outcropping of rock amid dense hazel till the fort's gates finally swung open, and a group of women came out to milk the cows clustered near the pickets. A party of armed men accompanied them, some continuing on to the springs. All seemed calm. Tranquil, even.

There would be milk. Cheese. Beef. Sion's stomach cramped. Boone's Fort would be home for a time. While Tempe healed he could act as scout if they needed an extra hand. The opportunities unfurled like a Patriot flag, full of promise. He'd pay his party in land, send Cornelius upriver to Fort Pitt and overland to Philadelphia, and wed Tempe if they could find a preacher or justice of the peace. The latter turned him weak-kneed. He spied watermelons in a garden patch just east of the fort, big as powder kegs. What a wedding feast they would have, even among strangers. Mayhap some fiddling and dancing. But for Tempe's leg . . .

Hope and haste got the best of him.

"Let's go in," he told Lucian at last.

26

We shall lay up provisions for a siege. We are all in fine
spirits, and have good crops growing, and intend to
fight hard in order to secure them.

—Daniel Boone

Tempe expected something grand, a good quarter-
mile of stout pickets linked by bulwarks of blockhouses, not this beleaguered structure susceptible
to the first assault. Her disappointment ran deep. But even
a pitiful outpost such as this was better than a worn saddle.

Blackened cornfields to the west told of a recent attack and
promised little meal to grind. Yet she couldn't rid her mind
of the notion of thick wedges of hot cornbread slathered
with butter. Turnips and potatoes. Maybe a melon or two.

She kept this in mind as they crossed the Chenoa River, the
horses adjusting easily to the sluggish current. The muddy
water made her wrinkle her nose, but it was blessedly cool, the
far bank holding the promise of safety. Healing. A full belly.

The sodden horses scrambled up the shore and picked
their way over unfamiliar ground, bypassing stumps and

grass burnt umber by the sun. Sion led, arms round her as he held the reins. She could hear the creak of leather thongs as the fort's front gate slowly opened.

A cow mooed dolefully, and then the fort's dogs began barking, the boldest curs rushing toward them and turning Cornelius's high-strung horse more dauncy. Seeing neatly clothed women in bonnets and aprons waiting just inside the safety of the enclosure—and staring—lent to Tempe's loose ends. Clad in a marrying dress now begrimed with a sodden hem, shorn of half her hair, she lowered her lashes.

Sion had taken a knife and slashed off her remaining braid, what little the rock hadn't severed. Now her hair hung to mid-back, hardly the lush waterfall to her hips of before. But any embarrassment was short-lived. One of the men who greeted them had a pegged head, evidence of a survived scalping. A shiver ran through her at the sight of all that puckered skin about his ears and forehead. The startling pate was bare and round as an egg.

Sion dismounted. Mute, Tempe sat on his horse as introductions were made and he shook hands with men she'd heard about but never seen. Richard Callaway. William Hays. Flanders Callaway. David Gass. Their women stood behind them, sober faced, taking her measure. Her leg was aching, the linen bandage in need of changing.

The bonnet-clad bunch was dominated by a tall young woman, babe in arms, two little girls hanging on her skirts. Tempe softened at the sight of them, reminded of James's sisters. But not one Boone did she see as her gaze scoured all present. What she'd give to meet Susannah and Jemima, Lavina and Becky. But would she even recognize them? The passage of time and all the changes it wrought stole away her gladness.

"I'm hoping for a doctor," Sion was saying quietly, sparing Tempe further unease by being terse.

"No doctor hereabouts," the elder Callaway said matter-of-factly. "This your wife?"

"Nay, Miss Tucker lives down along the Shawnee River. Her family inn-keeps there."

Gass flashed a yellow-toothed smile. "The Moonbow?"

"Aye," Sion answered for her. "I aim to return her there as soon as she can travel."

Her heart squeezed at the finality of his words. So they'd part company at the inn. Try as she might, she still couldn't recall their tense exchange in the caves. Wouldn't she remember if it had been heartfelt? All that filled her mind was the horror of finding Raven gone and the ensuing deluge of rock and mud. The heavy stench of it still seemed to cling to her. She longed for a good soaking, but she doubted a decent tub could be found in so sparse a fort.

Hays looked at Sion's party with an appraising eye. "We're in need of a few more guns. Since the June siege we've been worn down to a nub."

The young woman in back of him spoke softly but distinctly. "I'll see to Miss Tucker." At that she passed the baby to the wrinkled woman beside her and shook the least ones from her skirts. Sion moved to help Tempe down. She swayed a bit, not trusting her leg, and clung to him longer than she should have.

"Nothin' but a hussy," came an overloud womanly whisper.

Stung, Tempe looked to the ground, mortification giving way to understanding. What else were they to think of an unwed woman among so many men? Hadn't she cautioned Pa about the very same?

The tall young woman turned on the whisperer. "What

does it matter how she's come here in the midst of so much wilderness, being in such obvious distress?"

Reaching out a welcoming hand, Tempe's protector drew her farther into the fort's dusty common. "We'll leave the men to their talk." Her chin nearly touched her chest as she looked down the length of Tempe's dress. "There's blood on your skirt."

Tempe flushed, beads of perspiration dotting her upper lip. "It's not what you're thinking." *That* had been hard enough to manage on the trail with so many men and so many miles. "It's my leg."

"Your leg?" The dulcet tone was soothing. "What about your hand?"

Hanging limply at her side, Tempe's hand with its missing nail was all but forgotten.

"You're in need of some comfort, looks like. I've got a pinch of tea. You can take it in the one china cup my granny gave me when I left Virginia."

The simple kindness blunted the other woman's ugly slur. Raising her head, Tempe took in the fort's enclosure where rows of cabins formed the north and south walls.

"Mercy, where are my manners?" The woman's finely freckled skin stretched across high cheekbones, as fair as Tempe's was sun soaked, the brim of her faded bonnet hiding the vivid russet of her hair. "My name's Esther. Esther Hart."

"I'm Temperance—Tempe, most call me."

"How come you to be with so many men?"

"It's a story . . ." She'd tell it in time, but now, thirsty and strangely winded, she held her tongue.

They walked on haltingly. Just when Tempe thought her leg would fail her, Esther thrust open a cabin door, and together they surveyed the dim interior. It was cramped with one room, its sooty fireplace made of rock. Tempe's eyes went immediately to the two loopholes along the back wall just big enough to ram a rifle barrel through. Behind her, one open, unshuttered window faced the fort yard.

The clanging from the blacksmith's forge ushered in the memory of Russell and the barn-shed. Swallowing hard, Tempe fought down the ache his memory always wrought.

"This here belongs to an old granny woman who's gone over to Harrod's to be with kin. We're right next to you. The men you come in with can bunk in the blockhouse down by the necessary."

Esther gestured to a rope bed and slab table and twin hickory chairs with deerskin seats. Gourds, big and little, held sundry things. Buck antlers and wooden pegs were home to a faded sunbonnet and beaten saddlebags, a fishing pole and hands of tobacco. Above was a loft. Tempe could see the outline of two hogsheads of water beneath eaves strung with strings of red pepper and dried herb bundles. All was fragrant. Quiet. The privacy seemed heaven sent.

"I'll make a poultice of oak leaves and dress your leg. But first a bath."

Tempe stared at her, disbelieving. Had they a tub?

"Once you're clean we'll use the water to wash your pretty dress."

Pretty? Esther, bless her, looked on the sunny side of things.

"I have something you can wear in the by-and-by."

She went out, leaving Tempe to shed her filthy garments and shake her short braid loose from its tie. In time Esther maneuvered a hip bath through the narrow cabin door, a man following with steaming buckets. This was heaven sent too.

"In time maybe we'll have us a tunnel leading from the fort to the spring like I hear they have at Logan's," Esther said, setting down soft soap before closing the shutters. "It's a blessing to have enough water, especially when besieged."

In an hour's time the warm bath had stripped away the grime and left Tempe's hair clean. Wrapped in a linen towel, she tried to make light of Esther's grave expression as she examined her leg.

"I wish Granny Mason was here. She'd know what to do."

The fragrant salve Esther applied bespoke familiar, beloved things that crowded the rafters of the Moonbow Inn. Tempe set her jaw as Esther bound the cut leg like Nate had done.

Soon clad in a borrowed, threadbare shift, Tempe waited whilst Esther retrieved more garments. A striped blue and cream petticoat and stays were followed by the sweetest shortgown Tempe had ever seen. Embroidered with tiny rosebuds, the pale ground was lemon-hued, a burst of civility in a roughshod fort.

"This belonged to my mother. She was a lady, a Virginian. She never did take to the fact that my Henry wanted to go into the wilderness. Word came last spring she'd died. I haven't had the occasion to wear her best gown, always bringing one child into the world or nursing another."

Tempe made a move to return the heirloom. "I couldn't—"

"It's good to see it be of use." Esther's smile disarmed all doubt, knitting Tempe's heart to her in unexpected ways. "I reckon that man who brought you in will smile to see you in something different. Sion, I recollect his name was."

Smoothing a sleeve, Tempe nodded as a quiet delight stole over her. Sion was foremost in her thoughts of late. Could Esther sense their tie?

"One of the scouts brung in a buffalo early this morning." Esther moved to the window and reopened the shutter to peruse the common. "We're set to have a little feasting and fiddling. Welcome you proper."

Tempe joined her at the window, a bit startled to see a fire, brazen and bright, crackling inside a ring of stones at the very heart of the fort's common. Lucian and two unknown men were minding the buffalo meat, laughing and talking as they worked. A good many people went about fort business, all strangers.

At last she voiced the question that had dogged her since she'd first come in. "Aren't the Boones here?" Given the fort bore their name, she'd expected Daniel would be the one to meet them at the gates. Her disappointment went deep.

"Captain Boone's likely out on a scout." Esther pointed a slim finger toward a far cabin. "That's his and Rebecca's place over there. Their two eldest daughters have up and married and live in that double cabin opposite."

Susannah and Jemima? Married? Why was she surprised? Younger than Tempe herself, they were desirable, accomplished women and bore the Boone name besides, a coup on the frontier. Likely they'd had their pick of suitors.

Her gaze roamed restlessly, assessing and dismissing men and women by turn, hope rising in her. But there was such a passel of people in the fort she was hard-pressed to name any of them Boones. At the gate more folks were coming in.

"You know the Boones well?" Esther asked, interest enlivening her pale eyes.

Tempe bit her lip. Was it possible to put such in words? "We were part of their party that made a try for Kentucke in '73." She couldn't say James's name. Couldn't relive in the simplest words their valley experience nor her heartache since. "I never thought to see Boonesborough."

Esther let out a rueful chuckle. "I'd not think you'd *want* to see Boonesborough. These poor people were dirty, lousy, ragged, and half starved when we arrived last fall. This year, harassed as we are by Indians, finds us little better."

"But at least you're all together, making a stand." Spying a near rocker, Tempe sat. "Now seems a good time to tell you how I come to be with so many men." In as few words as possible, she shared the tumult of the past month, reliving the caves and how they'd ventured to the middle ground. Esther listened, asking few questions.

"You picked a fine time to arrive. We were under siege till Colonel Bowman and his men marched in from Virginia. Here lately the country's as quiet as I've ever seen it." Esther picked up a comb and began working the tangles out of Tempe's hair. "We're down to fifteen guns, though I can stand up to a loophole good as any man. I'm guessing, since Mister Morgan hired you on as guide, you can say the same."

"I'd rather cook and tend children than rifles and one too many men." As Tempe said it, the cabin door pushed open and two little girls entered, the eldest toting the baby, a fat fist in her mouth.

Esther smiled a welcome, gesturing to the tallest daughter. "This here's Ellender, my oldest, and then Isabella. The baby's Frances." Esther sighed good-naturedly. "Nary a boy in sight."

Tempe reached for the baby, settling her on her lap. Ellender seemed glad to relinquish her burden. "They've grown used to the thunder of the guns, I expect."

"If one can grow used to such. They've spent the better part of this year hiding under the bed playing with their dolls. We're hoping this fall to return to our farm. We settled out a few miles from here. By some miracle our wheat and corn was still standing, so my husband, Henry, brought it in to share. There'll be some roasting ears tonight at supper. And bread."

Mouth watering, Tempe wound a lock of the baby's sweat-dampened hair around one finger, unwilling to leave the cabin but knowing she must, and trying to dismiss the slur she'd heard at the fort's gates. At least she no longer looked like a hussy, clean and modestly dressed, save her bare feet.

The little girls were regarding her with something akin to wonder, as if the bedraggled woman they'd first seen was altogether different from the one who sat before them.

She surrendered to the sweetness of the moment, the weight of the baby warm and pleasurable in her lap. This could be her babe, her least'un. She felt an unbearable urge to kiss the infant's flushed cheek. She finally did.

Esther ceased her combing. "You need a babe of your own, Tempe Tucker. And if you stay on here more'n a day or so, there'll be suitors lined up all the way to the river to oblige you, Sion Morgan or no."

27

I thought it was hard times—no bred, no salt, no vegetables, no fruit of any kind, no Ardent Sperrets, indeed nothing but meet.

—Josiah Collins

Tempe . . . Tempe Tucker?"

The feminine voice swung Tempe around. She faced the young woman whose curves and comely features were but an echo of another time and place. "Jemima Boone?"

"Aye, all growed up, and now a Callaway." Teary-eyed, Jemima rushed forward and enveloped her in a humid, sweat-scented embrace. "Let me look at you." She stepped back, hands firm on Tempe's shoulders. "If you aren't a sight to behold. Prettier than a summer's morn too, even more than when—"

A flash of pain darkened her eyes, and her voice faded. Tempe well knew what James's sister was thinking. There was no need to finish. Tempe forced a smile, determined to move past any awkwardness. "So you're a married woman, Susannah too, Esther tells me."

"Aye, we get on with the business of living out here. One never knows what a day will bring." Jemima smoothed her bodice where it joined her skirt. "No least'uns yet, though Susannah has a baby girl, little Betsy."

"I'm glad to hear it. Needs be more womenfolk around."

Jemima locked eyes with her. "And you? You married to one of those men I hear brought you in?"

Obviously talk spread like fever in the confines of the fort. "Not married, nay." The words all but caught in her throat. She tried to keep the lingering sadness from her tone. "One day, maybe."

"Well, beware a stampede of lonesome men." Jemima gestured toward a chair. "Let's sit a spell. I've heard tell of your folks' inn along the Shawnee River. People say the fare's better than any ordinary in Virginia."

"People are kind. We do what we can." She bit her lip as pain seared her leg when she took a seat. In light of the wretched conditions at Boonesborough, life along the Shawnee seemed almost idyllic. "There's little Indian trouble that way so far out, but I don't expect the peace to last." The handbill flashed to mind—and Russell's involvement with the British, whatever that entailed. "I'd rather hear about you."

Jemima was smiling now, clearly bemused. "You likely know about our canoeing the river last summer and being took by Indians."

"Bits and pieces, mostly how your would-be husband rescued you."

"It makes a fine tale in hindsight, but I'd rather not repeat it. Pa cautioned me against going and I should have heeded him. It's a wonder you made it here safely. How long you aim to stay?"

Tempe raised her shoulders in a shrug, gaze falling to her leg. Leaning forward, she raised her petticoat. "My hope is to get home soon but for this."

Kneeling, Jemima unwrapped the linen bandage about her calf, her features stoic despite the sour odor and sight. "It needs some tending, for true. I know just the trick." She rose and headed toward the door. "I'll be back quick as I can."

Her disappearance allowed Tempe a moment to collect herself. Turning her face away from her leg, she fastened her gaze on a far wall made bright with a tangle of bittersweet vine.

Being here was bittersweet.

She saw James in Jemima's face. Heard him in the cadence of her voice, that distinct lilt true to all the Boones. Though James was long gone and Sion was larger than life, her heart still ran after James. What man would want her, given that? What truehearted woman pined for a lost love while a whole, warm-blooded man was hers for the taking? Dismayed, she swiped a tear away with a callused hand.

"Tempe Tucker?" The gentle question brought Tempe's head around. James's mother spoke from the open doorway. "What's truly ailing you? Your leg . . . or your heart?"

Tempe blinked. Another tear fell. Rebecca came forward, a little more lined, streaks of gray silvering her dark hair, and lay a soothing hand on Tempe's shoulder.

How was it that Rebecca knew, after so long, what Tempe's heart held? Was it so plain she missed James? Dare she confess the half-crazed thought that she'd come here hoping to find him? That in her heart of hearts, her dreams, she'd not buried him in Powell Valley, that some stubborn part of her refused to let go, preferring he live on, solid and beloved and enduring as the ground beneath her feet?

The truth was Boonesborough was full of Boones. But not James.

In Rebecca's left hand was a small basin of elm bark ooze. Tempe had a notion to tell her not to bother, that Esther had tried the same. But maybe Rebecca needed to do this. Maybe Tempe needed her nursing as well.

Looking considerably leaner than she'd been in Powell Valley, Rebecca knelt on the hard floor. The black-haired woman who'd birthed James, nursed and rocked him, and watched him grow then given him over to death, tended to her in silence.

In a kinder, sweeter time and place, Rebecca would have called her *daughter*, celebrated grandchildren and freedom and life beyond fort walls. But here and now, in the sore silence, she could only try to mend her leg and touch her heart. One of life's most painful mysteries was that time moved on, with or without you. Those left behind loved and laughed and resumed living as if you'd never been at all.

"It's good you came to be here." Rebecca spoke softly as she worked, her liver-spotted hands gentle. "Many a time I've wondered how you fared. I hoped you'd marry, start a family someday."

Tempe bit her lip, unable to answer.

"That's a good man who brung you in. Well, one of them." Rebecca's half smile turned her almost girlish. "That Sion Morgan reminds me of Daniel. You could do no better."

Studying the petticoat of Esther's borrowed dress, Tempe fingered a finely sewn seam.

"It's no accident he brought you here. It's time. The Lord made a way and you came." Rebecca's voice held acceptance, both a grieving and a letting go. The ache would never fade, this Tempe knew. But somehow Rebecca had come to terms with it.

"I thought by now I'd join James." Swallowing, Tempe forged ahead. "I've been reckless in those woods, hungering to see him again."

Rebecca looked up, understanding in her gaze. "You've got too much life in you yet. It's not your time."

Tempe took the words in, forgetting her leg, thoughts swinging from James to Sion. Maybe she'd stay on right here, spare herself parting with Sion at the inn . . .

Jemima returned just then, Susannah in her wake bearing little Betsy on one hip. Tempe opened her arms to James's eldest sister, the one who'd cried the longest and loudest at his passing. Little Lavina came in next, now almost as tall as Tempe herself. Did she even remember her beloved older brother?

Soon they all were crying quietly, undone by the moment. And then Jemima, ever good-natured, brought their weepiness to a halt. "Best shush lest the men bust in here thinking we're under siege. Besides, it's a glad day when Tempe returns to us. Reckon we can convince her to stay on at this stubborn fort—or will she slip away with her black-headed borderman?"

They laughed as Rebecca finished with Tempe's leg. Little Betsy began making a fuss, arms open to her granny, wanting some attention.

Tempe looked toward the open window, wondering where Sion was, what he was doing. And what if she did slip away with her black-headed borderman?

Betimes Sion was as hard to read as one of his surveys. For a few halfhearted seconds Tempe pondered what was to come.

But the future was hazy at best, and she'd take what came moment by moment, savoring the humble hospitality of this beleaguered outpost that was, at the moment, standing strong.

Esther Hart was something of a miracle worker. Sion had heard what a fine shot she was. Fresh from the summer siege on their station, the men were generous with their praise, recounting every detail of Boone's onerous run to Virginia for powder. But it was Esther's marksmanship he remembered now—and her miraculous transformation of Tempe.

The late-summer dusk lent a dreamlike quality to the fort enclosure, softening the choking dust and harsh edges of the white oak pickets. When Tempe emerged from a far cabin, Sion realized how much he'd missed her in the few hours they'd been apart. Whether by her continual quiet companionship or his own growing need of her, she'd become as near and dear as the seams of his linen shirt.

Unprepared for the sudden charge in his middle at the sight of her, he lowered his gaze to the ground. But the impression she made remained. Hair caught up atop her head. A delicate dress. The grit of dirt replaced by a rosy glow. And he wasn't the only one who noticed. More than a few men looked her way. Lingered. Tempe stayed beneath the eave of the Hart cabin.

He was barely aware of Esther coming up alongside him where he was minding Beck near the smithy, till the babe she held gave a little cry of discontent. Esther offered him a small smile, bouncing the child on her hip. "I wanted to talk to you about Miss Tucker."

His chest tightened. He lowered his head with the intent of listening.

"It's her leg. The gash is deep. I'm no doctor, but it's causing me to fret."

His high spirits sagged. He looked up again, finding Tempe hemmed in by two men in the span of his and Esther's short conversation. In so small a fort, it didn't take long to sort out who belonged to whom. Or not.

"Is it true there's no doctor at Harrod's—or Logan's?" he asked.

"None to speak of. Just an old granny woman due back any day. I put Miss Tucker in her very cabin."

"Any preacher hereabouts?"

Her brow creased. "Do you aim to bury her—or marry her?"

He nearly chuckled at Esther's honest jest. When he said nothing, she continued on. "There's Squire Boone near at hand. But we don't stand on ceremony in the wilds. Any God-fearing soul can say the words over you till you come by a true preacher."

Though he was open to the notion, a wilderness wedding seemed to slight Tempe somehow. His marrying Harper had been hasty, if legal. He didn't want Tempe to get any inkling he'd leave her, no proper tie to hold him. The Lord's blessing was something he craved. Mayhap Nate's Scripture spouting and Tempe's gentle devotion were wearing him down.

The babe reached out a dimpled hand and grabbed the leather strap of his powder horn. He took the horn off and gave it over, wishing he had a little barley sugar instead. She held it wonderingly, gnawing on the wooden spout plug with tiny teeth. He knew it was snug and no powder would spill, though Esther looked a tad wary.

The thought of his own babe cut in, sudden and sharp. His child had never drawn breath. Sion had fought the strange mourning that followed, wondering how a heart could grieve for a child never held. But maybe it was as Nate said. *For thou hast possessed my reins: thou hast covered me in my mother's womb. I will praise thee; for I am fearfully and wonderfully made: marvellous are thy works; and that my soul knoweth right well.*

"She's far too comely for her own good," Esther told him, eyes on Tempe across the way. "Bad leg or no, you'd best stake your claim."

"I will." He pried his powder horn away from the tiny girl gently, only to set her a-howling again.

At his approach, the men on either side of Tempe melted away. She finally noticed him, the pleasure in her eyes giving way to uncertainty and a guarded hope.

Mindful of her leg, he motioned to a bench near the west blockhouse wall. He wanted to take her hand, stake his claim as Esther said, but the fingers nearest him were splinted and the others were buried in the folds of her skirt.

"I hardly recognized you," he said in a stab at conversation. "I mean . . ."

Her answering smile assured him he'd not misspoken. "Well, there's no mistaking you."

He rubbed his jaw. Though he'd tried to clean up, he'd gotten no further than shaving. "I'll be out on a scout come morning. Be gone two, three days. Whilst I'm away"—he forced lightness into his tone—"try to fend off these fellows. They're nothing but a wake of buzzards."

She chuckled, fingers plucking at a rosebud on her sleeve. "Should I tell them the mighty Morgan said so?"

"Aye, if you like." He rested Annie against the log wall. "It's your wound I'm thinking of."

She sobered, all levity gone, staring at her skirt as if she could see to the injury beneath. "Ma would know what to do."

Her heartfelt words couched a dozen different things. Homesickness. Weariness. Resignation. Regret. She knew her wound might be mortal. She might not ever reach her family.

I am not the least afraid to die.

She was on the verge of saying it again. He could sense it. If she did, he would reach out and still the words before they left her lips.

He swallowed past the tightness in his throat. Twice now he felt he stood in the gap between her and James. She was leaning toward dying. He could feel it. And not only leaning, she welcomed it. The contrary notion sat sourly inside him, so at odds with his newfound hopes.

The twang of a fiddle sounded. The posted lookouts glanced down from their picket perches at the noise. Heartfelt seconds ticked by. Sion was in no mood to dance. But Jemima was partnering with her new husband, Flanders Callaway. Susannah and her groom, Will Hayes, joined in while Rebecca and Daniel watched from the shadows.

Sion had seen Daniel talking with Tempe earlier outside the Hart cabin and wondered what they'd said. It had to do with James, no doubt. Always James . . .

Tempe's expression turned poignant. "Betimes I wish life wasn't so chancy. Seems like we try to squeeze in little bits of living between trying to stay alive."

It's only hardest right now, he nearly said. But it wasn't. All of life was a frightful risk. If they weren't bedeviled by Indians, it was illness. Accident. Heartbreak. Separation. What did they have but this present moment?

No doubt the other unfettered men thought the same, for one young, scar-faced fellow came near and called Tempe out as the fiddler struck a reel. Sion watched as she lowered her lashes, declining with a demure smile. His resistance roared.

Did she have to be so downright fetching in her refusal?

Taking Annie back, he struck a sterner pose in order to keep all comers at bay.

"If I could I'd dance with you." Shoulder to shoulder with him, she leaned nearer to be heard over the raucous music. "Only I don't know if you dance."

"It's been a long while." He'd not attended a proper frolic in years. But he enjoyed a good bow hand, and while this fiddler was not the musician Russell was, he still managed a lively tune.

As it was, he felt a sweet contentment just sitting beside her, knowing she was safe from ambush and not out on the trail. Nate approached with two trenchers in hand, one piled high with fried venison collops, the rest buffalo so well roasted it fell off the bone. Tempe exclaimed in delight at the buttered corn, green beans, and cornbread. Sion felt a bit giddy himself at the abundance. Cucumbers and onions and slices of watermelon waited on another table. They didn't have much, but Boonesborough had combined all they had. A welcoming feast, truly.

"You two all right?" Though Nate included them both, it was Tempe he looked to for answer.

Tempe smiled up at him, inviting him to sit. Disappointment shadowed Sion like a cloud when Nate obliged and took a near bench. Nate cared for Tempe like a daughter. Who was Sion to wish him gone? Still, the need to be alone with her was strong, if being alone in a fort full of people was possible.

What he really wanted . . . He gave in to the nagging temptation. What he really wanted was to take her by the hand, away from prying eyes and the noise, and lead her to her cabin, where he'd shut the door and slip all the pins from her hair . . .

Freshly washed, a few strands had defied Esther's careful coil and fell in wayward wisps about Tempe's flushed face. That flush—could it be fever? Blood poison was never far from his thoughts. He shoved the worry away, but it took root, further shrinking his hopes.

She bowed her head as Nate said a prayer, but she ate little, further alarming him. Soon she was clapping in time to the music whilst he finished her supper and his, watching as Cornelius squired every woman present, proving himself an able dancer.

Someone had rolled out a keg. The chain carriers were partaking of some spirits between sets, and Sion hoped Cornelius would continue to act the gentleman. Lucian sat with a burly black man, two women with them. Lucian belonged here on the frontier, a free man, not enslaved by the hard-to-please Cornelius. This injustice bedeviled Sion too.

His mind drifted to matters within his ken. He needed to ride to Harrod's Fort and enter his land claims as required by law. Till the claims were entered, they were invalid and up for dispute.

Paramount was taking Tempe home again. But first she needed to heal. Daniel had asked him about scouting in the meantime since two of the fort's best guns had been killed the month before.

Lord willing, in the midst of all that, he'd woo her.

If he could stay alive.

If she was willing.

28

The Indians shot arrows on the cabin roofs, and set
them on fire . . . then fortunately it commenced raining.

—STEPHEN COOPER

Two days later Tempe stood outside the open doorway
of the east blockhouse, listening to Sion's scouting
report. Small roving bands of Shawnee had burned
several outlying cabins and fields west of Boonesborough, pulling up fruit trees and destroying a great quantity of cribbed
corn.

"I've not come upon any loss of life, but there's sign the
enemy's headed north," Sion finished.

"It'll be a lean winter, what with the loss," Boone replied
matter-of-factly. "The trouble's far from over. My guess is the
Shawnee are making for their camps on the Scioto, gathering
fresh supplies and preparing their warriors for another strike.
It's not called Indian summer for naught. There are only
three forts left standing in the whole of Kentucke. Logan's,
Harrod's, and here."

"Do you have enough provisions to hold?" Sion asked him.

Tempe moved away into the blinding sunlight of late afternoon, wanting to spare herself the answer. Precious little salt, scant powder and lead, and few men . . .

Stopping near Beck, his neck lathered and sides blackened with sweat, she spoke warm words to Sion's faithful mount, wishing she had a carrot or apple. He nuzzled her hand as if searching before she moved on around the fort's perimeter toward the Hart cabin.

Door open, Esther sat sewing, one foot extended to rock the cradle the baby slept in. Her girls played with their cornhusk dolls nearby, their round faces shiny from the heat.

Tempe longed for a shade tree. A cool creek. A breeze that wasn't blocked by pickets. She'd seen a graveyard outside fort walls, but Nate had cautioned her to stay inside the fort. She didn't tell him it was Sion she looked for on the horizon and that she longed to be free, not pent-up like livestock.

Stooping, she took a long, lukewarm drink from a gourd dipper hanging above a water pail before stepping over the threshold of the Hart cabin.

Esther greeted her, her cradle pushing ceasing. "I saw Mister Morgan ride in. Any news?"

"Plenty of sign." Tempe didn't want to alarm her. What if Esther's homestead was one of those burnt? "I'm just glad he's back safe and sound."

She took a seat in the rocker, ready to take the baby in her arms, be of use. Her leg was throbbing, and the pain seemed to go bone deep. Sometimes in the night she cried herself to sleep. But she wouldn't speak of it, not in light of pegged heads and a fresh graveyard.

Tempe admired Esther's work. "You piecing a quilt?"

Squares of various fabrics, some fancy, some plain, caught

her eye, a pleasing blend of Tidewater finery and frontier homespun. Tempe stroked a square of deep-purple velvet.

Esther smiled her serene smile. "It's your marrying quilt."

Tempe looked up. "My *what?*"

"The women in the fort—the Boones mostly—gave over a bit of fabric so you'd have a lovely keepsake. But you can't leave till it's finished."

Touched, Tempe tried to summon words enough to honor the gift. She looked toward the common to see Sion leave the blockhouse. Her heart turned over in such a rush it stole her breath. "There's been no talk of a wedding."

"Talk's hardly needed." Esther plied tiny, even stitches with linen thread. "I've seen the way Mister Morgan looks at you. It's just a matter of time."

Time. A knot formed in her throat. Her leg told her time was against her. She sensed Esther was holding this quilt out like a promise, to offer hope. Hope of healing. Love. A more settled life.

She still wasn't sure of Sion. He felt obligated to her, determined to bring her home, deeply concerned about her leg. Those heated kisses shared along the Green seemed so long ago they had the feel of a dream, yet they'd kindled a fire she feared couldn't be put out, at least on her part.

She wouldn't argue Sion's intentions with Esther. Best leave him to the Lord.

⁂

The steaming kettle on the hearth seemed to sing in the emptiness of the blockhouse. Sion poured hot water into a basin and cooled it down with spring water from a bucket before pulling his shirt over his head. The supper smells still lingered, but Lucian had long since washed the crusty skillets and dirty plates.

Night set in, bringing with it a blessed sense of privacy. By day, everyone knew everybody's comings and goings within fort walls, but beneath the stars they all turned to shadows, gaining a measure of solitude.

He was used to life behind pickets. Fort Henry, being so large, hadn't the cramped feel of Boonesborough. But all that had filled his head during his days along the Ohio were powder and lead and scouting. Not Tempe. Not courting. He'd tried to block the memory of their feverish kisses along the Green River till he was worn out with the effort. She was obviously still in love with James Boone. He couldn't compete with a hallowed memory. Not till she'd buried her past and moved on.

But had he moved on from Harper? Hadn't he once silently sworn he'd take no other wife? Risk a woman in the wilderness? Risk his heart of so much hurt? Why this maddening double-mindedness regarding Tempe? Even now he felt torn with need, burning with the desire to map out a life with her.

He soaped his chest, his mind churning with plans. He'd prayed more than one honest prayer of late, asking for the Lord's hedging and blessing. He had no idea what Tempe's reaction would be when he laid his proposal out before her.

Finished with bathing, he pulled on a clean shirt, wishing for decent breeches and silver knee buckles and shiny shoes. But buckskin and linsey would have to do.

"Well, what have we here?" Cornelius entered, silent as a cat. Sion could smell elderberry wine in the humid air. A dark stain soiled Cornelius's fine linen shirt. "No more rank buckskins?"

Sion didn't reply, reining in his irritation.

"My guess is you're going courting. If so, I have it on good authority that two of the fort's backwoods blossoms would welcome your suit."

Sion rued the condescension in his voice. Cornelius dallied with these hardy women, mayhap raising their hopes, but thought himself above them all.

"Nellie Saunders and Charity Wade are ready to light on you like a duck on a June bug." He rambled on, words slurring. "Though they may be fond of you, they are not fond of Miss Tucker, who they feel is little more than a common camp follower—"

"She's no camp follower."

At the ire in Sion's tone, Cornelius made a wide circle around him as he started for the steps leading to the blockhouse's second story. "Touchy, are we?"

"Where Miss Tucker's concerned, aye."

Sion already knew at least one of the fort's women shunned Tempe on account of her keeping company with so many men. He owned it looked questionable, but never had she behaved in an unseemly manner. As for the other females, Esther and the Boone women were kindness itself. They shared Tempe's spirit, that natural competence and stoutheartedness that had first drawn Sion's notice.

He heard Cornelius shuffling around upstairs, soon to be abed and snoring, or so he hoped. Nate was outside smoking with some of the fort's men. He wasn't sure about Lucian and the chain carriers.

Leaving the blockhouse, he heard Nate's unmistakable laugh. The flicker of grease lamps and tallow dips shone through the cracks of the cabins. He aimed for one, glad to see a light on, the door partially open. Was Esther visiting? Nay. She was singing a lullaby next door. The low tone tugged at him, revived some long-lost memory of his own buried boyhood along the Watauga.

With every step nearer Tempe's stout wooden door, he felt addled as a boy. Mayhap it was the moon's alluring rise or the anticipation of seeing her again after two days out, but he wanted to cover her with kisses, unleashing that eager response he'd first set loose in the secrecy of the sycamore tree.

He stood on the stoop, breath coming a bit thick, and peered into the cabin. Tempe sat on the puncheon floor, skirts in a swirl about her, playing with Esther's two little girls. Unaware of him, they walked and danced their battered dolls about, having a make-believe party with acorn cap cups and parched corn.

It wasn't till Esther came out of her own cabin that the spell was broken. "A pretty picture they make," she remarked before calling her girls and shooing them to bed.

"'Night, Mister Morgan," Ellender said with a lisp, glancing up at him shyly.

"Good night, Miss Hart," he answered, smiling down at Esther's eldest.

The door remained open. Left alone with Tempe, Sion all but forgot what he wanted to say.

"Sion . . ." She looked up at him, mayhap a bit flustered at being on the floor. When she made no move to get up, he realized she couldn't, not without help.

He reached down and lifted her gently to her feet, that nagging worry overtaking him. He had half a mind to tell her to pull up her skirts so he could examine her leg himself, but that would kill any decency between them and give the fort's wags plenty to chew on if found out.

The scent of herbs was strong. Esther continued to treat her, both of them weary of awaiting the old woman's return from Harrod's. The pale, strained look on Tempe's face as she favored her leg fanned his fears.

Motioning for her to sit in the rocking chair, he straddled a stool. "We need to leave for Harrod's as soon as you're fit to ride."

Relief softened her features. Did she think he meant to leave her? "I'm fit. It's not far."

"A hard day's ride or so. We'll break it up if we have to." First he'd see how she took to her own mare, or they'd double up as they'd come to Boone's.

"Why Harrod's?"

"You need to see that granny woman. I need to see about registering my surveys here rather than return to eastern Virginia. Harrod's has more provisions for our trip back to the Moonbow, besides." His plans came out rapid-fire, overwhelming her. He read confusion in her face. Swallowing, he said what was foremost. "We need to find a preacher."

Her eyes widened. "A preacher?"

"Aye, to marry us."

Her skin pinked. His own face felt feverish. She looked . . . startled. Didn't she recall his proposal to her in the caves?

"Don't you mean to ask me first?" she chided softly.

"Your kiss was answer enough."

"Along the Green?" A wistful half smile was followed by a laugh. "It's been so long ago I misdoubt you remember much."

"Oh, I remember, all right." He extended a hand and swung the door shut, nearly snuffing the tallow dip on a near table. Let the fort's wags have a heyday with *that*.

His arms went round her, gathering her out of the rocking chair. She felt so small. Wilted. Lonesome, even. When she settled in his lap, her mouth brushed his ear. "I need to be outside these walls."

He understood. He shared her pent-up feelings, that odd bursting inside to be unfettered. Free. Liberty, for some, trumped danger.

"We'll leave at first light," he murmured.

"Will Nate and the others come too?"

"I haven't asked them." At the moment it hardly mattered. "Boone agrees now's the time to go, with Colonel Bowman being in the country and things calmer."

She looked at him wonderingly, her fingers tracing the sun-hardened lines of his jaw. Feather light, her touch tickled and teased all at once. He leaned in slightly, lips brushing the little bare hollow of her shoulder. She shut her eyes, fingers falling to his linen-clad chest. Bestirred, the both of them.

Easy, reason urged.

But it was sweet. A holy moment. A promise of what was to come.

Their foreheads touching, he took a breath. This close, the rosebud stitching on her bodice rose and fell in a fetching swell. He drank in the clean soap scent of her, his hands cupping the back of her head, finding the pins he longed to pull free.

"Marry me, Tempe."

She looked into his eyes, her own so full of emotion it rent his heart. Was she thinking of James? Feeling she'd betray him by accepting Sion's sudden proposal? He sensed a reluctance in her that made him stumble. Was she unsure of him? Their future?

Was he sure? Or just buckling beneath the need and emotion of the moment?

Her kiss held no reservations. The feel of her arms about his neck was like a balm for all his own heartache. He loved her. He'd never loved anyone like her. Not even Harper, whom he'd wed more out of a sense of soldierly duty and youthful desire. This . . . this was different. Tempe was a truehearted woman.

But could she love him back?

Bidding Esther and the Boones goodbye was not an easy task. In their few days together, she and Esther in particular had forged a friendship that defied their short acquaintance.

"I'll not rest till you come back this way," Esther said. "Tell your borderman that there's plenty of land for the taking over by the Harts on Cedar Creek."

In a feat only an accomplished woman could manage, Esther presented Tempe with her marrying quilt. "It's a mite smaller, as I ran out of time to finish, but it's plenty big enough to wrap your firstborn in."

They embraced, then drew apart. Rebecca and her grown girls came next, bidding her a hasty goodbye if only to hold their emotion in check. The warmth and strength of their arms was something Tempe wouldn't soon forget.

Once they'd passed through the fort's gates, Tempe didn't look back. Her heart felt as sore as her leg. But for Sion and his beguiling plans, she'd be completely undone. Harrod's was before them, then home.

She sat her mare comfortably the first few miles, keeping in mind the journey was short, though sometimes she felt they were back on the Green. Cornelius and Lucian brought up the rear, the chain carriers in the middle. She rode between Sion and Nate, Sion leading. Without the equipment, the pace was far faster.

At last they traversed the Great Meadow, that rolling, blue-green grassland so different from the rocky, watery Shawnee

River country. The three forts formed a triangle of sorts, Harrod's being the largest, then Boone's. Logan's seemed the runt of the litter. If more trouble came, Tempe prayed all would survive. Thrive.

"Logan's is made of sterner stuff than you think," Nate told her. "After the last siege, the Indians started calling it Standing Fort."

Any mention of Indians turned Tempe's thoughts to Raven. A hollow place had formed inside her at his leaving. His betrayal, Cornelius said. She tried to keep her half-blood friend in a favorable light. He hadn't hurt them, had he? He'd just abandoned them. Or was there more to the rock slide than she thought?

Still, she longed to know he was all right. Maybe he'd gone back to see Russell, was even now at the inn. Would she ever know?

Toward dusk, when she could go no farther, Sion called a halt. Mare's tails were clouding the blue of the sky, promising rain on the morrow. A clap of thunder turned the horses skittish, reverberating like an unseen heavenly drum. Uneasy, Tempe scoured the sky for lightning. She'd seen trees shredded by such.

Sion took charge of her, erecting a brush shelter covered by a hide so she wouldn't get wet.

"I won't melt," she said quietly.

"I'll make sure you don't," he returned with a wink.

The wind picked up, shaking her humble bower as they ate supper, and they all hunkered down as the wet splashed large drops on hat brims and tin cups.

They'd come halfway to Harrod's. She took comfort in the fact they'd seen no sign. She worried some about Sion's equipment hidden along the Green, all that he'd abandoned to hasten her to Boonesborough. But as the night unwound, a plan was hatched to recover the tools of their trade.

"Me and Spencer'll go," Hascal told them, looking at Cornelius as he sat smoking nearby. "If you can part with Lucian for a spell, we'll make good time and meet up with you at Harrod's before September's out."

Sending him a mulish look, Cornelius paused in his pipe smoking. "What makes you think I can be without my man-servant?"

Privy to the exchange, Lucian looked hopeful, wrenching Tempe's heart. She knew how he longed for his liberty, even if it was but a few days of freedom from his overbearing master.

Spencer elbowed Hascal, mirth riddling his words. "What with all the petticoats at Harrod's, I misdoubt you'll notice he's even gone. You got distracted somethin' fierce at Boone's."

At this even Sion chuckled. Bristling, smoke pluming, Cornelius stared the chain carriers into silence. "What say you, Lucian? Can you stomach these scalawags in the far reaches?"

"Yessir," came the polite reply.

"And you, Morgan? Any objection to their returning our equipment posthaste?"

"Given you get to stay at Harrod's while they bushwhack their way west, I'd say the rest of us have the better part of the deal."

Seemingly solaced, Cornelius leaned back against a beech tree. "I've given some thought to going upriver rather than overland once they return. A flatboat seems preferable to facing the Gap again."

"So be it," Sion said. "That's where we part company. I'm bent on Shawnee River country."

Tempe looked to Nate standing watch a few rods away. She sensed he'd stay on with them and head south. Riding up the Ohio River was risky at such a time, though she didn't blame Cornelius for wanting to take the river route.

As for her, Nate, and Sion, if it came to that, they'd journey on, and she'd return home a married woman if she was willing. Pondering it, she looked down at the tonic in her tin cup.

Was the inn still standing? What of Pa's future if she and Sion wed? Sion needed to know the truth of Pa's past, though the burden seemed Pa's to tell. Would Sion even want her once he learned she was the daughter of a murderer, and the harm done to a fellow surveyor at that?

Spirits plummeting, she bent her mind to kinder things. If all went well, she and Sion could carve out time for themselves. Watch for the moonbow. She'd show him the secret chamber behind the falls. There'd be talk of where to settle. He was leaning toward Green River country but was considering Esther's invitation.

The details came hard and fast, like the rock slide. Pleasure melded to confusion. Was she willing to let go of James? Her desire to join him? Or would she choose life? Sion?

She might heal. See home. Marry.

Or not.

29

My wife and daughters were the first white women
that ever stood on the banks of the Kentucky River.

—Daniel Boone

You gonna tell her?" Nate queried at their change of
watch. "About her pa?"

The quiet words held a strange urgency. Nate had
been after him to relieve Tempe of the burden of her secret
ever since they'd come out of the caves. But Sion resisted.
"I've held off, hoping she'd trust me. Tell me herself."

"Tell you her pa's a wanted man just so you can tell her
he ain't?" Nate looked perplexed.

"Aye, something like that," Sion answered, struck by the
ridiculousness of the situation.

"It mighten go bad for you if you was to wait and cause
her more heartache."

Though stabbed with guilt, Sion shrugged. "I'm just trying to build trust."

Nate shook his head. "Well, you're goin' about it wrong-
headed."

"If she's not told me by the ceremony—provided we can find a preacher—I'll spill everything."

"If I was you, I'd be askin' for her pa's hand before I stole his only daughter away."

"With the good news I'm carrying, he won't begrudge me getting things backwards."

With a sigh, Nate ambled off to camp just as the rain switched from a steady spatter to an outright drenching. Water ran off the brim of Sion's hat, and his worn shirt was soon sagging against him. Annie was dry at least, wrapped in an oiled skin. Keeping his powder dry was paramount, though he doubted there'd be trouble, what with the lack of sign and the weather.

Still, instinct wouldn't let him settle. It was Tempe he was most vigilant about. Their future. He'd begun to allow himself a vision of what that might be like, the shadowy outline of the coming years taking shape, bent in the direction of his dreams.

He wasn't much of a farmer, though he could plow and build fence and bring in the harvest. For her he'd raise a fine cabin of logs, but in time, with his surveying, he could afford brick. His desire to run the line, go on a scout, seemed second best. It was Tempe he wanted. A home. Children.

Humbled by all that was before them, he felt gratefulness take hold. He murmured a silent plea.

Lord, let it be.

Mornings were hardest. Her leg, stiff from sleep, seemed as lame as Russell's. Though she hadn't told Sion, her wound had torn open slightly from her long stint in the saddle the day before. Scooting out of the bough shelter, she looked up into a sky lit by dawn. All around her the trees were dripping, but other than this it was still. She missed birdsong. Sunlight. The sky seemed to scowl.

She put one foot forward. She must relieve herself or burst. Gimp-legged, she limped into the brush, realizing Sion hadn't woken her to stand watch in the night.

Through dawn's hush the sudden stirring of the horses sounded like a warning bell. They were uncommonly nervy, stamping and snorting farther back in the trees where they'd been hobbled. She paused. A bear or fox could scare them . . . or was it something else?

Wary, bladder aching, she moved on in search of privacy. Her gun was more walking stick, a crutch. Who was standing guard?

The watery woods ahead of her released a shadowy shape. Her sleepy senses sharpened.

Raven.

She held tight to her rifle as he came toward her, unsmiling. His hair was shorn on the sides, a topknot of feathers declaring his allegiance. But it was his paint that stilled her heart. One side of his head was black, the other a garish red. Confused, embarrassed, she felt a warm trickle down her bare leg beneath her skirt. She opened her mouth to greet him—but couldn't. Voice gone, she broke into a spasm of yellow-bellied trembling.

The new morning was split open by the crack of gunfire and fiendish yells.

Whirling, she turned her back on Raven to see someone fall. Nate? The smoke of the guns clouded the heavy air, choking and blinding her.

A cry built inside her, and then Raven's fingers digging into her shoulder forced her to the ground. He crouched beside her, his harsh words filling her ear.

326

"Stay down or they will kill you." At that he stood, yanking her gun from her before striding toward the panicked horses.

Pushing up from the wet grass, she began limping in the direction of the camp, where men fought hand to hand. Jelly-legged, she fell down in back of the shelter Sion had made for her.

Lord, please. We've come so far . . .

Raven was shadowing her again. She turned and raised a hand to deflect what was sure to come. The tomahawk at his waist glinted, the sharp edge bloodied. It was with the butt of her own rifle that he struck her, sending her sprawling backwards into thorny brush.

⁂

She came to, rain on her face. The sky tilted and spun, gradually clearing of clouds as she lay on her back, her battered head as sore as her leg. Thirst parched her insides, making her first swallow excruciating. Slowly she raised her good hand. When she touched the sore place on her scalp, her fingers came away red.

What of Sion? Nate? All the rest?

A stone's throw away lay Sion's pocket compass—the land stealer—its glass face shattered. Beyond that was where they'd camped and been attacked.

She pulled herself to her feet, willing herself to stay standing, and stumbled into what had been a ring of dozing men a short time before. Nate's hunting knife lay in a clump of trampled grass. All else—bedding, gear, weapons—had been taken in the frenzy of ambush. All the horses gone. A trace of spent powder hung in the damp air.

Leaning into a tree, she listened, half expecting Raven or another warrior to come finish her. She'd rather that than relive the pain. The shadow of that day in Powell Valley sounded in the deepest part of her.

First James . . . then Sion.

She was cursed in love. Twice bereft. Nauseous, she knelt down in the place Sion had lain sleeping, the grass matted down. Signs of struggle were everywhere. A frantic mingling of footprints. Broken laurel. Her own shelter destroyed. A few steps to the right was a young haw where the bullets had cut down the greenery. Blood trailed on the limp leaves, turning her cold.

Numb, she began backtracking and retrieved Sion's compass as a nickering farther back in the trees gave her pause.

Her mare?

Hobbled—one might say hidden—Dulcey regarded her a bit wild-eyed. Of herd mentality and stripped of her companions, the nervous creature looked as forlorn as Tempe felt.

Had Raven left her horse to help her?

She stood on the spot Nate had last stood watch. She expected to find him there, stretched across the grass, eyes open and unseeing. But for the knife and compass, it was like she'd dreamed all of them up.

Pressing a hand to her aching head, she wandered about like a broken compass, looking for fallen men, sure someone had been tomahawked and killed. Each downed log or clump of brush left her more sick, thinking it was a body.

What would she do if she came across Sion? With her wounded hand, she could only grieve him, not bury him. She didn't even have a sheet like they'd wrapped James in at the last.

A lonesomeness like she'd never known hovered. She looked toward the settlements, miles distant, indecision astir inside her. Should she ride back and enlist help? Nay. With so few guns, none could be spared outside the three forts. Bowman's men had gone north, leaving the fragile stations to fend for themselves. Had Raven and the war party taken Sion and the others south?

She had a horse but no gun. A bad leg. A throbbing head. And no time to waste woolgathering.

Calling softly to Dulcey, she waited while the mare picked its way toward her gingerly. She tried to mount. Failed. Her strength was spent. Up she went again, but short of the mark. Dulcey waited patiently, tail swishing. Tempe let go of the reins, slid her arms around the mare's sleek neck, and wept.

Sion had heard of running the gauntlet in the Indian towns, but he doubted they'd live to see it. The dawn ambush, only hours old, was already sketchy in his memory on account of his gut-wrenching thirst and the terror of the present. His every thought was for Tempe.

Fate—God—had allowed him one last look at her. Through the bluish haze of rifle fire, he'd spied her near Raven, desperation and disbelief scrawled across her comely face. She'd been standing unbloodied apart from the fracas. But what had become of her was anyone's guess. She was not a part of the long snaking column of men and horses now heading south.

The leather thongs binding his wrists from behind were so tight his fingers were benumbed and tingly by turns. He was at the head of the line, just behind the warrior he knew to be Five Killer. Armed with war club and tomahawk, his quiver full of brass-tipped arrows, he was a punishing sight.

A quick glance over his shoulder earned Sion a swift jab in the side by the brave just behind. But it was worth the blow seeing Nate farther back. He was bound in a neck noose, his face gray as linen. Still alive, at least. Sion wasn't sure about the others. He knew Hascal had taken a bullet to the arm in the ambush but didn't know how badly he'd been hurt.

Chest streaming with sweat, Sion marched on, his heart a-gallop, legs burning with exhaustion. Up a wooded slope they climbed, branches stinging and slapping his face and neck, the whine of insects a discordant song. Wending through towering trees, they came to a notch in a steep ridge. The trail thinned at its crest, leading them along a cliff with a sheer drop too narrow for horses.

They had crossed some invisible border into territory Sion had never seen. Disoriented, he grappled for his bearings. A second look back cost him another blow but told him the party had divided. The horses were gone, and it was just a body of warriors and captives on foot, making their way along that precarious drop above a shimmering emerald valley far below.

What of Tempe?

They should have been at Harrod's by now. Safely behind pickets. Having her wound dressed. Searching for a preacher.

The line lurched to a halt. All turned for an unhindered look, leaving Sion time to account for his party, Lucian at the column's tail. Unbound, he was carrying Tempe's pack-saddle.

Cornelius had stumbled and halted the march. Though Sion understood little of what was said by his captors, one word wove a frequent pattern. *Squaw.* The Indians had taken to calling Cornelius that, belittling him for some grievance or another.

One warrior took a plundered canteen and approached Sion first, offering him a drink. They'd had little water. Though he was parched with thirst, he shook his head, gesturing to Nate and Cornelius and the others just beyond. Hands bound, Cornelius drank from the canteen the warrior held. And then, in a stunning display of impertinence, he spat a mouthful of water back at his captor.

The Indian's flintlike expression hardened. In one agile, unremorseful move, he unsheathed his scalping knife and drove it hard into Cornelius's middle before sending him over the cliff's edge. The look of surprise and horror on Cornelius's face as he fell was never to be forgotten.

Sion shut his eyes. Harper's death, every detail, was resurrected in Cornelius's last rash act. This had been a brother's attempted revenge. Final retribution. But oh, at what a cost.

There was a brief pause before their tramp resumed, the gaping hole in the column that marked Cornelius's place carrying a warning to any who dared trespass on an Indian's pride.

⁊

They descended into the dense shade of a shriveled creek bed with water enough to hide their passing. The mossy stones were slick and sharp, the rushing water blessedly cool. Twilight shadows brought on the wink of fireflies. The sting of insects ebbed. The captives were herded into a grassy meadow near a spring that gurgled and tumbled over high rocks.

Nate ended up near Sion, but the axemen and Lucian were kept separate. The Indians seemed to shed some of their hostility and hurry, talking among themselves while a few warriors stood guard.

"By heaven, how long d'ye think they'll bedevil us?"

A stitch of sympathy pierced Sion's stupor at Nate's worn question. Sion raised his gaze to the mountain they'd climbed over, their rocky trek marred by thirst and Cornelius's death. Buzzards were already circling, denying Harper's brother a proper burial. The wolves would come next.

With difficulty he said, "We'll soon see the Chickamauga towns if my instinct's right."

Nate hissed a sigh. "Why don't they just scalp us and get it over with?"

"Don't you recollect what we heard at Fort Henry? One white man's life is worth a hundred horses. That's what we'll gain them in trade goods."

"Horses be hanged. They mean to burn us alive, I reckon, if my instinct's right."

Sion didn't doubt it, though he was most mired by Tempe's whereabouts. Had Raven spared her? Taken her the other direction with the horses when the trail forked? He wasn't sure. There'd been too many Indians, and the warrior trailing him was bent on keeping him facing forward as if certain he posed a threat.

"Reckon little missy's still with us?"

Sion stared at him. Betimes Nate had an uncanny ability to read his thoughts. "I pray so." He could barely get the words out.

A few of the warriors began emptying Tempe's pack-saddle. Watching, Sion simmered. They were making a small festival of her belongings, one holding up a pair of stockings and garters, another her indigo dress. Laughing and murmuring, they divided the spoils—comb, hair ties, her Psalms and sewing kit. The hoecake Esther had packed was devoured. Had it only been yesterday they'd left Boone's?

A blue jay shrilled. The Indians' voices grew muted as exhaustion overtook him. Sion felt bewildered at his missing compass and rifle, the familiar, reassuring weight of powder horn and shot pouch. The sun was no longer a reliable guide. It slipped out of sight behind a vast wall of dark forest that had no end. He felt a terrible solitude, a keen lonesomeness borne of Tempe's loss.

Nate was whispering again. "I heard tell of two of them red men. Five Killer is leadin' and Big Jim is rear guard, all the worse for us."

"The both of them were in Powell Valley."

"Aye. The Boone massacre. That's what nettles me so."

Sion looked down at his bound hands. A bold notion leapt into his head, but the rawhide tugs rubbing his wrists raw mocked him. "I'm going to try to make a run for it."

Nate ran a hand over a week's growth of whiskers. "I'll wager you and Lucian have half a chance. Me and Spencer and Hascal . . ." Resignation tinted his tone. "For all their axe wieldin', them boys ain't sharp-witted. And I'm slow as molasses in January. I don't have any hankerin' to join poor Cornelius, but it was over right quick, I'll give you that."

Quick and merciless. Cornelius, volatile as a powder keg, had met his match. Nate's danger lay in the fact that he was old and he was slow.

"I ain't sure where he ended up," Nate said, mournful. "But I won't rest easy if I don't know for certain if I'll see you again."

"I aim to run and get my hands on a gun and free you."

Nate's eyes were a glittering green. "I ain't talkin' about the here and now but the hereafter."

Sion's chest knotted. Wanting to offer some reassurance, if only for Nate, he spoke the first verse that flashed to mind. "'For God so loved the world, that He gave his only begotten Son, that whosoever believeth in Him should not perish, but have everlasting life.'"

Wonder washed Nate's face, but it was short-lived. As if aggravated by their low talk, a warrior came from behind and yanked Sion to his feet. Shoving him forward, the Indian herded him toward a sapling, where he was tied with leatherwood bark for the long, uncertain night.

※

The longhunters would come as soon as the fall hunting was better and the rivers easier to ford, the wilderness having spent itself on a long, lush summer. But not one soul did Tempe see as she sped south as if pulled by some invisible string. When she came upon a seam of brightly colored clay and a rock besmeared with war paint, her heart nearly tore in two. Bright sky blue. Pale green and royal purple. The colors of the moonbow. Sometimes a chief would leave his own personal sign, often blood red.

Another war party had been this way, mixing their colors here, perhaps the same warriors who had ambushed them. She moved on only to draw up short.

Tromping in a thicket a few yards away was a wild hog, its button eyes menacing. She tensed, aware of her empty saddle holster. With a shudder she nudged the mare's flanks with her heels, the hog's fearsome tusks firmly in mind. If she but had a gun . . .

Her stomach growled an empty protest. Come October there would be grapes and pawpaws and nuts. Persimmons abounded but needed a hard frost before sweetening. She yanked her thoughts from her hunger to more important matters.

Her mare was showing signs of foundering. Had Dulcey eaten too much cane? A great burning was rippling up and down Tempe's leg where the wound was chafing with her constant movement. Disheartened, she murmured a prayer and pressed on, paying attention to the scant sign the war party had left. She refused to sink with panic when she came to a fork in the trail and the Indians seemed to have divided.

Wounded and without a gun and provisions as she was, what hope did she have of overtaking them? Raven had left her the mare at least, but her frantic flight courted calamity and every sinkhole in sight. If she reached home it would be naught but a miracle, sure as their Lord walked on water.

Pa, please . . .

She formed an impassioned plea long before she saw the first watery bend of the Shawnee and his rockhouse home. Would he listen? Go with her?

She remembered Sion's calculations from days past. Boone's was thirty leagues, some ninety miles, from the falls and inn. She'd covered half that the day of the attack and was now on the last leg of the journey.

She'd ridden most of the night by the light of the moon, till her head lolled on her chest and she'd fallen to the ground, sleeping in the grass where she lay. She'd come awake to the mare crunching cane along a creek.

Now, with the cobwebs clearing from her head, she revisited every secreted memory of Sion. The dark tilt of his hat. The rich timbre of his words as he'd read Herrick and the Psalms in her pain-clouded daze. The drop of her stomach when he looked at her. His calm confidence, be it facing a swollen river or the passing of a war party. The dimpled impressions in his large hands from countless lead balls. The tender way he spoke her name. His uncommon memory for laying off the land. His kiss. She dwelt on the details, branding them into memory till she knew them by heart.

Landmarks, beloved and familiar, began to crop up as

if calling her name. A sulphur spring. A trammeled deer path. The biggest elm she'd ever seen, bigger even than the divine elm at Boonesborough, its roots matted with moss and drooping daisies. The music of the river and a horseshoe-shaped boulder left her eyes smarting.

She'd not been home since the flax harvest. Now mid-August, the river was at its most fordable. She chose the narrowest place, the sun bedazzling the water and blinding her. She shut her senses to the daylilies and the trumpet vine and the excited warble of birds. Nothing could slow her, distract her.

Abandoning Dulcey, pushing past her pain, she started up the embankment beyond the fording place, senses quickened to the smell of a chimney fire or any flash of movement among the trees ahead. But all that met her ears was the dull roar of the falls as her eyes adjusted to the denseness of her own beloved woods. She would see Pa as soon as she could, but first . . .

Was the inn still standing?

30

The miseries of that hour cannot well be described.
—Colonel Robert Patterson

They were running now on this third day as if trying to hasten past some unseen enemy. A full-out, leg-shattering sprint. Nate had been put at the rear of the column, the chain carriers in the middle, while Sion maintained his position behind Five Killer. He wasn't sure about Lucian. Tethered by the neck and wrists, this time in front, Sion ran behind the young chieftain, every coppery feature engraved on his conscience.

Five Killer wore his hair long, his hawk feathers fluttering in the fickle breeze. Gleaming with bear grease, he wore only loincloth and moccasins, as unencumbered as Sion felt weighted by shirt and leggings. Bereft of his own weapons, he longed to pluck Five Killer's British-made tomahawk and scalping knife from his belt.

A nameless river flowed to their right between steep bluffs that took them up and down deer trails, testing their agility and endurance. He had eaten and slept little, tied to the sapling as he'd been, thoughts ricocheting between Tempe and his plan of escape.

Methodically, he'd made a study of his captors, fifteen all told. All formidable and easily riled. Five Killer had that air of authority he'd witnessed in Daniel Boone and Ben Logan while the other warriors were a hodgepodge of features and habits. His own guard, a bowlegged, gaunt giant, seemed to take peculiar pleasure in punching Sion with the muzzle of his gun when Sion made a move not to his liking. Beneath his linen shirt were myriad welts and bruises, but the fate of James hung squarely in his mind, giving him no cause to complain. Other than Tempe, it was Nate Sion was most worried about.

The grit of dust clogged his throat, the river an ongoing temptation. If they turned him loose he would drink it dry. All this movement left him strangely exhilarated and depleted at once, a throbbing mass of tension and vexation. At another vicious jab to the back, he wanted to crush his guard with his bare hands. *Love thine enemy* was the farthest thing from his mind.

At noon they halted in a valley tinged russet, a prelude to fall. Hascal fell to the ground, face red as an orchard apple. Spencer, so winded he was choking, collapsed against a shagbark hickory. And Nate . . .

Sion looked back expectantly. Scoured every tree and bush and moving figure. A great chasm began to open up inside him. Tiny pinpricks of panic told him searching was in vain. Nate was not at the end of the column.

Nate was gone.

☙

Something in Tempe's spirit gave a warning. Were there warriors here? In these very trees? She longed to still the tumult of the falls and just listen. Sion had done that well, standing so still he seemed made of rock, so attuned to all that was around him she felt he sensed the slither of a snake across the ground. With the falls turning her deaf, she relied on sight alone.

Scrambling up the bank toward home, she favored her gimp leg and hand, more mindful than ever of Russell's limp. A crushing longing stole over her to be reunited with the ones she loved. Sion foremost. Ma and Pa. Russell and Paige. Even Nate and Lucian and Esther had found a home in her needy heart.

The ground was dry, rocks and brush biting into her good hand as she climbed upward, staying off the familiar path. The slant of the sun foretold noon, but no savory odors carried on the humid air, no ring of axe or anvil. The closer she drew, the more she was aware of nothingness. Life carried a palpable rhythm, and she felt its absence even before she gained flat ground and a break in the trees.

There in the clearing sat the Moonbow Inn, burnt to a dusting of gray ashes, a few heavy timbers lying partially charred. Gone was the dogtrot and barn-shed. Only the springhouse and cabin chimneys, made of river rock, still stood.

Her heart lurched. She gave a strangled cry. "Nay . . . nay!"

Beyond the gaping emptiness spread the trammeled, blackened corn and flax fields. The ash hopper in the yard was tumbled, water troughs overturned, fences down.

The noise of the falls, so soothing before, turned mournful. She picked her way through the rubble, craving something recognizable. Save for a few nails of Russell's making, the destruction was complete.

Next she sought mounds of earth. Gravesites. Over and

over the ground she walked till she was convinced her people weren't here. Hadn't been burnt or buried.

Thoughts of Pa crowded in, and then her everlasting, choking need of Sion cut through her grief. She'd tarried too long here, but in her shock and dismay at finding her home in ruins, she'd forgotten her empty belly and slow-to-heal wounds. It was Pa she needed. Only Pa could help her.

Retrieving Dulcey, she made straight for the rockhouse. The trail beneath her was as known as her own name, but her whole world was off center, the inn—her internal compass—as shattered as the land stealer in her pocket.

Lord, be You here?

The Almighty seemed far away, unmoved by wounds and war, hatred and heartache. Her earthly father, holed up in a cave, imprisoned by his own misdeeds, might be missing too. And though she wanted to shout and call to him and end the agony of not knowing, his name knotted in her throat till she couldn't breathe.

Turning loose Dulcey, she tramped through brush and around boulders to reach the rockhouse, overcome when she heard the hiss of the ladder as it left the ledge and plummeted to the ground.

By the time she reached the top, great silent sobs tore at her. Glad she was of Pa's bearish embrace, smothering her tears. Amazement filled her at the nudge of a wet nose. Smokey stood wagging her tail, clearly at home in their lofty perch. Pa had likely hoisted her by rope.

"I wasn't sure what became of you." Pa held her tight, the fury of her cut lip no longer between them. "I could hardly live knowing I'd sent you away so sorry-like. Do you forgive me?"

She nodded, moving past what seemed of small consequence. "I saw the inn—what's left of it. Where's Ma and Russell? Paige?"

"Safe on the Watauga, if there's anywhere safe." He drew her to the back of the rockhouse. "A war party of Cherokee and Shawnee set fire to the place a fortnight after you left. Russell refused to repair any British guns and stood his ground like a proud Patriot. He threw the muskets in the river. Over the falls." There was pride in his voice, a hard-won admiration. "The Chickamauga wasted no time in burning down the inn. I hid your ma and Russell and Paige behind the falls till I could see them safely through the Gap."

"Yet you came back."

"If I'd gone with them, it would have been to a hangman's noose. I had no wish to leave you besides."

She drew apart from him. She needed to speak of Sion but hardly knew where to begin. Kneeling, she hugged Smokey next, glad for the feel of the dog's rough tongue on her tear-wet cheek.

"What's with the surveyors?" He was staring at her splinted hand, a dozen questions in his eyes. "They didn't abandon you in the midst of the trouble?"

"Nay. We were ambushed a few days ago." The suddenness of it haunted. "Sion Morgan and the others were taken south. Raven was with the war party—"

"Raven? He'd been with you, I thought."

"Till the caves, aye." She stood and drew up her skirt to reveal the gash beneath. "We went exploring, Sion, Raven, and I. There was a rock slide. Raven disappeared." She paused in the phrasing, certain he'd spared her in the ensuing ambush. "And then without warning, he was with Five Killer and the Chickamauga between Boone's and Harrod's."

"You reached the settlements? They're still standing?"

"Barely. They're all low on provisions." She lowered her skirt. "A colonel and his regiment came through but didn't stay long."

"With the war blazing in the East, George Washington can ill afford the loan of men." He began reviving a fire from a few scant coals. "Your leg needs dressing. I'll see to your hand next."

"There's no time. We have to find Sion, his men—"

Defiance twisted his face. "The very surveyors who work for the Loyal?"

"Pa! They're good as dead if we don't go after them. You know the Indians hate surveyors—"

"Aye. But 'tis like asking me to aid the one who wronged me. The one I killed."

She stared. Rarely did he speak of his crime, and yet he'd just admitted the gravity of it. "If you help Sion's party, maybe Virginia will grant you clemency—pardon."

"Likely this man Morgan will haul me to gaol. The courts."

"He's a good man. A just man." Her voice shook. "Do what is right—"

"And risk my daughter besides?" His eyes held hers, tender and flinty by turns. "What is this surveyor to you? This Sion?"

She dashed her tears away with her good hand, forcing the memory of James to retreat. To lose them both . . . "He's to be my husband."

"You love him?"

Her eyes filled again. "Aye, like James." But this wasn't entirely true. Loving James had been new, almost sacred. Uncommon sweet. With Sion it was more seasoned. But both were deep. Rich. Enduring.

She shifted her gaze to the front of the rockhouse, ever wary. Daylight was draining away. She wanted nothing more than to blot out all the heartache and fall down on the buffalo robe bed bunched along one rock wall and sleep.

"I'll dress your wound."

Heartsick, she stared at him. Was this all she could expect? She bit her tongue to keep from lashing out at his foolishness. His heartlessness. Yet as he concocted a poultice, he asked careful questions of all that had happened since the ambush. What sign had she seen? Where did she lose their trail? Who had made up the war party?

She tried to keep the despair from her voice, but firmly fixed in her mind was Ma's little leather book now turned to ashes. The Reckoning bore the names of one too many would-be Kentuckians and countless surveyors. She'd tried to purge from her thoughts their terrible fates, but they'd rent a gash in her mind like the gash in her leg.

"You're in a bad way."

His concern was making her antsy. She had no time to spend on a wound. Many had fared worse and lived.

"You belong overmountain with your ma."

When he'd finished with her leg she made light of her hand, looking to the rifles but knowing they'd be of little use to her. How would she pull the trigger? She took the lightest one anyway, communicating her intent with a look. He made no move to stop her, instead gathering a canteen and provisions, meager as they were. It was Ma's overflowing table she missed. Platters of fried fish. Mounds of hominy and gravy and green beans. Hunger made her light-headed.

Down the hanging ladder she went, gun in the crook of her arm, without another word to Pa. She didn't trust herself to speak except to spew ugly words that couldn't be taken back.

It took precious minutes to trade horses. The mare she

exchanged for Pa's gelding. It took to the woods with a readiness she sorely needed, allowing her to eat of the rockahominy he'd given her. She felt light as dandelion down, her time spent on the trail whittling her away.

There was naught to do but retrace her steps. Return to the place she'd lost the war party's trail. Pray for direction. Protection.

Miracles.

※

Their days had faded to a bewildering sameness, but Sion's emotions stayed fevered. He felt he'd lost his way, like a hapless boy separated from his father. Again and again he glanced back, praying Nate would reappear, earning another blow each time he looked. But the battering of his body was in no way like the battering of his soul.

He could not ask the chain carriers what they'd seen or heard. The Indians were careful to keep them apart, paying particular heed to Sion as if they were reserving him for some singular purpose. When his dread was heaviest, he knew Nate had been right. Once in the Indian towns—Chota or Toqua or wherever it was they were headed—they meant to burn him.

This alone eased his anguish over the old man. If Nate was dead, he'd been spared the torment of the stake. Sure of what lay ahead, Sion forced himself to eat the bear meat and deer collops, keeping his strength, studying his captors, praying for an opportune moment.

The warriors were growing easier now, their talk and mannerisms less guarded. How many days since the ambush? They'd come to another nameless river so shrunken by summer they forded it without pause. That night they camped near a lick tramped down by game, summer's flowers on the wane. The weather took a turn, a drenching rain soaking them as if ushering in autumn. Strangely chilled, Sion watched as a fire was built of deadwood, smoke pluming low till the weather cleared.

Hascal and Spencer were looking lean and sunburnt, their clothes in tatters. He caught their questioning stares, their unvarnished fear. They kept glancing at him as if expecting something. Some help. Some action.

Sion recognized his and Cornelius's saddlebags as two warriors brought them forward. They'd waited till now to divide up the spoils, intent as they were to leave Kentucke's middle ground. His chest clenched at the realization of what they were about to do. When the fire's flame grew hotter and brighter, the bags were opened and the contents spilled out. Ruthlessly, dark fingers dug through the belongings and deemed them worthless. Cornelius's detailed maps of the Kentucke territory, his own precious field book with countless notes and computations, the hard-won warrants for the surveys—they were fed to the fire till it blazed with the heat of the noon sun. Watching the destruction, Sion willed himself not to flinch. His work with the Loyal Land Company was finished. Staying stoic, he bled inside.

His focus narrowed as Cornelius's flask was passed from warrior to warrior. The blood-warming spirits—brandy— chased away the damp in a way the crackling fire could not. He bent his head, wanting to make peace with Cornelius's death and his own conflicted feelings.

Tied wrist and ankle, he tried to make sense of the Indians' expressive, singsong talk. He knew a bit of Shawnee, that strangely mellifluous tongue, but little of the nasal Cherokee.

Five Killer and Sion's guard, with his dangling ears slit and ornamented with silver baubles, were in a heated exchange, their rapid gestures slicing the air as they stood to one side of him. Were they arguing? About him? Sion shifted, the wet ground beneath him more mud puddle.

He was so weary he simply wanted to lie down on the ground and sleep. With a bittersweet pang, he recalled Tempe's nightly ritual, so hallowed in memory when it had become almost routine before. He could picture her redding up the camp, preparing branches for bedding, chewing a sassafras twig to sweeten her breath. She'd close her eyes in what he thought was prayer after combing out her hair, her back to them in a show of modesty, and rebraid the winsome plait the rock slide had torn in two.

What had Raven done with her? He'd seen them together at the last, sensed her unspoken heartache over Raven's duplicity. He understood the half-blood's shifting allegiances. Raids were being made on the Cherokee towns by North Carolinians, bounties set for Indian scalps. Raven was caught in the conflict. And so was Sion.

He took a deep breath, inhaling smoke, ignoring his bruised ribs. The Indians' rifles leaned against a forked pole a few feet to his right. Mist was curling in about the meadow, making it difficult to draw a bead or aim with any accuracy. The time had come. If he failed to break through, failed to make his escape, instant death would follow.

Lord, grant me speed. Be mine shield.

He struggled to his feet, requesting to be untied. The nearest warrior stared at his outstretched wrists, the tugs knotted tight, and likely thought he meant to make water. With a glance at Sion's guard and the other surrounding Indians, the warrior sliced the tugs free, ready to oversee him at knife point while he relieved himself a few feet away.

Before the cut tugs touched the ground, Sion swung at the Indian with all his might, knocking him into the fire. With bull-like tenacity, Sion plunged through the midst of the unsuspecting warriors in his path, fire to his heels.

The damp twilight was rent by fierce yelps as the Indians came after him, howling their protests as he made for a copse of hickories.

Now was Spencer and Hascal's best chance to do the same. He hit a curtain of mist, one Indian so close he fancied he felt his clutch. The thud of footfalls and snap of breaking brush resembled a small army on the run.

To confuse them he darted to the right. The way was slippery but he was gaining ground, his need for Tempe driving him. He knew the Indian mind-set. For all their outrage, their furious pursuit, they'd respect him if he got away. They'd not call him *squaw*.

Down into a gully his strained legs took him, the way trammeled by buffalo and other game.

Thou art my hiding place; Thou shalt preserve me from trouble; Thou shalt compass me about with songs of deliverance.

The Scripture, a favorite of Nate's, sprang to mind unbidden.

He ran on, barely aware he was headed east. Toward the Moonbow. New life. Tempe.

If Tempe lived.

31

As we came along on Rock-Castle the path was narrow
and along a precipice . . . the horse rubbed against a
sapling . . . and pitched him over the precipice into
the river.

—Francis Jackson

For miles Tempe had felt a crawling at her back, a sensation of being shadowed. Six hours ago she'd left Pa and the rockhouse, riding hard south, distressed the rain had stolen away any remaining sign of the war party. She longed for an imprint of a rifle butt in the soft earth, the passing of Indian ponies unshod. Anything telling.

At the fork in the trail where the war party had divided, she cut right. She knew to stay off the main traces, backtracking in spurts to confuse pursuers, walking atop deadfalls and in streams. Pa's gelding was fleet but noisy. Overcome by the shadowy feeling, she finally slid to the ground and grabbed the halter, pulling her mount's head down and backing off the trail into the bushes.

She waited for the shadowy sensation to take shape, listening for a soft, moccasined footfall or stirring of brush. Her gaze swung wide then lowered. There, crouched in the growth like a lamb with a hawk going over, she spied something pale and still.

Her heart clenched. Nate's tobacco pipe?

She'd taken notice of it early in their journey. Fashioned of polished wood, not simple clay, it bore a bent stem stamped with a maker's mark. The pipe had brought Nate hours of enjoyment. Far too valuable to be tossed aside, it lay in the weeds. She bit her lip to keep her sorrow in check, restraining herself from reaching for it.

Beside her, the gelding grew less quivery, ears less taut. She reached up a hand and stroked its sleek side. It wasn't until the foreboding passed that she let her fingers curl round the pipe bowl, unleashing an avalanche of memories. Nate chuckling. Nate quoting Scripture. Nate praying. Nate being . . . Nate.

She felt deep in her being he was gone. That henceforth only his memory would warm her. Spirits sinking, she remounted and rode on. Was this a senseless chase? Had they all gone the way of Nate? The pain in her leg was no longer paramount. Sorrow welled instead.

Dusk closed in, the shrinking light drawing her eye to bits of cloth left hither and yon on brambles and brush. Cloth used for patches in someone's gun? Aye. Whose, she didn't know, but it marked the way plain.

When it was well past twilight she sought shelter in a cove, a little pocket of green hidden away from the Warrior's Path. Back against a willow, rifle across her lap, she prepared to listen and catnap as night drew the curtain closed.

Exhausted, she fell into what seemed more unconsciousness than sleep, not waking till the next day's sun foretold late morning, hours past the time she'd meant to rise and ride. Her head was full of dreams—bad dreams—of Sion, so dire that not even daylight could dispel them. Her sense of danger, always high, was quickening. It seemed she was on the verge of some greater calamity than any she had ever known, more hurtful than James and Powell Valley, of greater consequence than all the wreckage that had come after.

She was of a mind to turn back.

❧

Only two warriors were in pursuit now, the fleetest of the bunch. Sion kept on with only one moccasin, having lost the other when the tug snapped. The ground became a gauntlet, tearing at the toughened soles of his exposed foot with every flying step.

Lungs heaving, he started to slow, his legs turning to molasses. Ahead was a thickset sycamore, recalling his and Tempe's tryst. He hid behind it, bereft of every weapon, hardly daring to believe his ears. Had the chase finally ended? He nearly bent over double in relief.

Drinking in great gulps of air, he straightened. Listened. Flinched. The swift whoosh of a well-placed arrow smacked into him, pinning his left shoulder to the rough trunk. The fletching was still aquiver when he grabbed the thin shaft and wrenched it free, grinding his back teeth to quell a fierce yell.

Blood spattered his filthy shirt, the flint tip of the arrow firmly embedded in the bark as it let loose his shoulder. Muscle and sinew convulsed and burned, sending a trail of fire through his whole frame.

He looked about wildly. Knowing at least one brave was ahead of him, he cut to the north, ignoring the pulsing agony of his body as his shirt changed from dingy cream to flaming crimson.

Like a hare he darted this way and that, jumping over

deadfalls and careening around boulders, running full tilt as night swept in, the beat of his heart pounding out two simple syllables.

Tempe. Tempe. Tempe.

Pa's gelding took her atop a rocky ledge with such sure-footedness she felt the daring creature had sprouted wings. At another time she'd have sought a less risky route, but the encouraging sign she found urged her on as much as circling buzzards pushed her back. She paused. Looked down.

Time and a pack of wolves had nearly turned Cornelius Lyon unrecognizable. 'Twas little more than the fancy shoe buckle that lay littered on the rock slab far below that confirmed it. But even at so sheer a drop, she would have known it was he. Given his quarrelsome nature, he'd likely outstripped the war party's patience.

The fall itself had not been the end of him. He lay upon what resembled a red quilt, his life's blood having soaked the ground beneath him. Denied a proper burial, he was left to the ravages of the wilderness.

Sickened, she turned away, the same nagging questions pelting her like buckshot. What if Sion was ahead . . . dead? What if she was to stumble across his unburied body? Too shaky to remount on the ribbon of trail, she led the horse along the sun-drenched ledge on foot, her every step a prayer.

He had gone miles and miles. Light-headed from a loss of blood, Sion slowed beneath a gibbous moon, ears still taut to any sound beyond that of a screech owl. God be praised, he'd gotten away. Had his chain carriers done the same in the confusion of the moment? Lucian?

His shoulder had stopped bleeding, but it was badly mangled. His shirt a red rag, he weighed removing his breeches, but the sight of so much pale skin might scare up more trouble. His usual leggings were packed away in his saddlebags, now Cherokee owned. Not all of him was as tobacco brown as his face and hands.

Pain pushed him beyond the point of hunger. Coming to a creek, he sat along the bank and cleaned both wound and shirt. The front of his shoulder was more easily tended, the back nigh impossible. Had he gotten all the arrow out? Or had it splintered inside him? Only time would answer. He needed Tempe's quiet tending, wherever she was.

He stumbled on, switching his moccasin from one foot to the next, his soles as sore as his shoulder. Toward midnight, when he felt sure he'd put enough distance between him and his captors, he came across a downed hickory, large enough to crawl into and lay down undetected. He slept, unsure if he'd awake.

The cry of a grackle jerked him from sleep. Daybreak. He crawled out of the hollow tree like some forest creature. Pulling himself to his feet, he continued on. A cluster of grapes made his breakfast.

Toward noon he found the Warrior's Path. A dangerous route, it was also his one hope of encountering a trader or longhunter. Smaller trails bisected it in places, but he headed east. Toward Tempe, if she still liv—

He cut off the thought with tomahawk-like swiftness, but even that took effort. His mind had turned to mush, and the mere thought of cornmeal, of eating, made him convulse with hunger. Chewing on a sassafras twig, he walked on till he came to the place he'd last seen Nate.

Sorrow had eaten a pie-sized hole inside him. That, coupled with missing Tempe and the fate of the chain carriers and Lucian, turned him more hollow. Then and there he repented of his prayerlessness. His pride. His hatred of Cornelius, God forgive him.

He might have half a chance to make it back to the settlements but for his wound. Fever had set in, turning his innards to cotton. He couldn't slake his thirst no matter how many springs he crossed. His heart seemed to beat clear up in his head, pounding out a punishing rhythm. And now, trail weary and worn with need, he was seeing things . . .

Just ahead of him down the trace came a bearish figure. Sion's wariness quickened, sharpening his gaze. A giant. The horse beneath this Goliath seemed too small to hold him, his rifle of uncommon length. Something about the set of his features—his expression—bespoke familiarity. But in truth, Sion had never seen such a power of a person. In his fever-addled state, the man seemed to dominate the trees and rocks and hills.

Sion wanted to get out of his way, but his sojourn had so sapped him his every thought was delayed. The buckskin-clad stranger had seen him, was even now riding slightly off the trace straight for him. Beside him, trotting with a bit of a gimp—could it be?—was Smokey.

Nay. His fevered brain was conjuring things. Smokey was leagues away, back at the Moonbow Inn . . .

The giant spoke. "Be you Sion Morgan?"

Sion heard a few cloudy words, but they failed to take root. Exhaustion and fever flung the question away. He stumbled over a stone in his path, his remaining moccasin coming free.

He bent to shoe his most tender foot, then straightened, head swirling before fading to black.

Pitching forward, Sion fell in a heap at the stranger's feet.

※

From her brushy perch, Tempe counted fifteen warriors . . . and two chain carriers. Nate and Sion were missing. And Lucian—where was Lucian? As she thought it, he emerged from the trees into a clearing where the Indians had made camp.

It was still light enough to draw a bead, but she was having trouble managing the rifle with her bad hand. Resting the gun in the crotch of a large laurel, she'd get one shot off if she was lucky. She wasn't aiming, just scaring. All she wanted was to give the three captives a chance to run. If she wasn't so crippled she'd risk two shots, reloading before the Indians took to the hills after her.

Lucian had the best chance of escape, being unbound. His captors had obviously taken a liking to him. He gathered wood and water while Hascal and Spencer sat tied hand to hand, the both of them scared witless, looked like. Frustrated and fearful of the worst, she wished she could simply holler down and ask the stricken boys and Lucian what had become of the missing men.

They were nearing the Indian towns. At a nearby creek a few of the warriors were washing off their war paint. In the fast-fading light their armbands and earrings and bangles gave off a fearsome shine.

Two hundred yards distant, she continued to look for signs of Sion and Nate. Nate's disadvantage was his age. But Sion . . . Sion was clever, and as good as the Indians at the Indian game.

For now she had to content herself with hiding in the clump of bushes, the rocky ledge biting her backside, and bide her time till the right moment presented itself. Pa's horse was well fed and watered and tethered to the bush just behind her, and blessedly quiet.

One shot and then she'd ride back toward the inn.

She blinked, vision sharpening at the sight of Five Killer at the edge of the woods. Nearby, she made out Big Jim, looking as hale and hearty as he'd likely been that day in Powell Valley, and entirely within her sights. She drew a bead on the both of them. If she could but muster strength in her hand . . . strength enough to aim true . . .

She braced herself for the flash in the pan. Writhing white smoke. The acrid stench of powder. With her good hand, she pulled the trigger. A deafening roar was followed by the spent ball kicking up dust near the Indians' cookfire, sending warriors scrambling.

Without waiting to survey the melee, she thrust Pa's rifle in its saddle holster and mounted in a rush, her leg and hand hardly slowing her. Nearly dancing, the gelding shot off like a bullet east, stumbling once as they careened downhill off the ridge's backside.

Father in heaven, help the captives get away.

She could do no more for the tattered remains of Sion's surveying party.

⁂

The aroma of rich venison broth nudged Sion awake. His memory of the bear-man was hazy—first his appearing and then his return, a deer draped over the pommel of his saddle. After that his focus narrowed to his own shoulder, consumed as he was by an unrelenting ache.

Flat on his back, unable to turn over or sit up or make water, he lay still. Listening. Praying. Willing his wits to sharpen.

"If you can stand this, you can stand anything."

The burning worsened as the stranger poured whiskey over the wound. Sion's shoulder seized, seemed set on fire.

"Arrow's poisoned . . . Tempe'll never forgive me if I don't bring you through."

Poisoned? Sion had heard of such, but this made him a believer. Though he was liable to die, he felt an odd peace. If he couldn't be in Tempe's hands, the next best were her father's. His future father-in-law. The man who'd fled Virginia over a crime he thought was a hanging offense. For all his bearishness, August Tucker bore Tempe's deft touch, the same crease in his furrowed brow, the same memorable cadence to his speech. And although Sion and Tempe's father had little in common, they'd found common ground in Tempe herself.

Sion's voice seemed little more than a frog's hoarse croak in the gathering darkness. "Where is she?"

August capped the flask of whiskey. "Your guess is as good as mine. She galloped out of my rockhouse a few days back, none too pleased with me but bent on finding you."

Sion's head whirled. So Raven had not harmed her but mayhap helped her get away? There could be no other explanation. Clenching his fist, he spoke past the pain. "She on foot?"

"Nay. Took my best horse without a by-your-leave—and a rifle."

At this, half the worry went out of him. "She's a hand with a gun, I'll grant you that. But she's tore up enough I misdoubt she'll use it." As if sensing his remaining disquiet, Smokey stretched out alongside him, her soulful eyes never leaving him. "How'd you find me?"

"You were easy enough to track with two men dead," August said.

"Two?"

"I come upon a man a mite older than me and buried him along Shawnee Creek a ways back."

Nate. Sion swallowed, grateful for the misery in his shoulder that made all softness retreat.

"I didn't see any violence done him. He looked real peaceful. Like he just got tired and laid down on the trail and went to sleep."

Could it be? Nate had often said he wanted to go easy.

I ain't so blessed that the Lord'll send a chariot of fire down from heaven to take me home like He did Elijah, but I'd be glad to go easy.

"But there was this other man . . ." August's voice sounded weary, as if the ugly memory wrung something out of him. "He died hard. Looked like the Indians didn't even want his scalp."

Sion pondered this. Cornelius had died as he'd lived. It was Nate's death he struggled with, their lack of a farewell. Nate had a heart ailment. All that running at the end, the threat of death hanging over them. Mayhap Nate just gave out . . .

He swallowed, the knot in his throat rivaling his shoulder. Abruptly, he changed course. "We need to find Tempe."

"Aye, we will. She's plucky. Tough as whang leather."

"You're not fretted about her."

"I'm more fretted about you." Setting the whiskey aside, August began tearing apart what looked to be a woman's petticoat. "This'll hurt some, but we need to apply witch hazel. Bind the wound tight. Let it draw out the poison."

Sion let him do what he would, no easier about Tempe. Would he ever know the satisfaction of telling her the good news about her pa? Best let it slip now lest he not have the chance. The words came choppy and breathless. "I have something that needs knowing."

August grunted. "You asking for her hand?"

Sion ignored the good-natured question. "You need to know you're not a wanted man in Virginia."

August's ministrations stilled. Sion filled the tense silence. "You may have beaten Frederick Ice and left him for dead, but he didn't die. He's alive to this day, or was when I left Virginia last spring."

Still August said nothing. Sion could only guess the gist of his thoughts. How to make up for years swallowed by the wilderness? A wary mind-set so ingrained he'd likely always call the rockhouse home?

With the beginning of a grin, August finished tending his wound. "You sure?"

"Sure as I'm laid out here with a hole in my shoulder."

August began to chuckle then, his broad chest shaking with a shuddering laugh. "Reckon the Almighty sent you into the wilderness to tell me that?"

"Nay. He sent me into the wilderness to wed your daughter."

Sobering, August cast an appraising glance toward the woods. "We'd best be finding her, then, though you should know we cache supplies in various places so she's not at wit's end. And we agreed long ago that if we were separated we'd return straightaway to the inn—or what's left of it."

"You've been burnt out, then."

"To the ground."

"What'll you do once we find Tempe?"

"Go join Harrod or Boone or Logan and hold the middle ground."

"We'll come along too, provided we can find a preacher."

Reaching out, August punched Sion's good shoulder. "You'd best get better right quick. Tempe's not one to wait. Patience is not her virtue."

32

Here we are all, by day; by night we're hurl'd
By dreams, each one into a several world.
—Robert Herrick

She was dog-tired. Discouraged. The trail had gone cold
after she came upon a dead campfire and some bloodied rags. Now just forty miles from the inn and near
the Warrior's Path, she pondered what to do. Russell and
Ma and Paige were east of the mountains. Pa was holed up
along the Shawnee. Sion seemed to have vanished from the
face of the earth. Her coming across Cornelius's body still
haunted. She feared Sion lay in some unknown spot, lifeless
and unmourned, and she'd never know. It happened to the
best of men. If not Indians, any manner of mischief might
have befallen him.

Her heart craved all she did not own at this present moment. A bath. Cool linen sheets and a feather tick. A hot
meal. Sassafras tea.

A kiss.

Shutting her eyes, she allowed herself one memory. Only one. She always harkened back to that breathless, startling first kiss in the hollow sycamore. Unending it had been, and yet not nearly long enough. His arms had wrapped round her, surprisingly strong yet gentle. She needed his strength. She craved the timbre of his voice. That way he had of subduing any situation, surmounting any obstacle.

Missing him came in spates, much like grief, upending her when she least expected it. She missed other things too, all distant.

The lure of Boonesborough was strong. But not because of James. She longed to be with capable women like the Boones and Esther Hart. Sharing her burdens. Her fears and tears. Any joys to be had. Instinct and prayer told her to go home even if home was no more.

"Come along, Nero," she told Pa's horse in an aggravated huff.

Snorting, full of cane, it looked fit for anything, but she herself was spent. Hopping on a downed log, she climbed onto the gelding's broad chestnut back and headed toward the inn, or what was left of it.

Was she dreaming? Just below the falls on the banks of the Shawnee came the whack of an axe. Pa? The sound renewed her flagging spirits, and she kneed Nero with a vengeance. Up the riverbank he scrambled, navigating oaks and elms just touched by autumn's paintbrush.

It was now late August. No calendar was needed. She could tell by the look and smell of the land. 'Twas Indian summer nearly. Her favorite season. A touch of frost would soon deepen the forest's color. It was the time they'd ready the inn for winter, the rock foundation banked with a thick matting of cornstalks and pumpkin vine . . .

Whack, whack, whack.

Her spirit quickened. Not Pa's familiar cadence with an axe, nor her brother's. Might some bold soul have jumped their claim?

Her leg hardly pained her as she abandoned Nero and started uphill on foot. Walking toward the noise, she smelled smoke and—could it be? Meat . . . bread. All known, beloved sounds and smells. Like the inn had not burned but was still standing.

She was hurrying now, praying it wasn't some dream and in her half-starved state she was touched with strange visions.

The figure in the clearing had his back to her, broad and bare, his skin the rich brown of chestnut. A sheen of sweat glazed him, evidence of the heat and his steady work. His dark hair was plaited and clubbed like the Boone men wore theirs . . .

Emotion choked her. In that heart-stopping moment the woodcutter turned around, a look of pure joy riding his handsome, half-bearded features. Dropping the axe, he opened his arms wide.

"Tempe."

She could not answer. Her hand went to her mouth to keep from crying out. She stumbled when she started toward him, her legs were so trembly. The shirtless stranger came toward her at a run, like a bear or charging buffalo.

Sion. Her Sion. Come home.

Wrapped in each other's arms for long moments, neither spoke. 'Twas sweet, this homecoming. A hallowed moment. She gradually became aware of her surroundings, of another noise that came from the little glen that used to house her gathering.

She tore her eyes away from that to look into Sion's face. To make sure he was whole.

Here.

He was drinking her in as well, a question in his eyes. His gaze slid from her face to her leg. Suddenly impish, she almost lifted a petticoat. "'Tis slowly mending. Should be well enough for our wedding day."

The lines about his eyes crinkled with mirth. "So you'll accept my humble proposal, then." He looked like he might laugh from the sheer joy of it. "Your father's given his blessing."

"He's here?"

"Aye, splitting shingles for the roof."

Her eyes widened. "Shingles? I see no roof—"

"All in good time, aye?" He tucked a breeze-tossed strand of hair behind her ear. "He found me when I was arrow-shot through the shoulder. If not for him . . ."

"I never thought I'd see you again."

"Nor I you."

Did she imagine the unclouded brightness in his gaze? It made him almost a stranger. 'Twas like a curtain pulled back on broad daylight.

With a halloo, August emerged into stark sunlight, looking at her as if she'd only been berry picking, Smokey on his heels. "About time, Daughter." His smile was warm and triumphant. "I'm not a wanted man but free, your borderman tells me. Seems likely cause for a celebration. Let's have us a wedding, aye? We only lack a justice of the peace, a few guests. Your ma and brother and Paige needs be sent for."

Free? She turned to Sion, read the confirmation in his eyes. Head full of questions, heart overflowing, she focused on one needful thing.

An Indian summer wedding. At long last.

A fortnight later, Pa returned with Ma, Paige, Russell, and a string of packhorses laden with supplies, the trace dusty with a few beeves and sheep. Tempe's family's surprise was plain to find men who had previously come by the inn gathered for a different purpose—a small army of them felling trees and hauling hearth rock and riving shingles. With the middle ground calmer, if only for the time being, they'd come because they'd heard the Moonbow had been burnt out. In a show of support they worked feverishly, their presence sending a message to the Indians that they were here to stay.

Squire Boone was among them. As preacher he would marry Sion and Tempe before going over mountain to lead another party to Boonesborough. To be blessed by a Boone was more than Tempe's heart could hold. During those frenzied autumn days of building and cooking and sewing a new marrying dress, Tempe wondered if the ceremony would come to be.

Two cabins were taking shape, not as large as the original Moonbow Inn but a start. Sion was taking extra care to hew log walls rather than leave the logs round. Alongside him Russell labored, gaze often straying to Paige as she helped Tempe tend the animals and build fence. Something had changed between her brother and Paige. Tempe felt a little loss that she'd missed the turning point of their courtship, and then gladness took hold. For the first time since Powell Valley, Russell seemed more whole, working away with little thought of his limp.

At last she and Sion stood beneath an ancient oak, its charred trunk a reminder of the fire that had ravaged the inn, the tree's brilliant foliage a testament to the coming cold. Bible in hand, Squire Boone married them with few words. Of those he did speak, each rolled over Tempe like a heavenly benediction slightly muted by the distant rush of the falls.

Their wedding eve, she and Sion sat on the rock ledge that had come to be such a part of her story. The mist was like a bridal veil, the falls more subdued in autumn. The air wafting around them held both warmth and chill. Indian summer bore a colorful, memorable welcome. Only the Almighty could have created such a night. Or maybe it was more the company she kept.

Through the trees came the sounds of laughter and the squeak of a fiddle as the wedding celebration ebbed. Wanting to be alone, they'd come here, not expecting any moonbow but granted one nonetheless.

Despite the moonbow's appeal, his first, it was Tempe Sion studied, tracing the arc of her cheek with a forefinger. She studied him in turn, wanting him to kiss her like the groom he was and snuff any worries about sitting on this rock so exposed. His rifle lay within reach, the shine of silver bewitching.

She said at last, "I wish Nate could have been here."

His brow creased, turning him more pensive. "I think of him often—Lucian and the axemen too."

"You think they got away?"

A slight lift to his wide shoulders. "Some captives want to stay. Not all have a Mistress Moonbow to return to."

The half smile she gave him was fleeting. And Raven? Was he even now on the Warrior's Trail? The war path? It had been surprisingly quiet. Too quiet, Pa had said as he finished chinking and daubing both cabins. There was a surprising absence of sign.

"Next spring when your pa goes to trade with the Cherokee, he'll make inquiries, see if they can be found."

She was glad of this, her mind turning a corner as she let go of the past. "Sion, I've been wondering if we shouldn't stay right here, at least at first . . ."

"Not go to Boonesborough, you mean." His eyes held a question she'd not been ready to answer until now.

"Not Boonesborough, nay. You could continue surveying, if not for the Loyal, then the settlers coming over the Gap and stopping by the inn. Maybe in time we'll settle out along the Green like you once said, or over by the Harts near Boonesborough. For now it's good to be near kin." She felt the need to stay close. Being on the trail had taught her many things, the importance of family foremost. "I want our children, at least our firstborn, to make his appearance right here."

"*His?*" He wound a long strand of her hair around a callused finger, his intensity making her insides spin.

She nodded. "A borderman needs a son, seems like."

"And if it's a girl?"

A flush turned her warm. "Then I'd like to name her Chenoa after the river in the middle ground."

He nodded, pensive. "Our son we'll call James."

She stilled. The earnestness in his expression moved her. "Sion James Morgan."

"Aye." As if sealing some sort of bargain, he caught up her hand in a mere skim of a kiss, a slight tingling arising from his whiskers on her open palm.

Done with courting, she stole her arms round his shoulders and circled his neck. She kissed him hard. The moonbow was nearly forgotten. There was just the two of them, the sheer delight of his presence, the reassuring scent and feel of him as she nestled in his embrace as his bride.

Together they looked skyward. The moonbow was shattering—mere bits of color in the blackness, a sort of bridge between heaven and earth—reminding her that even on the darkest nights there was a glimmer of hope, of promise, however hazy.

Sion's low words were nearly lost beneath the tumult of the falls. "Best bid the moonbow good night, Tempe Tucker."

She smiled and held on to hope. Their hard-won future loomed bright. "Tempe Tucker *Morgan*."

Keep Reading for a
SNEAK PEEK

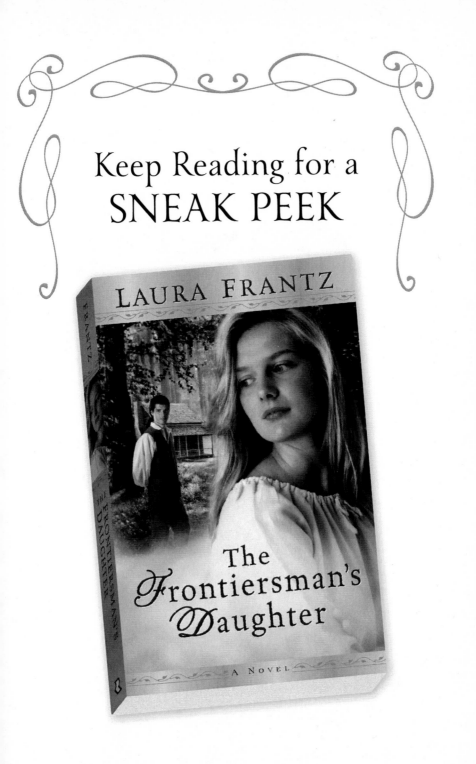

LAURA FRANTZ

The
Frontiersman's
Daughter

A NOVEL

1

KENTUCKE, INDIAN TERRITORY, 1777

In the fading lavender twilight, at the edge of a clearing,
stood half a dozen Shawnee warriors. They looked to
the small log cabin nestled in the bosom of the greening
ridge, as earthy and unassuming as the ground it sat upon. If
not for the cabin's breathtaking view of the river and rolling
hills, arguably the finest in the territory, most passersby would
easily dismiss such a place, provided they found it at all. The
Indians regarded it with studied intent, taking in the sagging
front porch, the willow baskets and butter churn to one side,
and the vacant rocking chair still astir from the hurry of a moment before. Six brown bodies gleamed with bear grease, each
perfectly still, their only movement that of sharp, dark eyes.

Inside the cabin, Ezekial Click handed a rifle to his son, Ransom, before opening the door and stepping onto the porch. His
wife, Sara, took up a second gun just inside. A sudden breath of
wind sent the spent blossoms of a lone dogwood tree scurrying
across the clearing. From the porch, Click began speaking in the
Shawnee tongue. Slowly. Respectfully. A smattering of Shawnee
followed—forceful yet oddly, even hauntingly, melodic.

Sara and Ransom darted a glance out the door, troubled by every word, yet the unintelligible banter continued. At last, silence came. And then, in plain English, one brave shouted, "Click, show us your pretty daughter!"

Within the cabin, all eyes fastened on the girl hovering on the loft steps. At thirteen, Lael Click was just a slip of a thing, but her oval face showed a woman's composure. Her pale green eyes fastened on her father's back just beyond the yawning door frame.

She put one cautious foot to the floor, then tread the worn pine boards until she stood in her father's shadow. She dared not look at her mother. Without further prompting she stepped forward into a dying shaft of sunlight. A sudden breeze caught the hem of her thin indigo shift and it ballooned, exposing two bare brown feet.

The same brave shouted, "Let down your hair!"

She hesitated, hearing her mother's sharp intake of breath. With trembling hands she reached for the horn combs that held back the weight of fair hair. Her mane tumbled nearly to her feet, as tangled and luxuriant as wild honeysuckle vine.

Woven in with the evening shadows was a chorus of tree frogs and katydids and the scent of soil and spring, but Lael noticed none of these things. Beside her, her father stood stoically and she fought to do the same, remembering his oft-repeated words of warning: *Never give way to fear in an Indian's sight.*

Softly she expelled a ragged breath, watching as each warrior turned away. Only the tallest tarried, his eyes lingering on her as she swept up her hair with unsteady hands and subdued it with the combs.

At last they were gone, slipping away into the wall of woods. Invisible but ever present. Silent. Perhaps deadly.

Evening was a somber affair, as if the Shawnee themselves had stayed for supper. To Lael, the cold cornbread and buttermilk that filled their wooden bowls seemed as tasteless as the cabin's chinking. Somehow she managed a sip of cider and a halfhearted bite now and then. Across from her, her mother managed neither. Only her younger brother Ransom ate, taking his portion and her own, as if oblivious to all the trouble.

Looking up, she saw a hint of a smile on her father's face. Was he trying to put her at ease? Not possible. He sat facing the cabin door, his loaded rifle lounging against the table like an uninvited guest. Despite his defensive stance, he seemed not at all anxious like her ma but so calm she could almost believe the Indians had simply paid them a social call and they could go on about their business as if nothing had happened.

He took out his hunting knife, sliced a second sliver of cornbread, then stood. Lael watched his long shadow fall across the table and caught his quick wink as he turned away. Swallowing a smile, she concentrated on the cabin's rafters and the ropes strung like spiderwebs above their heads. The sight of her favorite coverlet brought some comfort, its pattern made bright with dogwood blossoms and running vines. Here and there hung linsey dresses, a pair of winter boots, some woolen leggings, strings of dried apples and leatherbritches beans, bunches of tobacco, and other sundry articles. Opposite was the loft where she and Ransom slept.

The cabin door creaked then closed as Pa disappeared onto the porch, leaving her to gather up the dirty dishes while her mother made mountain tea. Lael watched her add sassafras roots to the kettle, her bony hands shaking.

"Ma, I don't care for any tea tonight," she said.

"Very well. Cover the coals, then."

Lael took a small shovel and buried the red embers with

a small mountain of ash to better start a fire come morning. When she turned around, her ma had disappeared behind the tattered quilt that divided the main cabin from their corner bedroom. Ransom soon followed suit, climbing the loft ladder to play quietly with a small army of wooden soldiers garrisoned under the trundle bed.

Left alone, she couldn't stay still, so taut in mind and body she felt she might snap. Soon every last dish and remaining crumb were cleaned up and put away. With Ma looking as though she might fall to pieces, Lael's resolve to stay grounded only strengthened. Yet she found herself doing foolish things like snuffing out the candles before their time and pouring the dirty dishwater through a crack in the floor rather than risk setting foot outside.

The clock on the mantel sounded overloud in the strained silence, reminding her the day was done. Soon she'd have to settle in for the night. But where was Pa? She took in the open door, dangerously ajar, and the fireflies dancing in the mounting gloom. She sighed, pushed back a wisp of hair, and took a timid step toward the porch.

How far could an Indian arrow fly?

Peering around the door frame, she found Pa sitting in the same place she'd found him years ago that raw November morning after his escape from the Shawnee. They had long thought him dead, and indeed all remnants of his life as a white man seemed to have been stamped out of him. His caped hunting shirt was smeared with bear grease, his deerskin leggings soiled beyond redemption. Except for an eagle-feathered scalp lock, his head was plucked completely clean of the hair that had been as fair as her own. Savage as he was, she'd hardly recognized him. Only his eyes reminded her of the man she once knew, their depths a wild, unsurrendered blue.

Tonight he was watching the woods, his gun across his knees, and his demeanor told her he shouldn't be disturbed. Without a word she turned and climbed to the loft, where she found Ransom asleep. There, in the lonesome light of a tallow candle, she shook her hair free of the horn combs a second time.

The shears she'd kept hidden since the Shawnee departed seemed cold and heavy in her hand, but her unbound hair was warm and soft as melted butter. She brought the two together, then hesitated. Looking down, she imagined the strands lying like discarded ribbon at her feet.

A sudden noise below made her jerk the scissors out of sight. Pa had come in to collect his pipe. Her sudden movement seemed to catch his eye.

"You'd best be abed, Daughter," he called over his shoulder, his tone a trifle scolding.

She sank down on the corn-husk tick, losing the last of her resolve, and tucked the scissors away. If she changed her mind come morning, they'd be near. Catlike, she climbed over the slumbering body in the trundle bed beneath her, surprised that a seven-year-old boy could snore so loud.

The night was black as the inside of an iron skillet and nearly as hot. She lay atop the rustling tick, eyes open, craving sleep. The night sounds outside the loft window were reassuringly familiar, as was her brother's rhythmic breathing. All was the same as it had ever been but different. The coming of the Indians had changed everything.

In just a few moments' time the Shawnee had thrown open the door to Pa's past, and now there would be no shutting it.

She, for one, didn't like looking back.

AUTHOR'S NOTE

Since I was a child, the death of James Boone has haunted me. I never imagined that particular event would work its way into one of my novels. While researching *A Moonbow Night*, I visited the spot along Wallen's Creek in Virginia thought to be the burial place of James Boone and party, only to discover another site that claimed to be the one instead.

At the time of the massacre, Daniel Boone was not a well-known figure on the frontier. Another young man who died with James that day, son of the wealthy Henry Russell, was the one who made headlines. James was rarely mentioned in newspaper accounts.

Sadly, little is known of Daniel and Rebecca Boone's first-born. In the words of John D. Smythe, "What should have been one of the richest pages of pioneer history is a blank." Given that, I took what is left to us historically and tried to capture James Boone's personality and presence, if only briefly.

As a young man of sixteen coming of age in 1773 and living in his intrepid father's shadow, James Boone must have been quite an interesting character. There are touching accounts of him accompanying his father into the woods when James was very small. Later, when Daniel Boone went off on long hunts and was gone for extended periods of time, James would have been his mother's closest ally and help about the farm. He likely filled a fatherly role with his many brothers and sisters. He might have had a love interest. Hardworking, of solid Quaker stock, he would have been a first-rate farmer and settler in his day.

The days leading up to his death are shadowy at best. We know that Daniel expressed confidence in James by sending him back to Castle's Woods to get supplies during that first try at Kentucky in 1773. We know that James and his small group made their way back but camped that fateful night only three miles behind Daniel's advance party. The site of the massacre itself is disputed. Just who found the slain party is also in question.

What little is known about that fatal October morning comes from the slave who escaped and hid behind a log and watched the tragedy unfold. It is said that James's mother, Rebecca Boone, gave linen sheets for the bodies to be buried in. The next spring, Daniel Boone returned to the gravesites and was overtaken by a severe storm. For years after, he was said to be visibly moved upon the mention of James's death. Daniel and Rebecca were to lose another son, Israel Boone, in the Indian Wars years later. What is perhaps most remarkable is that Daniel Boone seems never to have held a grudge.

There are many sources that enriched my research and writing, these being foremost: *Women at Fort Boonesborough* by Harry G. Enoch and Anne Crabb; *Boone: A Biography* by Robert Morgan; the Draper Manuscripts; and a great many other sources, too numerous to mention here.

As an author of fiction, I often take what history hands me and use it to the story's advantage without staying true to actual dates. Though there are early accounts of longhunters and surveyors in the region of Cumberland Falls, settlement was slow in coming. It was held sacred by many Native American tribes, and in early 1780, Zachariah Green and his companions endured a rough river ride and abandoned their boat to the falls, which inspired the scene of Sion Morgan doing the same. Not until 1800 did the Commonwealth of Kentucky grant two men Cumberland Falls along with two hundred acres. Later, in 1850, Louis and Mary Renfro bought four hundred acres, including the Great Falls of the Cumberland, and built a cabin there, inviting visitors to fish and enjoy the beauty of what historian Richard Henry Collins called "a succession of scenery as romantic and picturesque as any in the state." The subsequent Moonbow Inn was destroyed by fire in the 1940s. But this spectacular setting lends itself vividly to fiction and was easily reconstructed in this writer's eighteenth-century imagination.

I invite you to visit my website, www.LauraFrantz.net, and also Pinterest, where I share maps and images of *A Moonbow Night* and the inspiration behind the writing of this novel, which was particularly dear to me since I am a Kentuckian.

ACKNOWLEDGMENTS

Recently I read an acknowledgment by Agatha Christie that sums up what I hope my humble stories convey: "To all those that lead monotonous lives, in the hope that they may experience at second hand the delights and dangers of adventure." I'm ever grateful that books have done that for me. I'm continually inspired by men and women like Daniel and Rebecca Boone, whose lives leave an extraordinarily rich historical trail for us to follow.

Special thanks to Jenny Q, Jenny Quinlan, for being the first to read this manuscript and for sharing her expertise and insight. *Historical Editorial* is all that and more! I look forward to working with you again.

For my great team at Revell: To editor Andrea Doering, who takes the finished manuscript and is able to read with an eye for making the story the best it can be for readers. Your heart for those who pick up my novels always inspires and humbles me. To my patient, ever-faithful editor Jessica English, who takes the timelessness in my novel and helps me nail down days, something I am not very good at! Heartfelt thanks to Cheryl Van Andel and the art team for covers that reflect the heart of my stories. Last but not least, to all those folks who comprise Revell's sales and marketing team, and the sales reps who place my books in brick-and-mortar stores—you all are the absolute best. And to the extraordinary Karen Steele, who can take a book and make it shine on her end once finished—many, many thanks.

Heartfelt thanks to my savvy agent, Janet Grant of Books & Such Literary Agency, who made this story possible and the two to follow, all standalone novels after the Ballantyne Legacy series. Knowing she is always in the wings, able to take care of anything needed, is remarkable.

Special thanks to the Friends of Boone Trace, Dr. John Fox, Curtis Penix, and all those who've worked tirelessly to preserve the trail Boone blazed in 1775. In the spring of 2016, I was able to walk a portion of this trace starting at Fort Boonesborough to Twitty's Fort in Kentucky, following in the steps of my hero and those settlers who braved so much to embrace a new land. It was during this trek that I met some of the kin of Kentucky's first settlers, including Jasper Castle, a direct descendant of the very Castle who settled Castle's Woods, where James Boone went for supplies in 1773, days before his death. To learn more about this vital preservation effort to keep Boone Trace alive, please visit www.boonetrace1775.com.

And last but not least, to my readers near and far, who are God's ongoing gift to me. What would my stories be without you?

I thank my God upon every remembrance of you.

Philippians 1:3

Laura Frantz is a Christy Award finalist and the author of *The Frontiersman's Daughter*, *Courting Morrow Little*, *The Colonel's Lady*, *The Mistress of Tall Acre*, and the Ballantyne Legacy series. She lives and writes in a log cabin in the heart of the Kentucky woods. Please visit her at www.LauraFrantz.net.